T0208444

HEREDITARY DEFECTS

HEREDITARY DEFECTS

Frank McGillion

Copyright © 2020 by Frank McGillion.

ISBN: Softcover   978-1-7960-8812-0
               eBook   978-1-7960-8811-3

All rights reserved. No part of this book may be reproduced or transmitted in any form or by any means, electronic or mechanical, including photocopying, recording, or by any information storage and retrieval system, without permission in writing from the copyright owner.

This is a work of fiction. All of the characters, names, incidents, organizations, and dialogue in this novel are either the products of the author's imagination or are used fictitiously.

Any people depicted in stock imagery provided by Getty Images are models, and such images are being used for illustrative purposes only. Certain stock imagery © Getty Images.

Print information available on the last page.

Rev. date: 02/18/2020

To order additional copies of this book, contact:
Xlibris
1-888-795-4274
www.Xlibris.com
Orders@Xlibris.com
805174

CHAPTER ONE

It was fresh and early in the morning when Doctor Allison Young drove her ancient blue convertible into the hospital car park. She had her choice of parking spaces though even at this hour there were quite a few cars parked there already. She switched the engine off, placed the car keys in her purse and sat for a moment or two to compose herself.

'What an unearthly hour to start a new life, Young,' she said casually to her image in the mirror as it looked down at her rather pleasantly. She didn't really mind though. Today was her first as the new Junior Registrar in hematology at The London General Hospital and the very least she could do to make it flow easily was to arrive early.

Disorders of the blood had fascinated Allison Young long before her days as a medical student when her interest had been consolidated. So, despite the reservations of some of her friends and family who felt that obstetrics or gynecology were still the obvious choices for a woman who wanted to succeed in hospital medicine; Allison had, typically, persevered and had successfully gained her post in the hematology department against stiff competition.

The one person who had supported her choice one hundred per cent throughout, had been her father. A former eminent and well-connected psychiatrist who had practiced in London, he was now a semi-retired country general practitioner. He loved his job and the lifestyle it brought with it and he would have been delighted if Allison had joined him in his small practice.

He loved his daughter too, however, and knew her intimately. If she wanted to be a hematologist then nothing would stop her -not him, not God himself if he'd tried - so he had done all that he could to encourage and assist her achieve her ambition.

Allison often wondered how her father could be so settled in the country after the years he had spent treating a wide range of people in both the private and public sectors. In his time he'd treated 'society' people, royalty, industrial magnates and infamous criminals. Quite a difference from the rural working and middle classes he now dealt with. She was thinking about her father as she stepped out of the car, closed the door and looked about her. Despite the freshness, it was a dull grey morning with a wry chill in the air, typical of late autumn in the Home Counties.

She gave an involuntary shudder and hoped that it was due only to the cold and not to any lingering doubts she may have about her suitability for her new post. For despite her smart, confident appearance and the complete faith she had in her professional ability, she knew that hospital medicine, particularly at this level, was a demanding business.

She was fully aware of the fact that inter-personal and medico-political skills, were every bit as important in the attainment of success in hospital medicine as professional aptitude.

While she had no doubts whatsoever about her professional ability, Allison had had her doubts about her ability as a politician and they hadn't quite gone. Politicians were meant to be controlled and compromising, not capricious and single-minded as she could be. She'd see.

In front of her stood the main body of the hospital, which concealed the modern ward and treatment areas, which had recently been added to it. It was a large building constructed of red sandstone with slim majestic sides, pointed frontage and elegant arched windows. It looked for all the world like a small Gothic cathedral.

She stared at it for a few moments absorbing its sense of history and its acknowledged fame as one of the foremost teaching hospitals in the country. How fitting that the well recogniszed standards of medicine that were practiced here should be housed in such an impressive setting.

Incongruously she thought for a moment on Ken; dwelt fondly for a second or two on how much he, with his interest in such things, would have liked the building. How he would have appreciated the finer points of its architecture.

A sharp sensation of loss held her momentarily. Then, with a shake of her head, she dismissed him. He was past, gone, over with. They were past, gone, over with. It was finished.

Taking a deep breath, which sent a surge of oxygen to every part of her slender 5'8", Allison walked briskly towards the main entrance to the building. Externally she was the picture of efficiency and purpose. Her long black hair was carefully tied back exposing her bright blue eyes and attractive determined face that had only the merest hint of make-up.

She carried her briefcase efficiently in her left hand and her pace was quick and regular. Internally, however, this picture of confident composure converted to a controlled but gripping nervousness. As soon as she was aware of it, she dealt with it.

With conscious resolution, Allison pushed the large revolving door firmly and followed it through entering the freshly modern reception area of the hospital. She remembered it vaguely from her previous visit when she had attended her second interview with Doctor John Bennet her new chief.

Bennet was an exceptional man who, perhaps because he'd known her father, had seemed as interested in Allison personally as much as he had in her excellent academic achievements and in her undoubted keenness for hematology. That much had been evident from the two interviews she'd had with him.

The first had been held informally at a hotel in town where they'd had breakfast together.

'A cheap enough way to check your ability to hold a knife and fork.' he'd joked, relaxing her before they discussed her background in detail. She had liked him a very great deal. "The perfect man and physician," she'd thought then and there and her opinion hadn't changed one bit since.

The second interview had been more formal, there had been a panel of four interviewing, and it had been held here at the hospital. She'd been so preoccupied with it at the time, however, that she hadn't given her surroundings her full attention. Consequently she couldn't remember now, precisely where Doctor Bennett's office had been. So she looked around for someone to ask.

She spotted the reception desk and while there was no receptionist on duty at this time, a nurse was standing there reading something. She was obviously too involved in what she was reading to have noticed Allison's entry. So, Allison walked over in her direction.

'Good morning,' she said, placing her best smile on her face. The nurse looked up and peered at her over gold-rimmed spectacles, which were perched precariously at the tip of her nose. She didn't respond. Allison walked closer.

'Hello,' she said pleasantly; 'I'm Allison Young, Doctor Bonnet's new Junior Registrar. I'm due to start this morning and I wondered if you'd be kind enough to direct me to his office?'

The nurse looked at her again, her grey-green eyes in a fixed quizzical gaze.

'Good morning, doctor,' she replied coolly, 'A bit early, aren't you? The clinical trial is it?'

Allison felt confused. She hadn't expected a formal welcome, but this was a bit much. It didn't take much common decency to be marginally pleasant to a newcomer, surely? Further, what was this about a clinical trial? Perhaps there was one going on in the hospital to test some new drug or other, but it would have nothing to do with her and the woman should have known that. She decided not to let the coolness of the nurse's response trouble her unduly and what Allison Young decided, she was usually able to attain.

'Yes', she smiled pleasantly; 'I am rather early. I tend to be that way. Better to have some time to get used to the place, adjust, have a look around and so on. After all, I expect to be here for quite some time. How long have you been here?'

The nurse continued to look at Allison with something approaching distaste. She ignored her question completely.

'Well, Doctor Bennet's secretary won't be in for almost another hour, I believe,' she said; 'I imagine you'll be comfortable enough sitting here until then.'

With that the nurse closed whatever it was she had been reading, placed it back on a shelf and without further acknowledgement of Allison walked out through the back of reception and down the long narrow corridor.

Allison was annoyed. She felt like calling her back, saying something about politeness, about respect for a relatively senior member of staff; but her discretion prevented that. She looked around to see if there was someone else who could direct her to Bennet's office as that, she recalled, was where he'd told her to meet him:

'Wait for me there if I'm not in,' he'd said. 'Make yourself a coffee. I'll leave the door to the secretary's office open. Claire will see to you if she's in before me. She's a secretarial gem.'

There was no one else in sight for the moment, however, and none of the hospital signs were particularly helpful. Allison decided that she'd just wait where she was until a friendly face appeared, one friendlier, at least, than the nurse's.

Allison had noticed her name tag: 'Jennifer Wright' it had said, 'Charge Nurse'. 'Well, Charge Nurse Wright,' she mused, as she checked her carefully manicured nails; I wonder if they're all as friendly as you at The London. I certainly hope not!'

With that she sat down in the small, neat, waiting area picking up a tattered magazine to while away the time. She looked at the clock. "So much for getting here so damned early," she thought to herself as she began half-heartedly to read an article about yet another alleged royal scandal. It was worlds away from her.

As the time passed, a steady stream of people began to come in through the door. Allison observed them, taking in their appearance and passively guessing what each of them worked at. A diversion from the snippets of the article she read with little enthusiasm. Apocryphal blue-blooded scandal was not Allison's scene, as with most things for a practical woman, the real thing was of more interest to her.

She noted that staff was leaving the hospital too, though not many, just a few who had probably stayed on later than the majority of the night staff who would have left earlier. Among those leaving she noticed Charge Nurse Jennifer Wright.

Allison watched her as she walked quickly down the corridor towards the door. There was no glance in her direction, no acknowledgement of any kind that they had met and spoken previously. A few yards before she reached the door however, the nurse stopped suddenly, allowing whoever was coming in to precede her.

A young man entered. He was tall, good-looking and wore smart clothes. But he had an air of disarray about him, however, a hint of something removed and uncertain. It was in his face, in the way he held himself, in the way his hair was untidily groomed.

It took only a glance for Allison to detect this. She was a shrewd assessor of people and the fact that he was extremely attractive didn't exactly hinder her observations. Something troubled this man. She was sure of it.

When he saw the nurse he stopped abruptly and the two of them began to speak quietly together. The young man seemed very earnest indeed and he seemed to be doing most of the talking. For a few minutes he seemed to be exposing the nurse to an inquisition so intense seemed his conversation, so rigid his posture. For her part she merely shook her head from time to time, though on one occasion she raised her hand and gently brushed it against his sleeve.

Allison was surprised at this apparent gesture of tenderness. She hadn't seemed the type. It did not seem consistent with the hard, severe, woman who had looked at her so piercingly and ignored her so studiously. Uncharacteristically she wondered, for some reason, if they were lovers and if this was the resolution of a lover's tiff. Perhaps The London had more to offer than medicine.

At length they ended their conversation and as Jennifer Wright left through the door, the young man made his way slowly and pensively along the corridor. As he passed Allison, he gave her a half-smile. It was a poor attempt at acknowledging her, but an attempt just the same. She smiled back and noted his pale blue eyes. They seemed tired and sad and somehow reflected his general demeanor.

In the instant their eyes met she confirmed her earlier diagnosis. This was a man in trouble; he was confused about something, hurting about it. She wondered what it was. Jennifer Wright, perhaps, or something else? Quite suddenly, with a spontaneity that took her by surprise, Allison found herself speaking to him.

'Are you all right?' She felt surprise which wasn't unpleasant even as she spoke and she wondered what on Earth had prompted her to do so. He stopped, turned around and looked at her.

'Sorry?' he said, 'Sorry, did you say something?'

'I just wondered if you were all right,' said Allison smiling almost spontaneously, enjoying his voice, its softness; 'you look a bit... well, peakish.'

'I'm fine, thanks,' replied the young man. 'Just a bit tired. Thanks for being so thoughtful, though.' He gave her a deep appreciative look and remarkably she felt her stomach tighten.

'Fine, then,' she said: 'I'm sorry I interrupted you. I simply -'

'- No, really,' he interrupted; 'it was good of you to express concern.' He pushed his hair back from his forehead and shook his head in what seemed an expression of resignation. 'I suppose I must look a sight,' he continued,' for you to notice. Thank you again. At least you look well. Very well indeed. You must be in the wrong place.'

His attempt at humor was made in a lifeless, unenthusiastic voice, but, even so, it impressed Allison that the man, so obviously distressed, had attempted to joke at all.

'Well, I must get on,' he said, giving her a final, tired smile. 'Thank's again for your interest. Goodbye.'

'Goodbye,' responded Allison, looking after him and wondering what on Earth it was that troubled him so much.

Allison crossed and uncrossed her legs as, having finished the article on the royals she turned impatiently to another. It was a feature on the female senator who was taking the United States by storm and this did hold her interest. She was a remarkable lady, a role-model indeed for any modern woman.

'Doctor Young?' Allison left the world of American politics to find a pleasant young woman looking at her. 'Doctor Young?' she repeated, smiling.

'Why yes, sorry,' replied Allison.

'I'm Claire Sillars, Doctor Bennet's secretary. I was expecting to find you in my office. I'm afraid that I assumed you'd find it, then I thought better....' She smiled very naturally and Allison liked her immediately. 'Doctor Bennet's late this morning I'm afraid. It's unlike him. Have you had a coffee or something?'

'Not really, Allison replied, 'but I'd love one.'

'Done! If you'll simply follow me we'll get you to some caffeine immediately.'

The blinds were pulled tight over the windows. What natural light there was, was on the outside and it was kept there.

'Good morning,' the Shadow Man said to his audience with an undisclosive smile, if the break of the line on his mouth could be called that.

It was early. The blue light of the projected slide lit up the screen. It was the only thing clearly discernible in the small, modern room. In the shadows a small group of two men and two women sat in silence. The Shadow Man spoke to them, his voice very quiet indeed. They had to strain slightly to hear him exactly as he intended. He addressed the slide on the screen without looking at it. And he addressed the small audience before him without looking at them. They were simply shadows to him. He was the only one visible.

The Shadow Man's voice was not only quiet, it was soft. Soft, with a subtle edge of threat to it, like the fine edge of a razorblade. And like such an edge, it gave the impression that it could cause a great deal of damage. That, if need be, it could cut and cut deep; as deep as was necessary to make its message felt.

And soft as pliable metal, the voice tapered to its point and stopped. There were a few seconds of silence, a pause where nothing happened, where movement was suspended. A switch was thrown abruptly with an audible click and the room was suddenly filled with light.

Of the four people visible in the room one, a middle-aged woman, was conspicuous by her dress. Unlike the others who were smart and formal, she was plainly and informally dressed. Her name was Annette Pallain and, an academic of distinction, she wouldn't have dressed up to meet royalty. This was literally true. She'd done it, or, to be more precise, she'd chosen not to.

All were seated separately about the formal rows of seats which normally would have held ten times their number. They were a distinguished looking group and, with the exception of the American, were very well-dressed and groomed. They were people to be respected. Each leant over the wooden ledge in front of them, the polished ledges that folded over, the ledges, which were purpose-built for taking notes.

There would be no notes taken here, however. No record of this meeting would be kept at all, except for the pictures and the figures on the slides. These would be kept, safe and secure, hidden in a vault until they were required again. The only other record of this meeting would be what remained in their heads where it was assumed to be as safe as any vault. As safe as houses.

'Will it work, Greg?'

The young woman's voice was the first to break the silence. She was attractive, very attractive indeed, with short, styled fair hair and bright blue shining eyes. 'Will we be able to exercise adequate control internationally given the diversity of the regulatory bodies involved; Japan, Western Europe, the US, Australia?' she paused as attention focused on her. She was comfortable with it.

'I know we're fine here, in the U.K., in the under-developed countries,' she continued; 'but can we really slip ourselves into these places? Bypass government bodies such as the Food and Drugs Administration?

'They're so well monitored, so sensitive politically particularly since azutobine.' The group all knew about that one - azutobine. The miracle 'cure' for AIDS which - having received rapid approval by the F.D.A.- had shortened life-expectancy of recipients to half.

'Yes', replied the soft voice with a harder edge to it. 'Yes, we can.' Silently the woman nodded her acknowledgement mutely accepting the authority of his reply, absorbing its hidden threat.

Another voice interrupted the silence, a male voice.

'At our last meeting, Greg, you said that there was something more that we required. We discussed it recently. Remember? Could we have your comments on the state of our colleagues?'

The man who now spoke was tall and broad-shouldered and he sucked, redundantly, at an unlit briar pipe. He was in his mid-fifties and had distinguished grey hair swept back to display a prominent forehead and piercing blue eyes. His question had been asked in a voice that told he had known respect, authority and power for many years. It was a sure voice, a voice certain of itself, just uncertain now of the finer details. The minutiae waiting to be clarified.

The tall slim man who had been speaking in the darkness was, in its absence, handsome. He had short black hair which fell back in waves of natural curls which enhanced his eyes. And those were deep brown eyes which, when they looked at you, could make you feel as solid as an oak tree or as ill-defined as dust.

He wore a fine woven dark suit with a waistcoat to match and a crisp white shirt with a blood-red tie. The gold chain of a pocket watch fell across his waistcoat. It seemed to count the seconds before he answered with his characteristic efficiency and precision.

'Certainly, Abe,' he said by way of reply to the older man's prompting. He knew that's what it was. He was being asked to include the others.

'We required another medical team here in London. Another hospital willing to undertake clinical trials into the anti-porphyric profile of Oviron.'

'Why do we need an anti-porphyric profile, Greg?' the woman's voice interrupted him again, unwisely. 'I thought we were going to market Oviron for the agreed indications, forget about it's supposed effect in porphyria that's only based upon...'

The Shadow Man continued speaking, interrupting her in turn and ignoring her question completely.

'We required two members of that team to know our ultimate proposals for Oviron. Two members who were also on a hospital's ethical committee. We required two senior doctors with power, respect and authority, and who are respected within and outwith their own hospital community.

'Further, they would either have had to sit on, or have direct contact with, the U.K.'s Medicine's Commission or the Committee for the Safety of Medicines.' He stopped for a few moments to ensure that what he was saying was making appropriate impact. It was.

'Ideally they would be motivated with something in addition to a pecuniary motive.' he continued; 'they would either be idealists or needy in some non-financial way as well as being financially ambitious.

'They would seek power through their idealism or needs, rather than through their bank balances per se. Their specific motives for doing so would be of no relevance to us, the only necessary condition was that they had them. The motives for the pursuit of power.'

'A tall order,' interrupted the young woman once again, her now softer voice breaking the flow of the monologue. Quiet, intense she continued; 'Where could we possibly find two such people?'

At The London General,' said the Shadow Man, every bit as quietly, looking at her. 'Or, if you prefer, outside, waiting, right now - early as it is - in our hospitality suite. Waiting to come and speak to us about their willingness to participate in our venture.'

'Who are they?' she asked with a tone of evident surprise in her voice.

'Professor Sir William Mostyn and an eminent colleague,' the Shadow Man said. He looked first to the man called Abe, the man who sat so casually with his unlit briar and who was the absolute authority in that room.

'Are we ready to bring them in?' he asked. He looked round the room, assessing mute opinion.

'Bring them in Greg!' It was a command not a question.

The Shadow Man left the lectern and walked to a telephone which hung on the wall. He pressed three digits and waited no more than three seconds until he spoke.

'Send them in,' he commanded in turn. He turned to his audience again.

'The two gentlemen will be with us in five minutes,' Greg Hoffman said. 'If I may, Abe...' he continued, deferring to the older man, 'I'd like Kathryn to leave us now.'

'Fine,' came the reply without further comment.

Greg Hoffman turned his dark brown eyes to meet the young woman's and defiantly she held them with her own for a moment or two. Then, flushing with anger, she turned away.

'Thank you, Kathryn,' he said, as she stood up and made her way across the polished pine floor towards the door.

As she opened the door and left the room Hoffmann's eyes took in her slim elegant body. He'd take care of her later. Her impertinence and her body.

Almost exactly five minutes had passed when there was a knock on the door. It opened and a robust young blonde woman in her early twenties walked into the room looking very confident indeed. She was followed by two middle-aged men. One looked perfectly relaxed, the other looked concerned. Not nervous exactly, but concerned and very, very serious.

'The two gentlemen,' the young woman said with a smile that shone with near sincerity as she stood aside to allow the men to be met by handshakes and quiet greetings.

As she quietly moved back to make her exit, she looked discreetly at the man called Abe. She flashed him a smile too, but it was not the same smile; this one was tinged with something unsaid but understood. Something dark.

Sir Abe's eyes acknowledged her smile briefly. His pipe was gone now as he stood, tall and erect and powerful, leading his guests to their seats like a shepherd.

Closing the door quietly but firmly behind her, the young woman finally left them with a last, direct look at the Chairman and Managing Director of Unicorn Chemicals Ltd, Sir Abraham Wilder.

Greg Hoffman knew that despite the hour, both men had enjoyed the full benefits of the hospitality suite. He could smell alcohol from the more senior one's breath and he observed the bulges in their briefcases where the expensive trinkets they had been given were stored. Gifts from the company. Bribes.

They were appropriate gifts, of course, nothing with the slightest aura of corruption about them. A solid silver plate, with the Hippocratic Oath inscribed in gold leaf. An envelope with a voucher for an edition of the Complete Oxford English Dictionary, which was bound in leather and ready to be picked up at the appropriate bookshop whenever they pleased.

There were envelopes containing cheques too. A cheque to cover the expenses of the trials, the clinical trials these men were going to organize by treating the patients in their care with Oviron.

The first man, the one who'd had just a trace of a Scots accent when introduced, had an envelope with a cheque in it written for fifty thousand pounds Sterling and made payable to The London General Hospital. Sir William Mostyn had a similar envelope with a cheque in it written for one million dollars American and made payable to a numbered account in Luxembourg.

Hoffmann found both men distasteful. He didn't like the smell of alcohol on the breath of Mostyn, particularly at this time of the day. He didn't like the cheques Sir Abe had authorised him to sign for them either.

Nor did he like the thoughts that would be lingering in their heads about the young men and women he had ensured his Personal Assistant had paraded before them when they'd had dinner near the company's London premises the week before. Just in case.

'Show them a good cross section of desirable flesh,' he had instructed her. 'A good cross section with a bad record for sexual discipline. Or a good one, if you think that's more appropriate.'

She had laughed at that and he hadn't liked that either; just as he didn't like these two necessary interlopers into their cartel.

What he did like about them, however, was the power these men held. The power to treat human beings as guinea-pigs. To do to and with them whatever you could convince them it was in their best interest to do. And to be rewarded for this power sometimes, sometimes adored, sometimes even loved. That he really admired.

Greg Hoffmann not only liked this about these men, he envied it and it made him almost hate them. "Narcissistic ambivalence",' he thought to himself, of himself, with his well-trained, sharp and reflective mind. And the smile that he gave them as he shook their hands made them both feel as solid as trees.

'What I shall do initially, gentlemen, is outline the guidelines we have for investigating new drugs in humans in the United Kingdom. Thankfully the legislation drafted by our insightful government and its Civil Servants in this respect is weak. It can be bent like rubber.'

As he stood addressing his audience in his pinstriped suit, dark rimmed glasses and monogrammed tie, Sir William Mostyn looked the epitome of the medical Establishment In fact, Greg Hoffmann knew that he was no such thing.

Hoffmann noted how he used the word 'humans' in a pejorative way. Mostyn evidently did not consider the people he was entrusted to treat as being more than simply a higher order of guinea pig. He added this to his mental dossier on

Mostyn. It told him that bit more about him. Not that much more was needed.

'Our investigations are controlled by the Medicines Act of 1968 and 1971 and the few amendments made to this in 1995. From your point of view, is that it really consists of a series of guidelines giving us the opportunity to apply our considerable clinical discretion to it.'

A smirk crossed Mostyn's face and it reminded Greg Hoffman of the look he had once seen on the face of a man in an expensive brothel in Bangkok. That man was in fact presently engaged in watching the proceedings in this room on a closed-circuit television screen. A fact known only to Hoffman and Wilder.

'There are a number of committees which sit to pontificate on these guidelines we doctors have to follow in administering foreign chemicals to our patients, one requires a certificate called a Clinical Trial Certificate. But if we're careful, we can proceed to test our drug, quite legally, on a wide scale without any such certificate. And we are both, gentlemen, believe me. Both clever and careful.'

Hoffmann listened with rapt attention now. As ever he had done his research, he knew that to legally carry out a clinical trial of a new drug on a significant number of patients, a certificate was required from this Committee. That there was a loophole, a way round this, he did not know. He should have been fully aware of this and he made a mental note to deal with that issue later.

'If applicants for a Clinical Trial Certificate are refused,' Mostyn continued in his monotone, 'Then they can appeal to the Government's Medicines Commission. But that, gentlemen, just doesn't happen. And as it doesn't concern me, so it need not concern you.

'And we can do even better than that. We can give whatever we want, to whomever we want, as long as they are ill and we say that we can possibly cure them.

You see, if, for example, in our professional judgement a reasonably ill patient will benefit from the administration of a drug, even though that drug has never before been given to another human being, then we can give it to them. We have that prerogative, that right.

'Thus, if Mrs Smith, say, is very ill indeed with a septicemia - my apologies, gentlemen, 'blood poisoning' - of a bacterial nature and we find that our present antibiotics don't work too well, then we can give her whatever the hell we want to.'

While Wilder and Hoffmann were nonplussed by the casual cynicism, others in the room were less impressed. Mostyn's colleague did not like any medical man publicly portraying such an attitude, even though he accepted that some held such views privately though he did not. The other man, for his part, thought it uncouth.

His name was Andrew Wills. A sales executive by profession, he believed that tact was always better than frankness. This attitude had enabled him to climb to the position of Sales Manager with Unicorn. And while he was not impressed with Mostyn's attitude, he admired Greg Hoffmann's expertise in hooking him. It was someone just like this that the Sales Manager required. He was the answer to a commercial dream.

As for the man who secretly watched Mostyn on the television screen, what he saw was a kindred spirit. He liked that. There were not many of them about.

'The decision to give Mrs Smith that drug, however,' continued Mostyn; 'is subject these days to what we call a hospital ethical committee's approval. The drug can only be given on what it termed a named patient basis; but, well...

well, if you chair such a committee as I do, you could give potassium cyanide to a child as long as it had a potentially terminal meningitis and you suggested that it had some chance of curing the infection.

'Alternatively, if he was ill enough and you could make a case for it, you could give muddy water rectally to the King of Siam. If you get my drift.'

With a few early morning drinks in him, Greg Hoffmann thought, Sir William Mostyn is not a very nice man at all. But then he already knew that, and he knew that he didn't need alcohol to be like that either. Mostyn just preferred it amongst other things. That was why he'd asked the sycophantic young Johnson, to approach the man in the first place. He had no reservations about Mostyn at all. The other man, however, he was uncertain about. He'd see. As ever time would tell. It always did.

'The same committee which grants Clinical Trial Certificates, also grants your Product Licenses as you know. These licenses, which you need to use your product in any given disease, seem rather restrictive. You have to supply the committee with a lot of information about your drug to gain its acceptance in just one clinical indication. Once again, however, we can bend the rules a little, with just a little effort.'

Mostyn stopped speaking for a moment, looked around and picked up a empty glass from the lectern. He needn't have worried. Beside it Greg Hoffmann had already placed another one full of the Malt whisky he knew Mostyn favored. Beside that was a small silver dish with an elegant cover and a smaller silver spoon. Mostyn looked at him and their eyes met. No trees now. Just an understanding of mutual needs.

'The drug AZT used in AIDS for example, before the discovery of AIF and the great azutobine was a perfect example of this. It was made exempt from formal clinical trials and was given a Product License extension without any problems because it was apparently so dramatically effective in its actions.'

Hoffmann eyed the man carefully. He did not like him one bit, but he did admire him. He knew his business and, cocaine and alcohol apart, he was a professional. A thorough one. He listened carefully as Mostyn continued:

'I need not stress, gentlemen, that when you get a license exemption on humanitarian grounds, you are in a perfect position to dictate market conditions. You have what you term - a monopoly.

'Another way of capitalising on such a situation is to use a third party to market your drug, but perhaps you know that? You may remember that some years ago there were some remarkable reports on a drug, called 'interferon,' that allegedly cured cancer. The company who had the ability to manufacture this drug weren't so sure. So, without disclosing their clinical findings, they sold the marketing rights to a third party, a body who actually sold the drug. Consequently the first company took actual profit without any potential blame when the drug didn't exactly live up to expectations.

Mostyn continued. 'You have, no doubt, considered setting up a small independent company to market Oviron. If you haven't, it might be worth thinking about. You could then consider and assess your own tenders for business, though I suppose you do that already.' Mostyn looked at Hoffmann and neither man flinched. The man watching the closed-circuit screen scribbled a few notes. Like Hoffmann, he too thought Sir William Mostyn a thorough professional. Unlike him, however, he did flinch. The physician was more informed in commercial matters than he liked. He preferred them innocent.

'What I'm saying, gentlemen, is that if you want your drug tested quite legally in those who are obese, or indeed porphyric; we can do it. And we shall do it. Allow me to summarize the steps you must take to do this.

'Slide, please.' As soon as Mostyn spoke the lights went out again and a perfectly prepared slide appeared on the screen. Like his predecessor at the lectern Mostyn addressed both slide and audience without seeing either.

'First: Obtain a Clinical Trial Certificate to test Oviron in humans in any disease you please.'

'Second: Demonstrate that Oviron works in that disease and obtain a Product License for that clinical indication.'

'Third: Provide some evidence that it works in obesity.'

'Fourth: Obtain a clinical trial exemption to test the drug in obesity. Show - by fair means or foul - that it works.'

'Fifth: Obtain a Product License extension for obesity. Sell your drug. Make a great deal of money.

'Lights please!' Mostyn said, leaving the slide on the screen so that the information on it could be perused at will.

'If you have initial problems working out what the drug is actually going to do to people give it to prisoners in the U.S. Or to children, if you prefer, in under-developed countries. Korea's a good bet, about ten dollars a head. Alternately you can give it to human volunteers or to patients on a named-patient basis. It's all perfectly legal.'

Greg Hoffmann knew that in fact they had done almost all of these things and that they had not all turned out entirely as planned.

The Korean orphanage data had proved unreliable statistically and they had lost a prisoner in the States. The man had obtained more remission than he had hoped as a result of taking the drug. He had died. And one volunteer. Well, that still had to be carefully monitored.

A named patient had also been given the drug, a pregnant woman, and the results were due any time now. He hoped they'd be good.

'You will appreciate, however,' Mostyn continued; 'That as far as your Industry is concerned, there are also agreed, though not legally enforceable, standards by which such things are done. As long as you keep to these standards you obviate the pressure which comes from certain political quarters for more restrictive legislation on your autonomy.

'There are standards and conditions, too, which you must fulfil to obtain your first license for your new drug's use. But only the first one. There are also standards, gentlemen, laid down by our patriarchs, for the appropriate marketing of all drugs old and new.

'Even if you break these standards, break this voluntary code of conduct, you are usually back among the big boys within a matter of months. You may, for example, be fined or expelled, for a few months from what's called the Association of the British Pharmaceutical Industry which Iain here will discuss with you. But that doesn't mean much. If you don't believe me, look at Lilley with Opren, or elsewhere, Distillers with Thalidomide.

Anyway, allow us at this point to introduce to you the standards the Industry has set itself and which my learned colleague here will explain to you. He is very straight, aren't you Iain?' said Mostyn looking at his colleague, 'So you can rely on what he has to say, even if you don't enjoy it.'

With this piece of studied sarcasm so typical of his jaundiced view of most things, Mostyn left the lectern and went and sat down with the others. He took his drink and the silver pot and spoon with him.

The second speaker was less pretentious than Mostyn, more direct and every bit as professional. He made his points clearly.

'In the United Kingdom, we have highly specific guidelines for the investigation of drugs on human beings. As Sir William has intimated to you, these are made available to us by the A.B.P.I., The Association of the British Pharmaceutical Industry. This advice conforms to government legislation but the emphasis here is more on how to go about things, rather than to stress the legal aspects of them.

'For example, we should know the chemistry of the drug thoroughly and how it affects every major organ of the body. In addition, we should know if it has the potential to affect our sexual function in any way or, particularly if given over the long term, know if it predisposes us to cancer or some other chronic or malignant illness. In general terms, with respect to the average drug, we would want to see how it affects us in any way at all after it has been administered to us for six months or more.'

Hoffmann studied this man carefully as he had studied many similar men before. Sometimes they had been greedy men, sometimes over-altruistic, sometimes simply innocents abroad. This one, somehow, was different.

His dress was conservative, boring, nondescript. His physical bearing, his tenor of voice, his presence nothing spectacular, ordinary. Yet there was something, something about the man ... He wondered what his vice was and unexpectedly an errant thought dropped through him like ice. He reminded him of his mother. She'd had the same distant look in her eyes, the same disquieting ordinariness. But Hoffmann had known the reason for that. He thought on Kathryn. Her body and her insolence. He felt a surge of emotion as the ice melted. He repressed it easily. He'd had years of experience and practice.

He could control what he felt, whatever it was, whenever he wanted to.

The speaker made his points without any hyperbole or innuendo of any sort. He looked, dressed and behaved in a perfectly conventional manner and his presentation reflected this totally. His talk was factual and was delivered professionally, without undue emphasis on any particular point. Given this it was difficult to believe that what they were doing was grossly criminal.

Hoffmann sought in vain to find the crack in the speaker's character. To find the line he could insert his wedge into even as he listened to him speak.

'Once the appropriate laboratory tests have been carried out in animals, human tests are carried out. These conform to a pattern. Which we like to describe in phases.'

'In phase one, we compare and elucidate how the drug acts in humans with tests previously carried out on animals. If there are any major discrepancies, we study these in detail. It is in this way, for example, that we ascertain the likely initial dose of a drug that should be used on the first patients.

'In what we term phases two and three, we look at the drug in either human volunteers or in human patients and this constitutes what we term a "clinical trial". By doing this we can ascertain how safe a drug is and define the optimum dose required to treat the condition for which the drug is intended.

'It is now that, if the drug has shown that it is safe and effective, we enter into what are termed phase four trials: these are trials which occur after the drug has been marketed, but where feedback of potential side effects is carefully monitored by those treating the patients receiving the drug. Such post-marketing surveillance, usually picks up anything which was missed earlier.'

He paused and took a sip of water from the glass before him. He looked at Hoffmann and the ice formed again in the Shadow Man; cold, brittle, something with the potential to cut. As Hoffmann breathed deeply and steadily the speaker continued, the sound of his voice adding layers to the ice.

'At this point, gentlemen, all adverse drug events have to be reported. All relevant medical personnel are then informed of these through a formalized process we call the 'Yellow Peril.' In other words, warnings written on yellow cards are sent to every doctor in the U.K., telling him or her to look out for these effects. They don't instruct them to stop using the drug however, simply to exercise their judgement.'

Mostyn stood up at this point and Hoffmann noticed the silver container in his hand.

'Come on, Iain, time's getting on. Get to the point.' He spoke, with a loud distinctive tone in his voice, a tone that Greg Hoffmann had heard from someone else, the person who was watching these proceedings in the hidden room adjoining this one. A financial genius with a problem that led to occasional bursts of, what were termed euphemistically, 'enthusiasm.' Just like this one by Mostyn, but not induced by drugs.

The other physician looked at Mostyn. 'I'll leave that to you, Bill,' he said quietly, 'I've an appointment to keep myself. I'm already late for it.'

'O.K.', Mostyn replied getting straight to the point, his mood erratic. 'One way or the other, we can ultimately influence or control every department and committee that we have mentioned.'

He paused for just a second, his natural arrogance and confidence enhanced by the rush the white powder had given him.

'And what do we want? You've obviously asked yourselves that question. The bottom line's simple, gentlemen, as far as we're concerned. Iain should have told you himself, it's his greatest wish, if not exactly my own. Make 'The London General' the most famous hospital in the United Kingdom. Europe if possible, and we'll get your drug to where you want it to be. We are, you see, altruists,' he said with irony. 'We believe we are the best hospital in Europe and we want people to know it. To come there to be cured. To put money into our research efforts and our staff. That's it gentlemen,' Mostyn finished with what he felt was a grand flourish. 'The floor's now yours.'

There was silence for a time and then the quiet controlled voice spoke once more as the shadows of the morning crept up the walls from beneath the window-blinds which were still drawn.

'We can supply the means for you to do that, Sir William.' said Greg Hoffmann as he sat thinking. Understanding now, at last, the other man's motive. He could have that if he wanted it. At least he could think that he was going to have it, which was the same thing. He was a naive misguided altruist with a criminal desire for excellence.

Hoffmann stood up at this point and formally thanked the speakers. He now had enough information from these two, to advance the movement of Oviron. To make himself and his company secure in their ambitions for the drug.

Unicorn Chemicals was something special to Greg Hoffmann. His *raison d'etre*. He felt he had been nurtured by it, taught its ways, fed its food, conditioned to its modes of behavior. Sometimes he felt he'd die for his company. He loved it almost unconditionally. It gave him his reason for living. A reason for doing and thinking things which, perversely, kept him occupied and made him lonely at one and the same time. His company supported Hoffman's greatest dreams -and great they were. It was like a mother to him.

As the two physicians indicated their wish to leave, Hoffmann stood up and looked at the three others. Wilder looked satisfied, Annette Pallain suitably interested, the other man spoke.

'One thing, if I may, Greg.' The voice was confident and easy. Andrew Wills was an athletic looking man with healthily bronzed skin, grey-white hair and he sported a small moustache.

'Yes, Andrew?' said the Shadow Man.

'Two things really, Greg. One, why do we want to run these anti-porphyric tests? Secondly, what about side effects and adverse reactions?'

'Allow me to answer in reverse order, Andrew,' said the Shadow Man softly and with respect. Wills was a capable man. That's why he'd been invited.

'To address your second point. Oviron does not appear to have any major side-effects or adverse reactions,' he lied smoothly.

'And the reason we want an anti-porphyric profile run on Oviron,' Hoffmann said solemnly, 'is quite simple. It is because we are going to use it to make The London General the most famous hospital in Europe, perhaps in the world.' he looked squarely at Mostyn as he said this and as he ended.

'We are going to use it, you see, to treat the future Kings of England.'

Hoffmann opened the door of the hotel room. Kathryn Meadowford was lying on the bed waiting for him. Never in the bed, always on it. Just as he liked. He walked over to the courtesy bar, opened it, and took out a small bottle of tonic water. He unscrewed the top and poured the drink into a glass, watching it effervesce. The meniscus flowed up to the top, foaming there at the rim, partially suspended in air.

'What do you mean by trying to create an impression in that company?' he said softly, with a menace as chilling as the ice in his drink.

'I wasn't trying to create any impression, Greg. I was genuinely concerned. This project means so much to us. Without it the company...'

'Shut it, Kathryn. What did you mean by trying to create an impression in that company?' he repeated as he walked towards her, the cold menace streaming through his eyes into hers. It excited her.

He took a sip from his glass, felt the tang of quinine.

'Nice,' he said, as he threw the rest of its contents over Kathryn Meadowford's face.

She drew herself away from him, curled on the bed. Vulnerable.

'God', she cried, 'What's wrong with you, Greg? For Christ's sake! We don't need this!' She cleaned the liquid from her as best she could. 'I thought there may be something human in you somewhere.' she paused, manipulating him, pressing the buttons to evoke the response she wanted.

'Can you love at all, Greg? I feel it you know. You know that, what the hell's wrong with you?'

Hoffmann walked towards her and threw the few remaining drops remaining in the glass into her face. Love her, how could he? How could he love anyone? He didn't know how to. He had never learned. As a child no-one had ever loved him.

They were driven quickly towards The London General by the driver from Unicorn who handled the company Bentley as if he were an explorative teenager with a responsive date.

Mostyn sat quietly looking out of the car window, reflecting on whatever he reflected on. His colleague sat beside him with more precise reflections. He was not at all happy about the morning's events.

Since the first approaches had been made to him by Sir William, he had been very uneasy about their collaboration with Unicorn. He'd reluctantly agreed to assist, as he genuinely felt that it would do a great deal for the hospital. He had been wrong. He soon discovered that the stakes were much higher than that. Very much higher.

Like it or not, he was now committed to continue on the path he'd naively chosen. All that he could do now was to carry out a policy of harm-reduction. Minimize the damage to those who would be victims. There were victims already, he knew that, he was one himself.

'You mentioned that you had an appointment, Iain,' Mostyn's voice slipped into his thoughts; 'Anyone I know?'

'The new Junior Registrar,' he replied, 'she starts this morning.'

'A pretty young thing, I thought. And Young too if I remember correctly - Allison Young?'

'Yes Bill, correct as ever.' Their eyes met and there was a transient hint of distaste there: a distaste tempered by tolerance.

'Thank you, Iain,' said Mostyn returning once more to his personal reflections.

He disliked the Gaelic rendition of his forename name - Iain -which Mostyn, amongst others, had addressed him by ever since their student days. He disliked it almost as much as he disliked the man himself. Like the name, however, they went back a long time and there was a bond between them which, somehow, had endured. Like it or not, in many ways, John Bennet was a man with his fair share of problems.

As Allison rearranged herself and Claire stood waiting to escort her to Doctor Bennet's office, she suddenly heard a familiar voice.

'Allison! You're with us. Great to see you. Sorry if I'm a bit late. Traffic. Good morning, Claire.'

It was Doctor Bennet. He was standing in the corridor with an overcoat over his arm, a bulging briefcase in his hand and a beaming smile on his face. As Claire walked away from them back to the office, he waved Allison over, shook her hand and he went along the corridor with her.

In the old-fashioned manner that she didn't mind at all, he put the arm with the overcoat still dangling from it protectively around Allison's shoulders. Like his young secretary, he was pleased to see her at any rate. Two to one against the Charge Nurse.

Despite her delight at seeing him, Allison noted that he looked very tired and drawn. A great deal more so since they'd last met. Working all hours, no doubt, she thought.

They walked along what seemed like a maze of corridors and finally climbed two flights of stairs at the top of which they found Bennet's office.

'It's the only way I can keep fit,' he said to her smiling. 'No time for anything else more exciting. Hope you don't mind.'

'Why, of course not,' Allison responded. 'I need the exercise myself.'

Just as they were about to go into the office Allison noticed the young man she had spoken to earlier in the reception area. He was standing in the corridor speaking with what appeared to be a junior doctor. Doctor Bennet noticed him too:

'Hello, Harry,' he said in a voice tinged with concern. 'How are things?'

The man looked over at Bennet, nodded in recognition to Allison and raised his hand.

'Hello, John,' he replied. 'much the same.' He turned back to continue his discussion with the junior doctor.

Allison pondered briefly on this familiarity. Sister Jennifer Wright had certainly found herself someone well known in the hospital. 'Harry', she thought briefly. The name suited him.

'Come in and make yourself at home,' said Bennet as he opened the office door for her and stood aside to allow her to pass. She entered and noticed how the light fell through the window, spreading a long dark shadow across the parquet floor. The shadow chilled her as she caught the early morning sun bright and warm at last beyond the window. She found a seat and sat down. Bennet closed the door.

CHAPTER TWO

The Society of the Mayflower Compact derived its name from the agreement drawn up by the Founding Fathers of North America who had drafted a political policy in this name for their new colony. Each member of the Society wore a tiny decorative pin in their lapel on the top of which was engraved the mast head of a ship. The pin was not an aid to enable members to identify one another there was no need for that as they all knew each other reasonably well. It was simply a reminder to them of the interests they pursued and of their historical origins.

The Society was quite open about its membership and a list of its members was freely available for perusal if requested; its members in turn were open about the Society itself and what its functions were. They were, quite simply, a group of like-minded people who had a keen interest in the historical evolution of the United States since the arrival of the pilgrim fathers in New England on The Mayflower in 1620.

They were also keen devotees of American history and culture in general and over the many years of their existence they had set up a Trust to enable selected students who applied to them to obtain adequate funding to take up any academic posts pertinent to the Society's interests.

They had, for example, funded master's and doctoral dissertations and theses and had privately published historical works with titles such as: 'The Identity of the Pilgrim Fathers;' 'Captain Christopher Jones - A Biography,' 'The Mayflower Compact and Our Constitution;' 'Our True English Heritage' and many others.

These were works for the historian and none made for popular reading. That, however, was of no concern to the Society, for these were works of great historical interest to the specialist and that's precisely what its members were; specialists. In a number of things.

In this sense, therefore, the Society was a charitable organization and its economic status was thus defined. It was also an organization given to the furtherance of academic research and excellence; an organization respected by those academics who had dealt with it either directly or indirectly. It was also an organization given to gross dissimulation. In other words it was a sham.

Of the one hundred and two current members of the Society of the Mayflower Compact - the same number as allegedly sailed on The Mayflower - only eighteen were members of the 'Society of the San Graal.'

The 'San Graal' was an elite group selected from suitable members of the parent society who while they knew virtually nothing of this other group's true aims and objectives; would have fully supported them if they had. Perhaps not all would have wholly supported the methods used by this inner circle to achieve their ends however. Nor, presumably, would they have unquestioningly shared the extremity of their political intentions. For the historical aspirations of the select individuals who were members of the San Graal went a great deal further than academic study and excellence.

They all shared a common goal which was based on their avid nationalism. It was not, however, the nationalism of conservative Americans, of the extreme right or left. Neither was it the supremacist type of nationalism of the type portrayed by the Klu Klux Klan, or the American League of Fascists. For the members of the Society of the San Graal, proud American citizens as they all were; were English nationalists.

Republicans all, they felt that the time had come to replace that Republic. And the way they wanted to do that was by re-introducing a monarchy to their country; a monarchy which would give the term 'special relationship' between the two countries a significant meaning. Not only did they want an Anglo-American monarch to replace their republic, they also had a particular person in mind for the job; a person who they believed qualified for that position in every respect; including that of blood line. Of heredity.

To any outsider particularly to members of the parent Society who may have had limited access to any formal documentation of the Society of the San Graal; to its audited financial records perhaps, its stated constitution, or to any other of the few pieces of recorded information on the Society which existed; its title explained its function. The 'San Graal.' 'The Sacred Cup'. 'The Holy Grail.'

Much as they'd have been surprised at such notable people having an interest in such a vague and mystical subject as the cup which allegedly held the blood of Christ, it would have been accepted as being no more than a slightly eccentric interest or a rather majestic name for another area of study for these amateur historians - the Arthurian legends.

Further, those members of the parent Society who expressed keen interest in the pursuits of this smaller group, were told that this was precisely what the Society of the San Graal was about.

The study of the grail legends as depicted by Chretien de Troyes' *Conte du Graal*, von Eschenbach's *Parzival*, Malory's *Morte d'Arthur* and other works which these had inspired.

This was an acceptable explanation and if the interested member expressed interest in becoming involved in these studies, there was adequate academic research which could be put their way while the Society scrutinized them more closely with a view to extending an invitation in due course to enter their circle if it when it was appropriate to do so.

After all, all of the members of the Mayflower Compact were financially sound, strongly conservative and certainly nationalistic; most, therefore, were potential candidates for higher things.

What such an interested outsider would have been initially unaware of, however, was the fact that it was not the holy grail which this society pursued but something else. Something a great deal more sinister. It was not San Graal - the sacred cup, which they pursued or held in preparation for its day of revelation; but Sang Raal - the blood of the king. Or to be more precise, the blood line or descendants of 'The King.' For the members of the Society of the San Graal believed that they had exactly that; a direct male descendant of the English monarch James I whose ancestors had sailed, together with a sister ship, *incognito* from Southampton, England on September 16th 1620 and who had arrived at Plymouth, New England on December 26th of that same year.

The Mayflower had been compelled to go ashore at Plymouth because the royal child had been born that day and his mother required treatment which could only be found on land. Consequently, the ship put to port on 26th December 1620 or, to be more precise when time differences were taken into account, December the 25th - Christmas day. A highly appropriate time for a king to be born.

And that bloodline - the Society of the San Graal believed -had remained intact ever since. That they had a genuine contender for an American throne they had no doubt. All that was required of him was that he found an appropriate wife and that his descendants could claim succession to the throne of England in due course.

After centuries of waiting that "appropriate wife" was now a distinct prospect. Further she was a naturalised American citizen who spent much of her time in Washington. Even more to the Society's liking was the fact that her elder daughter could one day be the next queen of England.

There were two men in the library of the building fronted by the blue door and one woman. They sat close together around the table where a week ago to the day they'd had their historical meeting. The woman was beginning to show signs of her age. She was in her mid-seventies perhaps but her voice was clear and uncluttered as were her thoughts.

'The Duchess has accepted the invitation,' she said crisply; 'I received her reply this morning. So what do you propose to do now?' The elder of the two men responded immediately.

'Precisely as we discussed,' he said, with a voiced imbued with authority. 'We shall have a relatively candid discussion with her, reassure her that the arrangements will be satisfactory. She doesn't have to be given all the details quite yet.'

'She's not stupid,' interjected the younger man softly; the heir apparent who had so recently smiled with total control at the applause which had come his way the week before. 'You'll have to be pretty convincing before she'll accept what you say. She has her advisors too. They're hardly naive.'

The elder man gave a grunt and raised his hand in a gesture which demanded complete attention.

'Precisely,' he replied; 'While naivety is not one of their major attributes; like most things that fact has its positive aspect. They would not, for example, wish upon their other royal charges an untreatable disease which has psychotic components to it. Would they?' He reached out his hand and lifted a large crystal goblet filled with iced water upon which was engraved a unicorn.

He drank from it and adjusted the pin in his lapel the one which designated membership of the Society of the Mayflower Compact. 'These people are realists, pragmatists. We can offer them the means of preventing that happening or, at least, of reducing the severity of the disease to a minimum. A minimum, however, which does not enable them to rule.'

'But surely, given that the drug is effective in treating the disease there should be no reason why they shouldn't succeed?' questioned the elderly woman as she looked the elder of the two men straight in the eye.

'Explain if you would,' he prompted the younger man, his tone being quite acceptable, quite usual.

His voice completely controlled and precise as steel the younger man gladly capitulated.

'I have neither medical nor scientific qualification as you know, Marjorie, but so far as I understand while the drug does indeed remove the signs of the disease, it neither completely cures it nor guarantees complete remission from the occasional attack.

'Further,' he continued; 'I believe that the drug itself has some side-effects which, in themselves, could be embarrassing to a future monarch. The bottom line is simply that a life-threatening disease can be treated, lives saved, but succession is out of the question unless people want to see their monarch occasionally behaving like a lunatic in public. That possibility, apparently, can neither be fully predicted nor fully controlled.

'The two boys fall into that category, their uncle does too.' he continued; 'Consequently the next in line to the throne is that uncle's elder daughter.' He paused allowing the woman to take on board precisely what he was saying. 'I am loved a great deal by that daughter's mother and in the not too distant future, unless I am very mistaken, we shall be married. I am also a direct descendant of James the First as is my nephew.'

'And can you be certain that she'll marry you given the change in circumstances?' asked the woman whose social contacts included many royals. She knew their ways, their princely foibles.

'Until now we have been unable to be married much as she desires it,' continued the younger man as he smoothed his deeply dark hair with his palm; 'But now? Well as you say, things have altered somewhat. I think a deal can be struck.'

Again, he sat back in his chair completely relaxed, as he received approving looks from the elder one. Looks which did not at all intimate the real truth of the situation. That was known only to a few.

'But even if this does proceed as you say, surely when the elder daughter marries, her children will succeed and we'll be no further forward?'

Not if she marries an American citizen,' said the young man having anticipated the question as he'd answered it often enough; 'particularly if it's my nephew. Then, not only shall we have the American monarchy we all want but we shall direct and control it and it will all happen within our lifetime. At least that of most of us.'

'But there's no guarantee of that,' continued the woman who though still perplexed, had not missed the allusion to her growing age. It was typical of him, to hurt when he could; 'Who's to know what the courtiers, civil-servants and other establishment figures over there will do? There's no guarantee...'

'Oh, but there is!' interrupted the elder man his face tightening with the tension he was beginning to feel. He hated inquisitions, explanations of things which he'd himself planned. The woman was needed, however, and she was part of them, had been for almost fifty years. Consequently he indulged her. 'There is, Marjorie, believe me. 'We literally have the power of life and death over them,' he continued in a monotone; 'They will hardly attempt to strike a tough bargain under such circumstances. If it became public knowledge then...' He made an appropriate gesture which was understood.

'Anyway, he continued, 'we are simply making them an offer which - as they say - they simply can't refuse,' he continued ironically; 'We're making the United States of America a part of the British Commonwealth of Nations. How could they possibly decline...?'

'Then, of course, there's the religious issue... You'll remember, Marjorie, of course you will that back in 1994 the Duchess of Kent converted to Roman Catholicism as did Frances Shand-Kydd that same year. Have you pondered the significance of that one? It's implications...? Can you really see a King who is welcomed as a family guest at the Vatican? God! Elizabeth and Henry would turn in their graves at the very thought and quite correct they'd be too.

Both the younger man and the woman looked at him carefully. They knew that behind the irony there was the clarity of fact. And the fact was that Sir Abe Wilder, Chairman; Chief Executive and owner of fifty one percent of the stock of Unicorn Chemicals was rarely ever wrong.

The first week passed very quickly for Allison filled as it was with all that was involved in her getting to know the hospital, her department and her colleagues. There barely seemed to be enough time in the day to fit everything into it, and, busy as she was, she loved every minute of it.

As she had anticipated Doctor Bennet was not only very bright but was also a very capable and excellent instructor. He was simply a gem to work with. There were frequent flashes of warmth and humor sprinkling his down-to-earth way of approaching things. This was an attitude she liked, respected and responded to and which reminded her from time to time of her father.

Whatever self-doubts Allison had experienced about her suitability for her post were soon dismissed by the well-deserved praise which Bennet and her other colleagues intentionally put her way. A marked contrast indeed to the cool reception she'd received from Jennifer Wright on her first morning. A woman whose immediate impression on Allison had remained and hardened.

She had seen the woman five or six times that week and not once had the nurse shown any sign of recognition. In a way she intrigued Allison who knew of the often uncannily close proximity of like to dislike, hate to love, sex to pain, life to death. Now and then she found herself wondering about her. She seemed an efficient woman and her status as Charge Nurse demonstrated the fact that she must have considerable professional ability. Her downright bad manners, however, were puzzling and there was, of course, the unresolved question of the good-looking young man.

Allison wondered about him too when she saw the nurse and about the source of the sadness she'd felt surrounded him. She appreciated that such ruminations were more apposite for a teenager than a supposedly mature woman, but she indulged them anyway. Where was the harm? She had made a mental note to ask one of her colleagues if they could enlighten her as to who he was and about his relationship to Sister Wright. Having so much else to occupy her, however, she never got round to it.

By the end of her second week, Allison had fallen into some sort of routine, erratic as it was. So when one of the other younger doctors, an already internationally known geneticist called Pamela Smith had asked her if she would like to go to a party on the following Saturday evening, Allison felt that she was well enough established to accept the invitation. She had hesitated initially though, something in her resisting the urge to go out and enjoy herself. Soon enough she realized what it was. Guilt.

In all the time Allison had spent in her only serious romantic relationship; neither she nor her erstwhile fiancee had done much in the way of serious socialising alone. Not that either of them had lacked the opportunity. Far from it. He had, however, been very possessive and didn't like to see Allison fussed over by other men. As this was virtually guaranteed by the combination of her striking good looks and her natural charm and vivacity; it meant that she almost never went anywhere alone socially in order to spare his over-active imagination and his feelings. In turn, though it was a needless gesture, he did the same. They were, therefore always together at the parties and the dances and the more formal occasions. And if for some reason they couldn't be, they rarely appeared at all.

It was this that Allison was still coming to terms with. The feeling that she was in some way betraying him even though it was now more than six months since she'd ended the relationship; six months in which she had asked herself daily if she had made the correct decision concerning him; particularly when she lay alone at night missing his presence, missing his comments on her day, missing him beside her, loving her as he had once. She had nonetheless fought her resistance and had done so very successfully. She was going partying unescorted for the first time in a very long time indeed and she was determined to enjoy herself.

'Who's going to be there?' she asked Pam inquisitively.

'Just a bunch of hospital people I'm afraid,' said the darkly attractive geneticist. 'There's no escaping it. Still, it will give you the chance to meet some more people who work here and to put some names to the few faces you probably recognize already. You never know you might even meet someone special.' Pam spoke cryptically with a smile on her very pretty face. 'Perhaps we could meet up for a drink beforehand and go along together?'

'Why, that would be marvelous,' said Allison, slightly too quickly as the geneticist was very observant:

'A bit nervous?'

'Just a bit,' agreed Allison with a touch of embarrassment: 'You see it's been quite some time since ... Well I've been a lone-wolf for some time now and between that and being new to the place...'

Pam interrupted her, she caught her eyes in her own; brown eyes, Pam held Allison's with them, then smiled deeply. 'Seven-thirty in Vintners Wine Bar.?'

'O.K.,' Allison replied as a large smile of pleasure and relief crept over her face. 'I'm really looking forward to it.'

'Done then,' said Pam. 'Now let's see if Mrs Bailley's pathology is ready yet. She's just about to deliver baby Bailley and we'd better know what's what before then. Come on party girl!'

Feeling happier than she had done for a very long time, yet wondering what exactly she had caught a glimpse of in Pam's eyes; Allison followed the cue of her colleague and together they made their way to the pathology lab. In her mind Allison pictured the very large and very expectant Mrs Bailley. She was a delightful woman in her early forties who had been over the moon at becoming pregnant so late in life and who, although she had two other children, was behaving as if this was to be her first.

Pam told Allison that it had taken Mrs Bailley a full three months before she had even gone to her doctor to have a pregnancy test carried out; so incredulous was she that she was actually pregnant. She had thought that the physical signs she was having were simply due to the menopause, few things being further from her mind than a pregnancy at this stage of her life.

In consequence she had only recently considered the possibility that her baby may suffer from Down's syndrome, the mongolism which is much more common in the children of older mothers. To establish whether or not the baby was so affected, the appropriate test had been carried out by removing a sample of the fluid surrounding the baby in the womb to ascertain if the gene for Down's syndrome was present.

Allison actively willed that the result would be negative, but something told her that it wouldn't be. As they opened the door and sought out the senior histologist her good humor fell away. This was the reality of hospital medicine, what she was paid for, and what she wanted more than anything else to do.

They found the histologist in a tiny room off the main laboratory. He was peering through a microscope, pen in hand, noting what he saw. Without changing his position he raised a hand in greeting, continuing to look at whatever it was which was holding his attention.

'Hi Bob,' said Pam; 'Do you have Mrs Bailley's results yet? We'd like them as soon as possible, if possible!' Pam's voice was light an inversion of her thoughts.

The histologist turned away from his microscope and looked at her: 'I'm afraid so,' he said. Allison's heart sank.

'Positive for Down's?' asked Pam flatly; absently running her fingers through her dark shoulder length hair.

The histologist nodded. 'Yes' he said; 'Afraid so,' and he handed Pam the written report which he had prepared and had waiting beside him. 'Pity that isn't it?' His attention had turned to Allison who though she had been involved with Pathology quite a bit hadn't met him before.

She nodded to him and simply said: 'Allison Young' They shook hands.

'Hello and welcome Allison,' the histologist responded, 'I've heard all about you. All of it good. I hope you're settling in.'

'Thanks Bob,' interjected Pam as she replaced the report and made her way to the door with Allison following. Once outside they stood in the corridor for a few moments. Allison was visibly upset. 'You can't afford this you know,' Pam said, noting her distress. 'Professional detachment and all.'

'But I can,' smiled Allison. 'Now and then.'

Pam gave her arm a gentle squeeze. 'Come on,' she said, 'Let's go for some coffee. I've a little surprise for you, or at least Doctor Bennet has. It should cheer you up. I meant to tell you before, but it slipped my mind. He wants to see you, correction us; this morning at eleven thirty. Good news, I assure you.' Allison was surprised.

'But what can he possibly want to see me about? I mean, what is there to discuss? Come on Pam, what's the secret?'

Pam held her forefinger to her nose and slowly shook her head.

'So impatient,' she muttered: 'Eleven thirty in Doctor Bennet's office. You'll find out then, lass and not a moment sooner.'

In an excited frustration, Allison persisted in sounding out her colleague, but to no avail. Her questions were met with a stony silence. At last she desisted.

'Eleven thirty?' she said.

'That's right,' replied Pam. 'Not a moment sooner. Or later.'

Together they went to the common room for coffee. It was better than the staff canteen, quieter and Allison had one or two things to think about.

When they entered, there were a man and woman already there whom Allison had never seen before. Before Pam had time to introduce them Allison noted that the man wore his black beard carefully trimmed, had a formal black suit on, wore pince-nez and a bow tie:

"Psychiatrist", she thought immediately.

'Alan Downie', said Pam, 'London's favorite psychiatrist. Brightest, best and bonniest!'. Alan turned to face Allison directly, his eye-contact exact.

'Allison Young!', he said with a warm smile that Allison liked. 'Pam's told me all about you. And forgive her by the way for her Scottishness and skittishness - brightest, best and bonniest. She studied for a solitary year at Edinburgh and came back with a lot of odd political ideas and even odder words. Allow me to introduce you both to Kathryn Meadowford. Kathryn's from Unicorn Chemicals. We're running a small trial for them with their new drug Oviron.'

They both shook hands with the woman whom Allison noticed was strikingly attractive and beautifully dressed in that peculiar female-executive way. The new female edition of the pin-striped suit, briefcase and umbrella.

What sort of tests are you running?' enquired Allison. 'I have some sort of professional interest - my father practiced psychiatry until he retired to general practice in the country some five years ago.'

'Oh, nothing too stretching,' said Alan; 'Some psychometric stuff, vigilance tests, possible effects on learning, spatial orientation, that sort of thing. Nothing new, but it makes a change from the usual things, breaks up the old routine a bit.'

'Formal controls must be getting a bit tighter now,' Pam said absently as she made towards a drawer in the corner of the room and opened it.

'How do you mean?' asked Alan.

'Well, I thought Oviron was an anti-viral or an antibiotic. They're doing a formal trial on it in various things up in Infectious Diseases. There's a mob of bacteriologists running around with petri-dishes and things.'

Allison suddenly observed with what amounted to shock that Pam had removed a bottle of Scotch from the drawer and was openly pouring some into the coffee Alan had poured for her.

'Want some?' she asked. Allison declined. A degree of silence fell around them but the others said nothing and Pam poured herself a generous measure. She replaced the bottle with no further comment.

'We try to maintain the highest standards in drug-evaluation in the world,' Kathryn Meadowford's voice was soft, quiet and compelling. 'We're not content, at Unicorn, to simply follow the minimal requirements for monitoring our drugs. We like to know everything about them. Everything. That's what Alan's helping us to do. The same with the people in Bacteriology.'

'It's worth a free meal anyway,' said the genial psychiatrist. 'Don't let anyone tell you these Industrial types don't try to bribe you. I've had two Indian curries at the Taj and a Chinese carry-out already. All at Kate's expense; and two free pens and a Unicorn Chemicals note-pad!' They all laughed as Alan flashed one of the cheap pens ostentatiously. Allison felt that the executive's laugh was forced. Intuitively she didn't like her. Silly perhaps, but Allison trusted her intuition and it didn't like what it saw. She didn't think that Alan was really this lady's cup of tea, or that the 'Taj Mahal' and Chinese carry-outs were Kathryn Meadowford's scene either.

'Were you never tempted to follow your father into psychiatry?' Alan asked her. His voice and demeanor was more serious now; more, she felt, a truer reflection of the competent professional that he undoubtedly was.

'For a time,' Allison said, 'I trained for two years, as a then lay-therapist with my father, but I found that I preferred hematology. I think I understand why, however, my training did that for me at least!'

Alan smiled at her again:

'Pity we lost you,' he said, 'Still we need good hematologists too. What's your special interest?'

'Porphyria,' Allison replied casually; referring to the rare blood disease. 'When I did my undergraduate dissertation on it, it hooked me. I thought then I knew how to treat it! A precocious notion indeed for a mere student. Still it interests me greatly.'

'Oh the Royal Disease!' exclaimed Alan. 'Who was it...? Charles the first, George the third, Bismarck...'

'Well done!' exclaimed Allison, there are not many of my colleagues who share this particular interest, it's quite rare you know.'

'I know, but it can have interesting psychiatric complications,' Alan replied. Then turning to Kathryn Meadowford he

continued: 'What's your background Kate? I've never got round
to asking you. Too busy eating those curries.'

Kathryn Meadowford's voice was audibly strained.
Something had clearly upset her. Allison assumed that it had
been Pam openly reaching for the Scotch. Even so she answered
the question evenly. 'I did business management at Harvard
Business School after doing my M.P.S. at Kings College here,
in London.'

'So, you're a pharmacist as well as business-woman,' Pam
said apparently impressed and sipping slowly at her drink.

'No, just a business woman,' replied Kathryn Meadowford
with a graze of a smile. 'An executive of Unicorn Chemicals.'

"Sharp," thought Pam; "Too sharp for my liking, Ms
Meadowford, executive". Without knowing it, Pam and Allison
had found another common link in their growing relationship.
Their instinctive and mutual dislike of Kathryn Meadowford
executive of Unicorn Chemicals; member of the Society of the
Mayflower Compact and more. A great deal more.

CHAPTER THREE

It was one of the grandest houses in Washington and it was rumored that some of the most important political, military, social and financial issues had been decided there, informally, by those representatives of the American establishment who attend social gatherings such as this one.

In terms of the guest list, this particular occasion was no exception. The gathering included some of the most eminent people from every facet of the capital's various power bases. It included too a British Duchess escorted by a relatively young businessman whose face, like her own, was known to millions. What these millions, and few of the people in this grand house did not know, however, was that he aspired to a power potentially greater than any held on Capitol Hill.

'Good-evening,' Duchess,' said Marjorie Sisley warmly; 'I sincerely hope you enjoy yourself.' There was need for formality here as Ms Sisley, being one of Washington's top socialites, already knew the Duchess very well on both a social and personal level. She had worked hard to do so and, given the assistance she'd been given, it was no surprise that she'd been successful.

'I'm sure I will,' responded the Duchess as her escort followed her to take Miss Sisley's hand.

'How is your latest book progressing?' asked the aging socialite with apparently genuine interest. 'My grandchildren are keenly waiting it. They love your recordings too.' The Duchess gave her one of her warmest smiles:

'Fine, thank you. They won't have too long to wait.' Miss Sisley smiled in turn:

'Good!' she said. 'I'll tell them that.' With that the Duchess and her companion went into the room where the reception was being held.

The room, filled with light and crystal; with brightly polished mahogany and fine paintings: was as formal and exotic as any the Duchess had seen in her home country with the exception of the Palace of course; and the brief memories that brushed through her at the thought of that pained her. So much had happened there, so much that had led to her marriage... . But there was no point in reflecting on that. It was, as they say, history.

The guests were indeed eminent people and not only that they were varied too. Among the usual dignitaries from the political, financial and industrial worlds; there was a fair sprinkling of show-business personalities as well. It was towards one of these -an Academy Award winning actress and her husband - that the Duchess and her partner initially gravitated. The actress was delighted. Not only was she genuinely pleased to see the Duchess, but it would do her public image no harm either for her to be seen in her company. Pity there were no photographers present.

The guests having all arrived, the room was filled with chatter and the frenetic atmosphere created by some of the greatest egos on Earth impressing themselves on each other. Few of the discussions taking place were of great import. On the other hand some were. In one corner of the massive room Marjorie Sisley was talking with two men; one of whom was a complete stranger to her. He was no stranger, however, to the Duchess, who, suddenly noticing him, excused herself from her Hollywood star and; puzzled, made her way over to him.

'Here she comes,' said the woman to her companions as Sir Geoffrey Dorrington pulled himself to his full height and prepared to play the part he'd already been so well rewarded for.

'Why Sir Geoffrey,' remarked the Duchess ignoring the other two people for the present; 'What on Earth are you doing here? What an unexpected, but pleasant, surprise.'

Dorrington smiled his professional smile, took the Duchess' hand and; in his courtly manner, kissed it.

'Well, Your Royal Highness,' he said with some discomfort evident in his voice; 'To be quite candid, I was kindly invited by Miss Sisley here as I'm visiting our mutual friend the gentleman beside me; Sir Abe Wilder, Chairman of Unicorn Chemicals - allow me to introduce you.'

The introductions were made, but they did little to decrease the Duchess' surprise at seeing her brother-in-law's personal physician at this particular location. Again she commented on that fact. 'Well it's quite a coincidence,' she said expectantly, still wondering at the physician's presence.

'Well there was another motive I must admit Madam,' said Dorrington as he met the intense blue eyes straight on. 'I was hoping to have a word with you, unofficially and quite discreetly of course.'

The Duchess was now even more bemused. 'But surely you could have done that through the normal channels?'

'I could have,' he replied cautiously; 'But I felt it would be more circumspect, more - eh - appropriate, if we could keep it strictly unofficial.'

The Duchess was rather alarmed now. By the strangeness of the whole situation, its much too neat coincidence and by the demeanor and conspiratorial tone of Dr Dorrington's voice.

'Is there something wrong?' she asked.

'I'm afraid there is,' replied Dorrington gently. 'Could we have a quiet word perhaps, Madam? In private.' The Duchess nodded.

'Of course,' she said, looking at Wilder and her hostess more than slightly confused now.

'The library's free,' Miss Sisley said. 'Will that be satisfactory?'

'Why yes,' replied Dorrington looking at his royal companion for approval. With some reluctance the Duchess agreed. If this turned out to be some trifle... .

'I'll take you there,' said the woman, her eyes bright with anticipation, her breath short with expectancy. The time was now. Within the hour they'd all know precisely how things stood with the main player this side of the Atlantic. 'I'm sure you'll find it suitable for your purposes.'

As she led the pair away, Sir Abe Wilder looked at them reflectively. He had little doubt about the outcome. Somewhere in the room he noticed another movie-star massaging his ego against an eminent politician's wife's adoring eyes. The encounter filled him with disgust. There were serious things happening in this place; things which would change the course of history and nothing the illusion-makers of Hollywood could produce could compare with what was happening right now.

Wilder saw the Duchess' escort looking at him. Wilder gave him a brief nod and unconsciously twirled the pin in his lapel round and round. The Duchess' escort did precisely the same thing.

Saturday evening arrived wet and blustering. Allison had left her car at home and had taken a cab into the town center. Drinking alcohol and the practice of medicine didn't mix in any way. The cab dropped her only a short walk from the wine bar where she was to meet Pam; her umbrella was hardly raised before she was folding it down again at the door of their rendezvous.

She went in and looked around. Vintners was an elegant place and the quiet murmur of subdued conversation filled the air. It was mostly couples who were there, either singly or in groups, but there were a few places where people sat alone. "Lonely people, some of these," thought Allison. Among them was Pam, sitting at a corner table by the window, sipping from a glass of what looked like Scotch. She caught Allison's eye, broke into a smile and waved her over.

Almost before Allison had sat down a young waitress had arrived to take her order. She smiled at the girl in an attempt to make her feel less servile. This was a habit of hers, based on some sort of unresolved guilt she felt about being served. Allison always felt uncomfortable with waiters or waitresses and had done so all her life. It was yet another thing to be sorted out in this new life of hers.

'A glass of white wine please,' she said. 'Well chilled if you can.' Before the waitress went off, Pam ordered another large Scotch for herself. It was evident she'd already had quite a few. Allison gave Pam her full attention as she spoke:

'Well,' said Allison, 'A lovely evening for a party. Thank goodness it's not a barbecue. Or is it?'

'Afraid not,' smiled Pam with effort, her eyes looking slightly red; 'Just as well or we'd need a very large tent.'

'Oh don't!' said Allison, trying to lighten things. 'I've hated tents ever since I went on school camp as a child. I'd rather stand in the rain than be enclosed in one of them. On that occasion it amounted to virtually the same thing. It's not a tent we'd need tonight. It would be a marquee.'

Pam met her eyes with hers. Her sad brown eyes which spoke volumes about her. When she spoke again her voice wasn't really slurred just tired sounding;

'Comte Francoise Alphonse Marquis de Sade 1740-1814,' she said incongruously. 'Pervert, prolific writer, soldier, aristocratic prisoner of the New Regime and immortalized through the term 'sadism'.'

Allison, slightly disconcerted looked closely at Pam, as she continued;

'Prolific pervert. Author of *Justine; Juliette; 120 days of Sodom* - you name it, he wrote it.' Pam fell silent, her dark auburn hair falling over her face and shading her eyes. She stared down into her glass and a tear trickled down her cheek and dropped into it.

Allison waited for a moment or two, allowing her to compose herself;

'You seem to know a lot about it,' she said.

'Oh no,' Pam responded looking at her, her eyes red now, very red with biting unshed tears, 'Not me.'

'Then who does?' asked Allison gently.

The Duchess had never felt more vulnerable. Not, at least, since she'd completed her therapy. She was glad now that she'd sought such help in the past, it would help her cope now, of that she was certain.

Having taken leave of her hostess because of a "stifling headache" she was now at her Washington pied-a-terre sharing the large lounge area with the man she loved. They sat close together on the leather *chaise longue* which, ironically enough, had been a house-warming gift from the hostess they had recently left in such a hurry.

'We have to face the facts, darling,' he said gently as he stroked her freckled nose with his calculating fingertips; 'In a situation like this, we're obliged to put our own interests to one side. It's...it's, expected,' he finished flatly in the tone he'd practiced so often in anticipation of this moment.

'It's expected...?' she replied, her voice breaking, 'By whom is it expected?' He looked at her, saying nothing, knowing that his look said it all. 'I've already sacrificed one relationship to the expectations of those people, I have no intention of sacrificing another. We have our plans, we're going to stay with them. The divorce will be finalized in six weeks' time. We'll get married a month later, that's time enough; for God's sake we've waited long enough already!' Again, he remained silent, putting his arm around her shoulders, pulling her to him. Her lips parted slightly as he pulled her gently closer, showing her regular white teeth, sparkling moist in anticipation. Their mouths met in a deep and intimate kiss.

He caressed her hair and ran his hand down her back. She shivered with pleasure and her fingers began to explore him, gently at first and then more urgently. He responded quickly and he began to undress her, enjoying the sensations and sounds of the silk, lace and nylon as they fell onto the floor leaving her full warm body naked. He tenderly licked at her breasts, felt them respond, felt her pulling him ever closer to her. His mouth began to explore her and she sighed with a deep contentment as slowly they became as one.

After their first consummation he walked slowly with her, upstairs to the bedroom. They could discuss the other issues later; right now there were other needs to be met, needs that, no matter how commonplace and basic they were, were more urgent while they lasted. Other things could wait.

'What time is it?' she asked sleepily, as she uncurled herself from him and looked lazily around the bedroom which had become much darker in what had seemed such a short time. He switched on the lamp on the table beside them, glanced at the clock which hung opposite as they both frowned in the sudden light:

'Twelve thirty-five,' he replied as he heard the telephone ring downstairs.

'Who can that be?' she asked abruptly, annoyed at the intrusion, as she pulled herself away from him, from his warmth and security. She blew him a kiss as she made her way downstairs to answer the damned thing. He returned the kiss, watched her go and then lay back into the pillow and vaguely reflected on how good things were. The muted voice speaking intermittently downstairs didn't distract him. The enormity of what he was on the threshold of achieving did.

About twenty minutes later his reflections were broken by the sound of her footsteps on the stairs. She entered the room and immediately he saw the distress on her face.

'What's wrong, darling?' he asked, genuinely distressed.

'They've told her,' she said; 'She's been told the same thing. What Dorrington said is true. They've just been to see her!'

His voice was barely controlled. This was the big one. The final shot. They had always known that her sister-in-law's reaction, if it went public as it had in the past, would be their coup-de-grace. If that didn't happen things would be that bit more complex; though the end would be the same.

'How did she take it?' he asked quietly. She walked over to him, sat on the side of the bed her blue eyes burning with emotion:

'Not too well, I'm afraid. She's already demanded another opinion from a top man in that area.'

'And who might that be?' asked the young man calmly.

'Someone from London, a Sir William Mostyn. She's asked him to repeat the tests independently and he's agreed to do so immediately. I do hope there's been some sort of mistake. God, if only the results would turn out to be different, some horrendous mistake... .'

'I don't imagine they will,' he replied; as he reached for her to comfort her. Knowing very well they'd turn out exactly the same as before.

The powerful black Saab drove through the dusk at precisely the correct speed. Inside Greg Hoffman sat at the wheel thinking. Planning again for the night ahead. Itemising time into columns.

Beside him sat Kathryn Meadowford, her long legs spread out in front of her erotically- crossed at the ankles. Each time she moved them they gave off a sharp static sound as sheer silk rubbed against itself.

'I want you to find out what the Japanese likes and offer it to him. Give it to him if need be.'

'Sure, Greg. Whatever you say.'

'Sorry?' said the Shadow Man quietly. 'I couldn't have heard you, Kathryn.'

'I said 'Sure Greg, I -'

'- You're a nice English girl, Kathryn,' he said, his voice firming. 'Not a Yank despite your impressive piece of paper from Harvard and your few years Stateside.

'Of course, Greg.' the woman executive said quietly.

'Can't hear you.'

'Of course, Greg!' she cried louder, almost shouting within the heat and shade of the leather-upholstered car.

'Better. We need the Japanese until our own man's fully in place in Tokyo. Find out what he wants and give it to him.'

As he spoke Greg Hoffmann slid his left hand slowly up Kathryn Meadowford's right thigh. He gripped her flesh tightly, his fingers digging deep into it. She gasped. A mixture of feelings rushed through her. One of them was pain, another pleasure.

'I'll do whatever's necessary.' she said breathing heavily, as she placed her hand over his, keeping him there.

'I know you will. Just don't enjoy ot too much,' Greg Hoffmann said as he gripped her flesh again. Tighter this time

'I'm sorry Pam,' said Allison, 'I really didn't mean to pry. There's no need to answer that at all, really. It's your business. A personal matter. Just like your drinking. No need to mention them.' Allison continued to speak using the psychiatric knowledge and staccato speech techniques her father had taught her to deal with people in acute distress.

'No, it's alright,' Pam said, very slightly slurred now. 'It's just, well I haven't spoken about it, not to anyone. It's never seemed appropriate until now. I don't mind.'

Allison's wine arrived together with Pam's large Scotch. The waitress placed them carefully on the table and placed the receipt alongside.

Allison tested the silence, waiting for an appropriate moment to lead the conversation. She lifted her glass and sipped. 'Lovely,' she said. 'Nice and refreshing. Just like the rain in a marquee. Do you enjoy genetics Pam? By the way what time do we have to leave? When are we expected? I hope I'm dressed O.K. Do you think so? Where did you get that brooch, it's lovely.'

By quick-fire, staccato questions, Allison had confused Pam just enough; enough, if she had done it properly, to lift her from her depression and delay her confidences to a more appropriate time. Now was the time to get her sobered up and off to the party. If she was able to. Not to hear the evidently sordid details of her love life.

'I… Eh! The brooch. It was my grandmother's,' said Pam. 'About the drink, well, everyone knows about that, Alison. Everyone at the hospital. Most of the single men there have taken advantage of it at one time or another and a fair few of the married ones too. I take pills too you know - tranquillizers.'

'Bloody hell!' Allison suddenly exclaimed. This shocked Pam, who thought her a nice pleasant middle-class innocent who would barely utter as much as a 'damn'. 'I've just realized,' she continued; 'This is the first time I've been to a party since I broke with my fiancee. He's a doctor too. Went into general practice. He wanted me to do the same, thought we'd make the ideal couple in a joint practice.' She laughed ironically; 'I didn't think we would.'

'Were you together long?' Pam asked gently, forgetting herself now just as Allison had intended her to do. "Bloody Hell" - in any context - was a useful strategy at times.

'Over two and a half years,' said Allison; speaking honestly now, seeing no more need for manipulation. 'Obviously some things were fine, it was really just his jealousy and possessiveness. I couldn't really handle that aspect and in the end I just stopped trying. I loved him though, a great deal. He was very gentle, very kind. Attractive too. Pity.'

This time it was Pam who let the silence linger as Allison, looking very sad and lovely, looked at her, inviting more comment. At length Pam spoke again.

'What was his name?'

Allison looked up at her without raising her head. Her deep blue eyes were wide;

'Ken,' she said. 'Ken Johnson.'

'You still love him, don't you?'

'A bit,' she reflected; 'Yes, I still do a bit I suppose. These things take time. More than the six months it's been.'

'I'm sure they do,' whispered Pam gently and they both fell into a comfortable silence as Allison took out her handkerchief and passed it to Pam. She wiped her dark eyes clear with it and smiled at Allison. An unspoken intimacy passed between them.

At length Allison shook her head and said;

'Well then, Doctor Smith, enough of the trials and tribulations. Tell me about this party and the wonderful time we're going to have.'

Pam took up her initiative;

'As I said, Doctor Young, it's going to be like some up-market nosh at work. The place will be filled with our colleagues, known and unknown and a few of their friends who, for the most part, will come from some other hospital. Fun eh?'

'Yes' smiled Allison genuinely; 'I'm sure it will be. Listen, you haven't even told me yet who's holding it, or where it is.'

'Oh, of course, I forgot to. It's in John Raynor's house. I don't know if you've met John yet, or his wife, Wendy. John came to us from Saint Luke's a few years ago - he still has a clinic there one day a week - he was as an outstanding success there as he is here. They're very up-market but really nice. John's a clinical biochemist, and will be part of our research team, an excellent man. He and Wendy - who's a financial-analyst with Grundfelds the Bankers - are holding this 'do' simply as a get-together. They do so once a year I believe. A sort of bean-feast. Should be okay.'

'Sounds good,' responded Allison looking at her watch. 'When do we go?'

'Any time you want.'

'Now?'

'Fine by me,' said Pam as she rose. 'Once I've cleaned up a bit.'

Pam, quite composed now, made her way to the toilet and Allison felt immense sympathy for her. She was a sad woman, sad and abused and not only by herself. Allison intended finding out at the appropriate time how this was and why. She didn't want to see a brilliant geneticist and a very probable close friend suffer in this way. Allison didn't like waste, waste of any sort.

Pam returned looking a great deal better. She picked up the receipts and made to go.

'Well,' she said, turning to Allison and feigning surprise; 'Coming or not?' With the largest smile she'd worn all evening Allison followed her.

The Duchess emerged from the library alone. Her face was ashen, its lack of color heightened by the redness of her hair. She was in a state of shock. What she had been told had not yet registered with her, but it was beginning to.

She made her way to one of the elegant bathrooms off the major hallway of the house; entered it and closed the door behind her. She stood there perfectly still for a few moments, then made for the wash-hand basin. She doused her face in cold water as the reality of the situation crept through to her.

She'd have to speak with her advisors first, of course, ascertain that what she had been told was correct and that its implications constitutionally were as she'd understood them to be. Dorrington's visit, after all, had been unofficial but no less dramatic for that. If what he said was true her life would have to change dramatically and she was not keen for that to happen just yet.

She'd fought hard to gain the freedom she now had and she didn't want to compromise it now; now that she was so near to marrying the only person she'd found meant anything to her since the tragic breakdown of her first marriage. She appreciated Dorrington telling her before the Court got to her officially. It was strange, however, that he'd taken the trouble to.

After all in her time she had hardly been his favorite member of the Royal Household. So why take the trouble to seek her out and prepare her for what was to come her way soon enough through official channels anyway? The thought only troubled her for a short time, however, as the implications of what she'd been told finally overwhelmed her and she leant against the bathroom wall and took slow deep breaths to compose herself. She'd been expecting an interesting evening. She'd got one.

Sir Geoffrey Dorrington was still in the library. He felt that his discussion with the Duchess had been highly productive. Sir Abraham Wilder sat opposite, listening to an account of the meeting and the more he heard the more his sentiments reflected that of his co-conspirator.

'So, she took it on board? Understood what you were saying? All of it?'

'As far as I could tell. She's a tough one you know?'

'I'd heard,' said Wilder as he rubbed his hands together in a form of self-congratulation. 'And what do you imagine she'll do now? Before seeking professional advice from her courtiers as it were?' Dorrington caught the trace of sarcasm in Wilder's voice, looked him in the eye, spoke with an uncharacteristic sharpness:

'Don't under-estimate any of them; The Duchess, her advisors... They're as sophisticated in these matters as you are in your field Wilder and I am in mine. I've taken one hell of a risk coming here, speaking to her. Don't think -'

'- I'm thinking nothing that hasn't already been anticipated,' interrupted Sir Abe. 'I asked you, Geoffrey, and I repeat myself; What do you think she'll do now?'

Intimidated Dorrington controlled himself. 'Seek out her nearest and dearest,' he replied calmly. 'Ask his advice, discuss things with him.'

'He's waiting for her at this very moment,' said the industrialist glibly; 'And he has all the answers to whatever questions she may put his way.'

Sir William Mostyn sat in the back seat of his Daimler. His chauffeur knew the road to take. He'd driven it many times before. He brought the car to a halt a few hundred yards from the premises. Saying nothing to his employer he opened the door and got out of the car. He locked the door behind him and walked briskly away towards his destination.

In the back of the car, bent over a line of cocaine, Mostyn was using a glass straw to snort the drug into each nostril in turn. In front of him was the ledge of the Daimler's bar laid down to hold his various paraphernalia and the crystal decanter of his beloved Scotch.

When he had snorted just enough cocaine, he poured himself another measure of Scotch. He knew precisely how much to pour, how much to drink and the speed at which to do it. He then took out a bottle of a carefully prepared combination of vitamin and mineral pills and swallowed them all at once.

By the time the chauffeur had returned with his purchases, Professor Sir William Mostyn F.R.S. was away somewhere where he would stay happily for some time before coming back down to Earth again to indulge himself in other ways.

They spoke for most of the night and it was near dawn when they finally slept. They didn't sleep for long, however. The impact of what she'd been told soon had the Duchess awake again, wondering precisely what was going to happen and how soon. She rose and her companion woke as she did so. His thoughts focused themselves immediately.

'Good morning, darling. How are you? Any better for the rest such as it was?' he looked towards the bedside clock. The red digital numbers read ten twenty-six.

She turned to face him as she tied the cord of her blue silk dressing gown around herself. Her face was still very pale, her eyes tired. Despite this she made every attempt to sound normal, even happy:

'I'm fine chum, how are you?' He smiled, "chum" was a sort of pet name which had developed between them. He knew that she was using it in an attempt to bring normality back to her life. That would never do:

'Come here,' he said softly; holding out his hand, touching her emotions deeply, encroaching on her vulnerability. Increasing her dependency on him.

She walked back to the bed and put her arms around him, he held her close: 'Why don't we deal with this today?' he asked her. She drew back from him and looked at his face her own an un-asked question. 'I can call a friend of mine who's an expert in these matters. If you have a word at least you'll know what to expect if things turn out as they could do.'

'Medically?' she queried.

'Constitutionally,' he replied.

'But we know that,' she continued her voice filled with weariness and fatigue. 'We've spent half the night talking about it.'

'I know darling, but there may be aspects we haven't covered.'

'Such as?' she pressed.

'God alone knows. But you do have your enemies at the Palace and I for one don't want something unexpected cropping up particularly through their media machines. Good God look at what they've done to... .'

'I know,' she interrupted; 'She can't do a damned thing now in public unless it's vetted into sterility. God, she's a latter day Sophia.'

'I'm sorry? Who was Sophia?'

'Oh, George the First's wife. When he succeeded in 1714 he kept her locked up in a castle, even though they were legally divorced.' The descendant of James saw the parallel only too clearly as she reverted back to discussion of the issue at hand:

'But this situation's different surely? Anyway, I have my own people to discuss this with. I intend contacting them later today.'

'You can trust them?'

'Of course I can.' He raised his eyebrows slightly a look of concern spreading slowly over his face:

'I hope so.'

'God they stuck by me through all that...' she hesitated searching for the appropriate word. 'Mess,' she said finally. There was no word better in any vocabulary to sum up the whole sordid business that had been the failure of her marriage. "God, if people had only known the truth about that. How the media could be manipulated by..."

'I know,' he interjected reassuringly; 'But this is different. We're speaking here about your daughter's potential succession to the British throne. You insist you still want us to be married. The complications could be... .' he shrugged, opened his hands helplessly. 'An independent word would do no harm. My friend would give us that.'

She thought for a few seconds, emotions of all sorts tumbled about inside her. There'd been enough exposure of private issues to members of the public. But if he knew this man, if he was discrete, it could do no harm. She would speak to her own people soon anyway.

'O.K.' she said, 'Let's see him.'

'It's a woman, actually,' he replied; 'Her name's Annette Pallain.'

'A relative of Rosemary Pallain?' the Duchess asked with surprise.

'Her sister-in-law. Annette is the professor of constitutional history and law at Yale and consequently is an expert in constitutional matters of virtually every country in the Western Hemisphere. Latterly she's been much involved in the former Eastern-bloc too. She has a particular interest in the British Constitution, however, and in England and the English in general.

'For any particular reason?' asked the Duchess still surprised at the woman's personal credentials, more than her academic ones. Her sister-in-law could be the next President of the United States.

'Oh she has a son in England,' he replied casually; 'He's a very gifted young man, believe me. I've met him once or twice. You'd like him. Anyway, you're happy to see her? She's very discreet and, anyway, we're simply asking "what ifs."'

'Yes. If you think it would be useful.'

'I'll arrange it. Now how about some breakfast? Beagles, cream-cheese and salmon sound O.K, with a gallon of strong black coffee?'

'I'm not particularly hungry,' the Duchess replied flatly, still reflecting on the wisdom of meeting with the senator's sister-in-law. Still; at least she had a son in England, so she was both a parent and presumably an Anglophile.

'You have to keep your strength up chum!' he continued.

Despite herself she gave a short laugh. 'All right,' she replied; 'Just a little.'

'I'll get it now,' he said as he rose, emanating that intrinsic confidence that she had grown to admire and to love.

Once again Allison found herself sitting in a cab, being driven through the rain in the general direction she had come from. At length she and Pam arrived at a large detached villa in a small cul-de-sac in one of the suburbs of the town. In apparent generous mood, Pam paid the cab driver, refusing any contribution from Allison with a quick; 'You pay next time.' They then left the shelter of the cab and rushed up the path to the door of the house. Pam pressed the doorbell and in a few seconds the door opened.

It was John Raynor who stood in the doorway, a tall, slim, intelligent looking man with dark hair who had the abstract appearance about him that so many academics are accredited with, but which so few have. Pam quickly introduced Allison to him, and John just as quickly ushered them in, and out of the rain. He took their coats and led them to the door of the lounge. Behind it they could hear voices. Dozens of them;

"The place must be full," thought Allison as John opened the lounge door. It was.

People spread through the lounge and out into the kitchen which was adjacent to it. It was evident that there was plenty to eat and drink and there was certainly no shortage of issues to discuss by the sound of things. No one payed particular attention to the newcomers and Allison scanned the room.

There seemed to be no one there that she knew. One or two faces that were familiar that was all. She would have to remedy that before the night was out.

Pam had left her for a few minutes to fetch some drinks and considering she had been recognized by a number of people on the way there and back, she returned in surprisingly quick time with a glass of Perrier water for herself and one of Chablis for Allison. Allison noted how observant Pam had been, remembering the wine she'd ordered in the wine-bar despite her distress. She appreciated it.

Again, Allison scanned the room for familiar faces and she saw Alan Downie deep in conversation with a very pretty girl in a very short skirt indeed. She'd catch him later at a more opportune time.

Suddenly Allison felt herself freeze a little. There, standing in a corner with a small group of two men and another woman, was Jennifer Wright! Despite herself Allison felt a little threatened. She had no rational reason to be so, but the woman's prior conduct had dismayed her and it continued to do so. She wanted to say something to Pam but she didn't know what. It would have sounded trite whatever she had said. So she said nothing.

She and Pam stood together for a few moments alone and then John Raynor and his wife, Wendy, joined them.

'So, you're Allison,' said Wendy. 'It's lovely to meet you. John tells me that you're both going to be members of the new research team, the Royal Disease, porphyria or something. I can never remember these strange words he's always using, though I pretend to all the time!'

Allison laughed. 'Me too,' she said confidentially. 'Though I'm never allowed to admit it. Even socially!'

That broke the ice for all of them and they spent the next ten minutes or so talking about all sorts of things from hospital life to the interests of John and Wendy's two teenage children. At length the host and hostess left them to circulate further.

'A lovely couple,' Allison whispered to Pam; 'Delightful.'

'I thought you'd like them,' she replied; 'Let's see who else you'd like.' She looked around the room. 'There!' she said pointing to a young couple who were obviously enjoying themselves. 'Indi and Claire, Doctor Bennet's secretary. Come on, we'll join them, they're great fun. Follow me.'

With that Pam dragged Allison off through the throngs of people who now stretched out through the open lounge door into the hallway. And Allison realized just how much better Pam was.

As the Duchess and her companion sat down to breakfast, by a strange synchronicity Annette Pallain was in the process of explaining the very constitutional issues that her nephew had referred to that very morning. She was, however, speaking about them in a context and in a manner which would never be repeated in public.

'Ironically perhaps,' she said, her voice paced and authoritative; 'given the situation we find ourselves in we have to refer initially to an act introduced by King George III. This is the Royal Marriages Act of 1772. It stipulates quite simply that any royal marriage should have the consent of the reigning monarch.' She paused, looked over her academically correct spectacles to ensure that due attention was being given to her. It was.

'This post-dates the Bill of Rights of 1689 and the Act of Settlement of 1701, the net effect of which was simply to keep the throne free of Roman Catholics. So much for our mother country's civil rights conscience - that act is still in place. The Holy-Father himself couldn't sit on the throne, though incongruously, due to one of the few liberal aspects of Canon Law, some of the British royals could sit on his throne. Anyway, I digress.'

Like her sister Rosemary, Annette Pallain had charisma. It took a different form from her sister's however. She had no trace of glamour about her and commanded respect and total attention only when she spoke. "A mind" was how she'd been often described and that's precisely what she was. She often stressed, however, that she was no "intellectual." She was far too pragmatic for that. When, as a student, she had read Fydor Dostoevsky's classic, Crime and Punishment; she had commented only that the Russian author had allowed the sun to rise and set twice in a single day. Moral, or indeed any other, speculative pursuits were neither her forte nor her interest. Fact was and that was what she was dealing with now. Historical fact, legal fact, constitutional fact.

'The last amendment of any constitutional import was made by George V who introduced a rather useful caveat to enable his heirs to marry English commoners, irrespective of social background within reason. Hence, I think, the royal problems of the nineties.'

'We have a situation, therefore, where the following factors have to be taken into account:

First of all, the reigning monarch must agree, or have agreed, to sanction the person who is to succeed. Secondly the union must be sanctioned by the ceremony of coronation, this being carried out by the Archbishop of Canterbury. Thirdly it must also be acceptable to the British Prime Minister. That simply,' said the historian; 'is that. Now let's look at these issues individually.'

Before she continued, Annette Pallain poured some water from the carafe which sat in front of her into a crystal glass. As she sipped from it the pin in her lapel glinted in the overhead light. The ship inscribed on it was distinctly visible for a few silent seconds before she put the glass down and continued to speak.

'If the information I have been given is correct,' mused Annette Pallain, again looking over her spectacles; 'the Prime Minister will agree to the union, otherwise this country's political and financial support for the United Kingdom will be severely compromised.

'Loans from the last World War are still outstanding and the interest rate on these is hardly fixed, nor is the time agreed for their settlement, but it could be. 'The situation in Ireland is beyond breaking point and a full-blown civil war is inevitable if our power brokers felt it an appropriate scenario to end that conflict once and for all. There are many in Congress and the Senate who are ready to demand the complete renunciation of any territorial claims Britain makes over that island.

'Witless they may be, but powerless they're not. They could precipitate a civil war and it wouldn't be confined to the country of Ireland, believe me. This is not without precedent either. In the 1950's the United States condemned Britain's attempts to re-possess the Suez Canal. An outcome made virtually certain by the rather clever machinations of the State of Israel. The British were disgraced, they wouldn't want a repeat of that.

'The Archbishop of Canterbury will carry out the ceremony of the Coronation. It will be the first time any woman has done so and she will be delighted to be so historically honored. Which leaves us with the agreement of the monarch.

'We anticipate that when the time comes we will have a monarch who will either not succeed or be effectively a caretaker of the throne until the new regent takes her rightful place. I believe there is a potent medicine available to facilitate that.' Not given readily to humor, Annette Pallain let others do the smiling for her.

'All of which brings us to the central issue. The question of her consort!' she paused, stretching the moment to breaking point. 'Well first of all, he's English to the core, despite his roots. As you know he hasn't even met the Princess yet but that's due to happen soon. He also has all the qualities required to ensure that meeting attains its ultimate objective.

'He has an excellent education Eton and Cambridge; is a British National and has charm, good looks and is well connected,' she paused here and stressed this fact to her small audience; '...very well connected indeed.

'He has also been trained in the art of making women very fond of him. You may find it difficult to appreciate, but it's not too difficult to do that, when you know how. Psycho-analysts do it with every patient they have. The technique is termed "transference." All it requires is that our Princess gets to know him as a confidante, spends a fair period of time confiding in him and that he treats her in a prescribed manner. We have, I'm told, already arranged the circumstances for that to occur. Her mother has no prejudice against psychotherapists, by the way, she's seen one herself!' Again, Annette Pallain allowed her audience to smile on her behalf. Like speculation, smiles were not her forte. That she had just demonstrated in an eloquent, informative and incisive manner. 'God bless the Queen!' she said ironically as she removed her spectacles, walked to a chair and sat down.

As Pam and Allison made their way towards the young couple, they passed Jennifer Wright and her coterie of friends. Allison looked over, but even if the nurse noticed her, she ignored her completely as usual. Determined not to let her presence disturb her any longer, Allison turned her attention to following Pam across the room. It was crowded and noisy and somewhat haphazard and Allison loved it.

An hour and a half and at least half a dozen chats with various groups of people later, Allison felt that she should go and freshen up. Obtaining suitable directions from a regular guest at the Raynor's home, she made her way out into the hall and went upstairs where the first thing she did was splash cold water on her face. It made her feel refreshed and rid her of her few party-acquired cobwebs. On her way out she gave her long black hair a quick comb and admired herself in the mirror:

"Not bad, Young;" she said to herself; "Not bad at all." Feeling happier than she had for a very long time, Allison left the bathroom and made her way downstairs again.

As she reached the landing at the corner of the staircase, she noticed someone who seemed somehow familiar standing at the side of the handrail directly beneath her. At first it was just a vague familiarity, but then she saw the loose untidy hair and the familiar tweed jacket. Her heart began to pound, her knees weakened.

She pushed her head forward for a better look, to make sure, to remove any lingering doubt. Through the noise and bustle she heard the familiar voice and saw the familiar gestures of the hands. As if someone had struck her unexpectedly, Allison sat down where she was. Of all things at this time. Just as she was starting to make her own way again, rebuild her life, find herself. It was Ken!

The engines of the Japan Air Lines Boeing 747 screamed into reverse thrust as it touched down at Heathrow Airport. Sitting at the front of the first-class section of the jet was a small Japanese man. He sat quietly with his hands folded one over the other. The day before he had been in the silence and tranquility of his country home in the ancient Imperial capital of Japan, Kyoto. Now he was coming to one metropolis from another.

Professor Yukio Yoshimura had flown from Osaka International Airport to Tokyo International. He had been met there by a member of Unicorn Chemicals executive staff and driven to the company's headquarters in the center of the city. This was for a brief discussion with some of the company's medical representatives. He had emerged from the meeting unimpressed and distressed and had been driven back to the airport in good time for his flight to London.

When he had cleared customs, he was met in the concourse by another representative of Unicorn. He remembered the details on the man's card:

"Greg Hoffmann: Director Sales and Marketing." As a sign of the professionalism of the company he was dealing with, Yoshimura had observed that the same information was given on the reverse side of the card in Japanese. This touch of professionalism and knowledge of Japanese custom appealed to him.

Yoshimura recognized Hoffmann immediately. He was accompanied by a woman. Greg Hoffmann approached him:

'Konban wa Yoshimura-San' said Hoffmann bowing from the shoulders before the Japanese: 'Good evening Sir.'

'Domo arigato gozaimasu,' replied Yoshimura. 'Thank you,' he responded formally as he bowed his head just a little. Hoffman responded.

'Allow me to introduce you to one of our product-managers - the lady responsible for Oviron - Kathryn Meadowford.'

'Why it's a pleasure to meet you, Miss Meadowford,' said Yoshimura in flawless English which had a North American twang. 'What a lovely young woman you are. Tell me, how did you two recognize me?'

Hoffmann wondered if he caught a hint of a smile on the lips of the Japanese's inscrutable face. He wondered, too, just what he was dealing with here.

Some ten minutes after she'd gone, Pam had noticed Allison's prolonged absence and went to search for her. She assumed that she had simply joined another group and she would find her merrily nattering away. Still she had brought her to the party and felt responsible for her. If a crowd of bores had collared her the least she could do was to come to her rescue.

On exiting the lounge, she almost immediately saw Allison sitting on the stairs. Her hands were resting on her lap. She wondered if she was feeling unwell. Without too much trouble she made her way up to her and asked her if she was feeling all right.

'Depends what you mean,' Allison said cryptically. Pam wondered what had happened. She followed Allison downstairs and kept close to her as she approached a small group of people whom she didn't know. One of them, an attractive looking young man, looked up, saw Allison and seemed shocked;

'Allison!' he exclaimed, stepping forward from the group to meet them.

'Pam,' Allison said hoarsely, turning to her friend; 'I'd like you to meet, Ken, Ken Johnson.'

Pam held her hand out and Ken took it murmuring something. But his eyes were not on her, they were fixed on Allison. He quickly removed his hand from Pam's and took Allison's. He lifted his other hand up to her face and gently touched it. It was an intimacy Allison did nothing to resist.

'My God, Alison, it's a surprise to see you here,' he said; 'But what a lovely one. How are you? Let's go somewhere and talk.'

With that he led Allison away in search of somewhere less public and Pam watched them go feeling helpless to do anything to assist her new friend. After all she didn't even know if Allison wanted to be with the man or not. In view of the way things had developed, however, she thought that perhaps she did. She ruminated with something inside her for a moment, something difficult. Then she went off to find herself a glass of Scotch.

Andrew Wills was standing admiring himself in the mirror of his *en-suite* bathroom, which was designer-built and a mere particle of opulence of the many in the up-market residence in which he lived. He was combing at his grey-white hair and moustache with redundancy and pulling at his lamp-bronzed skin while he waited for his wife to finish dressing. His wife was less pretty than he was handsome, a great deal so. And while this had caused some problems some years ago, he had held their marriage together for the sake of their single son and by judiciously obtaining elsewhere satisfaction of the needs he no longer wanted met by his wife.

She too found outlet for her needs, but they were different now, different from what they had been. Her husband's inattentiveness had contributed to that, perhaps even wholly caused them.

'Come on darling,' Wills called; 'Hurry up, I don't want to be too late. My real business with these people will be on Wednesday evening, but I've got to meet one or two tonight. To break the ice.'

His wife took a last look at her mildly made-up face in the mirror. She didn't put too much make-up on, it didn't make much difference. She pulled her girdle tighter, that didn't make much difference either. She was plain and plump and she wished she could do something about one or the other or both. She didn't know that her husband, Mr Andrew Wills, Marketing Manager of Unicorn Chemicals had a sample of pills, in his briefcase, which were the answer to at least one of her problems.

'Come on darling,' he said, as he finally ushered his wife out of the door. 'Let's get going. Fast!' As they sped away towards John Raynor's house in their silver Mercedes, the Wills' looked a successful and happy couple. Even if they were a little mismatched appearance-wise.

After a brief search the only place that Allison and Ken could find to be alone together was in his car. It was a carefully modelled white sports convertible given to him, as far as Allison knew, courtesy of a very generous father. It was something Ken was very proud of and he kept it in mint condition. Constrained as they were within it, it gave them the isolation and quiet which they needed to talk.

From feeling that she had finally broken the bond that held her to him, Allison was now beginning to feel other things. Perhaps she still cared for him more than she had been willing to acknowledge. And as they sat in the dark together with the rain falling around them, she felt secure and close and warm. And she wondered.

'I've missed you Allison,' he said. 'Things have been pretty bad you know. Not the same without you. Have you noticed my absence at all? Have you?'

Allison was quiet for a time. She didn't mind him speaking like this, like a child. He only did it when they were close and intimate. She knew him well. Very well.

'You know the answer to that Ken,' she said softly. 'There's no need to fish. 'Of course I've missed you, we were pretty close you know. Or had you forgotten?'

'No I hadn't.'

'Well then, it's a pointless thing to ask.'

Ken remained silent for a few moments before he spoke again his tone lighter;

'How's hospital life?' he enquired.

'It's good. Just as I'd hoped it would be. And what about general practice?'

'I'm enjoying it, though I'd still like it better if I was sharing it with you.'

'Give it up Ken!' she exclaimed, annoyed now. 'You know we went over this time and time again. It wasn't possible for me, you know that.'

'I do now.'

'What do you mean?' Allison knew what he meant, but she wanted to hear it despite herself.

'What I mean is, that where I couldn't accept it before, I could now. I mean it Allison. It's all very well me enjoying my job and carving out my chosen career, but without the woman I love it doesn't amount to much. Does it?'

'I'm not sure,' Allison replied, sensing a change in his mood, a sudden softness in him she hadn't seen before, an almost boyish helplessness. 'I'm not sure of a great deal these days Ken, except that I love my work and I want to continue with it.'

'If we were back where we were, then there would be nothing to stop you doing that Allison. I mean it.' He turned in his seat and looked directly at her. She could feel his breath brush against her face, see his eyes glinting in the errant twilight which penetrated the darkness around them.

His voice changed, deepened;

'You know you're looking particularly lovely this evening, Allison. Very special indeed. Beautiful.'

'Why thank you Ken,' Allison felt faintly pleased even though she knew the compliment was more contrived than meant, came more from the groin than the heart.

His voice changed tone again;

'We must do this more often,' he continued with the irony she had once loved. 'What more could a man ask for than lovely weather, lovely surroundings and an even more lovely woman to share them with?'

'How very gallant,' she responded, sharing in his humor; but more cautiously now and trying to lighten the tenor of the conversation. 'Yes, it is lovely isn't it? At least it's snug and secure.'

'I think so;' continued Ken. 'Pity we couldn't be too. Isn't it?'

'Be what?' asked Allison looking at him.

'Snug and secure, Allison; you and me.' She felt him move closer to her, not in any physical way, but closer nonetheless, dangerously so.

'Oh let's not discuss anything like that just now Ken. Relax and enjoy yourself. Can't you? We?'

'Of course,' he said quickly, and she sensed rather than saw him looking hurt the way she knew so well. The way he always had when things didn't go as he wanted them to.

'Of course, we can Allison, I'm sorry. Tell me what's been happening at home with your mother and father and Oscar. How are they? I should have asked before.'

Allison was amused. 'Oscar' had been Allison's pet cat years ago and had worn very well until he had climbed into her mother's spin-drier unnoticed. A few dozen revolutions later and Oscar had emerged very unwell indeed. This incident had occurred last time Ken and she had visited her parent's home. How typical of him to remember it and introduce it so mock-seriously.

'They're all very well thanks, including Oscar!' she said; 'though Dad's still complaining that he can't find any reliable locums from the younger generation, thus justifying his hectic workload which he complains about all the time but really loves.'

'You would never consider taking over there would you?'

'Never Ken. I love the place and always will. I had a very happy childhood there even though my father was up in London most of the time. Life in the hospital is so different though. More immediate in many ways, more...I don't know.

Just different. I'm afraid the practice will pass into new hands when Dad goes.'

'I suppose I could always apply for the post,' remarked Ken apparently jokingly. 'Even though I'm from that incompetent younger generation who knows so little.'

'Goodness me!' mocked Allison; 'Country practice would kill you Ken Johnson and well you know it. No nightlife, no exotic restaurants, no cinemas or theatres; no grand buildings to admire. What would you do there except medicine, like my father does? That wouldn't do you at all. You'd be no good at it. All work and no play. Never!'

They fell silent for a time. Ken took her hand in his. From the first moment they came this close, Allison knew that some of the old magic was still there. She could tell that Ken knew it too, felt it.

She had mellowed a bit by now and sensing that the atmosphere had altered in some way they were both quiet and didn't speak. The rain pattered on the roof of the car intensifying their closeness. The noises from the house were faint and distant.

Allison was aware of Ken looking at her. She could feel his eyes scanning her face, absorbing her into them. She looked up and met him. There was some sort of recognition there and she felt a tightness in her stomach. A tug of excitement. Still they said nothing

Allison could feel her heart thumping and was aware of the sudden shortness of her breath. She glanced up and met Ken's eyes again in the car mirror. He gave her a soft, intimate smile which lit up his eyes. She felt a tingling sensation run through her.

He raised his left hand to her face and gently stroked her cheek. His right hand he placed slowly on the back of her head, rubbing his fingers through her fine, dark hair. He pulled her close. His right hand moved gently down her neck, caressing it, sending shivers of pleasure through her. She didn't resist. Their lips met and joined. The kiss was deep, intimate and sensual.

Just then the door of the house suddenly opened and a beam of light from within spread out into the night and partly lit up the inside of the car. Within seconds Allison heard footsteps and was aware of someone passing by the car window. As she gently tried to disentangle herself from Ken's arms she looked out of the window and saw a face staring in. It was Jennifer Wright.

The look on the nurse's face was a study in horror. For a moment or two she seemed to be transfixed by the sight in the car and then she abruptly turned away. Allison pulled free of Ken's arms and reflexly tidied her hair.

'What's wrong?' he asked.

'Oh it was just one of the nurses from the hospital,' Allison replied. 'I dare say she isn't used to seeing London General's doctors behaving like that. Particularly in cars.'

Ken laughed quietly. The sound was pleasant and full and one which Allison remembered with fondness.

'She's probably jealous,' he said, still amused. 'Tell her I'll bring a friend along next time.'

Despite herself Allison laughed too. The thought of Jennifer Wright sitting embracing in a car, or anywhere else for that matter, was amusing. 'Perhaps, thought Allison I'm what the politically correct might call a "lookist!"' The thought amused her. She peered out through the front window and could just make out the nurse's silhouette, standing on the pavement beneath the dim glow of a street lamp.

As she watched, a car drew up beside Jennifer, a door opened and in the light which came on inside the car she could see outlined the handsome young man who'd entered the hospital looking so distressed on her first day there. Just as Jennifer was pulling the passenger door closed he leaned over and kissed her;

'Well, well,' said Ken who was also watching; 'She doesn't seem to need my imaginary friend after all. Does she?'

'She certainly doesn't,' agreed Allison, surprised at the feelings the encounter had evoked in her so suddenly and unexpectedly. She remembered the few brief words she had exchanged with the man; the look in his eyes, the smile he had directed to her, the attempted joke.

'I suppose I'd better go home soon,' she said abruptly; 'Early start tomorrow and I have a report to prepare.'

'I'll drive you,' said Ken.

'No it's alright; I'm here with a friend.'

'A friend?' Ken interrupted sharply. Allison felt a disturbing sense of *deja vu*.

'Yes, Pamela Smith,' she said sharply. 'I don't imagine you remember her. You only just met her, albeit briefly, about twenty minutes ago. She's a geneticist at the hospital.'

'No I don't remember. Sorry,' responded Ken, 'I only vaguely remember being introduced to someone. I was too surprised and happy at seeing you to notice who. I suppose you have to go back with her?'

'Yes I must. Really. Don't worry, I'll mention that your car has only two seats!'

'You could always sit on my lap...' remarked Ken suggestively.

'Not when you're driving.'

'Some other time then doctor. Yes?'

Allison turned and looked at him. She smiled wanly;

'You don't give up easily Ken; do you?'

'I'll call you if it's O.K.' he said.

'Do that,' said Allison. She kissed him quickly on the cheek, then rushed from the car to the door. It wasn't closed and she went back into the party to find Pam. She found her standing with two junior doctors they had met earlier. Pam was drunk. Very drunk indeed. Allison approached her;

'Are you coming Pam, coming home?'

'Sorry, Allison,' Pam said grabbing her friend and embracing her; 'I'm staying. Why don't you stay and enjoy yourself. Please, if you can? If you can with these...' She stopped abruptly. 'Why don't you?' she continued, slurring her words more than just a little now. 'Please Allison, stay, just a little longer.'

'I'm sorry, Pam,' Allison replied; 'I really am, but I can't. I wish I could, Pam, but I have to go. You take care of yourself. Someone can call you a cab later. Do take care,' Allison said softly, squeezing her friend's arm gently and hoping with all her might that she would.

As Allison went in search of her hosts to thank them for their hospitality, the outside door opened and she saw Ken go out with his car-coat on. At the same time three new guests arrived. One was a tall, slim, darkly attractive man who to Allison's surprise exchanged a few brief words with Ken and shook his hand. The other man was an elderly Japanese.

The Japanese man took a slow, absorbent gaze around the room and his eyes met Allison's. He smiled briefly at her. She felt somehow privileged and smiled back a little self-consciously. It was the third person, however, who surprised her. With the two men was Kathryn Meadowford, the Unicorn Chemicals executive. 'The Unicorn Lady' as she had heard someone at the hospital unkindly label her. 'The Oviron call-girl.'

Allison waited until John Raynor had returned to the lounge before approaching him and thanking him for the lovely evening. He took her hand warmly.

'Listen Allison, we're having a little 'do' here on Wednesday evening. We'd like you to come. It will be nothing like this - more formal. Perhaps more fun for you?'

'Well, I don't know, John, I...'

'John Bennet will be here and he specifically asked me to invite you. Will you come? Yes?'

'Why, in that case, of course,' Allison said, puzzled at herself being in such sudden demand socially and in such exalted company.

'Great,' said John Raynor. 'I'll send you a formal invitation but there's no need to R.S.V.P. Just turn up at eight. I look forward to it.'

'So do I,' replied Allison, still bemused by the invitation. 'And thank Wendy for me will you? It's been a lovely evening.'

'By the way, how are you getting home?' John asked her.

'I'll call a cab if you don't mind.' said Allison.

'Never. Just a moment.' John Raynor went away and returned with two junior doctors Allison and Pam had spoken with earlier.

'These two will see you home safe and sound. See you Wednesday.' With that John left and Allison was standing with Gerry and Michael.

So it was that Allison found herself being driven home by the two young doctors she and Pam had socialized with earlier. Michael was very withdrawn and studious and had said virtually nothing all evening. All Allison really knew about him was his name and that he worked in Pathology. The other, Gerry, was a dark haired, attractive young man who was a gynecologist and great fun.

As they drove noisily away from the house, Allison noticed a large dark car - a Daimler - sitting in the shadows. There was a faint outline of the driver in the front, but the back windows were impenetrable so she couldn't tell if there was anyone in there or not. She wondered who it belonged to, who was in it, what they were doing there.

'Everything O.K.?' Gerry enquired.

'Fine', said Allison, who felt a bit flushed with all that had happened and a little awkward too. She gave the dark car a last glance and turned her full attention to the pleasant young doctor.

'Good,' he continued. 'I was just telling our colleague here how you intend finding the etiology of acute porphyria within the year.'

'The cause could be easy, the cure's the problem,' remarked Allison drolly. 'That'll take a bit longer. Eighteen months say!'

The laughter the remark elicited relaxed Allison again. Just then a very flash silver Mercedes sports car passed them, driving fast in the opposite direction. Gerry looked at it with obvious envy;

'I hope you don't mind being seen with a very junior doctor in the oldest banger in town,' he said to her.

'Well I do mind,' teased Allison, 'but no one will see us at this hour.'

'Did you enjoy yourself?' asked Gerry quizzically.

'"Interesting" is more precise,' replied Allison; 'I found it interesting and very enjoyable.'

'Really?' persisted Gerry.

'Really' Allison assured him, 'Yes, really!'

'Good.'

They spoke for a while about various things, then fell into an easy silence as they approached Allison's flat. As she left the car and said good night, she turned round on impulse and asked Gerry a question;

'Do you know Jennifer Wright?'

He looked at her, surprised at the unexpected question;

'Why yes, Allison, she's Charge Nurse on ward six. Neurological. In fact I saw her at the party this evening. Why do you ask?'

'Oh I just wondered, she seems an odd sort.'

'In what way?' enquired the young doctor.

'Oh nothing really. Just a couple of times I've tried speaking to her and been cold-shouldered; nothing important. Not that important anyway.'

'Oh, she's only been that way since her breakdown,' added Gerry with his friend nodding his agreement in the back seat.

'Breakdown!' exclaimed Allison. 'What breakdown?'

'Oh sorry,' Gerry continued; 'I thought everyone knew. Her sister-in-law was killed in a car accident about six or nine months ago. It affected her very badly. Come to think of it Allison, you look very like Jennifer's sister-in-law. I met her once at some party or other. Intriguing.'

'Anyway, Jennifer was just coming to grips with it when her niece became very ill. The two things together were too much for her. She had a breakdown. She's not fully back to normal yet, a bit moody still, but she's getting there. She was a bundle of fun before that happened. I imagine she'll fully recover soon now. Alan Downie thinks she will.'

'Oh I'd no idea,' said Allison, feeling very guilty and almost alarmed. 'I must be off,' she said abruptly. 'Goodnight.'

'Goodnight,' responded Gerry but not his friend Michael who simply smiled and nodded his head in agreement.

As Allison walked the short distance to her flat, she ruminated on what she'd just been told;

"Poor woman;" she thought; "I've made all those ill-informed judgements about her. She's probably the way she's been with me because I remind her of her sister-in-law. Of course, the look on her face when she saw me in that car..."

"Thank goodness she's got someone to care for her in her boyfriend or fiancee or whoever he is." The thought of the young man reminded her of Ken and his attentions that evening. She dwelt on that for a few moments, confused, her feelings mixed. She thought on Pam. Her feelings mixed more.

The Duchess sat alone in the small study of her Washington home. She was waiting for Annette Pallain to arrive and spent the time writing some letters. Only her security man, who she paid for from her own income, was in the house. He was entrenched in the spare bedroom having been fully informed by the Duchess about the credentials of her visitor. He was happy enough that she presented no threat. Some were to friends, others to social and personal contacts who she liked to deal with personally rather than through her personal secretary. However, as she wrote with her normally friendly and effusive style, she was far from feeling that way.

The wait for Professor Pallain was all the worse because she'd be meeting the woman alone. Once again her future husband was off somewhere on business and - though she normally didn't mind this, as they lived quite independent lives - she was not too happy about meeting a stranger to discuss such a delicate matter without someone else there, someone she knew. Still, the woman had been well vouched for. If nothing else it would be interesting.

The door-bell rang at precisely the time agreed and the Duchess heard her security man walk down the hall to answer it. She heard it open and there was a brief interchange of voices. He'd be taking her coat now if she had one with her. Moments later there was a knock on her study door, it opened and she was introduced to Annette Pallain. As the security man left them alone, the Duchess directed the other woman to a seat and sat down herself:

'Well,' she said smiling to the woman; 'I've heard a great deal about you. You come highly recommended.'

'Thank you,' she replied informally; 'I believe you wanted to ask me a few questions on some theoretical issues concerning the constitution of your country?' She was very composed and the Duchess found it difficult to make an immediate assessment of her, something she was normally able to do very quickly indeed.

'Yes Mrs Pallain,' she replied evenly; 'there are one or two things I'd like your opinion on. I have a friend who is considering writing a work of popular fiction which would involve some highly speculative accounts of changes in the British Royal Family's current lines of succession to the throne. She'd like to give an accurate account. Even though it's fictional, I'd like her to do so too. It does lend credibility to the work. Don't you think?'

'Indeed,' replied the professor; 'In what way can I help?'

'Suppose,' the Duchess said; 'just suppose that something tragic happened... .'

Annette Pallain prepared herself to answer as the Duchess spoke. The content of what she had to say was already prepared. However, the way that she conveyed her information was almost as important as that content. As the duchess completed her statement she replied with feigned concern and unfeigned, but well disguised, cynicism:

'In such a tragic event the constitutional issue is quite simple as I'm sure you know. Your elder daughter would succeed to the throne. Does your friend's plot involve any other issues which may be relevant? It could alter things.'

'Suppose, continued the duchess; 'that the princess' step-father was a U.S. national, would that alter things at all?'

'Not in the least,' replied Pallain.

'And if there were children from that union, they I presume would neither make any difference to the princess' position nor have any formal position at all constitutionally.'

'Absolutely correct,' the academic said, waiting, predatory.

'And if the princess were to marry,' the duchess went on; 'would there be any restrictions on who her spouse could be, if she intended succeeding?'

'That's a more complex issue,' said the academic; 'there are a number of possibilities here. Allow me to address them one by one.'

'Of course,' replied the Duchess sitting back, relaxing a bit. As Annette Pallain relaxed herself and began the work of dissimulation and misinformation that others would continue after she'd prepared the ground. And in matters like this one she was an excellent gardener.

Allison let herself into her flat and looked around the room. It was pleasant and well furnished but at times it was very lonely indeed. She sat down on a chair with her coat still on and wondered what she was going to do when Ken phoned her. Would it be any different if they gave it another go? She made her way to bed hugging the pillow close and letting the images of Ken, Jennifer Wright, her boyfriend, Pam, the London General and the varied events of the evening tumble through her head. Her most prominent thought though was about Ken. Could it be different? Would it be? Did she want it to be?

She was still wondering when she fell into a dreamless sleep. Outside the rain continued to fall around her and the man in the black Daimler had now joined the party Allison had so recently left. He was looking for Pam. For some diversion. He needed it. He had a great deal on his mind.

CHAPTER FOUR

A few minutes after eleven thirty Alison presented herself at Doctor Bennet's office. Pam was already there chatting to his secretary Claire Sillars. Claire was a very pretty young brunette who had achieved her high secretarial position due to the combination of her vivacious personality, her unswerving loyalty to the hospital, her sheer hard work and her excellent administrative and secretarial abilities. She was particularly caring and protective towards Doctor Bennet whom she adored.

'Good afternoon Doctor Young, Doctor Smith,' said Claire warmly; 'Doctor Bennet won't keep you waiting long He's having a word with Sir William before seeing you. I'll let him know you're both here.'

As the young woman said this, Pam visibly flinched and while the secretary buzzed the intercom and spoke to Doctor Bennet, Allison's bemusement increased a thousand fold, not only because of Pam's reaction.

Professor Sir William Mostyn was not only the big noise in hematology, both nationally and internationally, he was a veritable eminence in the area. He was also a very eminent man in the medical world in general; and - as hospital superintendent -his was the final word on all hospital matters.

"Why?' she wondered, 'was he there too? What on Earth could someone like Sir William Mostyn find of interest in her?" She looked at Pam seeking an answer, but Pam frustratingly avoided her look, giving her no hint whatsoever of what may be in store for them.

Incongruously, Allison ruminated briefly again on Pam's morning drink of Scotch - was it a 'one off' or was there a problem? This was not the time for that particular matter, however, if appropriate to do so, she could address that issue later. Meanwhile she wondered why was she here to see these two eminent men. Allison began to become slightly apprehensive. Was something wrong? Surely not. Was it her intuition again?

The buzzer on the intercom sounded, making Allison start. She heard Doctor Bennet's electronic voice say something to Claire and a moment or two later she and Pam were ushered into the main office. From behind his desk Doctor Bennet rose to greet them:

'Good morning, ladies,' he said, 'Allison, allow me to introduce you to Sir William whom you no doubt remember from your student days.' He turned to Mostyn and introduced Allison by name. Mostyn nodded to Allison, said hello to Pam whom he obviously knew, and smiled at them both. Otherwise he was non-committal. 'Sit down, please,' Doctor Bennet directed them to some chairs close to his desk.

'I suppose, Allison, you're wondering what this is all about. Allow me to enlighten you. First of all, however, let me ask you what you know about acute intermittent porphyria. Feel free....'

With that and a gesture of his hands which invited her to speak, he sat down. Bennet leaned back and waited. As quickly as this the floor was Allison's. She was centerstage.

Rosemary Pallain looked at her image in the mirror. Unlike her sister's - unlike the very plain Annette's - it was a good one.

A good one in every respect and she was proud of it with some justification. She was about to chair a Senate committee which had been set up specifically to investigate the alleged financial contributions to terrorism that her fellow citizens were being blamed of. Such a committee would normally have been held in Congress and have been cross-party. Indeed there was just such a committee being held there. But Mrs Pallain had called this one as a matter of urgency and she wanted it to be discussed both at senatorial level and among her own people.

The British had been rambling on about this for years as a result of NORAID; but their problems had been put into stark perspective by the allegations which had led to a politically intriguing affair, where, it was alleged, eminent American Jews has contributed significant sums to the Israeli terrorists who were now active in what had been the once occupied territories after the Arab-Israeli war of 1967. Only ten days ago there had been a massacre of Palestinians in their homes on the Golan Heights and this had produced outrage and condemnation in the Arab states in the Middle East and in most other neutral countries East and West. Most importantly it fired the anger in more radical Muslim countries where the threat presented by Islamic fundamentalist groups was becoming progressively greater and more real than it had ever been in the United States of America.

Since the recent tragedy, there had been two terrorist-led atrocity attempts by such groups working in North America. The first had been unsuccessful, but the second had succeeded precisely as planned. Thirty-two American citizens had been killed in a bomb-blast. The issue was critical. It could cost her votes from the Republican delegates.

Mrs Pallain was close, very close indeed to being nominated as presidential candidate of the Republican Party for the forthcoming presidential election. The pretty dismal showing of the Democrats' alleged best over the past few years; the pervasiveness of 'political correctness' above sheer common sense; the health reforms, the new social care policy, an inconsistent foreign policy and, more specifically, the general ineptitude of the administration; had alienated a great many people and had left the way wide open to a Republican victory. In short, within a year and a half she could become President of the United States.

Rosemary Pallain was very precise about how she described this possibility to the many audiences she addressed. "The first female President who would be elected democratically" was how she put it, much to the satisfaction of her supporters and the chagrin of her adversaries. That there were a great deal more of the former than of the latter in the country at large was fact. It was not only the polls that told her that, it was her supporters themselves and some of them knew exactly what they were talking about. This meeting was very important to her therefore, one of a number of obstacles she'd have to steer herself around before her nomination. She'd need support of course and where better to get that than from the select senatorial group she was meeting soon in the building fronted by the blue door of the Mayflower Compact.

There hadn't even been time for stage fright as Allison began to speak. 'Well...' she started, clearing her throat: 'The porphyrias are a group of metabolic disorders which are not at all common in this country but are more so in, for example, South Africa.

'Acute intermittent porphyria is one of them - a serious one. It is a familial, genetically inherited, disorder - it occurs for example in the European Royal family - in which the patient has severe generalised attacks intermittently which can, on occasions, be fatal.

'We're not certain as yet precisely what precipitates these attacks, though we do know that alcohol, barbiturates and certain other drugs can do so. We're not certain either what the primary cause of the attack is, though it's generally widespread and involves the cardiovascular, respiratory and peripheral and central nervous systems. This suggests a widespread disturbance of something neurological.'

Mostyn interrupted her: 'And what do you think is primarily responsible for the generalised pathology manifest in the attack?'

'I don't know, Sir. It's possible that one of the chemical forerunners of hemoglobin may do something to the tissues and make them respond abnormally as they do in the acute attack. The production of these forerunners is increased in the disease as you know, both when measured in blood and in urine.'

'And if what you postulate is true,' Mostyn went on in his controlled reassuring voice; 'How would you go about determining that fact? And what are your thoughts on the possible treatment of the disease?

'With respect to treatment, I've some ideas, but first I'd like to have an attempt at defining the primary etiological factors, the main causes of the disease, I've some ideas on that too.'

And you think that you could define these at the level of complexity you would wish?' asked Mostyn with mild interest.

Allison hesitated; 'It would take a fair bit of work, Sir, but given the proper facilities I'd initially look to see if these primary metabolites were in any way active physiologically...'

Just as Allison was about to fall into full flow with her theory, Sir William Mostyn raised his hand to stop her. He turned to Doctor Bennet with an approving smile on his face and said;

'I'm convinced, John. You'd can tell Doctor Young what we have in mind. Unfortunately, I don't have the time for the theoretical lecture on porphyria which I'm sure she's desperate to give us. I've got to catch a meeting at Government House then nip off and fetch the kids from school. It's end of term. I suppose I could miss the meeting, but if I miss the children, well... what would the poor little brats do?'

Doctor Bennet turned to Allison; 'As you know Allison, Sir William is widely known for his research activities in hematology in general. Recently he has been awarded a significant sum of money by the M.R.C. towards setting up a research project to look into the origins of acute porphyria. That's why you're here.

'Pamela, as you know, has already had considerable experience in genetic studies in this area and has already published a couple of papers on that aspect of the disease. We would like you to join her and a few other members of staff in setting up a much more comprehensive research team on the subject. In addition to the formal research experience which would be invaluable for you, you would be able to obtain an M.D. thesis from the work. What do you say?.'

There was a great deal Allison wanted to say. 'Why me?,' for example, or 'Do you really think I'm good enough?' Instead she simply said:

'I'd love to.'

The product of a solid W.A.S.P background; as a law student at Harvard aged seventeen, Rosemary Littleton as she had been known then, had a keen interest in history. American history in particular had fascinated her, some said later it had *enchanted* her. As a consequence of this she had prepared and submitted a monograph to an established historical academic journal. It had been entitled "James I of England and the Origins of American Democracy." To her surprise and delight after heavy editing it had been published.

One morning a few days later a letter had arrived at her flat in Harvard requesting her to contact a society in Washington called the Mayflower Compact. The young Rosemary had never heard of it. But it had heard of her. Long ago. She duly contacted them and was invited to visit the Society in Washington accompanied by whoever she wished. After having checked out their credentials, which were impeccable, she gladly agreed to visit the Society during that summer's vacation.

To accompany her she chose a close male personal friend she'd had since childhood; Arthur Pallain, also a gifted major in law, but with a background of old money and a driving political ambition which Rosemary at that time lacked. The visit had been very successful indeed. She had liked the members of the Society and they had liked her. It was the best move she'd ever made in her life.

Ten years later the successful attorneys Rosemary and Art Pallain, who had by now married, were not only established members of the Mayflower Compact but also of the inner Society of the San Graal. They were, in other words, two of the most privileged people in Washington and also two of the most politically extreme, ambitious and ruthless.

Within another ten years they had both become duly elected republican members of the Senate. Before the next decade of their lives were over they hoped to be at home in the White House with Rosemary as President and Art as the First Man. "The King and Queen of America" some of their supporter's had dubbed them. With an unknown but uncannily ironic accuracy.

Rosemary was not the only one in her family who had been successful. Her son, who had been named Charles after Art's grandfather, was completing his education at the University of

Cambridge in England. He'd attended public school there too. Eton.

Art's brother too had done very well for himself and the family, not so much academically but in business. He had become a multi-millionaire by the time he was in his mid-twenties and had excellent financial and social connections. Art was very proud of his brother. Proud of his financial acumen, his ancestry and, in particular, of his future wife. He had good reason to be. She was an English duchess and she was very much in love with him. It was against this background and with the enormous prospects that the future held for her and her family; that the senator reflected on the issues likely to be raised at the unofficial but powerful committee she was due to chair in ten minutes time.

'Fine' Bennet said to Allison with enthusiasm; 'Put your preliminary ideas down on paper and send them over to me as soon as possible. I'll have a look at them and pass them on to Sir William for approval. And, by the way, our first research meeting's tomorrow at four o'clock - so get something prepared by then. There's an international conference on Hematology in Vienna in a month's time. I'll expect you to attend if we can arrange funding.' With that he indicated that the meeting was over.

Bennet ushered the two young doctors to the door. As he did so, Sir William suddenly spoke again;

'Oh Pamela,' he said, 'If I could have a quick word with you please. The genetic studies. Just a brief word, up in my office' Pam stopped abruptly and Allison felt that something was troubling her.

'Oh, one more thing, Allison,' Doctor Bennet said, seemingly spontaneously, just as she was about to leave. 'Or to be more precise, two. The first is, would you pop along sometime next week to psychiatry and take some blood from a patient of Alan Downie's? Do you know him?'

'Why, yes. It so happens that we met this morning.'

'Good. He'll tell you which patient...Ben someone I believe. I want a complete work up on the specimen. Everything. O.K.? We think he might be a bit anemic.'

'Why, of course. And what's the other thing, Sir?'

'Other thing?'

'You said that there were two things.'

'Oh, yes! Mrs Bailley's Down's test. Perhaps you'd break the news to her, Allison. Again any time you're free to do so next week will do. Thank you.' With that, and a final smile, he closed the door and returned to his office. Allison wondered why she couldn't simply go and do these things now and why wait for "next week". But something distracted her attention from that issue.

She saw Sir William Mostyn walk away with Pam towards his office on the upper floor and Pam walked beside him listening carefully to him as he spoke to her with what seemed incipient intimacy.

In the small outer office, Claire was typing away quite happily. She looked up as Allison re-entered and she smiled:

'All's well, I hope,' she said.

'Yes,' she replied. 'Well, not all,' she thought, 'but most of it.'

Rosemary Pallain listened to everything that her advisors had to say on the matter and at times that understandably had been in conflict with her own ideas of how the party should express itself publicly on this issue. It was a sensitive one.

The Jewish vote was small in absolute terms. The Jewish lobby, however, both in the Senate and in Congress, was another matter altogether. But so too was that of the so-called "minority groups" and since Arafat's conciliatory moves on the international arena which had stuttered back and forth since way back in '93 the Arabs had suddenly become part of those minority groups, even though there were few Muslims and even fewer actual Arabs resident in the United States.

The momentum from the recognition by the P.L.O. of Israel and of the latter's willingness to ultimately accommodate all of the territorial demands of the 'legitimate' Palestinians as the P.L.O. were now referred to; had spilled over into North America. The sudden upsurge in Zionist terrorism had been anticipated, but not the fall-out that had spread to North America. Her own people were being killed by terrorist bombs and Rosemary Pallain had to decide who to back. She had to decide who could be persuaded to put more marks against her name on a ballot paper.

She left her office and walked to the meeting-room in her usual confident way attracting many male and a few female looks some of quite blatant lust. She knew they said that she had it all. She wanted to keep it and add some more.

As she'd been instructed the week following her meeting with Doctor Bennet and Sir William Mostyn, Allison made her way to the psychiatry department. She found Alan Downie just finishing a ward round, though she never felt that the term was appropriately applied to this branch of the medical profession.

Although she hadn't said to Alan and never would; one reason Allison had not followed her father into psychiatry was because of the general conditions prevailing in that branch of medicine, both in the private and public sectors.

Contrary to many prevailing contemporary views, Allison believed that most psychiatric problems were rooted in certain early childhood experiences and that they could be dealt with often by simply speaking with the patient and changing their social conditions. This was rarely possible to achieve because of the numbers of patients who had such problems and because of the financial constraints in both sectors. This was another reason she had opted for hematology. There had been another, however, too.

As a child Allison had been fascinated by both biology and history and it was when she became aware of the existence of a very bizarre and very rare blood disease which ran through the genes of the European royal family - the Royal Disease or acute intermittent porphyria - that Allison found her true métier.

She had read with wonder as a child, how this strange and exotic illness had given rise to legends as diverse as vampirism and lycanthropy, or werewolfism. The signs of the disease - abnormal hair growth, avoidance of sunlight and reddish 'glowing' teeth in some instances - showed features associated with such mythologies.

In the Middle Ages in particular, people, undoubtedly with this illness, were feared in this context. This would have been particularly so when they exhibited symptoms of mental disturbance too, as indeed more than one of England's kings had done for this very reason. Charles the First and George the Third as Alan Downie had known.

Allison had specialized in hematology, therefore, partly with a view to discovering the secrets of this singular disease and she had started her efforts while still a student, demonstrating that a form of the disease could be emulated in animals by administration of a particular drug. She had also hypothesized certain possible approaches to treatment of the disease. It was mainly this rather exceptional dissertation that had attracted Doctor John Bennet and then Sir William Mostyn to this rather exceptional young woman, for very special reasons.

As Rosemary Pallain sat down to chair her meeting in Washington, the current Vice-President of the United States had just finished a late lunch which he shared with three others in a fine London restaurant.

His dining companions consisted of his personal secretary -a friend of his, Chuck Fitzimons, a hard-living, quick talking bulk of a man; who was himself a Democratic Senator - and Charles U'Prichard, Private Secretary and confidante of the Prince whom the Vice-President was to meet in private this evening prior to his formal visit to the Palace.

It was U'Prichard who spoke now very much aware indeed that this man who had achieved a great deal both politically and in his former glamorous profession; had been treated pretty poorly by his former President. He was looking good now, however, in the Democratic ratings, his inner toughness and incisiveness pushing through the political fog the President had attempted to hide him in.

'So the latest polls are causing you some concern, are they?' asked U'Prichard; 'I'm afraid that, at least in the United Kingdom, opinion polls are no more accurate than a bent arrow. Our past few general elections have taught us that. Are they any better in the States?' He nibbled at an errant piece of celery as the Vice-President replied with a voice which in itself commanded authority.

'I guess not,' he said in a thoughtful tone; 'But we are looking pretty pushed. The Country like Mrs Pallain and I, at least, don't have her style. Or her good-looks.'

U'Prichard smiled, a smile as unfathomable as a Japanese koan: 'Perhaps not exactly,' he said tactfully; 'but your Party do have some fairly realistic policies. Another term would enable them to be implemented. No?'

'Yes it would. However the voting public don't always vote on policy; particularly back home. As you appreciate our presidential system is not quite the same as yours. It's more geared to personality than policy. You can be thankful you don't have that problem. It's like showbiz at times.'

'Oh but we do have that problem,' continued U'Prichard neutrally; 'Thankfully not so much in our government elections, but we are, after all, a constitutional monarchy. We have that problem there, as you'll appreciate.'

'Yeah, I guess you have,' responded the affable American; 'But surely that doesn't influence the voting behavior of your electorate?' The Vice-President was interested, he remembered only too well how the Republicans had plugged into the British Conservative publicity machine in a spirited, but unsuccessful attempt to learn some lessons some years ago.

'It most certainly can do,' replied U'Prichard; 'Our political loyalties in this country are inextricably linked to that fact though few would acknowledge it publicly. It's a subtle link, historically forged, but real enough for that.

'Of course our monarchy has no public position on whatever political parties choose to do, though occasionally by implication they can pass unofficial comment. There are no such problems in a republic of course, nor, I imagine would you want them.'

'It would make the War of Independence look pretty stupid,' replied the Vice-President to the nodded agreement of his companion.

'So you wouldn't want a monarchy then, would you?'

Both Americans looked at U'Prichard carefully. The man was not making casual conversation, the tenor of his voice told then that. But they'd be damned if they knew what he was getting at.

'Excuse me, Charles?' quizzed the senator on first name terms with U'Prichard already; 'Are you trying to make a point here? If so I'm afraid it's lost on me.'

'Me too,' added the Vice-President absently, as he weighed up the Englishman afresh.

'I am,' replied U'Prichard calmly.

'And precisely what is that?' the Second in Command asked directly.

Taking another bite at the celery U'Prichard told him.

Alan Downie welcomed Allison with obvious pleasure and, obviously knowing why she was here, he took her immediately to a room where a very withdrawn patient sat in a chair looking out of the window, responsive, it seemed, to nothing. Allison was surprised to discover Kathryn Meadowford present in the room - she wondered what she was going there.

'Good afternoon, Miss Meadowford; would you excuse us please.' Allison said. The executive made to say something, hesitated then simply said:

'Very well,' and left the room.

'This is Ben O'Grady,' explained Alan. 'He's been like this for a week or so now haven't you Ben?' As Allison prepared her syringe, he rolled up the shirtsleeve of the man, who was almost wholly withdrawn.

'This is Doctor Young, Ben. She'd only going to take some blood to run some tests. It won't hurt. I know you can hear me in there old chap, so don't worry. We'll get you well soon.'

The man remained almost totally withdrawn as Allison stuck the needle into his subclavian vein, the large deep vein which runs wide and long along the arm just above the elbow. As she withdrew the man's blood she wondered what had happened to him, what had precipitated his prolonged psychosis. She made a mental note to ask Alan later.

As she pressed the withdrawn blood into a heparinized bottle to prevent it clotting, she observed that Ben was trying to say something. He was now looking at her with some clarity.

'What is it Ben?' she asked hopefully. 'Come on, Ben what is it? What do you want to say? What are you trying to tell us?'

Ben's eyes flickered with life for an instant and then became vacant again.

"At least he's coming back" she thought and felt pleased. Intuitively she liked this man. They'd get on well when he returned to them.

As she left the department to take her sample back to the laboratory Allison noticed that Kathryn Meadowford was sitting in the waiting room.

'Waiting for what exactly' she wondered. She exchanged a brief nod of recognition with her. Then dismissed her from her mind.

* * *

Although incredulous, the Vice-President's face tightened as U'Prichard spoke about his quite fantastic suspicions. His latent political instinct, however, found something here, something which - however bizarre - just might be true. A terrier at a corpse, he never let go if there was something to hang on to. And if what this man was telling him was half-way correct, he'd see the White House for another term yet. With or without the incumbent President.

Essentially what he was being told here, albeit in less than well-defined terms, was that there was some sort of conspiracy occurring which concerned his fellow Americans attempting to destabilize the British Monarchy or something to that effect.

That, of course hadn't been precisely what the Private Secretary had said. More words to the effect that:

'Some of my very good sources in your country have intimated to me that there may be some well-connected groups there who are not acting in the best interests of the British Royal family.'

When pressed he had said little more, but the name of the Mayflower Compact had been mentioned and this rung a vague Republican bell with both politicians.

'Those bastards rake a hell of a lot of lettuce into Republican coffers,' Fitzimons had pointedly commented; much to the obvious chagrin of U'Prichard's sensitivities on the use of the English language - or so it appeared by the look he gave the man the Vice-President and other friends fondly named "Bucks Fizz."

'I've hear about them every time I've been on a campaign but they're innocent enough. A group of elite historians or something. They've too much money, too much concern about how things were and too little political sense.'

U'Prichard liked the man immensely, but a word he used had stimulated his curiosity. 'Is any elite group wholly innocent?' he asked; rather foolishly.

'Is the monarchy wholly innocent?' retorted Chuck.

'Of what?'

'Of the abuses of power and privilege society bestows upon them or that they bestow upon themselves?'

'The Prince isn't,' responded the Private Secretary with a smile as the Vice-President grinned.

'Let's cool it men,' he said.

'There's nothing to cool,' said U'Prichard calmly.

'Except possibly these Cromwellian fellow citizens of mine,' continued the Vice-President.'
'Oddly enough, I doubt very much if they're that at all,' said U'Prichard cryptically. 'I doubt that very much indeed.'

* * *

Just after lunchtime that same day, Allison went along to see Mrs Bailley to break the news to her about her test. She sat down beside the bed and asked her as cheerily as she could how things were.

'They're fine doctor,' Mrs Bailley said, patting her bulge proudly; 'I hope he arrives soon though before I burst!'

Allison smiled gently;

'There's been a slight problem,' she said; 'The test for Down's syndrome was positive. The baby will be mongoloid.'

Mrs Bailley barely moved. Her face showed only a transiently visible response to the verdict. A slight contracting of her eyes, a subtle wince of pain for her child.

'I thought it might be,' she said; 'I was prepared for this. It doesn't matter.'

'And your husband...how will he feel? And your daughters?'

'The same as me,' the woman said, rather too quickly. 'We all knew the risk was there, ever since the infection I had treated at Saint Luke's. The doctor there mentioned the possibility, that's why we had the test done. We'll love him just the same, doctor. 'Won't we?' she said as she patted her swollen abdomen again. A few warm tears formed in her eyes and began to trickle down her face.

Allison, who was never overly sentimental was quite touched, and she squeezed the woman's hand gently as she rose to go:

'I'm sure you will,' she said. 'I'd best be off now. If there's anything you need just let me know.'

'Thank you doctor,' said the woman quietly. 'I've got all I need as long as he's fine otherwise.'

'He will be Mrs Bailley; I'm certain that he will be.'

As she made to go Allison suddenly realized what Mrs Bailley had just said. She turned back;

'I'm sorry Mrs Bailley, but you just mentioned an infection. What was that? Tell me about it.'

'Oh it was nothing really, doctor. When I must have been early on in my pregnancy I went to see my own doctor because I had pain passing water...you know.'

'Yes...' Allison encouraged. 'We call it dysuria.'

'Well, the doctor took some tests, a water sample, some blood, you know; and a week later I was sent to Saint Luke's. It seems I had some infection or something. Anyway I was given their new drug and I was as right as rain. I'd have gone back there to have my baby but they don't have a baby ward there do they?'

'No,' Allison said; 'they don't. And what did your doctor say had been wrong with you?'

'My own doctor?'

'Yes.'

'A bladder infection. He said they were common in women.'

'Yes they are,' Allison responded. 'By the way, who is your doctor Mrs Bailley? Your own doctor.' Allison was aware that she should have taken the trouble to discover this previously.

'Why Doctor Johnson,' the woman replied, making Allison's heart thump hard.

'Ken Johnson?' she muttered.

'I don't know doctor. Could be. He's Doctor K. Johnson right enough of The Practice in Neilston Road. Do you know him?'

'Yes I know him,' Allison said to the woman as she left her. Not mentioning that she had almost married the man.

Rosemary Pallain emerged from the meeting very pleased with herself indeed. Under her stewardship, they had reached a highly satisfactory conclusion and a formal statement of the Republican Party's position would be issued accordingly. It would state simply that there was indeed evidence to support the fact that money was going from the U.S.A. to support acts of Zionist terrorism.

With perhaps a few minor exceptions this money was not, however, going from the Jewish populace. It was, incredibly, coming from a "black budget" established by the current President of the United States in order to subvert the Middle East peace initiatives to which his public relations men had contributed more than he had. The proof of this corrupt political activity existed in documents supplied from "reliable sources" in Wall Street, the Chamber of Commerce, the Federal Tax Department and elsewhere.

The reason the Democrats wanted this instability to continue was as simple as it was cynically horrific. They intended re-defining Middle East settlement, to include both extreme Jewish and Muslim views. They had drawn up a "peace-plan" to achieve this objective to which they were convinced both sides would agree.

This would enable the Golan Heights and the other still disputed areas to become "neutral" by the simple expedient of a shared-territory agreement being implemented and policed with vigor by the military of certain countries in the U.N.

Those non-Jewish and non-Islamic members of the United Nations who had no vested interest at all in the area would look after it and enforce peace there. A number of such states had already been approached, discussions had taken place incognito, and an outline plan had been agreed.

It was a plan, however, which would be unacceptable to any Republican president, it would legitimize the criminals in Lebanon, it would be a palliative to Iraq and an overture to Iran. Consequently, it would require another term of Office by the Democratic incumbents in order to be ratified. It may indeed stop the bombs, but what self-respecting electorate would be party to such a sell-out?

The Republicans would call for a Congressional Hearing on the issue and that would lose itself in the maze of credible documentation and media coverage Mrs Pallain's colleagues had promised to lay. By the time this Hearing was called, let alone arrived at any conclusion, the issue would be irrelevant. She'd be in the White House as President.

There was another thing too. Her brother-in-law would be stepfather to the future Queen of England and her perfectly groomed and fully Anglified nephew would make this young woman an excellent escort. To be more precise a "Consort" was the term; when the time was right.

As the committee had unanimously agreed to the adoption of an initial press-leak, followed by the official Republican statement, someone had asked what the project should be called. 'In the tradition of the past few decades,' said Rosemary Pallain, 'it has to have a "gate" somewhere. How about 'Ziongate?'' she smiled. As with most things this extraordinary woman suggested, her suggestion was adopted unanimously. Ziongate it was.

Early that same afternoon Mrs Bailley gave birth to a little boy and by the time Allison had popped over to see her in a free moment she was already surrounded by her family.

They were making such a fuss of her and the baby, that Allison didn't bother to intrude. She merely attracted the proud mother's attention and gave her a wave. Mrs Bailley beamed back a very contented smile. Despite everything, she and her family seemed to be very happy indeed with the new arrival. Allison wondered what the new antibiotic had been that they'd given the woman at Saint Luke's. It had obviously worked, but had it presented complications. For a moment Allison realized that she'd heard Saint Luke's mentioned in some other context recently; but in seconds the thought had slipped from her mind.

There was the meeting of the proposed research group to attend at four, and as Allison rushed along to the office where it was being held, she felt quite apprehensive about how she would perform. She was confident enough in her own ability in this respect. Such confidence, however, only came from a thorough understanding of her strengths and weaknesses and one weakness she was very aware of was her relative inexperience in formal research matters. She had been trained as a clinician not as a research scientist; something of course she hoped to remedy soon.

If, as Doctor Bennet had implied, she should manage to obtain her M.D. degree as a result of her proposed research, she would be well on the way to achieving this latter distinction. The 'Doctor of Medicine' degree was awarded for original clinical research and would be visible proof of her ability in that respect if and when she obtained it. Still that was at least three years away and the meeting was now. First things first.

Already in the room when she entered was Pam. She looked slightly disheveled and distraught and Allison wondered what was wrong with her. Alcohol sprung to mind, alcohol and alcoholism. There were four others there who Allison had seen around the hospital though she didn't know them by name. Pam briefly introduced them. As son as she could, however, Allison drew her to one side:

'Did you get back from the party okay?' she asked quietly.

Pam looked at her directly. 'I got back,' she responded with a trace of what seemed like sadness in her voice; 'Sorry if I had a bit too much I... .'

Another three members of the group arrived, interrupting their conversation, this included John Raynor, followed after another minute or two by Doctor Bennet. Coffee arrived on a trolley with a plate of biscuits on it and, exposed to such luxury, the group got down to business.

The meeting was about half way through when Doctor Bennet asked Allison if she would like to outline, for the information of the group, her ideas on her proposed research into acute porphyria. She cleared her throat and, fingers crossed mentally, she did so;

'Well,' she began; 'As you all know, in acute porphyria there is an increased production of the chemicals which combine to form hemoglobin. As you also know, there are certain pathological states associated with the sudden attacks of this disease which seem to be highly specific to it. Of these, I wish to specifically consider, at present, the neurological disorders.

'I propose to outline a series of studies which should demonstrate whether or not the increased level of the chemicals which combine to form hemoglobin, which occurs in acute porphyria, could cause toxic damage to the nerves thus leading to the neurological signs and symptoms of the disease and their psychiatric manifestations.'

Now in full flow, Allison continued to outline her proposals and her theories. By the time she had ended it was evident that she had impressed her colleagues with her scientific acumen.

True to form, Doctor Bennet made little comment on her presentation. He rarely did when things were obviously of a high standard and came from an established member of his staff. His brief; 'Thank you Allison,' was, in itself, one of the best professional compliments she'd ever had.

Allison left the meeting feeling very good indeed. Her proposals had been well accepted and it had been agreed that she would receive all of the budget and the facilities she had requested to carry out her research.

As she walked along the corridor with Pam, she expressed her amazement at this; 'Porphyria's obviously in vogue.' she mused.

'*Harpers and Queens*' more like,' said Pam glibly. 'This is up-market research.'

Allison laughed enjoying the *double entendre*. 'Well, I just hope I can do justice to what I've been given. It isn't always this easy surely, to get a budget and facilities, particularly for such an obscure disease.'

'No,' said Pam, 'It isn't.'

They discussed the possibilities which the group held with respect to finding a possible cause and cure for porphyria and the prospect excited Allison greatly. Pam, however, despite her usual good humor seemed preoccupied with something else.

As they turned a corner in the corridor, Allison suddenly caught sight of Jennifer Wright walking in front of them. She felt an uncanny impulse to go and speak to her, to attempt to establish some understanding or common ground. Pam noticed her interest in Jennifer and frowning a little enquired discreetly;

'What is it about Jennifer that interests you so much Allison? What was it exactly that transpired between you two? You seem to have been terribly affected by her in some way.'

'Oh it's nothing in particular,' said Allison; 'It's just that we got off on the wrong foot together and I would like to rectify that. I felt somehow that she took an immediate dislike to me for some reason.'

'Why don't you then?' asked Pam. 'Why don't you do as you say and rectify it.'

'I will,' replied Allison, her immediate opportunity gone now that Jennifer had turned off and disappeared into her own ward. 'When I get the opportunity.'

The lay-out of the wards was something Allison liked about the hospital. They diverted off from a central corridor into their own smaller corridors; off which were the patient's rooms. Some of these were individual, some had beds for two or four people. It gave the balance of openness, community and privacy which Alison felt a modern hospital should have.

'Come on,' continued Pam looking at her watch; 'Time for a quick coffee before ward round.'

'But we've only just had some coffee!' protested Allison.

'I know,' laughed Pam, 'but we mustn't get too used to quality stuff like that. Better to keep ourselves exposed to our usual brand.'

Laughing with her, Allison acquiesced and agreed to join her for another quick coffee;

'You should know what too much caffeine can do to your nervous system,' she jokingly warned Pam, then her lightness suddenly dropped as she realized that Pam's 'quick coffee' probably meant a shot of Scotch.

'Oh, go on doctor,' smiled Pam. 'Let's have your proposed research plan for assessing the origins of caffeine addiction in Pamela Smith. As if there weren't enough problems that way already!'

'It might come to that,' replied Allison, trying not to sound diffident and pulling some coins from her purse. 'Allow me at least to buy you some and watch you self-administer it, as a first step.'

'You're on,' said Pam as they headed for the common room and its machine standard cafe au lait. Pam, of course, used the drawer too. Allison watched her, feeling very helpless and very sad. As she looked she wondered what pills she took and where she got them from. She hoped it was by prescription.

* * *

The Vice-President had spent two hours discussing the matter with his colleague over drinks. As the tonic had bubbled to flatness in their respective glasses they had put out a few feelers to people they could trust. In particular they had confided in and obtained information from, solid personal contacts they had in the Intelligence Agencies. The response had been surprising and informative. What U'Prichard had intimated to them was not in the least incredible. Senator Rosemary Pallain was a member of a society called The Mayflower Compact as indeed was her husband and a number of other prominent republicans.

There was nothing wrong in that of course, but some years ago, under the Carter administration, The Society had been looked at by two of these agencies at the then President's request immediately after his problems in Iran. There was talk of some Republican collusion in the way the issue had been presented to the American public. It had angered the President enough to request the enquiry and the Mayflower Compact had been duly investigated.

While there had been nothing which would survive the tests of a Federal Court there had been rumors, nothing official, but credible rumors just the same - off the record - that this historical society was more than it appeared to be. Some said a great deal more.

As the information flowed to them and as they discussed it with each other; the fact that there may be some degree of truth in what U'Prichard had intimated to them crept through the two men. In due course after their final contact had given his opinion and without a further word being said, they exchanged looks of mutual agreement.

The Vice-President lifted the telephone. He spoke four charged words to the Secret Service man who had answered immediately: 'Get me the President.'

Later that afternoon Allison received a call over the intercom system requesting her to contact Doctor Bennet. She did so and he asked her to come round and see him in the general medical ward as soon as she could. She was there within minutes and when Doctor Bennet arrived he led her immediately to the room of a young woman of about twenty years old.

The young woman looked very distressed indeed and as she lay looking very lethargic in her bed, she didn't seem to be fully aware of where she was. Allison noticed immediately that her breathing was labored and she appeared to exhibit signs of a slight muscular tremor.

'This is Miss Goudie, Vikki Goudie,' said Doctor Bennet.

'Miss Goudie,' he continued, addressing the young woman, 'This is Doctor Young, she's come to take a look at you.'

The young woman looked up, but still didn't seem to be fully registering all that was happening around her. Doctor Bennet motioned for Allison to physically examine her which she duly did.

Allison was puzzled. The woman showed muscular weakness, her breathing was labored and she had tenderness in her abdomen. She was also exhibiting an elevated blood pressure and heart rate and was very definitely confused. Allison noted too, patches on the woman's skin where the pigmentation had darkened somewhat.

Allison stood back, reflected on things for a few seconds then gave her a further, very thorough, examination. The results were no different. She had no definite idea of what was wrong with the patient, though she certainly knew how she would propose treating some of the signs and symptoms she was presenting with.

She made the woman comfortable, pulled back the screens round the bed and approached Doctor Bennet who was standing a few yards away speaking with a junior doctor. She smiled at him. He nodded in response. It was Michael. One of the young doctors from the party. Allison wondered what a pathologist was doing here!

'Well Allison,' asked Doctor Bennet when he saw her approach; 'What do you make of Miss Goudie?'

'Not much I'm afraid,' replied Allison. 'Her signs are very generalized, but don't seem to form a cohesive pattern; not one that I'm familiar with anyway. There's obviously large-scale neurological involvement, both central and peripheral and she's significantly hypertensive with a prominent tachycardia. Has a neurologist looked at her?'

'She's just come from Neurology at my request,' said Doctor Bennet. 'First thing this morning. They couldn't make much of it all either, so you're not alone. No ideas at all?'

Allison looked at him and gave a little frown;

'Well there was one thing...' she said uncertainly; '...but I don't imagine....'

'What was that?' asked her chief.

'Her skin,' replied Allison; 'It was pigmented in some of the more exposed areas. At first I thought it may be the start of a fungal or Herpes infection or something but...'

'And?' urged Doctor Bennet.

'Well, it was distributed as if she may be sensitive to light to some degree and if so, given her other signs and symptoms....' she hesitated.

'Go on, Allison.'

'She doesn't have acute porphyria by any chance? Surely not!'

'Well done, doctor!' said Bennet genuinely pleased with his young protege. 'She does indeed. How would you confirm that diagnosis?'

'By having porphyrins run on fecal and urine samples; possibly a liver biopsy, if strictly necessary.'

'The former has already been done and was positive,' commented Doctor Bennet. 'Your first exposure to an almost classic case of a very rare disease, Allison; one in which you have a special interest. Let's see what we can do for her, shall we?'

Allison wondered if and how the attack had been precipitated and asked Doctor Bennet.

'I've no idea. Perhaps the girl's relatives are here. Have a look, and if they are, have a word with them while I have another look at our patient.'

Doctor Bennet then continued speaking in a more solemn tone;

'The most immediate problem we have here, is that of how to get the blood pressure down to near normal limits. None of our usual agents seem to be doing much and we have to normalize it fairly soon. Give it some thought.'

Allison returned to the woman's bedside and exchanged a few comforting words with her. Though still confused looking and unresponsive, she seemed to appreciate this and gave Allison a subdued smile. Allison looked pensive;

"How can we get your blood pressure down to normal?" she wondered. "What's so different about it that it won't respond as it should to the drugs we normally use?"

After absentmindedly straightening Vikki's bedclothes, Allison went off to find the young woman's relatives, still pondering this very critical question. "How," she asked herself, again and again, as she had as a student.

The ward sister told Allison that there were in fact a couple of members of Miss Goudie's family in the ward at present, even though she was not being allowed visitors. Allison said she'd be down immediately to speak to them. She rushed downstairs to the waiting room and, as she did so, a brief vision of Jennifer Wright's male friend crossed her mind. She dwelt on it for a moment or two, then let it go.

Vikki Goudie's mother was sitting in a side-room off the main hospital waiting-room. Beside her was Vikki's younger brother, a youth of around sixteen who looked very much like his sister.

'I'm Doctor Young,' Allison said to them both; 'I wonder if I could have a word with you?'

'Of course doctor,' said the woman. 'How is she? How's Vikki?'

'Stable,' said Allison, hoping she was correct. 'I'd like to ask you a few questions concerning Vikki's attack, how it came on, what happened before it and so on.'

'Of course doctor,' said the woman, as Allison closed the door to give them privacy.

'Well then...' Allison began. 'What happened precisely, when did you first notice that Vikki was unwell?'

'Well I'm not certain,' said the woman pensively. 'I think it was the morning after the party...wasn't it?' she said to the withdrawn looking young man at her side.

'I suppose it was,' he muttered.

'So there was a party?' Allison said.

'Yes, a little celebration for Vikki's aunt, my sister, she's back from Australia on a visit. We had a few people round and...'

'Did Vikki have anything to drink?' Allison asked; 'Any alcohol at all? It could possibly kill her,' she finished solemnly.

'Yes. We were told it could kill her,' said the woman.

'So none at all?'

'None at all, doctor.'

There were a few moments silence broken by the sound of the boy's voice speaking softly;

'Well...a little bit.'

'What?' asked Allison sharply. 'What do you mean a little bit?'

'She had a little bit to drink,' said the boy sheepishly. 'Just a small amount of vodka.'

'She never did!' said the girl's mother. 'Vikki'd never do that.'

'She didn't know,' said the boy. 'I slipped it into her drink... just a small nip of vodka...wouldn't do harm to nobody.'

Without waiting to hear any more Allison stormed out of the room. 'I'll speak to you later,' she said angrily to Vikki's brother as she rushed to a telephone.

'Doctor Young here. Doctor Bennet please,' she said to the operator. She reached her chief almost immediately.

'Vikki Goudie,' she said breathing hard. 'Her brother slipped her a Mickey Finn at some party. Vodka. Her attack's been precipitated by that. The girl didn't know.'

'Silly little bugger...' said Bennet, calmly. 'He could be responsible for manslaughter. Still at least we know what's happened. Stupid...' He didn't finish the sentence.

Allison met up again with Doctor Bennet in the ward, where after getting Vikki's confused version of events, they concluded that she had in fact drunk spiked orange juice and tonic water.

As she was about to leave the ward, Doctor Bennet again beckoned to Allison;

'I would like you to have a word with another young lady. She too was admitted from Neurology this morning. Her neurological problems have been discovered to be a result of a, as yet slight, cerebral hemorrhage. She has a brain tumor. We have been asked to keep her here for a day or two and assess if and how far this has spread before surgery becomes a realistic option. I want you to look for metastases. See if and how far it's spread.'

Allison was handed the case notes and taken to the little girl's room off the main corridor of the ward by Doctor Bennet. He introduced the girl to her as Tina. She was a pretty little thing, just over six years of age and as far as Allison was concerned, an example of the most distressing type of case she had to handle.

There was no need this time for any examination. She was a very sick child indeed who, within a very short period of time, would either make it or not. It was well established what was wrong with her. It was now simply a question of seeing how serious the extent of that illness was and assessing if she could be appropriately treated by established methods.

They had a brief chat and Allison explained to the child in simple terms what tests she was going to have carried out. In her experience this always made the patient feel secure no matter how young they were. She was a very bright little girl, who despite her illness, chattered away almost constantly. Allison liked her and, before she left, she assured her she'd be back personally in a few day's time to see her again once the test results were known.

Returning to the small office she had to herself - a rare privilege and one few hospitals other than The London could offer -Allison read over both sets of case notes again. She paid particular attention to Vikki Goudie's drug regimen. She couldn't understand why the young woman's blood pressure and heart rate had remained so high. By any standards the drugs she'd been given should have brought them close to normal levels at least.

She glanced through little Tina's file too, though there was nothing there that she didn't already know or hadn't already guessed. There was something about it, however, which seemed somehow familiar to her, something about the case which she felt she should have recognized and didn't. She couldn't work out what it was. No matter, it would come to her in good time.

She looked again at Vikki Goudie's file, tried to remember all the relevant reading she had already done on the subject of acute porphyria, both before and after her student days. What could be so different about it that the blood pressure remained elevated even after high doses of drugs which should have reduced it. She knew the disease well, very well, why couldn't she work it out, why?

Suddenly, and quite unexpectedly, a possible answer occurred to her. Allison had first considered this particular option when writing her dissertation on the disease. Now it came flashing back to her. The reason it was raised was probably different from the usual ones, the ones the drugs already used treated so well. With a sense of excitement spreading through her she impulsively reached for the phone and called Claire. The phone was answered on its very first ring.

'Oh hello, Claire, it's Allison Young here, is Doctor Bennet free? Could I have a word with him? Over the telephone would be fine.' Allison held on for a few seconds and then Doctor Bennet was speaking to her.

'What is it, Allison, something come up?'

'Yes, Sir,' replied Allison, scarcely able to control her excitement. 'I think I know how we can lower Vikki Goudie's blood pressure.'

'How?' asked her chief, with a tone of contained urgency she had never heard in his voice before; thought it incapable of.

* * *

As he waited quietly in anticipation of the President's characteristic voice; the Vice President looked at his friend the senator a man he trusted more than all the rest of them. They had been friends since childhood and they thought that they'd seen and heard it it all. They hadn't. Their eyes met again and they shook their heads in disbelief:

'An American fucking Monarchy!' the senator said incredulous as the Vice-President listened for his connection to be made to the Oval Office. 'My grand-children will love this one!'

A young woman's voice came onto the line and he recognized it. He didn't like her one little bit, she'd joined the Oval Office staff straight from her first flush of what passed for Hollywood stardom. She'd already made a few advances within the White House Staff by the simple expedient of insulting senior military officials. A position she justified by incongruously defining herself as pacifist.

'The President's unavailable,' the voice said; 'Anything important?'

The Vice-President paused, rethought his options, wondered what in the name of God had scuttled into the White House and decided that it was time to do things his way. 'Yeah,' he replied to the trumped-up starlet; 'I wondered if you had a copy of *The King and I*. If you could get a copy over to me. You know, the one with Yul Brynner?'

'You what?' the confused voice came back; as the senator smiled with a deep satisfaction and the Vice-President hung up.

'I think we could do it if we had some of the new atrial naturietic factor, ANF,' said Allison with just a tinge of excitement still in her voice. 'As we probably don't, I think we could do the same job by using a combination of phentolamine and a lower than usual dose of propranolol.'

'Explain,' said Bennet in his no-nonsense, professional voice. Allison did.

Bennet listened to Allison attentively and without interruption. When she had finished he said quite simply;

'It makes excellent sense. I'll try it myself. We don't have any ANF to hand, few people do - despite its proven efficacy - and the hospital ethical committee may have to agree to its use given that it's for an unregistered procedure. I may also need permission from Miss Goudie's family. However, it's well worth the attempt with the other drugs. If you're happy enough I'll go ahead and arrange it now.' He didn't mention that he'd already had this idea; from reading Allison's student dissertation some weeks earlier. He fully believed it would work, but not quite in the way that Allison thought.

Allison was excited she would soon discover if the treatment she had suggested for the young woman would work. Dismissing all extraneous thoughts from her mind, she became the clinical physician quickly and formally and she was soon walking briskly towards the girl's room. Just before she entered the appropriate corridor she gave her fingers a quick cross.

She accompanied Doctor Bennet into the ward. They made their way to Vikki Goudie's room accompanied by the ward sister. Vikki was still half-asleep and the sister roused her gently by softly speaking commonalities to her as she drew the screens around the bed. Doctor Bennet approached the young woman, sat on the bedside, and took her hand.

'Good afternoon, Vikki. How are you? Let's have a little look.' As he continued speaking, Doctor Bennet gave his patient a quick examination, using his stethoscope and his hands gently and professionally to reach what both he and Allison knew was a foregone conclusion. 'Much the same,' he said. 'Now, let's get you better, young woman, that's why we're here.' As he spoke he gestured for Allison to make an examination of the frail looking young woman which she duly did.

Still the difficulty in breathing, still the blood pressure pumping high above normal and still the heart racing. As a nurse entered the screened area with a medical trolley, Allison's heart began to race too. Within the next few minutes her seemingly inspired suggestions could save this young woman's life; then again they may not. She betrayed no emotion, however, keeping her professional face intact as Doctor Bennet continued speaking to Vikki;

'What we're going to do Vikki, is give you two drugs which should soon get things back to normal. We're going to have to give you these by injection which I hope you don't mind - you're not worried by injections I hope,' Doctor Bennet continued smiling. 'We get many patients who prefer being ill to a quick prick in the arm-not you I imagine though. Correct?'

'Correct, doctor,' whispered the distressed girl forcing a smile.

'Good. Right. As I inject you, Doctor Young here will take your blood pressure. I hope you don't mind that either - we get patients who object to that as well - it makes us wonder sometimes what we can do not to upset them.'

Vikki gave a short weak laugh as Doctor Bennet lifted the prepared syringe from the medical trolley, checked the level in it, gave it a little squirt and took his patient's arm. He gently caressed the skin to raise a vein for injection. Allison took her other arm and winding on the sphygmomanometer she put the stethoscope in her ears and began to monitor the blood pressure and pulse rate of her patient.

Given the experimental nature of their procedure, a more formal method of carrying it out had been briefly discussed. The insertion of an intravenous catheter to inject the drugs and directly measure blood pressure had been considered. So, too, had the attachment of Vikki to an electrocardiograph machine to measure changes in her heart in detail.

The attendance of an anaesthetist with resuscitation equipment in case of respiratory collapse had also been discussed. These considerations had all been rejected, however, in favour of the more relaxed setting of the ward and the simpler techniques familiar to the patient. A relaxed patient responded better and if things did go badly, the anaesthetist and his resuscitation equipment were only a hundred yards or so away waiting, with interest, like everyone else now, to see if Allison's theories were clinically viable.

'Sister tells me that you originally come from Norfolk...' began Doctor Bennet as he slowly began to inject the combination of drugs into the young woman's vein. 'I used to visit Norfolk a great deal...' he continued, distracting her from the procedure, but not giving her the opportunity to respond. '...a lovely county, one of the finest in the country and that's not just my opinion but my wife and daughter's as well. In fact my daughter...'

Carefully Allison listened and watched and almost immediately noticed a change in her patient's vital signs. The heart rate was slowing, the beat becoming more regular, the blood pressure was dropping. She began to feel very excited indeed.

Still speaking about the beauties of Norfolk to his patient, Bennet looked over to her. She met his eyes and nodded. 'Normalising,' she said quietly. '185 over 120, 95 bpm.' She continued giving the revised status of the blood pressure and the heart rate in bpm - beats per minute. By doing this she also let Doctor Bennet know he should continue injecting. Their aim was the ideal normal 120/180 for the blood pressure and 70 beats per minute for the heart rate. Anything near to these would be a major success.

'A bit of sailing on the Broads, of course, is my idea of a break, but my wife is a dedicated landlubber....'

'155 over 115, 80 bpm,' said Allison.

'...she won't go anywhere near a boat. I once had difficulty convincing her to travel on the cross-channel ferry...'

'150 over 100, 77 bpm. Falling.'

'...anyway, once I'd finally convinced her to do so, she enjoyed the trip so much that she asked me if I could take her sailing on the Norfolk Broads!'

Doctor Bennet removed the syringe from under the sterile swab he applied to its point of entry.

'130 over 85, 72 bpm,' continued Allison. '125 over 82, 72 bpm; steady at 125 over 82, 72 bpm.' She looked at the still talking Doctor Bennet, his eyes met hers;

'125 over 82, 72 bpm, steady...' she said, '...steady.' He winked at her.

'How are you feeling, Vikki?' he asked. 'Fine, Doctor,' she replied. Allison had rarely felt better in all her life. It had worked.

Allison noted how Doctor Bennet continued his casual banter with Vikki as he made repeated observations of her respiration, her coherence of thought, her memory and her general demeanour. She was highly impressed by his professionalism and learned a great deal from it.

When they finally finished and left Vikki in the capable hands of the nursing staff Allison took Doctor Bennet to one side;

'I'm still a bit puzzled, Sir,' she said.

'Yes?'

'The boy said one Mickey Finn - one vodka did this to her.'

'So you said,' replied Bennet.

'She must be very sensitive to it. It's not usually that critical. Not one drink.'

'That's what he said. Your very own words.'

'Yes, Sir, that's what he said.'

'Well it must be the case then,' said Bennet with uncharacteristic certainty in the veracity of the brother's statement.

Later in the afternoon, as she left the hospital, Allison noticed Pam walking along an empty corridor. She made to call to her, to join her, but as she approached she stopped. Something was wrong. Pam was lurching. Drunk it looked like. She seemed to be stifling sobs too. Allison stood still and watched and wondered, as the brilliant young geneticist made her way along the corridor unsteadily and went out through the revolving doors.

There was something else too, which left Allison a little confused. As she stood still watching Pam leave the hospital through the doors, she heard voices quiet but urgent, approaching her along with steady potent footsteps - the footsteps of two men. Despite herself she couldn't help but overhear what they said;

'It may work, Geoffrey, I don't know yet. We'll find out soon enough.'

'And if it doesn't William...? It was you who messed up the tests in the first place. If you hadn't been so incompetent then...'

'There's no point going over all that now. It was the technician's fault. He's been dismissed long since. We must take it from here. We can explain it adequately to his Private Secretary this evening. I'll do that...it's not too difficult to explain to a lay-man, even one as informed as he is.'

Allison realized that it was Sir William Mostyn speaking to someone, someone she didn't know, hadn't heard before.

'Even if it doesn't work we can pretend that it does. We can give that impression. We discovered how to only today. I knew that the girl…'

As the men turned the corner they saw Allison and immediately stopped talking. Sir William nodded to her, smiled and walked on.

'Evening, Sir William,' she said. The other man, who was striking in appearance and immaculately groomed, initially looked alarmed then ignored her. They walked on in silence out through the same doors that Pam had left from. It was only then that Allison realized that Pam may try to drive home in the state she was in.

Allison rushed outside, but Pam was nowhere to be seen. She heard a car drive off and hoped it wasn't Pam's. After a further look for her colleague, she made her way to her own car. It had been a long day and she was going out tonight to a dinner party.

* * *

As the White House starlet was asking various members of the staff what the political significance was of the movie *The King and I* the Vice-President and the senator had elected to pay a visit to the American Embassy.

They soon ascertained who gave medical back-up to the Ambassador and his staff and arranged to meet with the doctor. By pulling a few of the strings which they were privileged enough to pull they arranged a meeting for that same afternoon though it was pointed out to them that they may have to wait for a time as he had a full quota of patients to see; but he'd fit them in. When they discovered that the doctor's name was Hilary Imran Thame. The two Americans wondered precisely what his origins were. Whatever they were they immediately nicknamed him, due to his initials as, "The Hit Man"!

Whatever concerns they may have had over Doctor Thame's pedigree the senator and Vice President needn't have worried.

He was true blue American himself and graduate of Yale Medical School the Vice-President's alma mater. They wondered precisely why such a well qualified man had decided to come to work in the United Kingdom but felt it wiser not to enquire about this except in the most general terms of their colleagues at the Embassy. They were told in no uncertain terms that Doctor Thame "preferred it here" and appreciating that it took all types to make up a world and that there were few feathers easier ruffled than Embassy staff's; they left it at that.

They waited in a well furnished waiting room where there was only one other person waiting. They could hear quiet sounds behind an adjoining door. Evidently the doctor was giving a consultation.

After about ten minutes the door opened and Charles U'Prichard emerged followed closely by a preoccupied looking Doctor Thame. U'Prichard saw both of them immediately:

'Hello gentlemen,' he said nonplussed; 'I'm glad to see you here.' With that he left, leaving the HIT Man looking at them.

'You know U'Prichard?' he asked in a quasi Anglified mid-Western drawl.

'Yes, sir, we sure do.' replied the senator.

'Would you please come into my office,' the HIT Man said to his final patient of the day. He looked stressed. 'I'll see you gentleman shortly.'

'Sure thing,' replied the senator as the door of the consulting room closed. 'Bet he wished he'd stayed in Yale.' he said. The Vice-President smiled.

* * *

As Allison made her way to the door of the hospital and home, she decided, on a whim, to pay a quick visit to Mrs Bailley whose ward was nearby. She went there pleased that the woman had seemed happy enough. Down's syndrome was bad, but certain people had the capacity to handle it and to live happy lives with their children, who were, despite their situation, lovely kids. Mrs Bailley was obviously one of these people.

She made her way to the woman's bed and saw the child's cot beside her where she could hear the baby awake, mumbling. Mrs Bailley was asleep, so Allison took a look at the baby, held its tiny hand in her own, looked at the delicate palm, at the delicate child as she slowly froze. It was normal! Not Mongoloid at all. Her first thought was that it was the wrong baby. The tests had been repeated, controlled they were fool-proof. It must be the wrong baby!

As she stood there in near shock, Allison heard a voice.

'He's lovely, isn't he, Doctor. You were all wrong I'm glad to say. What a little beauty he is.'

It was Mrs Bailley. When Allison saw her eyes, their color tones, she knew that the baby was hers.

Allison drove home in confusion. There must have been some mistake made about the child. She'd see the histologist, Bob Innskip, in the morning. She'd mention the fact to no-one until then, no-one at all. What a lot of suffering they had caused that woman and her family for nothing.

Above her the moon hung quiet and solemn, its light spreading into the sky until it was lost in its vastness.

* * *

With professional tact of their own, which more than matched any physician's the two American politicians asked

Doctor Thame what contacts he had with eminent hematologists both in the U.K and elsewhere. The Hit Man was concise and to the point.

'I'll assure you gentleman that there's only one worth consulting on either side of the Atlantic. No matter what problem you're concerned with - and you don't feel too free about telling me that - it seems;, but then I'm no Democrat, so who am I to complain about that? Yup there's only one man.'

'And who would that be?' the Vice-President asked quietly.

'Why Sir William Mostyn, of course. Rumor has it that he attends to royalty. See him if I can't help you gentlemen. He's at The London Hospital.'

'Thank you Doctor Thame we might just do that,' said senator Chuck Fitzimons as the two Democrats rose to take their leave.

CHAPTER FIVE

Harry Wright lived in an imposing detached Victorian villa which seemed at first to be much too large for him and his daughter. It would have been, but for the consulting rooms he had there in addition to the living accommodation. It was a very impressive house; indeed a beautiful one. It was the sort of house Harry loved but which he now found difficult to manage on his own.

It had a large driveway with a double garage to the front; all of which was tastefully set off by shrubs and flowerbeds. It was in an ideal situation for just about everything you could think of and it was a perfect place to live.

The interior of the house was as impressive as its exterior. And this morning Harry was showing a middle-aged lady around it; she had a neat trim figure, bright grey-blue eyes and dusty-fair hair. He was interviewing for a receptionist-come housekeeper and he spoke to Mrs Marianne Mawson as he attempted to show her the house and also describe the medical work she'd have to do at one and the same time.

Marianne had come to him highly recommended by a close friend of his; and he'd given her the interview on the basis of a brief telephone conversation. This, therefore, was her first view of the house and their first view of each other. So far they had got on very well and had immediately felt at ease with one another. Marianne was a Scot with a pleasant, practical, matter-of-fact manner which Harry liked immensely. She asked him how long he'd stayed there;

'Oh, we moved here five or six years ago when my daughter was only an infant,' he replied. 'I have two rooms out back which I use for consultations; the remainder are family rooms. Would you like coffee or something?' he asked.

'Yes please,' Mrs Mawson replied, smiling a self-confident, but not overbearing smile. 'Perhaps I could get it? I'm here to be assessed on how well I can do this sort of thing you know. Now's your chance to find out!'

'No need really,' laughed Harry gently but with effort; 'I'm well into equality in domestic tasks,' he smiled; 'I'll get it, even if it's just this once.' He walked towards the kitchen and the woman with the pretty fair hair and the bright twinkling grey-blue eyes followed him, admiring him as if he were some errant son.

'I'm really quite domesticated you know,' he went on. 'At least as far as making coffee is concerned. But I'm far from being the "New Man" I'm afraid. 'I can boil a decent egg and make a slice or two of toast.'

Mrs Mawson smiled warmly, he was putting a brave face on things. She knew, from her past employer that Harry was going through a rough patch at present and that he'd been through rough patches before.

'Just a touch of cream,' she said after him. 'No sugar and no need for toast or a boiled egg!'

Harry turned and grinned at her, he did like her:

'Right,' he said, 'coffee coming up.'

Dressed very formally in her black cocktail dress, black stole and her best silver jewelry, Allison felt just a little more nervous than she normally did before any formal occasion. While she was a gregarious woman by nature, she preferred informality to formality, casual chat to serious conversation, buffets to sit down meals. Having said this, she was looking forward to her dinner party a great deal indeed and was excited about what was in prospect for her.

Doctor Bennet had kindly offered to pick her up and take her there, mentioning that it would be a pleasure to do so as his wife was indisposed and he would enjoy accompanying such an attractive and gifted young woman. Allison smiled at his flattery, accepted his offer with alacrity and sat now, looking out of the window of her flat, waiting for his car to arrive.

At seven thirty, prompt, it arrived and Allison had a final look at herself in the mirror, swiftly appraising her image. It was fine. She looked good and she knew it.

During the drive to John Raynor's house Allison asked Doctor Bennet precisely who would be at the dinner party.

'Some people you know John and Wendy, Sir William, myself and you, of course,' he said with a tease in his voice. Allison smiled, though she hadn't considered the possibility that Sir William would be there. Exalted company indeed.

'And some people you don't know. A few of the senior management of Unicorn Chemicals - I think you've already met one or two of them at John's party.'

'No,' said Allison truthfully, 'I didn't. I left quite early. The only one I saw there from Unicorn was a woman called Kathryn Meadowford who knows Alan Downie quite well.'

'Don't know her,' Bennet said. 'Surprising.'

'Why?' asked Allison.

'Because I thought I knew them all,' he said, his tone seeming different, a touch brittle. 'Evidently I don't.'

* * *

Harry left the room and soon Marianne heard the sound of cups rattling and cutlery being taken from a drawer. Within a few minutes Harry was back in the lounge with a tray containing two fine porcelain coffee cups and a matching pot steaming with fresh coffee. It smelled lovely, a deep fresh Columbian brand she saw from the packet which he'd inadvertently placed on the tray, superb.

Harry poured; and the lovely rich aroma spread throughout the room: 'First of all the appointments book.' he said, lifting a thick leather-bound ledger and showing it to Marianne as he sat beside her.

Immediately he spoke, the phone rang. With a bump Harry placed the coffee pot back on the tray and walked to it.

'Hello,' he said. 'Doctor Wright speaking.' He listened for a time and said nothing. A grim, determined look tightened his face. 'I'll be right over.' He looked at Mrs Mawson helplessly. 'I have to go on a house-call,' he said; 'I am sorry. Do you mind waiting here for half-an-hour or so...I won't be too long?'

'Why, of course not!' said Mrs Mawson warmly as she surveyed the room around her and decided just how it could be arranged to suit her adopted doctor if she was fortunate enough to get the position.

'See you when I get back.' Harry said with a forced smile; 'Help yourself to whatever you need.' With that he went to a small cloakroom, pulled on a driving jacket and went out of the door into his car and drove off.

When the sound of the car had gone it was very quiet indeed and Marianne Mawson sat looking at the two unused cups on the tray wondering what to do with them. She drank both with deep pleasure as she sat for a while looking around the lounge which was traditionally furnished and which had along one wall a beautiful chaise-longue.

In one of the corners there was a Regency mahogany cabinet on top of which was a framed photograph of Harry's former wife. She went over and looked at it, she had been a very beautiful woman and he and his daughter had lost her. She shook her head at the fickleness of life and turned away to look further at her surroundings.

She went over to the table the coffee-pot had been placed on and poured herself another cup. It tasted almost perfect. She sat down again and looked at a Victorian grandfather clock which stood ticking away relentlessly in the corner. She checked it with her watch. It was probably a century old, but it was absolutely on time.

The day had brightened quite a bit, so she walked through the expansive and very modern kitchen and went out into the garden and sat on a seat on the patio which had been built there. Like the house, the garden was beautiful and it was beautifully maintained. It had a long carefully tended lawn which ran down to an area which had been left intentionally untended and which was overhung by a number of large spreading trees including a large chestnut and two beeches.

She sat there for a time flicking through the appointments book which she had taken with her and she mentally noted that Doctor Wright had a patient due at ten o'clock. She finished her coffee and went through to the kitchen to wash up and assess how it could best be put in shape if that was going to be her responsibility in the future.

At length - while she was still studying his appointments ledger which was not in perfect shape by any means - she heard a noise at the front door; a key fumbling in the lock. She put the ledger down and went back through the lounge to the entrance hall. The door swung open:

'Hello; still here?' Harry said; giving her a lovely smile.

'I am, Doctor Wright. Now, let me get you a fresh cup of coffee and this time I mean that literally.' Harry smiled again this time his eyes shone with a trace of a sparkle. He knew a gem when he saw one.

'I think that perhaps we could make things a bit more formal.' he said.

Marianne looked at him and smiled brightly; 'I've got the job?'she asked, looking expectant and delighted.

'You've got it, if you want it. When can you start?'

'I want it and I can start right now, Doctor Wright, if you've no objections. You have a patient due in ten minutes, I see; you'd best get yourself ready. I'll get the place ship-shape in five. What's your normal procedure for seeing patients? For settling accounts and so on? Would you like me to re-arrange your system or implement it as it is?'

Harry looked at her with what was almost relief, totally convinced now about the correctness of his decision. He'd found a gem alright. She'd do the job well. 'We'll, keep it as it is,' he said. 'It works - just!'

* * *

They drove in silence for a short time until Doctor Bennet spoke again, his voice back to its normal tone. 'Did you know that there's a possibility that Unicorn's drug, Oviron, might just have an anti-porphyric action?'

'No, I didn't!' exclaimed Allison with surprise and immediate interest. She wondered why this hadn't been mentioned to her before. 'In what way?' she asked.

'It seems to inhibit the activity of the enzyme ALA synthetase in the liver of all mammals including humans.'

Allison immediately wondered how Doctor Bennet knew this. Surely no such studies in humans had been carried out on the drug? Nor could she see how they could have been - at least justifiably. She was fascinated, however, and let Doctor Bennet continue uninterrupted;

'If your theory about the etiology of the disease is correct, that it's due to over-production of ALA, then Oviron given long-term might control it by keeping this enzyme functioning at normal levels.'

'Which could lead to a remission of symptoms,' mused Allison; 'And even permanent remission of the disease...if what I am postulating is correct and the drug does this effectively. My God, Doctor Bennet. What a remarkable discovery...if it works!'

'John,' Bennet said quietly.

'Sorry?'

'Drop the formalities this evening, Allison. Call me 'John.' It's more in keeping with your status as a brilliant academic. And with the tone of a dinner party.' He smiled at her and she warmed to him again as she had in the past. The strangeness which had clouded him had gone.

Allison noticed that they were approaching John Raynor's house now. She began to feel a little nervous again. Doctor Bennet's disclosure had excited her greatly, however, and it kept the nervousness at bay. She was still reflecting on his comments when the car stopped and the engine was switched off.

'I wish there was some way we could try Oviron on Vikki Goudie,' Allison said suddenly.

'There is Allison,' Bennet said looking at her. 'If, in your professional opinion, you think it's going to help her, perhaps save her life. In such an instance you need not require formal clearance except from our own hospital ethical committee.'

'I'd like to try it, John,' she continued; 'God, it could revolutionise life for these people. Release the most severe cases from a neurological and dermatological prison cell.'

'You might just get the chance,' he replied. 'We'll talk about it later.'

When John and Wendy Raynor met Allison at the door this time, it was immediately evident that things were going to be a great deal different from the way they had been just so few days before. This had already been intimated to Allison by the cars she had seen parked in and around the extensive driveway. She recognized three of them.

The black Saab she'd remembered seeing as she left the party and the silver Mercedes sports car they'd passed as she'd driven away from the party with Gerry and his friend in his 'banger'. There, too, was the Daimler, the one she'd seen that night too; the one with the darkened windows. She was certain it was the same one. She reflected that there were no 'bangers' here. These were quality cars, all of them, which usually meant quality people. And, for whatever reason, she was one of them.

For the first time since her invitation, Allison began to really wonder why she'd been invited here, and why, for example, if the intention was to discuss Oviron informally over dinner and drinks, why Pam and Alan Downie hadn't been included in the guest list too. Allison wondered what she had to offer which was so special.

Both John and Wendy looked magnificent in their evening wear. John wore a white tuxedo which in Allison's experience suited only some men and he was one of them. Wendy wore a white silk evening gown set off by what looked like an emerald brooch on her left breast with a matching set of earrings. They made a stunning couple and they welcomed Allison and John Bennet warmly, as if genuinely delighted to see them;

'Come on in, both of you,' John Raynor said. 'Only one more to arrive and that's us at full complement. The others are already here.'

'Oh, I hope we're not late!' Allison said as the soft sound of voices conversing in another room spilled through to her.

'Why, of course not!' Wendy reassured her. 'The others were just a little bit early, that's all. Come along, I'll take your things then bring you in to meet them.' Allison handed her stole to Wendy and, as she took it away, John Raynor led her into the guest room to meet the other guests.

Since the death of his wife Harry had lost his enthusiasm for running the practice in the singular way that he did. Charging patients on an ability to pay basis for example and not hesitating to send them elsewhere for treatment if he felt it apposite.

Harry sent his patients to all sorts of professionals if he felt that he could not help them himself and some other therapy could. The one thing he never did was send a patient away without any hope at all.

He had in the past referred patients to osteopaths, acupuncturists, homeopaths and herbalists, aromatherapists and reflexologists; as well as to his more conventional medical colleagues. On one occasion Harry had even "referred" a patient to a professional astrologer. The patient had thought that it might help - so Harry advised having a go. The outcome had been satisfactory. 'An eclectic approach,' was what he termed it.

Harry also ensured that every one of his patients disclosed as much about their personal lives to him as they felt comfortable in revealing. He knew that the origins and prognosis of most illnesses were to be found in domestic and social conditions as much as in any pathology of the body itself and he incorporated this knowledge into his medicine.

By lunchtime, at one thirty, Marianne had the house and the appointment book in some sort of order and ready for the full reckoning she'd give them in due course. She noticed that Harry's accounts were badly kept, but she was unable to do much about this except ask him if he was going to attend to them or should she find someone else to do so.

'I'll get round to it sometime,' he said as he made to go out for a quick swim and an even quicker sandwich before his next patient was due. 'Sometime soon.'

Marianne doubted that he would. She knew that he needed someone to manage his finances and indeed his life. She could do what she could for him, but what he really needed well... She almost wished that she were twenty years younger and available!

Harry swam his usual twenty lengths of the local pool swiftly and efficiently. Breathing easily he came out, showered, then dried himself with his large bath towel. He had a fine muscular body which stood six-foot one in his bare feet and he had a fine spread of close-woven fair hair across the front of his chest.

When he'd dressed he went to the small shop where he always bought his lunch - two slices of sesame seed bread filled with a mixed salad and chicken. These he ate as he drove back home for his afternoon surgery. It was not much of a lunch-break, but it was all that he could manage and all that he wanted.

It had been different of course when Ann had been alive. Then he'd wanted lunch-breaks to last forever sometimes; and sometimes he'd never even managed a solitary sandwich. He'd been sustained then by more than food and drink. Still those days were gone now, gone for good. And he drove on home munching at the lettuce and the watercress, ruminating on other days and on his daughter and on the financial situation of the practice.

Yukio Yoshimura walked slowly along the street with his chauffeur-driven car driving slowly along beside him. It was being driven by a Vietnamese, a man who had borne untold hardships in fleeing from his country after the fall of Saigon and who now worked happily as a chauffeur with Unicorn Chemicals U.K.

The chauffeur had originally been a musician by profession, but damage to his hands during his flight to the West and safety, had put paid to any possibility that he may pursue that particular talent ever again. He had been a harpist and the fingers which had once strummed over the strings of the harp, now held the steering wheel of the car firmly; as firmly as the deep affection he felt for Yoshimura-San - the man, above all, whom he admired and revered.

Yoshimura walked a little further, looking now and then at the sky, the clouds, the moon, searching it as if looking for something.

At length the driver stopped the car beside him. The window rolled down slowly, electrically;

'Nam'ji desu ka' he said to Yoshimura. What time is it?

Yoshimura looked at his watch and smiled;

'Domo,' he said. Thank you. Yoshimura stood while the driver got out and opened the door. He got into the back seat and sat looking out of the window, still looking deep into the sky as the car drove off to the dinner party where he would meet his colleagues, old and new.

The first person Allison recognized was Kathryn Meadowford. She was looking as confident, well groomed and lovely as ever and was standing beside the tall, slim, dark man she had noticed her arrive with at the party. They were both talking quietly to a slightly smaller man who sported a moustache and had short grey-white hair.

She soon noticed Sir William Mostyn, drink in hand, standing talking to a very plain looking woman indeed whom Allison had never seen before. He seemed filled with animation as he spoke with her. It was evident from his eyes, however, that he was bored and it looked as if the woman was too. Even as she watched, he put his drink down on a tray as a waiter passed and lifted up another.

In a corner of the room two men were talking, one of whom was vaguely familiar to Allison though she couldn't quite place him. He was a tall man, also moustached and looking nothing short of magnificent in his evening-wear complete with cummerbund. He was talking to another man who was equally impressive - a shorter man with broad shoulders and grey swept back hair and who sucked at an unlit briar pipe. This man turned and looked at Allison the instant she entered the room. His piercing blue eyes seemed to see right through her. Strip her naked.

At this point Wendy appeared beside her and, with John, she proceeded to take Allison and John Bennet round to make the necessary introductions. It was only when she was formally introduced to him that Allison remembered Sir Geoffrey Dorrington. He had been the man she'd overheard speaking with Sir William Mostyn in the hospital corridor.

'Delighted to meet you,' he said to Allison, making it clearly obvious with his look that he was quite the opposite. 'Hope you enjoy the evening.'

'Yes, do that, Allison,' Sir William said to her, placing his hand, the one without the drink in it, on her bared left shoulder and keeping it there. It made her feel uncomfortable. It was Wendy Raynor who intervened;

'Goodness, Allison!' she said, pulling her away from Mostyn's grasp; 'I must introduce you right this minute to Greg Hoffmann from Unicorn. He asked me to grab you the first moment I could. He'll never forgive me if I don't do it now.'

Money, as such, was not a problem Harry had. He had shown a prodigious talent for financial matters while still relatively young and indeed had considered banking, economics and accountancy as possible professions prior to his opting for medicine.

This talent had not deserted him and he had become very comfortable indeed by judiciously playing the Stock Market. Rather than deal in shares proper he dealt in 'futures'. This way he could make a great deal of money for a small capital outlay and if you were good enough and fortunate enough you could do very well indeed. He had been and had done so.

By early evening he had seen another five patients, only one of whom was causing him some concern. This was a patient with a depressive illness who, despite psychiatric help, had failed to improve much at all. Harry had seen him at the man's wife's request and he suspected that his illness was not psychiatric in origin but organic.

He had sent him off for some tests and they had revealed a large degree of brain degeneration consistent with localized blood vessel wasting. There was little Harry or anyone he knew could do for the man and this fact depressed Harry. He would continue to see the man, however, but ensure that his fee would be appropriately adjusted downwards. The only hope the man had left was Harry himself and Harry wouldn't allow him to lose that. At least he hoped he wouldn't.

As evening fell and dinnertime approached Harry told Marianne to go on home to her husband. This was something she was loath to do, much as she loved the man, while she was still up to her neck in receipts, appointment slips and columns of figures. At length she agreed to go, leaving Harry to pay a visit to his daughter in hospital and then return home to a solitary dinner; one at least which she'd prepared for him and which was, for a change, more than substantial.

'Just heat it up in the microwave. Setting number eight for four minutes,' she had said. 'And eat it all, please!' When Harry returned home after seeing Tina he did neither.

Allison allowed herself to be led away by Wendy still feeling Sir William Mostyn's fingers on her shoulder warm and moist and lecherous. It didn't overly bother her however, surprised as she was at his behavior. He'd obviously had a drink or two too much, you could tell by his eyes. They were very red indeed.

Wendy led her towards the tall, slim, man with the dark, curly hair. He moved away from his two companions to come and meet them; 'Allison Young!' he said to Allison's surprise; 'I've heard a great deal about you. My name is Greg Hoffmann. I'm Marketing Director of Unicorn Chemicals. I hope you're going to become more involved with us and our product, Oviron.'

Allison was intrigued immediately by this interesting man. Not only was he very handsome indeed and spoke with a direct, quiet and authoritative voice; he also had a great deal of charm and what she could only term charisma. Not given to a great deal of sexual fantasy, Allison realized that with this man it would be tempting to indulge in a bit. That made her think on Kathryn Meadowford and she glanced quickly in her direction. The executive stood staring at both of them and she had a look on her face that would have made the Mona Lisa frown.

'You know, it's quite a coincidence you being here. In more ways than one. I know it's quite natural with you working in John Bennet's team and our interest in hematology and Oviron - but there's another connection - another link between us.'

'And, what is that?' asked Allison, genuinely interested by this fascinating man.

'A friend of mine was treated by your father when he was in practice up here in London. She had some problems which were soon sorted out. It's a small world.'

'It's certainly that. But how did you know that it was my father who treated your friend. I mean "Young's" a pretty common name - even in the Medical Directory.'

'When I spoke to John Bennet about you - when he told me about you, your research work and your father's background; then it clicked and I wondered if the Young was the same one. I asked my friend and she told me that it was. So there we are.' His smile would have melted lead.

'Oh,' said Allison, 'I see. And how's your friend now, if you don't mind me asking?'

'Very much better thank you,' Greg Hoffmann said about his mother. 'Yes, very much better. Anyway, I hear that your research interest is in the field of acute porphyria. How close do you think you are to finding the cause of the disease, the cure?' As Greg Hoffmann proceeded to make Allison feel as tall as a pine tree his eyes took in everything around him despite the fact that they rarely seemed to leave her own.

As Allison, fortifying herself with a glass of sherry, launched into an account of her research for Hoffmann; Yukio Yoshimura entered the house and shook hands with John and Wendy Raynor. He gave each of them a short bow and handed each a small carefully wrapped gift. They were delighted and, after taking his coat from him, they led him, in his immaculate evening wear, in to join the other guests. Wendy went off to tell the caterers to have the meal ready for serving soon and John led Yoshimura into the spacious guest room.

His entry caused a momentary silence, which was soon broken by the tall man with the briar pipe walking over to the Japanese and bowing briefly before him, before he shook his hand and started speaking to him with great animation as if he was very important indeed. The reason for this was quite simple. He was.

Yoshimura's face lit up with an apparent delight as he scanned the room with his eyes and noted every tiny detail. Once again he met Allison's eyes and smiled. The smile told her that he remembered they'd 'met' before. His eyes also met Kathryn Meadowford's and she too knew that they acknowledged their meeting. The meeting that hadn't turned out as she and Greg Hoffmann had planned.

While she was still quite enmeshed in conversation with Greg Hoffmann, who was asking an incredulous Allison how she felt about a trip to New York - to visit the subsidiary of Unicorn there where they were running further biological screens on Oviron in its context of its anti-porphyric properties; Wendy announced that dinner was just about to be served. The guests made their way to the dining room which adjoined the lounge and which Allison hadn't seen on her previous visit to the house.

It was magnificent. A large mahogany table was surrounded by matching chairs in Regency stripe and the whole scene shone with light and with the sheer brilliant quality of the tableware.

The silverware glinted soft sharp shades, which blended perfectly with the sprays of prismatic light which reflected from the cut crystal wine glasses. The dinner plates and bowls were made from a fine porcelain china; and were finished with a sparkling gold rim. Allison was enchanted. She had rarely seen anything more beautiful even in the often very expensive restaurants Ken used to take her to.

She was escorted to her place by John Raynor and found herself sitting between the grey haired man - Sir Abraham Wilder as she discovered - and the little Japanese, Yukio Yoshimura. The men introduced themselves to her, Yoshimura stressing with a lovely smile that they had already met before. He was pleasant, very pleasant. She didn't know if she would be able to say the same of Sir Abraham Wilder.

Allison soon fell into easy conversation with Sir Abraham. The man was erudite, eloquent and charming and though she instinctively didn't like him, she did find him intelligent, amusing and entertaining.

'So you see,' he said. 'If you analyze the statistics very carefully you see that we can justify the use of drugs in the Western world by virtually every illness you could mention.' He continued with a slight change in the tenor of his voice, a more personal element creeping in, a confidential element, almost intimacy. 'Say, for example, we have a very large group of people who are ill due to depression or unhappiness, for example, or a large group who are potentially going to develop all sorts of illnesses in the future because of the way they are behaving.'

'As with smokers,' Allison interrupted.

'Exactly, my dear,' the large man said, touching her arm in a patronising manner and pressing it reassuringly. 'Then if we can cure that illness, that cause of depression and prevent the potential future development of those illnesses, we have achieved a great deal at a personal, social and economic level. No?'

'Why, of course!' Allison said. 'If we could do it. Are you suggesting to me that you've found a drug that actually works in smokers?' she said.

'No,' said Sir Abe. 'Anyway, what do you think causes the combination of most unhappiness, desperation, proneness to illness and general debility in the Western world today?'

'Poverty,' Allison said, immediately.

'Obesity...!' corrected Wilder with a look of disdain.

'But the drugs we have to treat that - the appetite suppressants - are generally very dangerous,' retorted Allison.' They can lead to all sorts of problems, even those registered in the past decade have their problems...murder for one!

Again Wilder smiled, patronising her. 'What other thoughts do you have on this group of drugs?' he asked.

'Amphetamine psychosis was a major cause of suicide in the sixties and other methods of controlling weight are too...' she stopped short and looked at Sir Abe closely. 'Are you telling me,' she said, 'that you've discovered an anti-obesity pill, a weight normaliser, a metabolic hormonostat? I've heard of such things, but... Have you, have Unicorn Chemicals, discovered a safe anti-obesity pill?' she asked once again on this strange evening finding herself incredulous.

'Not my words,' said Sir Abraham Wilder looking at her closely. 'Yours.'

Allison was astounded and it was some time before she realized that the Japanese man, Yoshimura, was speaking to her.

'The prospect seems to be remarkable to you, Doctor Young,' he said. 'Why is that? You don't think it's possible to do; or possible to do safely?'

'Well, I... I'm no expert on such things, of course, but... well, we know it's possible to suppress appetite, a number of drugs do that all of them, in my view, potentially dangerous.

'We know that it's possible to reduce weight actively. The hormone thyroxin would do that for example, but again not safely... so I suppose that's what it is. It's not the concept, it's the safety aspect. That's what's difficult to accept. There are so many factors associated with weight control...'

'As there are with all other aspects of our metabolism.' Sir Abe interrupted.

'Of course,' Allison agreed. 'But hunger and appetite are so basic, physiologically and psychologically. To control them by chemical means safely seems to be... well, simply remarkable. It's like producing a safe and predictable...' She looked for a suitable term.

'Aphrodisiac?' finished Sir Abe. 'Sexual activity too is "so basic" as you say, physiologically and psychologically.'

'Yes,' said Allison, inwardly smiling at the man's perspicacity. 'Precisely.'

'And there isn't one?' he asked in a mocking tone which made all three of them laugh.

'Not that I know of,' Allison responded, as she directed a quick unconscious look towards Greg Hoffmann who was deep in conversation with John Raynor, Kathryn Meadowford and John Bennet. 'Not to my knowledge, anyway,' she said. As Hoffmann's eyes left his dinner partners' and met hers Allison wondered about the truth of what she had just said.

Yoshimura embraced the topic of conversation Allison had been having with Sir Abe. The Japanese spoke with a quiet, thoughtful cadence to his speech which commanded attention and respect.

'The economics of the drugs industry is a fascinating subject, indeed, Miss Young. As you may know we Japanese have the highest consumption of drugs per person in the developed countries and it would seem that this is a good thing for us.

'On average we appear to live longer than the rest of the developed world, but I'm not certain that this is all attributable to our avid consumption of drugs. After all, the Portuguese live long enough and they only consume an eighth of the pharmaceuticals that we do per person per year. I think our longevity is due mainly to our way of life, to our diet and to our genes which have been well selected by mother nature.

'Anyway, enough of that. What is your precise speciality, Doctor? Myself, I was a general physician before I went into the Public Health Sector. I am now the equivalent of the head of your Committee on the Safety of Medicines or the Food and Drug Administration; I've now more or less retired from that service, not quite yet perhaps, but almost. Your speciality is...?'

'Hematology,' replied Allison enchanted by the man; 'I work at The London General - as a junior registrar - under Doctor Bennet. My research interest is acute porphyria.'

'I see,' Yoshimura said. 'How very interesting. Doctor Bennet's with us this evening I notice. I believe that you are going to run a screen on Oviron in porphyria?' he said, turning his attention to Sir Abe.

'Why, yes, Yukio-San,' Wilder replied. 'We've already studied it in chemically induced porphyria in rats and between you and me and the gate-post there have been other results which look very promising indeed.'

'Ah, yes,' said the Japanese, sipping at his soup gracefully. 'The gate-post. We must see how the drug does in rats before we try it in people. What made you think of such a singular indication for your drug? I thought it was going to be an antibiotic or an antiviral?'

'Both, we hope, Yoshimura-San.,' responded Wilder; 'We found by accident that one of the patients on our initial screen was a latent porphyric,' continued Sir Abe in a totality of untruth; 'She responded well to the drug, her hematological profile altered - hence our screens.'

'Could I see those data? In confidence of course, as a courtesy?' asked the genial Japanese.

'I'll see what I can do,' Wilder replied quickly, no pause, no hesitation needed to consider what he was saying. No need. He had already worked out his strategy.

The conversation drifted on to other things and at length, when the meal was over, the group drifted through to the lounge for coffee and drinks.

A few exchanges were made between various people and Allison but there was only one person that she really wanted to talk with, to be close to again; and enjoy his pulsating charisma. Greg Hoffmann.

After a decent interval had passed, allowing both of them to circulate a bit, Hoffmann approached her;

'It's done,' he said.

'What's done?' Allison asked with expectancy.

'You're coming to New York in a month's time for three days to see our laboratories there. I've okayed it with head office and Doctor Bennet. Satisfied?'

Allison was dumbfounded, but didn't want to act naively. 'If John Bennet thinks it's a good idea, then it's fine by me,' she said assuredly as she churned inside for all sorts of reasons.

'Great!' Hoffmann said. 'Have you been Stateside before?'

'Only on vacation,' Allison said; which went unqualified by "When I was three and went to Disneyland with my parents".

'To New York?'

'No, Florida,' she said, truthfully.

'Well, don't you worry about a thing, because you'll be well looked after. I'm going with you. I'll show you around myself.'

A mixture of emotions ran through Allison all at once and as she felt them race through her she saw that Kathryn

Meadowford was looking at her in a way which said that if looks could kill she'd be dead.

She met the woman's look and gave her a social smile. The Unicorn executive turned away and was immediately pounced upon by an overactive and rather drunk-looking Sir William Mostyn. He was enjoying himself immensely and so too, now, was Allison.

Allison spoke with Greg Hoffmann for as long as she decently could and the impression he made on her was no less fascinating. He was a very handsome man indeed and he excited Allison just by standing close to her, listening to her or speaking to her in that quiet, calm voice of his.

He spoke little about his work, more about the travelling he had done in his job which had taken him to just about every country and major city in the world. At a more academic level, he was quite fascinating too. Allison learned that in addition to his formal business qualifications obtained, like Kathryn Meadowford's at Harvard Business School, where he had in fact met and recruited her, Greg Hoffmann had other academic talents.

He was, for example, a qualified psychologist, holding a Master's degree in the subject from Yale University. He was, too, highly informed about contemporary European and American literature, a subject that Allison knew little about but was fascinated by. And, to add to it all, he was something of a gourmet, having spent some time in Paris formally studying food and its intricacies. Between all of this and his athletically-honed good looks, he was, all in all, quite a man indeed.

It was only when Allison began telling him about herself that she realized that despite all that he had told her about himself, Greg Hoffmann had not once mentioned his childhood. She had begun with an account of hers as usual. He hadn't mentioned his at all. It was as if it hadn't existed.

When it was no longer possible to hog Greg without being impolite as she saw it, Allison went to look for Doctor Bennet. He was standing talking to Yukio Yoshimura and she approached the two men and was welcomed by them.

'I take it that you've heard you're going to New York?' Bennet asked her with a smile.

'Why, yes!' exclaimed Allison. 'It came as quite a surprise...'

'And Tokyo,' interjected Yoshimura. 'I have agreed with Doctor Bennet that you will come to Tokyo directly from New York. You see we are very interested in the various proposed uses of Oviron and Doctor Bennet tells me that it's been used also with some apparent success in one case of acute porphyria. He also tells me that you're the resident expert on the disease and I'd like you to come and talk to us on this, at the Medical Association in Tokyo.'

Allison looked at Doctor Bennet and wondered what all this was about the drug's use in porphyria... a repetition of Sir Abraham Wilder's comments at dinner, his own in the car.

'While you're in Japan, you can come and stay with my wife and myself for a day or two at our home in Kyoto. If you'd like to. It's very different from Tokyo - or Ebo as we knew it before - more traditional. It used to be our Imperial Capital. It's a place I think you'll like. You can fly from Kennedy to Tokyo International and then I'll join you for our flight to Osaka. We will then take the train or drive together to my place in Kyoto. How does that sound, Doctor Allison Young?' said the Japanese with a warm smile.

'Magnificent,' Allison said in breathless honesty, 'Absolutely magnificent.'

'You're rapidly becoming a real jet-setter Dr Young. First, of course, there's work to be done,' said Bennet bringing Allison back to earth a bit because by this time she'd virtually left it. So much so soon. 'That takes priority. But I'm sure your trips will be well worthwhile. Talking of which, are you ready to go sometime soon, Allison? Home I mean,' he laughed; 'I have to myself,' he said looking at his watch. 'I'll run you home if you're ready to go now.'

Allison appreciated that she was being politely asked to leave with John Bennet, but she didn't mind. She'd had a lovely evening and she was sure the people left had important things to discuss without her.

'Yes,' she said. 'I'm ready. It's been a wonderful evening.'

'Good,' said John Bennet as he took Allison by the arm and went to excuse himself and her to his hosts and the other guests.

Allison made the usual formal noises and noticed as she said her farewell to him that Sir William Mostyn had quickly sobered up and was now quite his normal self. The only 'goodbye' of any note, however, was said by Greg Hoffmann, with the look he gave to her. It was for her only and it made her tingle like a bell-chime in winter time.

As they were just about to leave in Doctor Bennet's car, Allison noticed the lovely sky and the large round moon, which delighted her. Then she noticed a rather grand car which had drawn up beside those already parked in the driveway. It was chauffeur driven with a man, very smartly dressed as far as she could make out, sitting leafing through a sheaf of papers in the back.

She assumed that he was some other industrialist until she saw something, something that put the whole evening into a different perspective. The car was carrying a Coat of Arms, one that even Allison recognized. With a turn of her neck she saw it completely as Doctor Bennet drove his car hastily away. The Coat of Arms which she saw was of the Royal House of Windsor... .

'Who's that?' Allison asked, abruptly. 'Who is that, Doctor Bennet, John?'

'It's the Prince's Private Secretary, Allison. It's about time you knew a little of what we're doing here. Let me explain it to you.'

Harry found himself once again having a sleepless night. Images of Ann and Tina kept coming to him each time he was about to fall over into sleep. They had been a very happy family indeed, too good to be true, and that was exactly how it had turned out.

Tonight in particular he couldn't stop thinking about Ann and the day he had proposed marriage to her. It hadn't been far from where he was now. It had been in a park which was close by, on a lovely summer's day when children were sailing on boats in the park's lake. This particular ghost was one Harry found it particularly difficult to lay and he decided there and then that it was about time he did something about it.

He rose, went and found his running kit and put it on. He made his way to the front door of the large house, opened it, and went out into the night.

The sky was filled with myriad stars and a large orange moon hung above him giving him enough light to see by when he ran beyond the reach of the street lamps. He shivered slightly in the night-time chill and then jogged a little until he broke a slight sweat. Then he began to run.

He ran at a steady pace along the deserted streets, his feet racing over the road as he made his way steadily and surely towards the park. He passed house after quiet house, shadow after empty shadow and the quiet empty shadows of this particular portion of his past ran along with him.

Finally, after running at his regular rate for about fifteen minutes he reached the entrance to the park. The entrance he associated with the lovely days of their courtship and with Tina's early childhood. Walks on Sunday, together, family walks. Gone now, for good.

The gates were closed at this time, so he climbed over the fence and continued to run through the pale moist grass towards the lake. His feet left imprints in the moisture but they were invisible even in the moonlight.

Soon he reached the edge of the lake where he stopped abruptly, breathing heavily, hurting a little physically as well as mentally, and letting thoughts and images of the past flow through him like water through the depths of the lake.

He knelt down and put his fingers into the water. It was surprisingly warm and he took them out and shook the drops away. He remembered Ann again and again, in particular, that day - the day he had proposed to her.

He began to cry. And he did so unashamedly. As he cried her name in this star and moonlit night, the tears of expressed grief ran down his face and dripped onto the ground. A few fell into the lake.

At length his tears dried themselves and he found a strange relief moving through him. He discovered the memories again, the days when he and Ann and Tina had been one, the sounds of the band playing in the bandstand, the sounds of children's voices, the sounds of an unseen happiness. They still hurt, but differently.

At length he felt composed enough to make his way back home. And he found that when he left the park and ran home again at a slower pace, he had left something behind him.

Something precious that had to be allowed to die and rest. At the very place where it had been born.

As dawn approached a fluff of grey-white clouds spread over the moon and changed the texture of its color. A breeze sprang up and blew waves across the lake and no-one saw them blow.

When he had finished his explanation, Allison thought that she understood something of what was going on. It was a possibility, no more than that, that a member of the Royal Family had latent porphyria and it was also possible that Oviron would prove to be an effective anti-porphyric agent. It was for this reason that the Private Secretary had turned up at John Raynor's home. To get an up-to-date account of the drug's action.

'But I heard Sir Abraham Wilder distinctly tell Yukio Yoshimura that the drug had been tested in a porphyric subject and that it seemed to be effective,' insisted Allison. He said that some patient had "responded well to the drug". You gave Yoshimura the same impression yourself. Is that the case? Has someone with latent porphyria received Oviron?'

'Not yet, Allison, but perhaps soon, perhaps soon enough. Young Miss Goudie perhaps.'

Allison was serious now; 'Then why, if you don't mind me asking John; did both Sir Abraham and yourself give the impression that...'

'Look, Allison!' Bennet interrupted with an uncommon irascibility; 'You must understand that what we are dealing with here is a great deal more sensitive and complex than you presently appreciate. You simply do as you're told to, as you are doing. Work hard, enjoy yourself and everything will be fine.'

'But...' Allison made to interject, but was herself cut off immediately.

'Otherwise we must seriously look at all you have achieved and review how we see your career progressing. You've come a long way in a very short time, young lady. Why don't you let it rest there?

'Now could we both be more constructive and address our work please? Could you manage in tomorrow a half-hour or so earlier so that we can take another look at Miss Goudie?'

Allison knew that discretion was always the better part of anything. Every time. And as this was a side of Doctor John Bennet she had never even suspected had existed before now, she used it. The man was under pressure, no doubt and something else too.... There was something else wrong with him. Something bothering this normally placid and controlled man.

'Of course, I'll be in and I'll let it rest there.' she said quietly. She didn't add "For now." Discretion, in Allison's book, didn't preclude her ultimately proceeding precisely as she intended to and with valor where necessary.

That night Allison lay in bed wondering what was actually going on with respect to Oviron and the hospital. It was all becoming a bit complicated and she was far too junior to be becoming involved in the high-power politics which seemed to be going on. And not just hospital politics either. A member of the Royal family who may be a latent porphyric! Allison wondered if "The prince" Doctor Bennet had mentioned only by title, giving away nothing else, could possibly be... She let the thought drop. As she'd been told in no uncertain terms. Keep herself to herself for now.

Even so... What was going on? And why the fabrications to Yoshimura? She lay awhile and let the thoughts drift around in her head. Vienna, New York, Tokyo, Kyoto - she couldn't believe it. And so they drifted until they came to find Greg Hoffmann. Then they turned somewhere else and things took on a different texture. She was restless for a while but in time she slept soundly.

CHAPTER SIX

Annette Pallain sat beside her sister on a seal-skin Chesterfield settee. The two sisters were situated directly opposite to Rosemary's husband, Art, who was sipping at a glass of Bourbon. Rosemary wondered what the Animal Rights' campaigners would make of her select piece of furniture and although one part of her was clearly alarmed by that prospect; the other didn't give a damn. Art downed the remains of his glass and walked to a drinks cabinet to replenish it:

'Careful honey,' his wife said maliciously; 'Mustn't have too many before the happy hour. Though I suppose this is it?'

Art smiled ruefully: 'Guess it is Rosie,' he said as he filled the glass almost to the brim with neat spirit; 'Happy as it gets at this time.'

Annette watched them carefully. It had never ceased to amaze her; never satisfied her purely rational and logical mind that two people could live for a life-time together. "Normal people perhaps, she though condescendingly, but not two independently minded and ambitious people such as these two.

"That, of course was the source of their success," she thought. "Put two bees in a honey-pot and one will work to make the other Queen. It didn't really matter who was who in that game though in this set-up the Queen was of the correct gender and put in a fair share of the work herself." Annette stopped thinking and began talking:

'O.K. Rosie, how did the meeting go? Have you arrived at your decision yet?'

'"Ziongate" would you believe,' said Art as he strolled back to his seat his head shaking with irony.

'Yes I would,' responded Annette; 'As a matter of fact I think it's a damned good name. It was me who suggested it in the first place.'

"Christ," thought Art as he sipped once more at his whiskey; "It's going to be one hell of an afternoon."

When Allison woke the following morning she felt very good indeed. She had enjoyed her evening at the Raynor's and despite the various conflicts which had seemed to have surrounded it the overall verdict was an unqualified success. She ruminated on it for a few minutes then suddenly a stray thought crossed her mind and her mood became more serious, more professional. She had remembered Vikki Goudie.

After her success in treating Vikki she and Doctor Bennet had ensured that the young woman was stable and they had left her in the capable hands of the nursing staff and returned to Doctor Bennet's office. For a time he busied himself making notes on the patient's file; meticulous notes, in which every aspect of the treatment they had administered to the young woman was carefully detailed. At length he closed the folder and looked up at Allison from behind the desk.

'Well, Allison,' he said. 'How does it really feel to see your theories work in practice?' Doctor Bennet seemed back to his normal self.

'It's marvelous,' she replied. 'I just hope she remains stable.'

'We'll keep her carefully monitored. Make sure, by the way, that you look in on her three or four times a day over the next week. She's an important lady for you. Your first presentation and publication.'

'Sorry?' asked Allison taken by surprise. Her chief looked almost expectantly at her. 'Sorry, Doctor Bennet, what do you mean?'

'I had a call yesterday from the chairman of the clinical section of the upcoming Hematology congress in Vienna,' said Bennet; 'Someone has withdrawn a paper on metabolic disorders and they need another speaker. I've suggested you. You can give a paper on Vikki Goudie's treatment. Unicorn have offered to pick up the tab, travel, hotel, and so on. Do it in style.'

'But I've never...' started Allison.

'No, but you have to sometime,' interrupted Bennet quickly anticipating her. 'You have two weeks to submit your draft,' Allison; 'You'd better get on with it. It's not long until the conference either, so you've quite a bit of work to do. I know it might seem a bit daunting - giving your first academic paper always is - but you'll get used to it in time. We all do, or to be more precise,' his voice lightened here and he gave her a smile, something which was becoming rarer these days; 'We all get used to being nervous. It's perfectly natural.

'You should bear in mind that it will also be a major step towards you getting a decent M.D. thesis. Academic presentations and publications are all very important for that too as you know, so get on with it young woman. Best of luck.'

With that Bennet rose from his chair, moved to the office door and held it open. He briefly nodded to Allison, ushered her out and returned to his desk. Allison moved out into Claire Sillar's room feeling quite stunned.

'Everything alright?' asked Claire smiling at her.

'Why, yes,' said Allison with a start. 'Yes, I think so.'

"There is no doubt that the President has sanctioned special funding to facilitate the peace talks between the Arab States and Israel.' said Rosemary Pallain with determination. There is nothing illegal nor constitutionally incorrect in this per se as you'll agree Annette.' Her sister nodded assent as Rosemary continued. 'However, it smacks of covert activity and is potentially a political bombshell."

Rosemary in full flow was quite an earful and an eyeful, even after all these years of marriage; and Art had momentarily stopped drinking his Bourbon. He watched his wife as she spoke and wondered why the genetic mix which gave Rosemary her strikingly good looks had failed miserably with Annette. 'Genes could do funny things,' he mused and this took his mind onto a completely different track. He coasted it while his so very gifted wife continued to hold court.

'Under normal circumstances these payments wouldn't constitute shit,' she said bluntly; 'However, given the popular response to the terrorist bombings and the general unease pervading the country as a consequence of these - the President is vulnerable. And he will continue to be vulnerable while these atrocities continue. We can arrange that. I guarantee it.'

Art gulped hard, swallowed a hard shot of his drink: 'You're not seriously telling me that you're going to back a quasi- terrorist campaign no matter how controlled or expeditious it may be politically Rosemary. Christ, do you realise -'

'- Do you realise that you're jumping to rapid and unjustified conclusions Art?' interrupted his wife sharply; 'Did I say that we were going to blow the fuck out of Fort Knox or the Washington State Museum?'

'I guess not Rosie; my apologies. I'm sorry. Please continue. Please.'

'Thanks Art;' said his wife giving him an aggrieved look which nonetheless spoke of her immense fondness for him. 'I meant that we can arrange for the President to remain vulnerable while the current political climate maintains itself.'

'How, precisely?' asked Annette who was hanging on her sister's every word.

'By leaking details of these clandestine payments to the appropriate people in concert with new independently leaked allegations about the President's extra-marital sex life.'

'What's the point?' asked Art; 'We all know he's screwed everything that has double X chromosomes. Christ, Rosie; he's even worse than our last paramour; it's alleged this one's even screwed one of his secretaries while she was typing a memo for him. And I believe it, though I can't imagine how it actually happened.' Art was light laughing; his wife was not.

'We're not talking double X chromosomes Art,' she replied with a hint of the venomoos; 'We're talking X and Y.'

Art thought about this for a moment: 'You mean the guy's a queer?' he asked incredulously.

'I think the term is "Gay" Art, interjected Annette as her eyes met her sister's in mutual understanding and her brother-in-law drank far and deep from his glass.

Allison left Doctor Bennet's room and made her way back to have another look at Vikki. She wanted to be certain that her patient was still stable and improving. The prospect of presenting a paper at an international conference so soon filled her with a mixture of deep apprehension and elation. 'God,' she mumbled to herself as she made her way to the ward; 'What a thing to happen, right out of the blue,' and she wondered, again, at the nature of all the things which had happened out of the blue thanks to Unicorn Chemicals. New York, Tokyo, a paper to be presented in Vienna - whatever next? Then, with a flick of her head, she dismissed the conference and the rest from her thoughts and wondered again how Vikki was faring now.

Allison paid her a brief visit and gave her an equally brief, but thorough examination. She was fine and Allison felt very satisfied with her patient's steady and maintained improvement. When she finally left Vikki, she made her way across the ward to pay a brief visit to the little girl Tina who was still very ill indeed.

The child lay quietly on her bed, staring about her, looking at the various bits and pieces in her room, being quite unable to concentrate on anything more substantial. As Allison approached, the child smiled in her direction.

'Hello Tina,' said Allison. 'And how are things with you? You're looking better. How are you feeling?'

'Oh, not bad, Doctor,' replied the child. 'It would be nice to get up, though. Go for a walk or something.'

'In time,' Allison replied. 'Take it easy just now, rest for a while and we'll soon have you going for runs not just walks!' Tina gave a brief laugh. 'If only that were true,' she said.

'Oh it will be,' reassured Allison. 'It will be. You'll see.'

'I hope so,' said Tina. 'But I don't think my father believes that or my aunt and they should know.'

'And why should they know?' asked Allison, a little confused.

'My father's a doctor and my aunt's a nurse,' replied the child. 'He's a very good doctor... or at least he was until...mum died.' She looked at Allison and started to cry.

'Go on,' said Allison grimly, taking her hand and holding it tightly; 'Cry as much as you want.' She knew there was little else she could do to help the child. She knew from Tina's case history that she had lost her mother and that the expression of her grief distressing as it was, was all that could usefully be done at present to ease the pain this caused her.

'You're not seriously telling me that our President is homosexual!' There was a touch of indignation about Art Pallain's voice which belied his stature as *bon viveur* and general man-of-the-world. The possibility that the President of the United States was bisexual appeared to rank equally in importance to Art along with the merciless genocide he'd recently seen firsthand of the black, white and colored populations of South Africa.

'I'm seriously telling you Art that we have access to documentation, photographs and sworn affidavits which state precisely that,' said his wife. 'Further, I'm seriously telling you that we can arrange for these to be released to the national and international press and media whenever its most expeditious. How does that grab you husband?'

'By the balls Rosie,' said the still astonished Art; 'But not nearly so hard as it's going to grab the Presidents'.
His wife laughed at that and even Annette managed a smile as she made her calculations and a mental audit of what precisely this could mean for them. All of them.

* * *

'What are you doing here?' a voice interrupted. 'I see my niece has been crying. Why is that? What's wrong, darling?'

Allison turned and saw Jennifer Wright looking at her with unconcealed disapproval as she made her way towards the girl. Allison stood up from the bed and watched in amazement as the nurse sat down and held Tina's hands. "Niece?" thought Allison, then she remembered the case file:

Tina Wright. Mother killed in a car accident. Father a general physician in private practice. Harold Wright. Patient has relative on hospital nursing staff. Jennifer! Harold Wright. Harry! In the space of a few seconds it all became clear to Allison.

Jennifer was Tina's aunt and Harry - handsome melancholy Harry - was Tina's father. He had lost his wife in a car crash and now his daughter was critically ill. No wonder the man had looked so distressed, no wonder he was so close to Jennifer. He was after all her brother. Not her boyfriend, fiance or anything else of the sort. The kiss she'd seen had been filial not amorous. They were brother and sister and Allison had put two and two together and made one hundred and one!

As she stood apart from the two of them working out the relationships and watching aunt and niece sharing intimacies, Allison decided it was time to have a word with Jennifer, to make the first move in an attempt to befriend her. She intended making certain that all that was possible would be done to get Tina well again almost impossible as this would be; and she decided that one step towards doing this would be to win the trust of the child's aunt. She waited a while therefore and then addressed herself to the nurse.

'I wonder, Charge Nurse Wright, if I could have a brief word with you?' she asked firmly.

Jennifer looked at her, her eyes still very angry looking: 'Anything you say, Doctor Young.' she responded, coolly.

'In my office then. In half an hour. O.K.?'

'Yes, Doctor,' said Jennifer. 'In half an hour.' She then turned her attentions back to her niece.

Allison said goodbye to Tina and walked purposefully away. Her footsteps sounded sharp in her ears as they clipped on the tiled floor. She found herself thinking again of the revised status of the man she thought had been Jennifer's lover. Harry. Harry Wright. General physician, brother of her one problem

in The London and father of one of the most tragic patients in
the hospital. He was also a widower, she thought, a very young
widower indeed. How sad. She found herself wondering what
his wife had been like:

"Come to think of it, Allison, you look very like Jennifer's
sister-in-law; same height, shape, looks, color of hair. Intriguing."
The words spoken by Pam's friend on the night of the party
filtered through her mind. She remembered them with an
almost unnatural clarity. They almost stunned her. She looked
like Harry's wife. Harry's? She meant Doctor Wright's. She
wondered what she was thinking about, wondered at the racing
of her thoughts, her sensations of conflict and confusion. But
she knew somewhere precisely what she was feeling. And what
it meant.

'The practice of homosexuality is forbidden by Roman
Canon Law in that anyone wilfully practising it is *ipso facto* -
by that fact alone - forbidden from receiving the sacraments.
That's as certain as Gratian himself and he was the man who
gave that Law its present form. And it's not only forbidden by
Canon Law. It's also forbidden by ecclesiastical law. So, no way.
Not if you're Catholic.'

Annette Pallain spoke with her accustomed authority and
despite the fact that she was with her immediate family she was
still fairly formal in her presentation of the facts.

'That's one thing Roman Catholics are not allowed to do,'
she continued; 'There's another that's of relevance here. They
can't succeed to the British throne. It would quite literally be
simpler for your average Catholic to become pope than to
become the King or Queen of England.'

'So what's the point?' asked Art looking at the double
strands she had woven and wondering how they'd combine,
what they'd mutate into in his sister-in-law's very clever head.

'The point is,' replied Annette; 'That these issues are highly emotive ones which if handled judiciously can be used to bring pressure to bear precisely where and when we want it.'

'I'm still not clear on what you're saying,' said a much more pensive Art; 'I'm not clear about the connection. What is it?'

'Allow me,' said Rosemary who stood up abruptly and began to pace the room while her sister and husband watched her with undisguised admiration.

'Despite the anticipated back-lash which is inevitably occurring against political correctness at its most absurd; there are still a great many sensible and liberally minded people who accept that no one should be ostracised or debarred from any Public Office or other role in society simply on the basis of their religious beliefs or their sexual persuasion within reasonable limits.'

'So,' said Art' 'We intend directing public opinion towards the injustices of the British Constitution and show how iniquitous it is with respect to religious bigotry. I can see that, particularly now that the Church of England is pretty sterile and so many lesser royals have converted to Catholicism.

'That's clear and it will clearly benefit us if we generate interest in the issue and suggest a reversal of that particular policy. But are we really going to defend and condone the behavior of a President who's allegedly homosexual? Where's the gain in that for us?

'Oh we only do that when he's no longer President,' said Rosemary. 'We only do that, Art, when we want to pick up all those liberal votes which will be floating about between the issues of Middle-Eastern terrorist's funding; the British Monarchy crumbling into chaos; and a Washington Duchess who will be vying for media cover space with a gay and broken President.

'Anyway,' Rosemary continued with a gleam in her eyes that bordered on the fanatical; 'If it came to it, I wouldn't object to an American regent being Roman Catholic. Not if I were President. That wouldn't bother me at all. And I will be President, believe me.'

'I know,' said Art as Annette nodded her agreement.

Exactly on time, Jennifer appeared at the door of Allison's office. Although the door was open she gave it a sharp knock and remained outside.

'Come in,' invited Allison smiling and pulling a seat out for her. 'Have a seat and forgive the clutter. It's only tiny but it has to do and anyway I've never been the tidiest of people. Can I get you a coffee?'

'No thanks,' said Jennifer, still cool. 'Why did you want to see me, Doctor Young? Something important? Something concerning my niece?'

Allison felt her heart sink a little. She had hoped the pleasantries she had put Jennifer's way would have softened her a little, but evidently they had not. She would just have to try harder and differently.

'Look,' she said. 'Since the morning I started here it seems that for some reason we've been at cross purposes. I'd like to change that situation, if only because I'm one of your niece's doctors and I don't believe that I warrant the view you may have of me. Perhaps you could tell me what that is so that I can perhaps correct it if necessary.'

Jennifer looked at her with something akin to amazement.

'I don't really have a very definite view of you,' she said. 'If it's of interest to you and if I may be frank, I must admit that when I first met you, you seemed rather high handed and pushy and I'm afraid that's the type of person I don't particularly like.'

'Anything else?' enquired Allison, flinching a little inside, but showing no sign of it in her response.

'No, nothing,' replied Jennifer, looking at her differently now; 'Nothing...in particular.'

Allison took a very deep breath, what she was about to say was risky. She wondered if she really should dare. She wanted to befriend the woman but was this the way? She decided that perhaps it was.

'Look,' she said; 'One of the junior doctors told me about your sister-in-law. He also told me I looked very much like her. Do you think that has anything to do with your perception of me?' Heart thudding Allison waited for the response; if it was a very angry one then it was perhaps no less than she deserved. Jennifer continued to look at her, ruminating on what she had said, looking and assessing. Then she spoke.

'I will have that coffee, Doctor Young,' she said. 'If you don't mind.'

'I don't and it's Allison.'

'Allison, then,' replied Jennifer smiling at long last; 'One sugar and a touch of milk.'

'On its way Sister Wright - Jennifer,' said Allison, returning the nurse's smile. 'I'll have one myself.'

The two women spent the next hour talking. Once the initial reticense had gone they fell into conversation easily and pleasantly. It meant that they both missed lunch - the conversation eating into their lunch-break - but that didn't bother either of them.

Allison reassured Jennifer that she was far from being the 'high handed and pushy' individual that Jennifer had thought she was and pointed out that despite appearances to the contrary she had been nervous as a thyroxic kitten on her first day at The London when she had met Jennifer for the first time.

'You know, Jennifer...' Allison said; 'It really was quite traumatic coming along here to The London and somehow having to find the composure and discipline to work in what, at times, is a very competitive and demanding environment indeed.

'My father told me ever since I was a little girl, that we should present ourselves in public the way we would like to be, even if we felt far from it. He said that if we did so, then in time we would come to be that way. I've never wanted to be forbidding or remote, but respected. Yes. That's all.'

Jennifer agreed and, in turn, went on to detail her own recent history which had been as terrible as Allison had imagined. She spoke of the awful time she, her niece and her brother had experienced after the accident and of how, when she subsequently learned of her niece's illness, she had experienced a minor breakdown. Most of all, however, she stressed the quite horrific pressures which her brother had undergone as a result of the whole thing and told Allison a great deal about him. A great deal that Allison wanted to know.

Art Pallain had known for at least twenty years that his wife had ambitions to become President of the United States of America. The ambition had suited her, it suited her style. But he hadn't ever believed that she'd get this close. Didn't think that the chips would fall for her as precisely as they had.

Oddly enough, Rosemary occasionally saw an astrologer, every time they were in London in fact she saw the woman - a petite attractive blonde thing that Art wouldn't have minded consulting himself - and the lady had predicted that Rosemary would make it to the very top. She'd also said the same apparently to the Princess of Wales so Art had his doubts.

There was no doubting of the fact, however, that Rosemary was indeed in sight of her goal and the audacity, determination and sheer inventiveness she'd shown in the past few months in particular - since she saw the opening for nomination and had made a run for it - had impressed him more than he'd ever been impressed by her. And he'd been impressed by her in many ways and for many years now. She was literally excelling herself and it pleased him a very great deal.

'Tell me Rosie,' Art asked his wife; 'What do we need now in the way of funds? Did you discuss that at your meeting?' he was perfectly sober now, no longer light. This was the professional politician not the doting and humorous husband.

'Yes we did discuss it honey,' she replied; but Annette here's the one to give us the low down on that. She looked at her sister and smiled. "What a nest of vipers," we are she thought; "And we carry one hell of a sting.'

'Harry is a lovely man,' Jennifer said to Allison. 'He's also quite brilliant and very idealistic. He has a very successful private practice as a general physician which he built from virtually nothing. He always felt that within the State system it was impossible to give some patients the personal attention they needed, so he works in the Private Sector. He often treats patients for nothing or next-to-nothing though if they can't afford his fees.' The woman was obviously besotted by her brother in a very healthy way. Allison could understand why.

'He has,' continued Jennifer; 'Incongruously for a medical man, a remarkable gift for financial matters and he has an avid interest in them. He's made a few very inspired investments over the years and generated a good deal of money from them - something he speaks about quite freely. Most of it's been ploughed back into his practice though, to help subsidize his poorer patients. He's no saint but he is, or at least was, the best, soft-touch medic around and his patients are devoted to him.

Comment stub

Allison listened attentively and quietly. She anticipated that the difficult part was about to arrive soon and indeed it did.

'Since Ann's death however,' said the nurse more carefully; 'And since Tina's illness, the practice has gone downhill. Oh, he tries hard enough, works all sorts of hours, but he can't really cope. Ann was a great help to him kept the books, knew his patients and so on and without her, and given the nature of Tina's illness, he's in a pretty bad way right now. He's a fighter though, always has been, just like my niece and I'm sure he'll come through in time.

'At present, he's really only seeing those patients of his who won't or can't go elsewhere and many of those he is seeing for no substantial payment. All in all, the practice is in a pretty bad way, but understandably all that concerns Harry just now is Tina. He loves her desperately and I just wish there was something more we could do. Both for her and for him.'

'If there is,' Allison said, with a fierce determination; 'Then we'll do it.'

'Thanks,' said Jennifer as she looked at her watch and rose to go; 'See you soon.'

'I look forward to it,' responded Allison with a smile.

As Jennifer left Allison's office Pam was approaching it. She noticed in passing that Jennifer had been crying. She popped her head through Allison's door and though she appeared quite sober, Allison could smell whisky from her breath.

'Everything O.K.?' she asked. 'Didn't see you at lunch.'

'Everything's fine.' said Allison.

'Made a friend or a foe?' enquired Pam lightly.

'I think I have,' Allison said cryptically; 'Yes, I think I've made a friend.'

'Good,' said Pam.

'Tell me, Pam,' said Allison. 'What do you know of Tina Wright's case; the little girl who was transferred to us recently for a hematological work up?'

'Yes, I know Tina, but not a great deal about her personally, if that's what you mean,' Pam replied. 'Only that she's very sick indeed and that her father's moving heaven and earth in an attempt to get her well again. I'm afraid poor Harry will have to do more than that. His daughter's in a very bad way as I'm sure you know.'

'"Harry,"' asked Allison surprised. 'You know him?'

'Of course, I do who doesn't here?' responded Pam. 'He's quite a favorite at The London. He did his residency here and was very popular with everyone. He was Doctor Bennet's protege at the time and it's rumored that the great man wanted him to stay on here, but he opted for Private Practice instead.

'He was popular with the rest of us too of course. He's quite a dish you know. Rich too, I hear, Stock Market impresario and things!'

'I know,' smiled Allison. 'I've seen him and heard about him.'

'Well,' continued Pam; 'You can appreciate the number of hearts he broke while he was here. They're uncountable and inconsolable. Still no-one had a chance. He was very much in love with his wife. In fact, they were inseparable and had been together if I recall things correctly, ever since early in his student days.'

'Did you know her?' asked Allison with what was more than a casual interest.

'Yes,' replied Pam. 'I was invited over to their home once. A little get-together for a few of the staff. She was a charming woman an excellent hostess, witty, vivacious; made you feel very much at home and wanted.

'She was very popular too, and very beautiful. They were a perfect couple. I don't imagine that Harry will ever find anyone like her again. Pity really. Still enough of that! Do you want to grab a quick snack before our out-patient's clinic, or had you forgotten that we had one?'

'No, I hadn't,' said Allison flatly. 'But I won't bother with a snack. I'm not hungry.'

As the two young women walked along the corridor, Allison felt distinctly down. She was pleased that she had at last made friends with Jennifer but for various reasons the information that had come her way concerning her brother had depressed her. For more reasons than she cared to admit.

As Allison walked to her meeting she glanced out of a window and noticed that it was raining. The sky was dull and grey, forlorn clouds moved across it quietly, blotting out the sunlight. As she walked HArry seemed to diminish in her thoughts and Ken replace him. Perhaps a mental mechanism, she briefly thought, suggesting what was attainable?

* * *

'According to the legend,' said Annette Pallain; 'The horn of the unicorn has magical properties, which is not surprising when you consider that it's a magical beast.' she stated logically.

'We, as you know, have our very own unicorn. And its particular magic is its ability to confer the gift of money; lots of it. If we do as it requests - a sort of mythic quid pro quo. And indeed, mythic is the operative word here, for our friends at Unicorn are very close now to dusting down a throne and polishing up a crown for a future Royal Head of America and they continue to need our help.'

Annette walked to a nearby dresser and picked up an envelope which was on it. She opened it and removed a cheque from it. One million dollars dead,' she said; 'A contribution to Rosie's campaign fund. And there's more where that one came from believe me.'

'And all we have to do to get our hands on that is help the Food and Drugs administration to swallow a little pill,' said Art thoughtfully.

'Oh a little more than that Art,' said Annette in way of reply; 'But that will do to be going on with.'

Allison had seen Ken once or twice over the past week or so and on each occasion she had tactfully rejected his advances to her. She was very confused by their relationship and while she was still very fond of him she wondered where it was really going. Once or twice she had captured a bit of the old sparkle from him and this made her wonder if there was a chance that if she put the work into it, it could work out.

"It would be so easy" she had thought on more than one occasion. Dear reliable Ken who apart from his now seemingly absent possessiveness, was very close to her and had been the only man to date she had ever really fallen for. But did she love the man whatever that meant? She was uncertain but thought that if she asked herself the question then she probably didn't. So what?

She would continue to see him as long as things remained uncomplicated. He was so devoted to her and anyway, perhaps given the fact that her career was so important to her she would never find anyone who would give her the illusory love she sometimes felt she sought. Perhaps it was only that anyway - illusory. Ken was a good man, a decent one who loved her deeply. She could do a great deal worse and as she cared enough for him before to even contemplate marriage then surely she could do so again.

After the success of their "clear the air" meeting, Allison met Jennifer a few times for coffee and found that she enjoyed her company a great deal and Ken had even been mentioned once or twice already. She could see that the vivaciousness Jennifer had formerly had was returning quickly and she looked forward to their get-togethers very much indeed.

Jennifer spoke a lot about Harry and it seemed that his life was dragging along from day to day miserably. Tina was now undergoing chemotherapy and this had distressed him even more. The drugs she was receiving were very toxic and the girl's hair was coming out by the handful and she was constantly nauseated, in pain and feeling very unwell indeed.

'Can't they simply operate?' Jennifer had asked Allison almost pleadingly on one occasion. 'Surely it would be worth the risk. The poor mite's suffering enough as it is.'

'It would almost certainly be fatal,' Allison explained. 'The tumor's located in a very sensitive area of the brain and the tiniest disruption would lead to almost certain haemorrhaging, brain damage and a highly probable death. They're doing the best possible, Jennifer, believe me. I wish as much as you do that we could do more for her.'

By comparison Vikki Goudie had improved to such an extent that Allison decided to discharge her the following day. She spoke to Doctor Bennet about this and, though initially uncertain, he finally agreed to the discharge and signed the appropriate papers.

When thinking about the case Allison found herself wondering and not for the first time; whether or not there was some rogue chemical substance produced in porphyric patients which might be responsible for the psychological disturbances associated with the disease.

Night after night she had read books and papers on the disease and related areas and as she read she developed the germ of an idea which soon blossomed into another theory which she decided she would duly discuss at their coming research meeting. She mentioned her wish to do this to Doctor Bennet who seemed very interested indeed. He agreed for her to do so at the next meeting of the group which was in a few day's time. For some reason obscure to her, she anticipated it with something approaching dread.

Annete Pallain had gone to bed and Art and Rosemary lay beside one-another in their grand extra King-Sized bed. "How appropriate," thought Art as he looked at his wife who was asleep beside him. Six hours sleep was all she needed and she'd already had one. He'd better get some sleep himself.

There was a lot to be done over the next few weeks and they'd better get it right. After all being First Man would suit him just fine. He would gladly settle for being second fiddle to a woman who was President and after all, that's what the astrologer had said last time they'd been in London. Art looked out of the window to the stars. Perhaps they weren't so dumb after all.

As Art slept the sleep of the just, Vikki Goudie was on her way home. She was delighted when she finally arrived there and with her mother and brother's help unpacked her clothes. She had only been home for a few hours when she felt unwell. She phoned the hospital and asked to speak to Doctor Bennet. He wished he hadn't signed the damned discharge papers in the first place.

Allison entered Doctor Bennet's office in response to his paging her; she saw that a number of the research team were there, including Pam and John Raynor. She looked expectantly at Doctor Bennet who had attracted her attention.

'We have a problem,' he said, 'Vikki Goudie's been admitted again. A major relapse. I think we might lose her.'

'Oh God,' said Allison, she seemed to be doing so well. What's happened?'

'She's had an acute exacerbation of her illness and we're at a loss to explain why or what to do about it. That's why I've asked all of you here. We must do something and soon.

'Miss Goudie's well-being is our first and most immediate priority, but in addition to that, if we have in any way contributed to this exacerbation of her illness by our treatment of her while she was last in The London, then there could be other problems, the least of which would be loss of funds for the research group.

Now, I'd like your opinions and comments, please. First, you, Doctor Smith,' continued Doctor Bennet looking at Pam. 'What do you think has brought about this relapse?'

As Pam began to speak, Allison felt a chill run through her. Her novel drug treatment. Had she contributed to Vikki's relapse? She wondered and she worried and when she, in turn, was asked to comment on the case, she had little new to offer:

'I would do the same again, drug-wise,' she ventured. 'I suppose the trauma of her being discharged could have precipitated an attack, but she was very stable when she left. I still think, given the circumstances, that we did the correct thing.'

'There's no question about the ethics of the issue, Doctor Young,' interrupted Bennet; 'The pros and cons were fully discussed by us and it was agreeed that she was fit to go home.'

'Well, I can't imagine what's happened,' Allison continued, puzzled, searching her mind for something she may have missed.

'Well, let's try and find out,' Doctor Bennet said. 'I'll see those of you concerned at ward round this afternoon. Until then...' He beckoned to the door and the colleagues left. Allison found herself standing alone with Bennet in the corridor. 'Come down with me, Allison, he said. 'We'll see to her now.'

When Allison went with him to attend to Vikki, who looked pretty ill and was now on a saline drip, she discovered that Doctor Bennet was intending to make an addition to their therapeutic regime. In addition to the two drugs that had worked successfully in the past he was going to administer Oviron.

She couldn't deny that the prospect interested her and even excited her, but she was unsure as to its advisability. She made her reservations felt to Doctor Bennet. Taking him out of earshot of their patient she spoke quietly and seriously:

'My one worry about giving it, apart from long-term toxicity,' she said, 'Is that it may set up a bio-feedback loop.'

'How do you mean?' he asked her.

'Well, as we know, it inhibits the enzyme ALA synthetase...'

'Which is why we want to give it in the first place,' he interrupted, 'to decrease the production of ALA.'

'That's right,' said Allison. 'But what if the lack of ALA production causes a stimulation of the enzyme in classic feed-back fashion and ultimately, in a few weeks or so, we end up producing more ALA despite the initial inhibition?'

'Then we increase the dose of Oviron.'

'We can't do that forever,' said Allison reflectively. 'Still it's only a theoretical possibility. Have there been any such positive feed-back results from the animal studies? There's none that I know of.'

'Not to my knowledge,' said Doctor Bennet, still ruminating, apparently, on what Allison had said.

'Well, at least that's hopeful,' said Allison.

'Yes, it is,' said Bennet, preparing a syringe and laying it beside a pale blue 100 milligram Oviron tablet. He looked at th etablet for a few seconds, lifted it and placed it in his pocket.

'You're probably right,' he said; 'We'll forget the Oviron.'

'So, it's all go,' said Allison brightly to Vikki, as she attended to her, preparing her for the injection as before. 'We're going to get you allright this time, Vikki,' she said.

'I hope so,' said the young woman, who was very laboured. 'I really hope so.'

Bennet approached with the syringe:

'This won't hurt, Vikki,' he said. 'Just the same as before.'

'It's a lovely time of year in Norfolk,' Doctor Bennet said calmly as he looked at Allison with a disconcerting look which was far away from here. 'I sometimes think I'll go there when I retire.'

And just as before as he spoke about the Norfolk Broads the blood pressure and vital signs returned to normal. Vikki was stable again, Allison once more vindicated. She felt pleased.

CHAPTER SEVEN

The research group had gathered in their usual meetings room and by now Allison felt perfectly at ease with them. No longer was she the novice, the new member of the group who needed guidance and direction in procedure. Without really noticing the fact she had become one of them, a fully respected member; a professional among professionals

'Explain it to us again, Allison, from the beginning, Doctor Bennet was looking at her carefully as were all her colleagues in the room. 'Give us a chance to consider the possibility of the truth of what you're saying. It does seem quite remarkable - perhaps a bit overly speculative. However, you know what you're talking about if anyone does. So let's hear it. On you go, continue.'

Allison cleared her throat and cleared her mind of everything except her theories and once again briefly explained her latest thoughts on this baffling disease to her colleagues;

'As you all know,' she began; 'there is an overproduction of the forerunner of hemoglobin called ALA in acute porphyria. When we test for this in the urine of patients in acute attack of the disease we find that it's concentration there and in the blood is even further increased.

'Now if we consider the nature of this substance we discover that it could potentially interact with itself to form a new chemical; attach itself to itself as it were to make a new compound. In theory it could do this in the body and it is possible that this new chemical unlike ALA itself could be toxic and cause some of the psychological distress we see in attacks of the disease.'

The room was silent as Allison walked over to the small blackboard and began to draw chemical structures on it.

'As we see,' she continued; ALA could combine with itself and form this chemical.' She pointed to the odd looking ringed-structure she had drawn.

'There is some evidence to suggest that this substance is present in people with mental illness and some authorities believe that it is responsible for some aspects of such illnesses. My contention is that it is present in porphyrics during acute attacks of the disease and is to some extent responsible for these.'

'Interesting.' muttered Bennet and a few heads nodded in agreement; 'And how would we test this theory, Allison. Could we take some blood or urine from a porphyric in attack and measure for the presence of this new substance?'

'Afraid not,' replied Allison. 'My calculations suggest that there is little if any of this rogue chemical in blood or urine. I believe that it is produced and contained within the cerebrospinal fluid and hence only circulates within that fluid as it surrounds the brain and the spinal cord. We wouldn't be able to measure it anywhere else.'

'So, in order to test this theory of yours, we'd have to take a spinal tap from a porphyric patient, preferably one in acute attack. Correct?' asked Bennet.

'Essentially correct.' agreed Allison.

'A tall order,' continued her senior. 'A very tall order indeed.'

'I'm not so sure.' Allison replied.

'Explain.' said Bennet, in his purely professional voice.

'Well, first of all, I don't believe the patient would necessarily have to be in attack. Even in remission there should be enough of this chemical in the cerebrospinal fluid to enable us to measure it.

'Secondly, I think we could obtain a spinal sample quite readily and ethically from a patient we have in London at present.'

'Vikki Goudie?' offered Doctor Bennet.

'Yes,' replied Allison. 'She's a bright girl and we've spoken a great deal about the possible origins of the disease she has. She's already volunteered to help us trace down the cause of her illness in any way she can. I'm sure she'd be willing to give us a sample of CSF if we asked her and carefully explained to her what was involved and why we were interested.'

'Are you not running a bit ahead of yourself, Allison,' interjected Pam. 'We can't really go about taking samples of CSF from patients unless we have very good and very ethical reasons for doing so.'

'I don't know, Pam. That's for others to decide. What I do know is that if what I say is true, then we could be well on the way to discovering a major cause of this very distressing, debilitating and potentially fatal disease. And when you have the cause you are within sight of a cure.'

"Well said!" thought Pam as she watched Doctor Bennet's face for any signs of the irritation he could readily demonstrate towards any of his staff who didn't quite match up to his very high medical standards. There were none. Instead he sat for a time ruminating then at last he spoke;

'An excellent idea, Allison. I'll speak with Vikki myself and if that's productive I'll put a proposal before the hospital ethical committee this afternoon when it meets. I trust your judgement, Allison. You could be on to something here - something else' he stressed, smiling now.

Andrew Wills admired himself in the mirror of his Mercedes as he drove to Sir Terence Sanderson's house. He looked good and felt even better. In the back of the car two young women were sitting quietly apprehensive. Under their raincoats they were dressed in the flimsiest of clothes silk and nylon, pink and black.

At their feet there lay a bag containing the utensils necessary for their few hours work. They had obtained these from their pimp after he had given them explicit instructions about their client's needs. They had already been well paid for what they were about to do and they would do it well.

Despite the fact that it was still relatively early in the morning, Wills knew that Sir Terence would be up working and that he'd appreciate the gifts he had brought him. The precise time of arrival had been arranged though Sir Terence's appetites were rarely determined by anything so irrelevant as time. One of the girls, the one who was less bright, less experienced, would probably need medical treatment later. That too had been arranged.

Sanderson himself sat in his shaded room where the closed curtains kept out any unwanted daylight and the light of a single 60 watt lamp bulb was his solitary illumination; at least in the outside world. But inside his head shone, shone as it always had with figures and the manipulation of them.

His latest brain-child was a small holding company called Sefarat Chemicals Ltd which was based in South East Asia. Sefarat was an import-export business, dealing in chemical raw materials and formulated drugs of various qualities. The good quality branded products from reputable manufacturers and the so-called generics which were sometimes not all they were claimed to be in terms of quality control or efficacy.

Sefarat was an on-going concern which could be financially controlled, in fact be virtually taken over along with the existing board of directors, for a considerable but highly reasonable sum of money. Sir Terence knew this because his son-in-law was on the board of directors and was responsible amongst other things for agreeing tender business.

Through this puppet director, Unicorn Chemicals could respectably take a controlling interest in Sefarat and use the company to market, sell and distribute Oviron. By being mere suppliers of the drug, Unicorn could be distanced from Sefarat in the event that something untoward happened, which it wouldn't.

Sir Terence rarely took chances and son-in-law apart he was taking little or no chance by 'taking over' this company. Anyway, his daughter's husband would never be a threat to him, he was too afraid to be. The pathetic boy. He had seen the consequences of betrayal first hand and he hadn't liked it one little bit. He had also seen aspects of Sir Terence's "little pleasures" and he hadn't liked them one little bit either.

Business in South East Asia was carried out very differently from business elsewhere in the world and Sir Terence was as au fait with its intricacies as he was with that of the most sophisticated and formal of the Western Capitalist nations. The man was a financial genius with just one problem. He was despised by all who knew him and by many who didn't.

The reason for this was simple. He was a sadist of the most extreme type, both psychologically and physically, and there were few people whom he had dealt with who hadn't experienced some facet of this aspect of the man. Sometimes, as with Hoffmann, this had been the experience of seeing Sir

Terence in action in some of the most sordid, seediest and most expensive brothels in the world; an experience few people could ever forget. To others, however, the experience of Sir Terence's peccadillos came in more indirect form.

Abuse of power, money, privilege and position, had all been indulged in and few had escaped his excesses in this respect, including his near family. He had however, gone too far on one particular occasion thinking that he could behave in the West End of London as he had in the South Central Side of Bangkok. He had been wrong.

By the end of the afternoon agreement had been obtained both from Vikki Goudie and the hospital ethical committee to take a sample of cerebrospinal fluid from her and to analyze it for the presence of Allison's proposed substance which the research team had unimaginatively nicknamed 'Substance X.'

The sample was taken by inserting a needle into the young girl's spine. This was done under local anesthetic and a small volume of the fluid which circulated within the spine was withdrawn. The only discomfort Vikki suffered was a severe thumping headache which came after and which thankfully didn't last too long. She had been well prepared for it and, thankfully, it was not as bad as she'd expected it to be.

The sample of cerebrospinal fluid was rushed to John Raynor's laboratory for analysis and Allison was informed that the result would be known in around twenty four hours. If it was negative for Substance X it wouldn't tell them much. If it was positive... Allison tried not to think on that.

A lot of money had been paid, a lot of hands shaken and a lot of promising words exchanged in eager ears. The result had been no prosecution of Terence Sanderson but effective disbarment from the City. For this financial wizard this was a terrible fate indeed and one he found most difficult to accept.

He did, however, find outlets for his genius in his work with Unicorn, where he'd obtained a major interest relatively recently; and by indulging his sadistic pleasures in any way he could.

The financial system Sanderson had devised in this instance was simple and brilliant as most of his systems were. Unicorn Chemicals would express some degree of doubt as to the advisability of marketing Oviron on such a wide scale as the demand created for its use in obesity had generated. The company would express genuine concern about the clamor that would come for the drug and this concern would come from those members of the medical and marketing staff who were as innocent as little boys in blue cotton night-gowns as to what was really going on.

In acceptance of this demand for control Unicorn would only market the drug in a very limited way - for the treatment of acute intermittent porphyria and for certain specific infections. These were hardly great money spinners but even so Unicorn would forego patent rights on the manufacture and formulation of the drug as a gesture by the Industry of charitable aims and royal assent.

They would supply it however, on a tender basis to the sole distributor in the Far East, Sefarat Chemicals; from where it would be re-exported back into the industrialized nations for widespread use in obesity. As Sefarat would accept tenders only from Unicorn, with one or two exceptions for appearances sake, this would net them a neat little profit.

The excess drug ex-U.K. that was supplied to Sefarat to meet demand, would be manufactured in Pakistan and exported to Sefarat via India and Russia where it would be paid for in hard currency. This would pass to London via Pakistan. The Indian company would receive vitamin and mineral products in payment from the Russians and the Pakistan company would officially record the manufacture and sale of vitamin and mineral products for exportation to India's starving and malnourished. A multi-million dollar market in itself. This 're-export and switch deal' was the ideal vehicle for capitalising on Oviron individually and collectively.

Before all of this was formally arranged, however, and before the public announcement of Unicorn's intentions it would be mooted that Unicorn were going to market Oviron in obesity, internationally and exclusively.

A three month advertising campaign would do that and they would, after all, have a Product License to do so. The share price of the company would rise by a significant percentage. A few million options traded at the right time in the appropriate way could add to any of the inner-circle's collateral quite readily.

The advertising campaign would of course be challenged by various medical authorities and Unicorn would accept their recommendations and ultimately withdraw the advertisements; but only after they had defended and procrastinated about them for as long as was necessary. This would be for as long as they wanted the ads to run in the media to achieve maximum public exposure and effect. By the time the medical opinion had its way, the public would be desensitised to any prospect of Oviron being a potentially dangerous drug and they would be clamoring to pour it down their throats.

Allison spent that evening with Ken at her flat. Despite her thoughts being somewhere close to Substance X much of the time, she had cooked him a delicious meal of prawn baked eggs followed by carrot and tomato soup, bacon fricassee and ending with a delicious yogurt mousse. They both sat sipping coffee and chatting idly, mainly about their work and colleagues.

At length an easy silence fell and each mused with their own thoughts. Allison was sipping a small brandy and its generous warmth made her feel very pleasant indeed. After a time, however, Ken spoke and even before she could make sense of his words, Allison could tell by the tone of his voice that he was in a very serious mood indeed.

'You know, Al,' he said. 'I think it's about time we made a few decisions, don't you?' Allison looked at him but didn't respond.

'Is it really fair for us to continue like this?' he went on. 'You know how much I care for you. I love you very much indeed. You know that. But this is difficult, very difficult. What do you say we get married? Forget any reversion to our former relationship. Marry me Allison.'

'Oh, Ken,' said Allison suddenly feeling deflated; 'I didn't think... . I do care for you, you know that, and I know that things are less than satisfactory as they are just now... but marriage... . I just can't seem to...' she paused seeking the words she couldn't find.

'Why not?' he continued. 'Give me one good reason why not.' He sounded upset, irritated, annoyed at her. This she knew was understandable.

'One reason,' he repeated. 'Give me one good reason why not.' Allison couldn't. She felt harassed.

'I just...' she said. 'I just don't know. It seems a sensible thing to do but...'

'But what?' interrupted Ken.

'I don't know, Ken. I just don't know.'

He reached over and took her hand. Moved closer and sat beside her, brushing her hair back with his hand and looking at her with a terrible intensity. Allison began to tremble, she was uncertain why. The phone rang.

Sir Terence Sanderson put his pen down. He was happy with his morning's work, such a lovely morning it seemed if he was to believe the weather report he had heard on B.B.C. Radio 6 News.

He heard his door bell ring. Bang on time! And knowing who it was he was filled with an urgent anticipation. He heard the sounds of voices as his man let Andrew Wills in with his guests. Sir Terence felt very strange inside. A sort of empty feeling held him, an exciting emptiness . He walked to his study door and unlocked it. His man would know to send the women to the room and to send Wills up here to him.

Wills entered, shook his hand, and spoke carefully:

'I've left them downstairs, Sir Terence. We've made all the arrangements. I thought, that I might just mention that what I've brought for you can be arranged as often as you want as long as you work for Unicorn.

'This in addition, of course, to whatever help we can give you or to any of your interests you may wish to pursue independently of us. I've been given carte-blanche to take care of things for you at this end. As often as you like, in total confidence.' The pale thin man looked at him and said nothing.

'Have you anything for us?' asked Unicorn's marketing manager. Sir Terence handed him a few sheets of paper. 'The perfect corporate man.' he said; '"Us" is it?' Wills said nothing; 'Most of it's here,' said the sadist; 'Just a few loose ends now.' He was becoming agitated wanted rid of this man. 'I'll attend to those later with Hoffmann and Wilder. It has to be at that level, you understand. You're not senior enough to bother with. You understand?'

Andrew Wills understood very well and feigned hurt. 'Very well, Sir,' he said, placing the papers securely into the briefcase that he carried: 'I'd better go now and let you get on.' He handed Sanderson a card with a telephone number on it. 'Just ring me at this number when you've finished and I'll be here within fifteen minutes and take your friends away.'

With that, Andrew Wills let himself out of the study and out of the house. As he drove away in his Silver Mercedes there was one phrase repeating itself in his head. "Sick bastard," it said. And Wills knew it was correct.

Excited, walking slowly, savouring every step he took towards the room with the quiet voices, Sir Terence Sanderson smiled as he walked actually showing his teeth. They glistened in the morning light which fell through the windows. For his mouth was watering, literally. Just as if he was anticipating his favorite meal.

Sir Terence returned to his study. He looked over a copy of his plan for Sefarat Chemicals. It seemed fool-proof. Was there any corner uncovered? Any edge revealed? There didn't seem to be. It may not be perfect... but then it might just be. He worked on the details for another hour before telephoning his son-in-law and asking him to fly to London that coming weekend. The boy didn't even ask why. Like others, he did as he was told when Sir Terence cracked the whip.

It was John Raynor's voice which met Allison when she picked up the phone and listened.

'Allison,' he said. 'I'd like you to pop over to the lab if you can. How does it suit just now?'

'Well, I suppose I could, John. Ken's here, he could run me over. Why though? What's the rush? Have you some news?'

I'd rather you saw it for yourself, dear girl. Coming?'

'Why, yes,' Allison responded, beginning to feel very excited indeed. 'We'll be with you in about half an hour.'

Twenty minutes later they were at the door of the laboratory. Ken who had been a bit tetchy about the interruption had reluctantly agreed to run Allison over and as they entered the laboratory he looked around quizzically. It was as if he was bemused by the bottles, jars, personal computers, elaborate electronic machinery and the pristine glassware that were the hallmark of a modern laboratory.

Allison made her way directly to where John Raynor was working and Ken followed her, still looking around seemingly bemused - or was it dismissive? - at the array of scientific esoterica.

'Hello, Allison,' John said with a smile; 'Come and have a look at this.' He was looking into an opening in a medium sized metal box. The purple glow of ultra-violet light spilled from the opening and Allison walked over and looked in.

'What do you see?' the biochemist asked her.

'Nothing much,' replied Allison, her heart beating fast. 'Just a plate with what looks like a layer of white powder on it.'

'That's correct,' said John. 'It's a thin layer chromatographic plate...'

'With a single pink spot on it...' Allison continued knowing even as she looked that this was precisely what she had predicted. The spot was her rogue chemical.

'Substance X!' said John Raynor triumphantly. 'It was there right enough. Just as you said it would be.'

'No!' said Allison now smiling incredulously. 'I don't believe it!'

'Yes,' said the clinical biochemist with a smile as broad as he could muster. 'Substance X!'

Simultaneously they reached for each other and hugged.

'Well done.' laughed John. 'My goodness, this will ruffle a few feathers in Vienna. Wait and see, you're going to be the sensation of the conference.'

Still holding tight to John in her elation, Allison turned her head to look at Ken. Her smile froze on her face and her stomach tightened in a spasm of anxiety such as she hadn't experienced in almost a year. He was staring at both of them with a peculiar look on his face a look she knew so well a look of all-consuming jealousy.

Sir Abe Wilder, briar as ever in hand, put down one telephone and picked up another. He had just finished speaking with Terence Sanderson. There was a smile on his face embroidered by Sanderson's comments on both his financial manipulations and by the few innuendos he'd given as to the similar expertise he'd shown with the two women Wills had brought to him. It was another weakness this of Sanderson's, his indulgence in boasting about his sexual expertise. He only did so with his friends, of course, but who could be considered friends by Sanderson, except, perhaps, Mostyn. They shared similar but distinctive tastes.

On the line now was another potential Knight of the Realm - a man who had overcome enormous personal and financial setbacks as a result of his father's financial promiscuity; to emerge as one of the great media barons. He could manipulate the press of the country as readily as Sanderson could two prostitutes.

'Hello, Kevin,' said Sir Abe amiably. 'I was wondering if you could possibly see it in anyone's interest, someone down there in the gutter-press perhaps; to have an exclusive on the Palace. 'The source would be from the Palace itself and concerns some secret medical treatment our future regent and his son are about to have within the next week or so. The treatment could not only save their lives it could also prevent their imminent insanity.'

Sir Abe waited, listened to the controlled excitement in his correspondent's voice. 'You could? He lit the briar with satisfaction. 'Excellent. I'll give you fuller details soon. Fine. Tell me how are things with you generally? How's the family?'

'Constant,' replied Kevin drolly.

Ken drove her home in utter silence. It was the old silence, the one Allison used to dread and which was Ken's infantile attempt to punish her for some apparent misdeed - in this instance her innocent expression of delight in hugging John Raynor.

She felt sorry for him knew that he couldn't help his crippling jealousy, but she knew too that she couldn't allow it to cripple her. There was a coolness and clarity to Allison's thinking now which she had never had before in relation to Ken. She sat quietly surrounded by his silence and for the first time ever since she'd met him it flowed over her completely leaving her untouched and, she felt, at long last free.

As they drew up at Allison's flat Ken silently unbuckled his seat belt and made to get out. 'A moment, Ken,' said Allison.

'What?' he mumbled, failing to meet her eyes, attempting to continue punishing her.

'I don't think you should come in,' she said squarely; 'I think we've probably run our course, don't you? It's time for change, for both of us. We can be friends if you want to, but no more. Call me if you wish once you've got yourself together. Take care, Ken. Bye.'

As Allison made to leave, Ken grabbed her by the arm.

'What's the hell's wrong with you?' he said. 'Just because I haven't said much, haven't congratulated you on your great bloody discovery you think that...'

'No,' Allison interrupted. 'It's not that at all Ken and you know it. For years you've been able to make me feel guilty. You've learned how to do and say things - or sometimes, like this evening, not to say things - which have had the same effect.

'You've managed to make me feel as if I've been doing something wrong when in fact I'm doing no such thing. I've had enough of it Ken. Enough. As I said, we can be friends if you want to be, but that's it! Now goodbye and goodnight.'

With that Allison left the white convertible and walked steadily to the door of her flat. She closed it behind her and sat down to compose herself. A brief sensation of pain and hurt held her for a time, then it lifted. It was replaced by a feeling of release, freedom and near elation again as she remembered;

'Substance X' she said aloud as she walked to her brandy glass gave it a short refill and raised it in a solitary toast;

'To Substance X and the start of a new life,' she said, smiling as she did so. Outside she heard Ken drive off. "Goodbye," she thought with sadness, relief and professional satisfaction running through her in equal measures with the spirit.

The polished mahogany table was headed by Sir Abraham Wilder and he was surrounded by the senior executives of Unicorn Chemicals Limited. At his side, and secretary to the meeting now being held, was Greg Hoffmann. At his side was Kathryn Meadowford.

Beside her Andrew Wills was seated who, along with the seven Regional Managers who controlled the sales operations for Unicorn internationally, completed the small group who were privileged enough to attend the meeting and be made privy to what was happening with Oviron.

The company was divided into seven major regions of operation. These were, the U.K., Western Europe and Ireland; North America; Latin America; The "SEA" Zone or South East Asia; Africa and other so-called developing countries; Australia and Japan; and Eastern Europe.

Normally there was a great deal of internecine politicking between these groups, particularly at the more junior levels of management. There, arguments over sales projections, allocation of production resources, supply of raw and finished materials, products which were allowed to be marketed, promotional campaigns which were allowed to be run and so on, were a constant and unnecessary irritant to the flow of normal business. People being what they were, however, it was one which little could be done about. Usually. There was none of that pettiness here.

Each of the Regional Managers took their cue from their Chairman and Managing Director and were one hundred per cent behind him in his carefully stressed statement about Oviron being a company product as a whole and not one subject to regional squabbles. They had good reason to be so committed very good reason.

*   *   *

For sometime now Allison had continued to see Alan Downie's patient Ben O'Grady whenever she could. He had gradually recovered from his psychotic illness and she was not surprised to find that, as she had anticipated when she had first met him; he was a very pleasant articulate and intelligent man indeed.

Ben was popular with the other patients and he did a great deal to encourage and assist those of them who were less fortunate than he was, who had chronic rather than acute illnesses.

What *did* surprise Allison was the fact that Ben had worked for Unicorn Chemicals and was still officially employed by them. He spoke little about his company other than to mention the fact that they had been very supportive of him during his period of illness and that he'd worked for them in the capacity of Clinical Research Associate - assisting in the carrying out and monitoring of clinical trials.

Obviously Allison found this aspect of particular interest and she asked Ben during this morning's visit what products of Unicorn's he had worked on and how many trials he had been involved in:

'Only Oviron now,' he said with some enthusiasm and speaking in the present tense. It was a forced enthusiasm Allison appreciated. It was Ben publicly expressing his "normality". She often found this with psychiatric patients and was saddened that they felt obliged to sanction themselves in this way. They felt a shame that was rarely theirs.

'I worked on other products prior to Oviron, of course,' continued Ben; 'But I now deal solely in Oviron. It could be a major product for us if its antibacterial action is more widespread than we first thought.

'We haven't carried out many formal clinical trials as yet, just one major one in Korea, a low dose study in children from an orphanage. I know it sounds a bit unconventional but children in institutions are prone to throat infections and they tend to get passed on, so it's an obvious place to study such a drug and the legislation over there isn't as strict as in the West. The other trials we've carried out have only been minor ones; more "studies" rather than formal trials.

'The main reason for the lack of clinical trials here in the U.K. is the documentation we require to generate in order to obtain a CTC - a clinical trials certificate. We don't have it all yet. We've completed a number of volunteer studies though mainly to test patient safety.

Allison listened carefully and with no little interest.

'It so happens that I was one of the first volunteers to take Oviron,'Ben continued; 'It's normal procedure for those involved with the research and development of the drug to try it out for safety first.

'This time I picked the short straw but it didn't do me any harm. My blood tests were perfectly normal, as you know, and I imagine that my split ejaculate was too. I cracked-up before we got the result of that back but I'm sure...'

'You're what...?' Allison interjected.

'My 'split ejaculate',' repeated Ben, smiling slightly, amused. 'Oh, come on, Doctor Young, you know what that is surely... it's standard procedure now in pharmacokinetic studies on new drugs.'

'I'm sorry Ben, but I don't know, Allison admitted. What is it?'

'Are you readily shocked?' he asked jokingly.

Allison laughed: 'No. Not really,' she said. It's that bad though, eh?'

'Yup,' said Ben, laughing with her. "What a change in him," she thought, "What a lovely man brought back from wherever by the devoted care and patience of Alan Downie and his team"

'Well,' Ben began. 'First you swallow the said drug and wait twenty-four hours or so. Then... well, then you are given an X-ray film and if necessary a book or something. You then go into a small cubicle and, eh, masturbate over the plate!'

'Oh!' exclaimed Allison, surprised and mildly shocked that she was hearing this.

'An assistant usually a nurse then uses a plastic spatula to split the ejaculate roughly into three different parts - sperm, seminal fluid and the rest.

'The concentration of unchanged drug or its metabolites in each of these portions is then measured. This way we can tell if it's safe to have intercourse while taking the drug. If the drug was present in sperm or seminal fluid it could affect a conception, produce a deformed child. We do something similar in women...

'I think we'll leave that for now,' said Allison, feeling quite enlightened. Then she changed tack: 'Did you ever have any psychiatric problems at all before Ben; ones you haven't mentioned to us since your referral here?'

'None at all, Doctor Young. I've been asked that once or twice before, as you can imagine. None at all, ever. And, before you ask, I don't drink to excess, I have no domestic, financial or other major problems and there is no family history of mental illness.'

'Ever drink too much? Take any recreational drugs; LSD, cannabis, cocaine, PCP, khat? anything...?'

'I've been asked that, too,' said Ben smiling. 'I once puffed pot but "I didn't inhale it," as someone once said. 'No! I've never done drugs. I'm a bit of a health freak. I don't even drink alcohol and I even have a mountain-bike and cycle to work. I've never had anything stronger than an aspirin in my whole adult life and even that under protest.'

'Except, of course, UC825-0,' said Allison without elaboration.

'What?' asked Ben, surprised; 'What's that?'

'Oh yes, you've had that,' she continued; 'That's your company's code for Oviron, Ben, remember? Unicorn Chemical's drug number 825, 'O' for Oviron. You've had Oviron, Ben, that's a drug though hardly a recreational one. How often did you take it?'

'Just once,' he replied, more reflective now.

'How long after that did you have your episode did your illness start?

'Why almost... Well, three days, I think,' said Ben, more serious now. 'Surely you don't think that Oviron caused -'

'- Split ejaculates indeed!' said Allison smiling at him non-committally changing the subject. She made a mental note

to have another complete hematological check run on Ben
O'Grady and another split ejaculate if he, and they, could cope
with it. She thought that he would.

Allison made her way back to her office via the ward where
Vikki Goudie was. Her intention was to look in on her, see how
she was doing. She had no idea.

'For once ladies and gentlemen it must percolate throughout
this company that we have a product here whose importance
transcends the narrow localized interests of any one geographical
area' Abraham Wilder for once had no briar in his hand as he
spoke. He didn't need it. There was stimulation enough in the
adrenaline that surged through his modest audience. There was
no need for nicotine.

'Oviron is not to be seen as a product solely for your market.
It is to be seen by all of you and all of the staff you represent as
a product for a global market. To this end - and for this product
alone - I am going to run things a little differently.'

The Regional Managers glanced around at each other; some
smiled some looked puzzled; one - Ilse Hempel of the Eastern
European Zone - kept her face blank, expressionless.

'I have decided that for this product, we will not have the
usual accountancy procedures which are normally applied in
any of your markets. You may apply them locally if you wish
to. I leave that decision to you. In general terms, though, I wish
the procedure to be changed for Oviron so that it reflects the
Group situation and not the local one.

'Our first major target markets for this drug are Great
Britain; The United State of Ireland; North America, Western
Europe and Japan. In that order of priority. I have had a system
devised by which each of you will be credited for the assistance
you can give to get Oviron into these markets irrespective of the
regions you normally represent. They can come later.'

There was general agreement and a degree of relief at this statement. Wilder had known that there would be. The competitive nature of his Sales Managers was almost instinctual.

'By this system we will assess your ability, your tenacity, your willingness to become involved in helping the company as a whole and all our regional differences will for the time being be suspended.

'I ask Greg Hoffmann to forego his role of Secretary to the Meeting for the moment and explain this system to you.'

Sir Abe turned to Hoffmann, beckoned him in the direction of the overhead projector and then said, 'Thank you, Greg.'

'The system I have devised ladies and gentlemen,' said Greg Hoffmann quietly, 'It is a very simple one indeed. We will take the total turnover of the company, of Unicorn Chemicals, and divide this by the total turnover of your respective regions. This figure will give us a measure of how much you contribute to the company. We will then take this figure as a fraction of the market target in dollars for Oviron in any given market...'

Hoffmann explained his system which was engineered to enable a fair comparison to be made between regional performances in terms of marketing Oviron.

'By this method we will be able to assess each region's contribution to our marketing effort and each region will be rewarded or penalized accordingly, as the case may be, with respect to future incentives.

'We demand one hundred per cent effort from all of you in getting this drug launched in the sequence we have outlined. It will be as evident to you as it is to us that your particular methods of contributing to this effort will, by their very nature, have to vary. But we can and will assess these centrally by the scheme outlined and we will see this as a reasonable guide with respect to the motivation towards our desired end which is supplied by local senior management and thus ultimately by yourselves. Are there any questions at this point?'

A deep and sudden silence fell. This was something different, something these people had never heard of before, a collective and concerted drive market-by- market. There had to be something going down here. There had to be some major reason for this and they wanted to know what it was.

Later that afternoon Allison spoke to John Raynor while they were both having a cup of coffee in the common room.

'How's Vikki Goudie coming along?' she asked him.

'She died half an hour ago, Allison. Cardiovascular collapse. There was nothing we could do.'

Allison was utterly shocked. She looked at him in disbelief: 'She died?' she said incredulously. John Raynor nodded once. 'My God,' she said. 'I never knew things were...'

'As I said, there was nothing we could do,' he interrupted, as he made to walk out of the room. 'Pull yourself together, Doctor,' he said as he placed his empty cup on the table and left.

As she stared after him, Allison remembered the little Japanese she'd met at the dinner party in the Raynor home. The very thought of the small courteous man somehow made her wonder about what exactly was happening at the hospital. She began to make an important decision. If what she thought might have happened to Vikki indeed had happened; then she needed proof. And that was going to be very difficult to find.

Allison left the restroom immediately after John Raynor and made her way down to what had been Vikki's room. Two nurses were getting her things together and were generally straightening the place out. Allison stood to one side beside the now redundant intravenous drip which had pumped vital fluid into the failing Vikki.

Hoffmann called for the lights to be lowered as he switched on the machine. He was back where he was at his best, his very best. In the shadows.

Later that morning she managed to collar Doctor Bennet in the corridor and she confronted him: 'What's the problem with Vikki Goudie, Doctor Bennet?'

'She's had a relapse, Allison. We're dealing with it. We're using your therapy again but this is a bad one a very bad one. I hope she pulls through.'

'Have you any idea what brought it on this time?'

'None at all,' replied her chief, looking her straight in the eye. 'Why, have you any ideas yourself?' he asked with an uncustomary bluntness a trace of sarcasm floating in his voice.

'The Oviron,' said Allison simply. 'That could have precipitated it, by simple bio-feedback. I told you before that...'

'And I told you before, Doctor Young, to just keep on doing what you're best at and leave the rest to those of us who are your seniors. Whatever brought this attack on, we'll discover the cause and deal with it accordingly.'

Allison was taken aback by the abruptness of his manner as he continued: 'As far as you are concerned, Vikki Goudie is no longer your patient and I don't want you attending her or even visiting her just now. Just let it be. Is that clear?'

'Perfectly,' said Allison firmly, unintimidated, looking at him with her fiercest determination. Abruptly turning away from her, John Bennet walked quickly away and Allison knew that she had spoken to a very worried man indeed.

Greg Hoffmann looked round the room, round the areas of the light and the shadows. There were no questions just silence behind which was the quiet hum of the overhead projector's cooling system.

'Now you will want to know the marketing strategy we are going to utilise for Oviron, our marketing plan. For once this is unique. It has never had a parallel in the history of our Industry and we have a glowing sequence of features and benefits which will guarantee, and I mean guarantee, the success of our product. Our sequence will be as follows:

'First of all, we will obtain a product license or its equivalent for Oviron's use in Streptococcal throat infections. We already have this in the U.K. as you know thanks to the second epidemic of Strep: A infection in a decade. We will then apply for a license for its use as a prophylactic in acute intermittent porphyria.'

A few exclamations of interest occurred which Hoffmann quickly quietened:

'If you refer to the document you have which is marked - "Acute Porphyria" - you will see there an outline of this disease and its incidence of occurrence in each of your regions. Please do not be disturbed by its low incidence. We have a premium product here for that indication and I don't just mean in terms of price.' His sales team looked at him. If not in terms of price how else could you define a 'premium product?'

'Before we obtain the Product License for the use of Oviron in porphyria we will obtain massive press coverage for the drug. And I do mean massive. This coverage will mention in passing that it has been observed in the few trials of the drug that have taken place in throat and dermal infections; that, in a number of patients, there has been an apparent associated reduction of weight precisely to their ideal weight.. It will be stressed that this has occurred without any change in eating habits or diet.'

There was more talking among the group, more interest, more adrenaline flowing.

'In the initial stages of coverage this will merely be mentioned, but it will then become a topic of correspondence and active promotion as interest in the drug peaks so that medical and lay-people alike are intrigued by the possibility of a drug than sculpt you into shape while you pig if you so wish to.'

The Shadow Man was flowing now. He was at his very best:

'At this juncture there will be a demand for formal clinical trials into this aspect of the drug's profile and we will defer to this demand and undertake these trials in obese patients and in normal, or almost normal weight, controls. We will find that the obese patients drop to their ideal weight, despite being able to continue eating as before and the same will apply to our control group. I don't need any soothsayer or astrologer to tell me this,' stressed Hoffmann; 'I know it already.' His audience were enchanted.

'The combination of the massive interest in the drug and its effectiveness in reducing weight will create massive demand for it both in Western Europe and in all developed countries internationally.

'By this time, be well on our way to having, or indeed will have, a license for the use of Oviron in acute porphyria with all that entails, which is a great deal. And we will have a premium price for the product which will have been negotiated with the Department of Health here, and which will set a precedent for other regulatory authorities such as the Food and Drugs Administration in the United States.

'We will then be in a position to offer to the next market on our list - the U.S.A. - a by now household name drug, which cures obesity without any need for dietary changes and at a premium price.' The sales people were delighted with this. He had taken them up, now he took them down.

'We will decline this opportunity,' ladies and gentlemen; 'And proceed differently. We will offer the drug to our competitors. Specifically to a company called Sefarat Chemicals.'

Again the murmuring started as the Regional Managers highly motivated by the scenario outlined to them now wondered why there was the proposed hold back and sell out. All their natural commercial instincts honed over years of competitive marketing told them to get in there and bleed everyone dry while they could. The scenario being outlined to them was incomprehensible.

Greg Hoffmann took a sip from a glass of iced water. He looked around the room, making everyone feel as if he was making eye contact with them in the shadows. Then he continued, playing his face cards as prepared; his Royal Flush:

'The drug will have been used in two senior members of the British Royal Family by this time, two members who suffer from acute intermittent porphyria and interest in it will be strong to say the least.' Again confusion, puzzlement and delight. 'You'll all appreciate why when you look at the possible outcome of that disease.'

Hoffmann continued speaking quickly and more loudly to stifle the spontaneous and open conversation which had broken out amongst the managers:

'The drug, however, may well show signs of toxicity when used long-term. We don't know yet for certain whether this will be the case or not. If it is, then we could have enormous problems with respect to liability claims. Having said this, we don't see how we can fail to have enormous demand for this product even in the absence of very long-term toxicity studies. Thus we shall progress our commercial plan in a way which is radically different from the assumed normal.

'We will forego our normal patent monopoly on Oviron and offer it to whoever wishes to purchase it from us. They can have the process patents and the drug itself if they want. We shall not market directly into such a hazardous market. If other companies or institutions wish to do that then that's up to them. We are happy to supply the drug to other sources, other companies, but we will not market it ourselves for the indication of obesity.'

Allison watched them as they went about their business clinically and routinely, erasing all traces of the young woman's presence. She wondered if the traces of a human being could be cleaned away that quickly and she wondered what Yukio Yoshimura would have thought of her thought.

As she stood aside while she spoke to the two women she unconsciously pressed her fingers into the tubing on the drip. As she did so a bubble of the liquid left in the tubing ran onto her leg. She bent down and reflexly brushed it away and as she did so she caught a characteristic odour just as one of the nurses spoke to her:

'We were very sorry to lose Miss Goudie, Doctor Young. She was such a nice young woman. Doctor Bennet said it was just one of these things. We were under the impression that you had her stabilised on her new drug regime.'

'So was I,' said Allison, as something tugged at her mind, something poignant and volatile, a fleeting unformed thought which left a trace of unease.

'Only yesterday she was talking about what she'd do when she finally got out of here,' said the other nurse. 'Thought she might study nursing herself.'

'Really?,' mused Allison, as the tugs pulled at her - something, something wrong, the drip, the smell from it, suddenly recognition hit her. The thoughts fell through her like a rainbow turned to fire. They were so incredible she couldn't quite accept them:

'What was in this drip?' she commanded. Both nurses stopped working and looked at her, at each other. Neither seemed to know what to say.

'It was intravenous saline,' said one, looking at the disposable bag and feeling threatened by Allison's tone. 'Doctor Raynor took charge of it. He asked for i.v. saline. The patient needed fluid.'

'Look, Doctor,' said the other looking around; 'I was instructed to get rid of these things almost an hour ago. I'd best get on with it. Excuse me.'

Allison considered removing the drip, having its contents analyzed, using them as evidence. She decided against such action. It was impractical to say the least and anyway, they probably had Vikki's permission on some piece of paper.

She stood aside and said nothing else. There was no great mystery here. She had her evidence even if it could not be produced in any court of law. They had run ethanol into Vikki Goudie to precipitate an attack of her porphyria, to test, no doubt, how Oviron was doing. And it had all gone wrong, very wrong indeed. The bastards had killed her.

She left the nurses to their tasks and walked away from the ward a changed woman. Why had they done this? And who precisely was involved? Who, Allison Young was determined to find out, had dirt on their faces while they portrayed them as clean? A prescient thought in more ways than one as Allison was to discover.

At this point in the proceedings Greg Hoffmann had to hold up his hand and ask for silence. This roller coaster was far too much for his marketing men. To actually give the product to the competition in the absence of established toxicity was, to them, akin to commercial suicide. In time they fell silent and he completed his presentation:

'I would ask you, ladies and gentlemen, to assist us wholeheartedly in selling Oviron to all third parties who request our product. All your work and goodwill must go into this and to assisting us in any way you can to have it available in the markets I've designated, for the indications of streptococcal throats, dermatological infections and porphyria as soon as possible.

'I appreciate that you must all find this marketing plan somewhat unconventional - a little bizarre perhaps - but please if you can't take it on its merits please take it on trust. Trust me, ladies and gentlemen. Trust us. We shall succeed with this product in this way, globally. We shall make many millions of dollars and you will all benefit from that. All of you. Thank you for your time, your patience and your attention.'

With that, and without giving anyone time for formal questions, Greg Hoffmann switched off the projector, removed the overheads and went back to his seat. As he sat down Kathryn Meadowford pressed his leg:

'Well done,' she whispered to him.

He didn't make any response. He just sat there knowing how confused these people must be and wishing that he could give them the whole truth not just part of it. On occasion, Greg Hoffmann's loyalty to his company extended to its employees. This occasion was one of them.

The questions would come he knew and he and Sir Abe would answer them adequately. But these people were professionals, thorough professionals, and they would know that there were things going unsaid. They didn't like taking things on trust - trust played no part in successful marketing and marketing was what these people were successful at. Trust they left at home each morning, when they left their families. And even then...

Yes, the questions would come and they would be answered, but when Greg Hoffmann caught Ilse Hempel's eyes and absorbed the look which she gave him, he knew that he had not fooled her and that this was probably true of the rest too. They would carry out his dictates to the letter, but they were not fooled, none of them. They would simply obey him. "And where," he thought, "Was the harm in that?"

CHAPTER EIGHT

Harry Wright was troubled. He scanned through the abstracts of the Hematology Congress which was to be held in the State University of Vienna. Of particular interest to him were those abstracts that made any mention whatsoever of anti-cancer agents. He was especially interested to see articles which discussed the effects of these on blood cell levels in patients receiving chemotherapy.

His daughter Tina was receiving what was termed "heroic" treatment of this type. But the only hero was Tina. Her blood count had fallen dangerously low and Harry wanted to discover if anyone had found a new method whereby such effects of these drugs could be diminished. Even more, he hoped to find some article or other pertaining to advances in the treatment of the disease that she had.

Cytostatic drugs were very efficient at killing rapidly growing cells such as those found in tumor masses. The problem was that they killed other rapidly growing cells too. The cells of the gut, hair, skin, blood and the immune system; all grew and were replaced very quickly and while cytostatic drugs killed tumor cells very efficiently, they killed the cells of these tissues too. This led to hair loss, nausea, vomiting and, worst of all - anaemia, a compromised immune system and a predisposition for potential infections which, normally harmless, could prove fatal if not controlled.

The ideal cytostatic agent would only act on tumor cells "magic bullet" style and indeed such target-oriented drugs and delivery systems were currently being developed by bio-technologists. The present state of the art however, was such that they were not refined adequately enough to be used clinically in Tina, so Harry had to look elsewhere to attempt to discover other ways of reducing the toxicity of the drugs she was receiving.

'He muttered to himself as he scanned abstract after abstract. There were one or two papers which seemed to hold some hope in this respect and Harry ruminated on whether he should contact the authors immediately by telephone, fax, modem or letter; or go to the conference itself and meet them personally. He decided to do both. You never knew who you would meet at these meetings and what work may be in the pipeline but unpublished.

He filled in the registration form for the meeting, wrote a cheque and enclosed the appropriate fee and placed the envelope with the rest of his mail for posting by Mrs Mawson who was by now well established in his home. He prayed he would find some glimmer of hope for his daughter in Vienna. It was a slim chance but a chance just the same. He could ask for no more.

Over the next few weeks Allison had worked very hard both in and out of the hospital attending to her patients, taking part in meetings, keeping up with current medical literature and preparing her paper for the congress in Vienna. This latter was still causing her some concern and she found herself preparing draft after draft of what she was intending to say without really being fully happy with any version of it.

Despite her anger at what had happened to Vikki and her continuing desire to bring down some form of justice on whoever had "experimented" on the young woman; no one had behaved with undue unease since the tragic event had occurred. All concerned had expressed their deep regret and when Allison had alluded to what had been in the drip Vikki had received, no one had appeared particularly interested.

When she'd taken the bull by the horns and specificality alluded to the smell of alcohol she'd noticed, Doctor Bennet had a very realistic explanation. 'The nurses would have run ethanol through the drip to sterilise it, Allison. That's all, it's standard practice with some of then here. They run saline or distilled water afterwards. Though these days drips undergo standard and intensive cleaning anyway. They sometimes forget that.'

"This may well have been true," thought Allison; But it didn't ease her suspicions about Vikki having received Oviron.

There had of course been an autopsy on Vikki and the details of this were on a computer data base that Allison had access to. As this included all details of any foreign excipients in Vikky's blood at the time of her death, it would tell Allison precisely what had been there. As she typed in the password, she realized that any found ethanol in Vikky's system would also be included in that file.

She accessed the data base and using the computer's mouse she scrolled down the list of hospital fatalities for that particular day until she found the one she wanted. "Goudie V.B." She clicked in and found the appropriate sub-directory. She accessed this and saw only four noted. "Propranolol (0.023%), phentolamine (0.045%) epinephrine (0.035%) and hydrocortisone (0.089%) and metabolites of same (0.132%)" There was no mention of any alcohol or Oviron in any form.

Allison wondered at this, could she have been mistaken? Very mistaken? Bob Innskip would have made the reports on the post-mortem blood samples and he was beyond reproach. Could his data have been tampered after he'd entered it?

Allison knew a great deal about computers and their software and she'd done a bit of relatively harmless "hacking" on her Personal Computer in her early teens simply for fun; this, until her father had caught her hacked into one of his bank accounts! She smiled at the memory, it had been fun and he'd taken it well. But this was no fun and withe her hacker's background she soon managed to access the command files in the programme and attempted to alter Vikky's data.

She couldn't. The data base would not accept any of her digital pleadings however sophisticated they were; and they were much more sophisticated she knew than any of her colleagues.

There was only one conclusion to be made. She had been completely wrong about Vikky and her suspicions of her colleagues had been completely unfounded. In retrospect her colleagues abrupt behavior with her had been fully justified. She'd been a stupid, interfering and highly unprofessional delusive. She felt ashamed as she clicked out of the directories one by one and finally switched the PC off.

In confirmation of her revised, and original, view of them; Allison's colleagues were more than helpful with suggestions and advice about the forthcoming conference in Vienna. Indeed Doctor Bennet even arranged for a room to be made available for Allison to give a mock presentation to a number of the medical and research staff and students. This took place complete with projector and slides and with testing and probing questions from said staff. It went well.

Even so, she was still lacking in confidence and hoped that she would reach the standard required of her at the conference.

After all, it was a very important step in her career and all the reassurances from colleagues that it would be fine -that her work was excellent - didn't mean a thing on the day.

During this same period Allison had approached a number of her colleagues about the case of Mrs Bailley's baby. All of them had been perplexed by her news particularly Bob Innskip the histologist. He found it literally incredible and didn't believe a mistake could have been made. He was at a loss, however, to explain how the positive result for Down's had been obtained.

As a consequence of his overtures and those of Allison a committee had been set up especially to investigate the case. It was chaired by Doctor Bennet himself. After much deliberation and investigation, the outcome was inconclusive. It was reluctantly agreed that some unfortunate but untraceable error had occurred as they did from time to time. This didn't satisfy Allison at all but that unsatisfactory outcome was the end of the matter as far as the committee was concerned. After all, the end result had not been tragic, no fatality or real damage had been involved, just a short period of psychological stress. Allison decided to take the issue further if she could when she returned from Vienna - first things first.

The lecture hall was full. It must have contained at least three hundred people. Allison sat nervously watching the numbers on the board which had lights portraying each presentation in progress as they counted themselves down to her presentation number - ten. She was sitting near the front and before her, almost within touching distance at the lectern of the lecture theatre, a small man with a goatee beard and bow-tie was reading a paper on some aspect of the hematological changes occurring in leukaemia. He was pointing to his projected slides and making comments on the graphs and figures they contained.

'When broken down by age and sex we find, using the Chi-Squared test, that these results are significant at the $p = 0.001$ level in both groups...' the man was saying. It was all that Allison could take in. He was number eight. One more to go and then it was her.

Her nerves were running riot flipping her heart, stomach, lungs and thoughts into somersaults. For the thousandth time she knew she was going to make a mess of the whole thing. She would forget her text, her slides would be messed up, the projector would break down, her results would be faulted... the list was endless and she wished she'd never come.

Then the delegates were applauding a slight woman who wore enormous glasses and a black skirt with a contrasting white blouse. Next thing Allison knew the lights had changed to presentation number ten and the Chairman of the meeting was announcing her name, hospital of origin and the title of her paper.

With legs as weak as distilled water and her insides jumping like an abused trampoline, she made her way down the endless stairs to the front of the lecture hall. To all who observed her Allison looked the picture of composure.

The hall fell silent and she stood looking at the vast number of delegates. She took a very deep breath:

'Acute intermittent porphyria...' she began, 'is a disease characterised by the increased biosynthesis of porphyrins and their precursor ALA...'

She finished and the delegates were immediately aware of her caliber they respected her and the findings she had come to present to them. She received long and appreciative applause at the end of her presentation and as she returned to her seat - still slightly shaky but feeling a unique high - John Raynor was sitting waiting for her with Doctor Bennet:

'Well done,' the latter said, simply. 'That was excellent.' Allison felt a thrill such as she had never known before. She had, she knew, academically arrived.

* * *

That evening, before dinner, most of the delegates congregated in the bar. A number of them came up to Allison and congratulated her on her presentation. Some were merely being polite, others had a genuine interest in her work and they exchanged views and results with her; promising to communicate and send copies of their own published work in relevant areas to her.

Allison enjoyed it all. There were some very eminent people at the meeting and here she was amongst them; if not quite yet a star attraction then not in the least out of place either.

People milled about and chatted and there were groups locked in intense and no doubt medical, conversations. Others were brimming with laughter - no doubt their conversations were non-medical!

She remained seated at a table with John Raynor and Pam who had both given papers at other sessions of the same meeting; Pam at the genetic session and John at the clinical-biochemical one. In between visits from the other delegates they gossiped among themselves, pleased that their presentations were over and that they'd gone so well.

Both Pam and John were particularly attentive towards Allison and both had taken time away from their own sessions to attend her presentation. They assured her it had gone off very well indeed and that she should be more than happy with it.

Allison knew that while they were being truthful. They were also consolidating her new-found status. She was well aware that after such a stressful event the tendency was for the presentee to hog the conversation seeking reassurance that things had indeed gone well; so she made a point of directing the conversation away from herself and towards their own presentations and the reception they had received.

Pam, in particular, had been very excited about the reception she'd received from her fellow geneticists. So Allison asked her what had transpired after her paper:

'They were all very excited about the work the research group is doing,' she replied excitedly; 'And they asked me question after question about our research. They were particularly intrigued by your finding of some rogue substance X in the cerebrospinal fluid, Allison, and some groups are already talking about looking for the equally rogue gene which could cause this to be produced. They all knew that porphyria was a genetic disorder. One delegate even asked me if - given Charles' recent decision to commission the building of a pyramidal museum of esoteric artifacts - our royals didn't have it themselves.

'There's a thought,' said John.

'It certainly is, laughed Allison sipping her small brandy with immense pleasure.

'I couldn't believe it,' Pam continued, also sipping gently at what Allison had counted as being her third drink. 'I've had offers to go on sabbatical to places as diverse as Budapest and Cape Town!

'They're fascinated by our work, especially the possibility of a genetically based bio-feed-back malfunction, with ALA being responsible for neurological damage. They believe that, if true, it could apply to Korsikoff's syndrome in chronic alcoholism and possibly to Alzheimer's. Lead poisoning too, was mentioned. The possibilities seem endless.'

'It certainly could account for some of these,' agreed John. 'Both alcohol and lead stimulate ALA synthesis and prolonged elevation of the substance - if Allison's hypothesis is correct -could lead to such damage in the central nervous system.' As Pam drank her fourth Scotch in a row, Allison wished that they were applying some of this theorising to her.

During the general chit-chat Allison noticed that in the professional setting in addition to the social one; John was a very accomplished communicator. SHe enjoyed his darting witticisms and poignant comments immensely.

So too, it seemed, did a number of the other delegates, as there was a constant flow of them to and from John; seeking no doubt not only his academic expertise, but also his expertise in the art of humor.

He was a very popular man and Alison could fully understand why. She noticed, however, that no matter how engrossed any conversation about his interests became, the subject of Oviron and Unicorn Chemicals was never mentioned. She presumed that they were confidential matters. And she now realized that's how they should be viewed and treated. Professionally at least she was growing up fast.

At eight o'clock precisely a hand-bell rang and the crowd, still milling about, moved collectively in the general direction of the dining room. It was time for dinner and the after-dinner speeches. Allison doubted if Pam would hear them when they came.

One of the top table speakers was Doctor Bennet. Allison had actually helped him prepare one or two sections of his speech and she fondly anticipated hearing herself quoted from the floor.

She sat down at a table with John and Pam and a few other people she didn't know. Introductions were soon made, however, and they began to chat amongst themselves as the waiters and waitresses went about their business efficiently, pouring wine and serving food.

Within a very short period of time Allison was completely relaxed and she sat back in her seat laughing at some very witty remark John had made to a colored delegate from South Africa, a country where porphyria was relatively common, though relatively unnoticed with that countries current problems. They had more on their collective minds there at present than an exotic blood disease. The delegate had responded in turn to John, thus the spreading amusement.

As she sat back with her hand to her mouth, Allison looked around at the crowd. It was good, this was the sort of life she wanted, this was what she had worked towards and would continue to work towards. Her eyes took in the people around her. All shapes and sizes, all animated, talking, buzzing with excitement. Suddenly she froze in her seat and waves of a different excitement flowed over her. A few yards from her, sipping from a glass of wine and looking very tired and pale indeed, was Harry Wright. He'd just arrived from London a day late.

It was approaching ten thirty in the evening when the three collaborators met together in the hotel suite. John Bennet took control of the proceedings from the clinical aspect, the Unicorn representative from the commercial one.

They were speaking to Annette Pallain, a lay member of the American equivalent of the British Medicine's Commission and the Committee on the Safety of Medicines - the Food and Drug Administration; The F.D.A.

Both doctors knew that Annette was an influential figure with excellent political connections. They knew that these were not for herself but for her sister whom she believed could become the first elected female president of the United States. She genuinely believed that her sister was an up-market version of the now aging Hiliary Clinton; with that ladies' formidable intellectual and oratorical talents and political achievements.

They recalled that Rosemary Pallain had the fading but still striking looks of Fawn Summers; the electrifying P.A. of Governor Oliver North; apparently Doctor Pallain's idea of the supreme patriot. It was a stunning combination.

It was for this very reason, Rosemary, that Annette was here and speaking to Bennet, Raynor and the representative of Unicorn Chemicals. She needed little convincing as to the clinical efficacy of Oviron, the envelope with the new subscription to her sister's putative election campaign assisted that.

But important ass he was, Annette Pallain was not sufficiently important in and of herself, to dictate the policy decisions of the F.D.A. Its infrastructure was too complex for that, no one individual could call the shots there. It required someone and something else. Something also relating to the highest office in the land. It required an approach, appropriately made, to the Office of the President of the United States himself.

Annette knew that the President's advisor on the F.D.A.chaired or was otherwise involved in a number of committees with a strong bias towards the health problem and the relatively new Medicare programme - a potent electoral issue given the shortcomings of the second stage of the revisionist view of the US health care system presently under way.

She knew, too that the North American Market for pharmaceuticals was massive; being second only to Japan with respect to the per capita expenditure on drugs. This was around the two hundred dollars per annum mark. 'A lot of lettuce.' as Art would have said. Annette also knew that this same advisor - pretty Evie Elliott -had a fascination approaching on the obsessional with European Royalty.

In fact Annette knew Evie Elliott fairly well, she'd met her at a few of the lesser Embassy "do's" in Washington and attempted to befriend her. Despite her attitude problem, Elliott was an attractive, clever woman with a penchant for american history. She'd recently asked Annette if she knew what significance the old movie "The King and I" may have had to the Vice President's recent visit to London where he had met some royalty.

Having no idea, Annette had ingeniously suggested that perhaps "The youngest brother" - as she termed the third son who was in the movie business - might have wanted an American copy or something. For some reason, Evie Elliott had looked flustered at that.

Anyway, for whatever reasons; Miss Elliott carried a lot of clout with the President and therefore indirectly, with the F.D.A. A formal visit for her to Buckingham Palace would be like the popular acceptance of "Creationism" to Christian Fundamentalists. It would please her immensely. And while the latter couldn't be easily arranged. The former could. Through contacts of Bennet, Raynor and the Unicorn executive.

With these things tumbling through her mind, Annette gratefully accepted another glass of orange juice and listened to what was being discussed. It was important. It could make her sister President. And Queen of North America.

A few hours later Allison walked across to a table in the bar where Harry was sitting alone teasing a glass of beer. She had told Pam and John that she wanted the opportunity to have a quick word with him, to introduce herself. Pam had offered to make the introduction, but Allison had declined her offer saying she didn't mind doing it herself.

Pam, still surprisingly sober and John had apparently gone off into the town with a group of the other delegates to visit some night-club or other. Allison approached this hauntingly attractive man wondering what she was going to say right up until the time she said it.

'Hello,' she said. 'You probably don't remember me. Allison Young. I work at The London General. I know your sister, Jennifer. We met briefly a couple of months ago at the hospital.'

Harry looked up at her his pale blue eyes penetrating her own and showing themselves tired and dissipated:

'Why, yes, I do remember,' he replied. 'You asked me if I was unwell or something. "Peakish", I think you said.' Surprising her with his powers of memory and observation. He stood up. 'Please sit down,' he smiled weakly. 'Can I get you something to drink?'

'A glass of white wine would be lovely, please,' said Allison; and Harry immediately set off to the bar. He brought her drink back, placed it on the table and sat down again.

'So what do you do at The London?' he enquired, making good eye contact, but looking tired, very, very tired.

'I'm a Junior Registrar, Hematology,' replied Allison. 'I'm working with Doctor Bennet, researching porphyria.'

'Enjoy it?' Harry asked her absently, still toying with his glass and obviously a bit at unease. 'John Bennet's a good man to work with, you'll learn a lot.'

'I enjoy it very much,' Allison replied. 'Medicine's what I always wanted to do,' She paused. 'Now I'm doing it.' She paused again, gauged him. 'I've attended to Tina,' she said quietly.

Immediately Harry's attention was all on her, his face a mask of concern and bewilderment. 'Tina?' he repeated. 'You've attended Tina? I never knew that!'

'Only in a limited way,' admitted Allison reassuringly, 'I've carried out her preliminary screens.'

'And? What's your prognosis, Doctor? The same as the rest?'

'She's very ill,' Allison replied sincerely; 'You know that.'

'Of course I do,' he said flatly; 'That's why I'm here. There are one or two papers which looked to be of potential interest with respect to Tina's illness and I was hoping to get the opportunity to discuss matters with the authors.'

'Have you managed to do so?'

'Oh, with one or two of them. I'd already contacted them, before the meeting,' said Harry, 'But there have been no dramatic discoveries, no sudden breakthroughs I was unaware of. There are one or two leads, one or two suggestions of things which might lead somewhere, sometime, but nothing substantial.

'It's very frustrating indeed to find that people are digging around in areas which could produce sudden and dramatic results in this area, but not knowing if and when they will do so. I've attended various meetings since Tina became ill - medical, bio-tech, surgical, even holistic medicine. All with the same outcome. Zilch!'

He paused for a few moments, collecting his thoughts, sifting them, changing their direction. He gave Allison a fine direct look, his blue eyes shining at her, covering her with a controlled affection: 'Anyway, enough of that,' he said,

'What are you doing here, Allison Young? Are you giving a paper on something spectacular, or are you just here for a bit of academic voyeurism?'

'A bit of both,' replied Allison smiling; 'Though I'm hardly doing anything 'spectacular'. I've already given my paper - on acute intermittent porphyria - and it seemed to go down fairly well. So now it's down to total academic voyeurism. Perhaps you could direct me as to what to look for in that way?'

Harry gave her a warm, embracing smile and looked over her face anew. He had relaxed a bit now and his good looks and fine features were more prominent. He tugged at his chin thoughtfully with his hand and gave a slight pensive frown:

'You said that you knew Jennifer,' he said.

'Yes, we get on well together. She's a treasure.'

'She certainly is,' agreed her brother. 'I don't know how I'd get by at times without her. She's solid. Always there when needed. Dependable.'

'I'm sure she is,' commented Alison. 'She does worry a lot about you, you know. I imagine that you must be very close to each other.'

'We are,' said Harry. 'I don't know if Jennifer mentioned it,' he went on quietly as his eyes searched Allison's face almost seeking assurance. 'but my wife was killed in a car crash and -'

'- I know,' said Allison.

'Well, after that Jennifer was solid. Then, well … when Tina took ill...'

'I know that, too,' Allison interrupted gently.

'You seem to know a lot Allison Young,' said Harry, still scanning her face, looking very vulnerable.

'I suppose I do,' Allison responded gently. 'Jennifer talks about her family often. We've become good friends. She really does care for you both.'

'I often wonder if I'm indulging in self-pity,' Harry said, opening further; 'Instead of just getting on with things … do you think I am?'

'No,' said Allison with certainty; 'You're consumed with grief and loss. It will take a long time for you to get over it. Lots of time. You're not wallowing in any self-pity; you seem to be fighting very hard for your daughter's life and not sparing yourself as you do so.'

He held her eyes with his and she could sense the emotions tumbling around inside him. Somehow she sensed just how special he was. 'You're quite a special lady,' he said softly. Allison flushed.

'Not that special,' she replied. quietly; 'Just concerned; particularly about a favorite young patient of mine.'

Harry searched her face again, smiled more warmly; 'Have another drink,' he said . Allison did.

The conspirators spoke for almost two hours. There were no real problems, at least as far as what they could acceptably achieve themselves was concerned. Annette Pallain would gather support for Oviron amongst those of her colleagues on the commission whom she could influence, directly or indirectly; and she would arrange for the F.D.A. to agree a clinical trial on the drug in Streptococcal skin and throat infections. Quickly.

This latter would be done as a supplement to the volunteer study she had already arranged on Federal Prisoners, with only one fatality, and that had been due to asphyxiation caused by a convulsion in a man who had presumably been epileptic. A life-term murderer, no-one had bothered a great deal about that one.

It had been the gifted Doctor Pallain, too, who had statistically analyzed the first extended tests of Oviron in humans, those which had been carried out by Doctor Chung Lo in an orphanage in Seoul, Korea. The children, each of whom had been credited with ten- dollars a head for the privilege of receiving the drug, had developed no distressing symptoms with the dose of drug administered to them. The odd unpleasant effect yes, the odd adverse transient reaction - but no permanent trauma, not yet anyway.

The only question unanswered was how viable it was to arrange a visit for Evie Elliott to the Palace at very short notice:

'No problem whatsoever,' said the representative from Unicorn, looking very serious and animated. 'Sir William Mostyn can arrange it, without any trouble. He has good contacts. He has a hook in the Prince's Private Secretary and, in a sense almost literally, in the Prince himself.' He didn't elaborate. There was no need to.

'Just tell us when you want it done and we'll do it,' continued the man from Unicorn confidently.

'I'll let you know,' said Pallain yawning slightly. 'Let's call it a night, folks. I have to phone home. My sister's waiting for a call and my brother-in-law won't get his bottle of Bourbon until it arrives.'

'Let's do that,' said John Raynor, as he looked at his namesake and colleague John Bennet and gave a short, conspiratorial smile. It was not returned. The executive from Unicorn kissed Annette Pallain "good-night" with platonic formality.

The afternoon of the third day of the conference was free and Harry had asked Allison to join him in a "surprise trip." She had agreed immediately and had found herself sitting in the foyer of her hotel ten minutes before the agreed time. She had no idea at all where they were going and the prospect delighted her.

She hoped however that perhaps they were going to the incongruously named Spanish Riding School; one of the most famous in the world and based in Vienna itself. Ever since she had begun riding as a young girl Allison had wanted to see the School and the allegedly marvellous horses they trained there for competition.

Although she had never taken part in dressage, she was enchanted by it and hoped that perhaps she would get the chance now to see some of the best instructors in the world as they trained some of the best horses to excel at that most precise and demanding of the equestrian arts.

She had arranged to meet Harry in the foyer of her hotel and before doing so Allison took great time and care over her appearance. After she had spent a long time in a very hot shower, she bundled her hair into a towel and set about making herself presentable.

By the time she had finished putting on her few traces of cosmetics, drying and grooming her hair and spraying herself with the expensive cologne she had bought from the Duty Free shop in London Heathrow; Allison felt that it was going to be a very fine day indeed.

Her wardrobe was restricted by what had gone into her suitcase; so she chose a deep blue cotton dress, a pair of short-heeled matching shoes and a lightweight red jacket which set off the blue perfectly. She pinned a silver Gallic brooch onto her jacket lapel and, almost forgetting to do so, she hung a fine gold chain around her neck and clipped it into place.

She looked in the mirror. The effect was stunning and she felt happy with it. She looked anxiously at her watch. It was a bit early yet but she felt she would make her way downstairs anyway.

She hadn't felt up to any breakfast at all not even a coffee and smiled when she realized that this was because she felt nervous. She lifted her carrier-bag, opened the door, had a last brief look around her room and stepped into the hotel corridor closing the door behind her.

Five minutes before their scheduled meeting time, Harry appeared in the foyer and looked around for her. He was dressed in an immaculate tan suit, brown soft leather shoes and a matching off-tan shirt and brown tie. His explorative fair hair flopped over his brow and he pushed it back time after time as his eyes sought Allison out. When they found her, a bright genuine smile lit up his face:

'Hi,' he cried, looking fresher than she'd seen him. 'Ready?'

'Why, yes,' responded Allison rising, 'Quite ready.' She rose and walked towards him. Unselfconsciously and perfectly naturally; he took her arm in his. He guided her to the waiting cab.

'Berggasse 19,' he instructed the driver. Allison realized immediately where they were going. It certainly wasn't the Riding School, but, if anything, the prospect thrilled her even more.

They drove for some time in a comfortable silence interspersed with casual chat. Then quite suddenly Harry turned to her

'Interested in psychology?' he asked.

'I am in Freud,' she said, with a grin.

'What do you know about Sigmund Freud?' he asked, incredulously.

'Oh, not a lot,' Allison replied, speaking with humorous irony. 'Just that he was an eminent and revolutionary psychologist who developed some very radical ideas about mental illness and its relationship to experiences in early childhood.

'He was something of a genius, I'm told, but I don't think that most people give him a lot of credibility these days, do they? His father's birthday fell on the same day as Bismarck's you know,' and Bismarck had porphyria!'

'You do know your stuff!' exclaimed Harry; 'I hope you're not going to tell me that Sigmund perished from porphyria in some Viennese asylum. It may explain many things...'

Allison smiled; 'No, he didn't have porphyria, which is just as well. And he died in London, if I remember correctly, but he lived almost all his life in Vienna. At Berggasse 19!'

'Yes,' Harry said, suitably surprised at Allison's knowledge as the taxi slowed down. 'Quite right, Herr Doctor Young - if you'll forgive the pun - that's where he lived.' Harry pointed to a terraced building as the taxi slowed to a halt. 'Berggasse 19. The place where one of the greatest minds of the 20th Century grappled with the problems of the mind and its illnesses. But I suppose you know all that!' he said to her, smiling.

'Yes, I do, but you know, just to look at it gives me a sense of something special. As you say, many people are less than keen on Freud and his theories now, though that's nothing new as they were always contentious.

'Even so, they revolutionized many things - the arts, social science, medicine itself, in many ways. And all of that revolutionary work was carried out here. As I say, it's something special. Thanks for bringing me.'

'He lived here almost all of his life, as you know,' Harry said. 'From 1891 to 1938 to be precise, the year before his death.'

'You seem to be just as well informed about him,' said Allison, impressed, in turn, by his knowledge.

'An interest of mine from way back,' replied Harry. 'Way, way back. I once thought on doing psychiatry myself, but opted for the safer pastures of general medicine. Psychiatric practice itself never appealed much to me. Still, my interest in Freud has always remained.'

'Great minds,' said Allison, cryptically, as Harry paid the cab driver and made his way towards the entrance to the building, now a complex of offices and apartments including the one that had been occupied for so many years by Sigmund Freud and his extended family.

Heading in through the door in front of the arched entrance, Harry beckoned to a flight of stairs bearing to his left. He indicated to Allison to climb them with him.

'An historical visit,' he said quietly as, together, they both walked up the stairs.

Allison was very impressed indeed by Harry's almost encyclopedic knowledge of Freud and his life and his work. Though she knew almost all of it herself, mainly from her father, he made it all seem so interesting and alive and he told her a few things which she'd never have dreamt of in relation to this very great man.

She discovered, for example, that, not unlike herself, he had specialised in anatomy and pathology - the study of cells - and that he had made important discoveries in these and in other medical areas. He had also discovered the anesthetic qualities of the drug cocaine and was indirectly responsible for its introduction into common medical practice as a local anesthetic.

Fact after fact poured from Harry and Allison was enthraled. This was as much by his enthusiasm as it was by the content of what he said, interesting as that was. She found herself from time to time, watching him as he spoke, absorbing him into her as he discussed some point or other with a seriousness and vigor which surprised and delighted her.

'I have an excellent new book on Freud which I've brought to Vienna with me if your interested,' Harry said. 'It's called *The Burglar of Bergasse*. It's a fascinating work. You can borrow it if you want. I'm sure you'd enjoy it.'

'I might just do that,' responded Allison with superior and ulterior motives; 'That might be interesting.'

When their visit was over she found herself back in a cab, with Harry still chatting away beside her. He had forgotten his troubles for a time and this pleased her greatly. She wanted to encourage him to talk, to keep his mind flowing away from his recent tragedies.

'And why did Freud come to London so late in life?' she asked him.

'He was a refugee as a consequence of the rise of National Socialism in Germany. He was brought there by Princess Marie Bonaparte. Now there's one aristocrat who probably had no risk of having porphyria. Am I right?'

'I've no idea,' laughed Allison. 'So you know that porphyria has been common in the European royal family - whatever next! What don't you know, Doctor Wright!' Harry flushed a little, warming Allison as much as himself.

'Anyway,' Allison continued. 'So, Freud lived all his life here and just a year before it ended he had to move all the way to London. That's sad,' she said; 'The move probably killed him.'

'No it didn't,' said Harry, becoming less animated, more withdrawn.

'What didn't?' enquired Allison; losing the thread a bit.

'The move. It wasn't the move to London which killed Freud,' Harry said softly.

'What was it, then?' Allison asked.

'A tumor,' he said quietly, 'A very nasty tumor.'

John Bennet used the international telephone in the hotel lobby and put a call through to London. Within seconds he was speaking to Sir William Mostyn:

'They want you to arrange the visit, Bill. This woman, Rosemary Pallain, carries a great deal of weight with the F.D.A. and Raynor believes that with appropriate overtures coming from within the Oval Office that Oviron will become the drug of the century if not the millennium.

'Having said that, I can't say I like all of this,' continued Bennet; 'It's a bit too much, more than I'd anticipated.'

'No-one asked you to like it John,' said Sir William in a clear, drug-free voice. 'Simply do it! You've got your money. You could be the superintendent of the most famous hospital in Europe. You could cure those unfortunate thousands you're always talking about. So, you don't have to "like" anything. You'll get your reward in heaven.

'I'll call the Private Secretary now and arrange a meeting. You can take it from me that a State Visit will be offered to that rather unfortunate Ms Elliott. We might even give her her own little crown and make her an honorary Duchess.' It was as close as Mostyn came to humor.

With that the phone went dead and Bennet turned away looking visibly upset. Things were well out of his hands now. He noticed that John Raynor was standing in the lobby waiting on him; "Watching" Bennet thought briefly:

'O.K.?' asked Raynor simply.

'Fine,' replied Doctor John Edward Bennet F.R.C.P.

They had dinner that evening at a restaurant within easy walking distance of their respective hotels. Harry made every effort to keep things cheerful, but it was evident that he was preoccupied again with thoughts of Tina. Allison fiercely wished that she could do something to ease his preoccupation, but she had no idea what.

She made as much conversation as she could and Harry responded in turn. They were not strained with each other at all, simply not flowing together as Allison felt they could be under different circumstances.

In an attempt to draw him out of himself again, she asked Harry about his interests, his hobbies and his practice. It was this latter which elicited the response from him, but it was the wrong sort of response. It seemed that he was very concerned indeed about it.

'It was all going so well,' he explained. 'I was very close to finding the ideal compromise between the private and public sectors. I really had things running well. I imagine my way of doing things was different, not entirely the conventional way, either medically or administratively, but it was working very well indeed and then... well, then the accident happened and Tina... 'He opened his hands out in a gesture pretty close to defeat and Allison felt his pain physically within her.

'Surely you'll be able to piece it all together again,' encouraged Allison; 'In a month or so's time, with a break perhaps and a little help, you'll get it back to what it was.'

'I hope so,' Harry said skeptically. 'But there's so much ground been lost. I really was on to a precise and fair compromise between these two diverse sectors in our society. The experiment was working... but it had to be kept turning over and I haven't managed to do that.'

'You'll do it,' reassured Allison. Some patients will have to go elsewhere. You'll get them back.' Harry responded.

'The books are in a mess...'

'You'll get them in order.'

Harry lifted his eyes to hers. They were blue, pale, deep and pain-filled, but they shone with determination and, Allison saw, affection in there for her. 'You're quite an optimist, Doctor Young.'

'I am,' replied Allison. 'That I am. I imagine that you're one yourself, when you take the time to think about it.' He reached over and held the tips of her fingers in his own. Waves of a breathless excitement flooded over her just as suddenly as a gust of wind in summer.

'And quite a woman,' he finished. A silence fell around them. Quiet, waiting for something to happen. At length Allison removed her hand from his and took a sip of her wine:

'The book,' she said suddenly, *The Burglar of Bergasse*, the new book about Freud. You promised you'd lend it to me. I'd really like to read it.'

'It's in my room,' Harry. said, more animated now. 'Shall I drop it over to you tomorrow or shall we go up to my hotel and get it after this?' Allison mused for a very brief moment.

'We'll go up and get it,' she said, her eyes sparkling light and her cheeks flushed with color. 'If that's O.K. that is, if you don't mind...'

'Fine,' said Harry, musing again on the menu, losing himself in it. 'What would you like for dessert? They do a lovely chocolate mousse here. Terrible on calories, but marvelous on the taste buds.' He was beginning to cheer up a bit again and Allison encouraged him.

'I think we can forget the calories this evening,' she smiled. 'Chocolate mousse it is.'

'Two chocolate mice then,' he said, flippantly. She laughed. Their eyes met briefly and held contact for a few stretching moments. Something special passed between them and part of it remained with Allison, almost hurting her. Making her wonder what this man meant to her and almost certainly knowing after such a very brief time.

They finished dinner with an excellent glass of brandy for Harry and a delicious local liqueur for Allison which they took with their coffee. Harry called the waiter and paid the bill and very soon they were out in the street and walking towards Harry's hotel. As they did so, Allison gently took his hand and he held her's as if it belonged there.

When John Raynor returned to his room it was well past midnight. He had spent a half-hour or so talking to Bennet in the bar, reassuring him, convincing him that what they were about to do was at least perfectly ethical if not to the letter of the Law.

As usual his "For the greater good" argument seemed to sway Bennet who was beginning to look like being the weak link in the chain. John Raynor hoped that he wouldn't do anything silly.

"Oviron would be for the greater good," he thought as he lifted the hotel telephone and put a call through to his stockbroker in London. The broker wouldn't mind the time - not with this sort of call.

John Raynor undressed and prepared for bed. When he was well settled, he lay down, switched off the lights and settled down for a good night's sleep. His thoughts tumbled about for a time, but they focused on one thing and it made him feel good.

"Yes, Oviron would be for the greater good. But it could be for the individual good, too. After all, what was the 'greater' but a large collection of individuals."

Allison and Harry walked along the thickly carpeted corridor of the hotel towards Harry's room. Allison's heart was pounding, her legs felt weak. "Worse than before the presentation," she thought to herself, uncertain of what she was doing, what would happen in. What she wanted to happen.

In no time at all they reached the door and he fumbled with his key inserted it into the lock and pushed the door open. He stood back to allow Allison to enter first, switching on the light as she did so. She looked around. It was a pleasant room; single, with toilet and shower *en suite,* a small bar, a television and a dressing table, two cupboards and a bedside cabinet with a lamp on it. There was also a solitary chair by the far wall and Allison walked over to it and sat down.

'Would you like a drink?' asked Harry. Allison considered him carefully, looked at him, his tired face, his haunted eyes, his new-found levity spilling through these.

'Just one. A small brandy, please,' she said and Harry moved to the drinks cabinet to get one out for her. He poured it carefully into a glass and handed it to her. She noticed that his hands were trembling slightly. "Tired," she thought; "The poor man must be exhausted."

He poured a glass of wine for himself and sitting on the edge of the bed he lifted his glass and said: 'Here's to Viennese mice!' He sipped at his wine and then placing it on the floor he leaned over to the bedside cabinet. After moving things around on it he retrieved a book from a bundle of papers within it. He handed the book to Allison:

'*The Burglar of Bergasse,*' he said. 'An interesting work that should dispel a few myths about Freud and create some new ones.'

Allison looked at the cover, at the blurb on the back, flicked through the pages. It was the author's name that caused her to exclaim: 'Good God, Harry,' she uttered in complete surprise and delight; 'You wrote it!'

'Afraid so,' he smiled almost sheepishly; 'You know, Allison, I wrote that two years ago, it's only recently been published. You're the first person I've shown a copy to. Thanks.'

'It looks interesting,' Allison replied warmly; 'Very interesting. I'll enjoy this. Doubly.'

'Hope you do,' Harry responded still sipping slowly at his wine.

They sipped at their drinks in silence until at last Allison rose and said she'd have to go back to her hotel. Inside she was in chaos and wished with all her might that Harry might just suggest otherwise.

He rose from the bed and walked over towards her. Allison was almost visibly shaking, waiting for him to take her hand again, hold her close, kiss her, love her... .

Suddenly there was a crashing sound and they both looked over in the direction of the bedside cabinet. The bed had moved when Harry had stood up from it and it had knocked over a photo-frame which had been standing on the cabinet top.

Reflexly Allison moved to pick it up and as she did so she turned it in her hands to look at it. It was a picture of one of the most beautiful women she had ever seen. A pain shot through her, a fierce, hot jealousy.

'Your wife?' she asked Harry quietly.

Yes. My late wife,' he replied.

'She's beautiful,' Allison said almost dumbly.

'Yes, she was beautiful, Allison, very beautiful indeed.' He turned away and poured himself another glass of wine.

Allison stood her ground for a few seconds, stunned, photograph in hand, wondering what to do.

'I'd best be getting along,' she said.

'Must you?' Harry asked, a distance in his voice now.

'Yes, I must.'

'Let me call you a cab, then.'

'No, it's all right. I'll get one at the door. The porter will see to it. Good night, Harry. Sleep well,' said Allison as, picking up her bag and the book he'd lent her, she made for the door.

'You too,' replied Harry, walking to the door with her. 'I've enjoyed myself today, Allison. Thanks.' He spoke awkwardly, as if he wanted to say more, but Allison was confused and in a rush to get out of the room and into the freedom of the air outside the hotel.

'So have I,' she said quickly. 'Very much indeed.' She rushed out of the room, went along the corridor to the lift and pressed the call button time after time after time. Tears of frustration filled her eyes, hurting them, hurting her. The image of the woman's face was burning in her mind as were Harry's words:

"Yes, she was beautiful, Allison, very beautiful indeed"

The lift arrived and the door opened with a ping. It was empty and she stepped inside. The doors closed and she descended, back to the ground, back to earth.

Allison walked quickly across the reception hall, out of the doors and into a waiting cab. She gave the driver the name of her hotel. As he drove off through the now dark streets of the city, the woman's face haunted her. How beautiful she was, how much Harry must have loved her. Allison caught her reflection in the window of the car. Pleasant enough, yes, even pretty. But no beauty. Ken used to tell her that, that he loved her because she wasn't classically beautiful. She was a good-looking woman. But she was no competition physically for what Harry had lost and still grieved over.

As the car drove through the city, moving slowly towards its destination Allison discovered that she had learnt a number of things today. The most important of these was how much she cared for Harry Wright and how difficult it would be to see that care achieve its desired fruition. Despite herself however, she knew that she usually got what she wanted and she wanted Harry Wright.

The night was dark around her, the shadows deep, as she returned to her hotel. And the moon shone soft within them.

CHAPTER NINE

The conference ended without Allison seeing Harry again. He was not evident at any of the remaining sessions or functions and he neither called nor left any message for her at her hotel. This hurt her deeply and consequently she found her attention wandering at the remainder of the sessions she attended. There seemed little that she could do to prevent this no matter who was speaking, how eminent they were, or how interesting the subject they were discussing was. One moment her mind was on some aspect of medical science and the next on Harry.

That she had become so wholly involved with him so soon amazed her, yet when she thought on it she understood why. It was simple. She had never met anyone like him. He was strong yet vulnerable, enthusiastic yet dispirited, idealistic yet practical to the point of desperation, particularly where it concerned his daughter. His attendance at the conference demonstrated this more than anything could. He was seeking out help at the highest level and rummaging among as yet unpublished medical work to seek help for her. It was a pity that he didn't seem to be finding it and that he didn't have more help for himself.

It was a pity, too, Allison mused, that he had not yet managed to get over the death of his wife. What did she expect however? The man had loved his wife deeply and you couldn't just switch something like that off as if it had never been there. What depressed Allison more than anything, though, was her belief that he would never get over it. And even if he did, well, Allison Young was hardly in the same league as his wife had been. That was more than evident. Almost uncannily she had total recall of Pam's words.

Both Pam and the very much more contented John Raynor noticed that Allison was more than a little subdued for the remainder of the meeting though neither of them had commented on the fact. Pam thought that it was related to the fact that Alliosn had been out with Harry and observed that it had been after this that the change in Allison had become evident. All considered, Raynor felt that it was not for him to pass any comment on Alliosn's preoccupations though he wondred whast they were precisely - at least not quite yet. For her part, Pam felt that any comment she would make could wait for a more appropriate time and place.

On the trip back to London on the plane Allison spoke very little. The flight was smooth and pleasant and they were served with an excellent meal and some excellent wine. There were a large number of conference delegates on the flight and there was almost a party atmosphere amongst them. Despite this Allison kept herself to herself and simply stared out of the window for most of the journey, reflecting on the scenery below and on her deepest thoughts.

When they arrived back at Heathrow they collected their baggage, passed through customs and went in search of a cab to take them into central London, all in a fairly muted way.

Pam noticed that as Alliosn went through all of these procedures she kept scanning the crowds around her. "Looking for Harry" she thought to herself. She was saddened to see her colleague like this and while she didn't know what had happened to make her this way, she determined at the appropriate time to find out.

On her first evening back at the flat after the trip Allison felt particularly alone and despondent. It did seem such an empty place and so isolated when there was no-one else to talk to and share things with. The conference, her paper, Vienna, Harry. She proceeded to unpack and get her things in order, looking through the many papers and pieces of paper and notes which she had brought back with her, trying to condense them into some sort of order.

When she had finished doing this she seriously considered giving Harry a call. She weighed the pros and cons of doing so for a very long time. Sometimes she even lifted the phone and put it down again. She ultimately decided not to call however. He knew her number and she felt that it should be his decision and not hers to make contact again if he wanted to.

She went to bed in a quiet and almost melancholic mood; and she lay awake for a very long time going through the events of the past few days. Images flowed over her of the conference hall, various delegates, the dinner and of Harry sitting alone sipping at his drink as she approached him. As sleep gradually descended over her, her very last conscious thought was of Harry sitting with her at dinner in the restaurant and of chocolate mice.

Allison returned to the routine of hospital work and to a number of letters praising her highly for the paper she had given at the conference and requesting further details of her work. There was also a letter from the editor of a learned journal asking her if she would be interested in writing a full paper on her work for publication. This was something which pleased Allison enormously. She sought Doctor Bennet's permission to do this and was duly given it. She set about writing the paper and between that and her other duties, she managed to keep her mind off Harry -at least for most of the time.

By now Tina had been transferred to another ward. She was still very ill indeed and no-one could really see much hope for the child. She was still receiving chemotherapy, but the dosage had been decreased as her condition had become progressively fragile.

Allison visited her as frequently as she could and each time she did so she felt a wave of anticipation flow through her at the prospect of the possibility of her running into Harry. As she visited outwith usual visiting times however, she thought it unlikely that they would meet.

From Jennifer, Allison learned that Harry had come back from the conference early and was working all sorts of hours in an attempt to keep his practice going and his patients well. He had made no mention to Jennifer that he had met Allison at the meeting, an omission which for fairly obvious reasons hurt Allison deeply. On her behalf, Allison volunteered to Jennifer that she'd met up with her brother at the meeting and had a drink with him; but she didn't elaborate. His sister seemed pleased at this and asked if they had made any plans to meet up again after they got back.

'Why, no,' said Allison. 'No, we didn't. That would be nice though.' She hoped that Jennifer didn't notice the fact that the question had caught her quite off balance.

'Pity,' said Jennifer reflectively; 'It would have done him the world of good. I keep telling him he should go out more often, keep his mind off things. You'd have been particularly good company for him too.'

'Why do you say that?' asked Allison.

'Well, it's been a good time now since Ann died and it's about time Harry sought out some more company - intelligent female company, like yourself.

'I know it's very difficult for him - especially with Tina and all, but he was such a mixer before, so enthusiastic about all sorts of things, medical and non-medical. You know, Allison, before all this happened his interests ranged from skiing, to sailing, to literature, to...'

'Freud,' interjected Allison.

'Why, yes,' responded Jennifer, looking at her with a bemused smile. 'How did you know that?'

'He told me,' responded Allison; 'He mentioned it in Vienna.'

'Well I never!' Jennifer continued; 'He's been so reticent recently, he hasn't spoken about much to anyone, let alone of his past interests. You must have made quite an impression on him. Did you?'

'I don't think so, Jen'.

'Why do you say that?'

'Simply because I don't think that I did.'

Jennifer looked at her carefully, gauged her expression, the tone of her voice...

'Mmm...' was all that emerged as she eyed Allison with a revised look. 'Perhaps you did, Allison,' she said cryptically. 'Perhaps you really did. I certainly hope so. Nothing would give me greater pleasure.'

At that she walked away leaving Allison wondering just what precisely Jennifer had meant.

The next few days flew by with Allison working very hard indeed attending patients, meetings, seminars and the rest of her duties. She worked herself as hard as she ever had and in doing so kept her mind occupied solely with medical matters. Jennifer had not spoken to her about Harry again and as yet Pam hadn't even broached the subject, knowing intuitively and by observation that Allison was very raw about it. Not to worry, she'd soon be off to the States and Japan. She wouldn't have time to think about it then.

When it began to leak to the media that Oviron could reduce body weight irrespective of any dietary restrictions they began to have a field day. The poorer quality newspapers had a number of misinformed and frankly ridiculous feature articles and headlines all on the theme that no one need ever be overweight again. Ridiculous as the features and inch-high headlines were however, they were essentially correct.

Even the more conservative broadsheets were very positive in response to their assessment of this aspect of the drug's action and it was difficult not to be sensationalistic about it. The Daily Independent, for example, carried the following article by their senior medical correspondent:

"Oviron: Could It Abolish Obesity"

"Oviron, a drug bio-engineered from transgenic cattle, was originally considered to be another unremarkable antibiotic. It is now potentially the wonder drug of the decade. Developed and marketed by the U.K.-based pharmaceutical multi-national Unicorn Chemicals Ltd for the treatment of bacterial infections, sources have informed us that it is likely to be effective too in the Royal Disease - acute intermittent porphyria. This has caused something of a sensation in medical circles as indeed has the claim that the drug is the means to 'an end to dieting forever.'

"It has been discovered that the drug has what scientists call beta-3 agonist activity, with a highly specific lipolytic - or fat breaking - action on brown fat-producing cells. This leads to a reduction in fatty tissue irrespective of what weight or what sort of diet a person is on.

"In theory, it is possible that you could take this drug and eat as much of whatever you want and still maintain your ideal weight. You could - again theoretically - reach this weight even if you were significantly overweight without any dietary restriction whatsoever.

"Oviron has been deemed a miracle drug by some, and one eminent nutritionist Doctor Richard Owen of the University of New Mexico has said:

"'With the discovery of this drug we have revolutionized nutrition overnight. If I had the authority to do so I would prescribe it for every single member of the human race including the malnourished and starving who could benefit from it as well.'

"Doctor Owen's rationale for the latter comment apparently relates to the fact that the drug makes energy utilization more efficient by in some way re-setting the energy 'thermostat' in our brains and it is also said to reduce the sensation of hunger in us.

"A senior spokesman from Unicorn Chemicals declined to comment at any length on this aspect of the drug's activity simply stating that while the company had applied for a Product License for use of the drug in this indication; as far as they were concerned Oviron was primarily used for and would continue to be used for specific bacterial (streptococcal) infections which were resistant to other anti-biotics.

"He also stressed that profit motive alone was not the major one behind Unicorn's success. The company's record demonstrated that its ethos was to work for the good of mankind not just to generate profits. If the indication [in obesity] was granted (and informed sources have suggested that it will be) by the appropriate government regulatory bodies; then, the spokesman said, Unicorn would think very carefully as to the best way to proceed with marketing the drug in this 'sensitive' indication. The company didn't want to create a populace of people taking pills instead of being sensible about eating.

"When questioned about the alleged efficacy of the drug in the disease which has debilitated at least two British monarchs - Charles the Second and George the Third, he declined to comment. An eminent haemotologist whom we contacted in London today however, while requesting anonymity; intimated that this aspect of the drug's profile would be of interest to the people who suffered from this rare but traumatic disease.

"When asked if this disease was evident in any of the current Royal Family he again declined to comment. This has fuelled speculation in the Tabloid press and we believe a statement from the Palace is immanent."

Greg Hoffmann read the copy very carefully. It pleased him the way a well- orchestrated piece of verse pleased its composer. It pleased him because it was effective and credible. And he had written it. He had also written the advertising copy for Oviron which, already printed, sat in one of Unicorn's offices sealed and secure awaiting distribution.

Andrew Wills Marketing Manager of Unicorn Chemicals, was less reserved in his comments on Oviron in obesity. He had called a special meeting of the senior international sales managers of his company; those immediately responsible to the Regional Managers who'd already been put in the picture with respect to Oviron by Hoffmann and Wilder. He spoke to them with the fervour he could always muster for such occasions:

'What does this drug mean for us ladies and gentlemen? What does it mean for Unicorn, for you, for me, for our husbands and wives, our sons and daughters, our extended families, our friends, our colleagues and the whole human race?

'I will tell you. I will tell you precisely what it means for every single human being on this planet. But first allow me to tell you what it means for you and for your loved ones, those nearest and dearest to you.

'For you, ladies and gentlemen and for those you love, it means in a word, security.

'Unicorn Chemicals as you all know, has struggled by for years on a handful of products of which only one or two are still within patent. We were obliged to invest hundreds of millions in biotechnology which to date has given us nothing substantial to sell. To be blunt this has meant that we've been walking a knife-edge economically. Our financial colleagues have been losing their hair in handfuls, the books have been balancing but the scales have been tipping; tipping so far that one day they might just tip over and tip all of you and your families over with them.'

The audience were captivated. After all, it was their livelihoods at stake; their material success in life was linked intimately to what this man was saying.

'Not any longer,' Wills continued; 'Now we are secure, will be, all of us, for the rest of our lives.

'So why is this? Why has Oviron done this for us? There is only one reason ladies and gentlemen - one single, solitary, reason. Greed! Base, human greed and its indulgence without due consideration as to its outcome in terms of cosmetic unsightliness or the threat of ill-health.'

There was a general outbreak of confused comments by the sales managers. They had all heard Wills speak before, knew he was an aggressive promoter of the products they sold that was his job. But this was over the top.

'For years now, 'Wills continued' 'The Food Industry has bombarded the general populace with foodstuffs which do a number of things. They give them immediate gratification of their uncontrolled and unrefined appetites; and they makes them fat unsightly and unhealthy.

'Those companies with the sense to do so have co-marketed the greatest misnomer of our commercial world - 'diet foods' - and have thus capitalized both ways. Make them fat get rich; make them thin again - or at least hold out the promise of doing so - and get rich too.

'This clever yet absurd monopoly on human stupidity and lack of self-control is now at an end. The era of "give them what they want then make them feel bad about it and give them something else and make profit either way" is at an end.

'Now, with Oviron, the obese can eat and grow slimmer. They can stay slim when they reach that weight; that weight which they've sought vainly to attain for years through spineless attempts at dieting. They can eat as much as they like of what they like and as often as they like. Not only will they lose weight they will also maintain their ideal weight when they reach it.

'If everyone takes just one of these little pills every day, then everyone can eat as much as they like and keep slim, trim, healthy and live a longer happier life. Diets, ladies and gentlemen, food control, the censoring of what we wish to consume, are things of the past.'

Andrew Wills stood back for effect. For a moment he distanced himself from his audience in a carefully planned manoeuvre devised to elicit their affection. Gone now were the reservations, gone the assumption that the Marketing Manager had been over-the-top. He was handing them the ideal product; one too, which as he intimated, would give them and their families financial security. Spontaneously one and all applauded him.

Charles U'Prichard and the Prince's Private Secretary; escorted Sir William Mostyn into his office where Sir Geoffrey

Dorrington was already present. He offered him a glass of sherry from a beautiful crystal decanter which the latter accepted with alacrity. U'Prichard knew all about Sir William's weakness for alcohol and other things. But this didn't concern him now. What did was his ability to obtain an adequate supply of the drug Oviron to start treating both of the Princes.

Neither Prince had as yet showed any signs of the disease other than the biochemical abnormalities the screen by Dorrington's team had shown and which, on the Princess' insistence had been duplicated by Mostyn's team. It could however, manifest at any time and the Private Secretary wanted the thing tied up and organized as soon as possible:

'You say that there may be problems with the government body granting a license for porphyria,' he said to Sir William. 'But as I understand it there is no need for a license. You can give it to both Princes on a named-patient basis.'

'You would like us to do that?' said Sir Geoffrey, gruffly, listening with interest. 'Obtain the drug on a named patient basis? It's out of the question!'

'Of course it is!' U'Prichard snapped; 'I didn't mean it literally. I meant that we could use a pseudonym, or simply obtain a supply of the drug and administer it. Surely that's not out of the question? Surely not, not for a potential future king of this country?'

'There could be a problem, Mr U'Prichard,' said Sir William smoothly as the sherry trickled down his throat: 'Unicorn are not too keen to dish out the drug willy nilly. And, what if something happened to the Princes, to either of them...?' He let his question hang in the air and the Private Secretary knew that some modification to their agreed deal was in the offing. He decided to take the initiative:

'Look!' he said aggressively to both men. 'I have already extended an official invitation to the Vice-President of the United States to come here. This was a request made by a representative of this company and which took a great deal of quick-footedness on my behalf. I also had to extend an invitation to that asinine Senator Pallain. If the Prince had guessed for a moment what the motive for doing so really was, he would have stopped the visit immediately.

'What more do these people want? You gentlemen know them, and you Mostyn, tell me you have assesed the drug's efficacy? Are you telling me that you would deny the future King of England his life. Would you? Or even more importantly, his sanity?'

'I said I was assessing its efficacy in the disease,' replied Mostyn and, in response to you last question - if that's what it was, no, we're not saying that. Quite simply, we have no control over the drug. That's wholly controlled by Unicorn, at least if you're talking about a preferential continuous supply. The only way they'd be able and willing to do that would be if they get the license for porphyria, then Dorrington would be able to prescribe it if necessary.' Sir Geoffrey nodded in grave agreement, a tough young bastard this U'Prichard, bright too; but they'd get the better of him soon enough.

Mostyn continued, slow, persuasive: 'They might help out meanwhile of course, but long-term...' Sir William's voice tapered off again as he ostentatiously put down his glass silently requesting the refill which he quickly received.

U'Prichard looked at both men closely, the ball-park moved: 'What do they really want? What do you really want out of this, Mostyn?' he asked, knowing that there was more here, more than was being said, more than was laid on the table. 'And you,

Dorrington, what's your position here? Are you interloping too?' I thought you had everything; is there something more?'

'How dare you!' Sir Geoffrey Dorrington said. 'How dare you suggest such a thing - if you don't retract that I'll have a word about you with the Prince himself. My only concern is for him -retract that slander.' said the Prince's personal physician.

'Retracted,' said Charles U'Prichard easily, knowing he had touched a raw nerve. That there was something afoot with the man. 'Which still leaves you, Mostyn. What do you want from all this? What, as the Vice-President would say, is your angle?'

'All Unicorn seem to want is that, given the radical nature of this drug, that it passes through the C.S.M. without delay. That's hardly unprecedented for a potentially life-saving drug. The anti-AIDS drug AZT for example did precisely this.

They want their Product License quickly and I agree with them in this. My own overtures to this effect have already been made to you. You carry influence, you can help them get it. Help us put the case for exemption to the Medicine's Commission. To obtain that, I'm willing to authorise the use of the drug in a patient we have who has acute porphyria; who is in attack now as we speak.'

'I'm not so sure about any of this.' murmured Dorrington who was duly ignored.

'And in return, what is it that you want precisely...?' persisted the tenacious Charles U'Prichard, directing his venom at Mostyn; knowing that this was sheer cover, bluff. There was something else going down here, but he didn't know precisely what.

'Just another glass of that excellent sherry,' said Sir William Mostyn with undisguised sarcasm.

Immediately after his meeting with Mostyn and the Prince's Private Secretary, Sir Geoffrey Dorrington went off to his office in Harlet Street and removed the carefully written letter of resignation from his desk.

It was dated one week hence and written in very strong language indeed. In it he expressed, not only his concern about the Princes' propective new course of treatment which was being taken against his "at present not fully informed" judgement, but also at the behavior of the Prince's Private Secretary.

Sir Geoffrey ended this creative work by saying that the major reason for his resignation was his considered opinion that he was not qualified to treat the princes' incipient disease and he felt that another physician could perhaps do more.

It was his duty to his Royal charges and his country, therefore, to resign and he would ensure that not a word of what was contained in the letter would ever emerge from his lips. As part of his deal with Unicorn, however, Sir Geoffrey would ensure that it emerged from someone else's.

Three days before the meeting which was 'resulting' in Dorrington's resignation, Vikki Goudie's mother had opened the letter carefully. It was from The London General and it requested that her daughter prepare to go in for a few days for further tests. It was stressed that this was purely routine and that all the details would be explained to her when she arrived at the hospital with Vikki.

The letter was signed by Doctor John Bennet and Vikki's mother knew that her daughter would be in very safe hands indeed. She went out and did a bit of shopping to get together the things Vikki would need for her short stay at the hospital. This time there was no chance anything would go wrong. There hadn't been a trace of alcohol anywhere near Vikki since the day of her discharge.

Greg Hoffmann sat with Ken Johnson in a small bistro. Both were drinking cups of *Cappuccino* and Ken looked very upset:

'Simply refer one more patient to The London General, Ken, one pregnant woman who no-one cares a great deal about, or at least, whose pregnancy is not the focal point of her life. They should simply have a relatively resistant throat infection which you say you can't treat by normal means and which may threaten the baby or the woman. I believe it would do that if she had a heart condition. No?'

Ken looked at Hoffmann. He spoke in a voice which was very distressed indeed.

'Yes, your correct, but it's not that simple. I did it with the Bailley woman because that was meant to be a one-off and it was easy enough. She didn't even know that she was pregnant and she had a genuine urinary tract infection. But another... it's not that simple, you don't understand.'

'But I do,' Greg Hoffmann said very softly. 'I do, Ken. I thought you enjoyed your occasional work for us. Found it rewarding.'

'I do, but...'

'Then you'll get us a referral within the week,' the Shadow Man said. 'Otherwise, you'll never work for us again.'

As he finished the remains of his coffee and made to leave, Greg Hoffmann placed an envelope on the table. He stifled the urge to pay the bill for the coffees too. 'And, by the way, Ken,' he said. 'Who ever said that it would be simple?'

CHAPTER TEN

Immediately after she returned from her trip, Allison telephoned Pam and asked her to meet up with her for a drink. She knew Pam rarely refused such an opportunity and as Allison habitually counted the number of drinks Pam had, she wondered how involved, if at all, Pam was in the intrigues Yoshimura had discussed with her in Osaka.

On her flight home Allison had pondered on the unthinkable and again it was becoming rapidly that. Unthinkable. She resolved to attempt, however, to elicit whatever information she could from Pam - if there was any to elicit.

They spoke briefly about a number of inconsequential things, caught up on some hospital gossip and discussed Allison's trip in some depth but little detail. They briefly discussed the Vikki Goudie case and Pam explained how once again in Allison's absence, her drug regime seemed to have stabilised the girl after she'd experinced an acute attack. What role, if any, Oviron had played in this was, as yet, unknown, but it was the perfect opening for Allison.

'How did you come to know of Oviron's prospective use in porphyria anyway?' she asked with apparenttly casual interest, watching her friend closely as she sipped at her third Scotch. Pam looked at her, her browm eyes uncluttered by conspiracies.

'Oh, Kathryn Meadowford was introducing one of Unicorn's new hospital reps to members of staff and I happened, for once, to be approached by her. It's not often that company reps want to detail geneticists like me.' Pam finished her drink and, refelectively, swirled what was left of the ice around the glass; 'Our dear Ms Meadowford asked me if I'd be interested in a drug they had which may be effective in preventing acute attacks of porphyria. I was of course and we spoke about the genetic aspects. She was pretty well informed as you'd expect. Apparently they're attempting to produce a transgenic animal model.'

'They are,' agreed Allison; 'In Guinea-pigs. I saw their attempts during my trip.'

'Anyway,' continued Pam; 'that was it. I knew Alan Downie was involved in psychometric studies and John Bennett had been approached too. Odd given what they had was primarily an antibiotic; but then, not so odd if it is active in porphyria.' As she caught the attention of the waitress she asked Allison the obvious question:

'Why do you ask?'

'I just wondered,' her friend replied, wondering if she should probe deeper, convinced that Pam knew nothing of any conspiracy.

For her part, Pam, still remebering Venna, waited her opportunity to broach the subject of Harry almost as eagerly as she awaited her next whisky. When she felt it appropriate to do so, she did it without any preamble:

'You seemed to be getting on well with Harry Wright in Vienna,' she said. 'Haven't you seen him since the conference?'

Allison looked at her evenly 'Well, no...' she replied, a bit too quickly. 'In fact, I haven't.'

'Whyever not?' Pam asked her. 'I imagine it would do you both good. A bit of company. Was there some problem...?'

'What do you mean by "problem" exactly?' Allison asked defensively, regretting the tone of her voice immediately.

'Sorry, Al, I didn't mean to pry.' said Pam as she drank her drink down, too quickly, in response, Allison knew, to the abruptness of her reply.

Allison met her eyes and smiled weakly 'I'm sorry, Pam I shouldn't have been so sharp. I'm still tired after my jet-setting. No, I haven't seen him. There's no definite reason. It's just that... Well...I suppose...' she paused, seeking the words.

'That you're feeling a bit vulnerable,' Pam said quietly, 'and feeling a bit more for Harry Wright than perhaps you're willing to admit.'

'Could be true,' Allison replied, turning away. She thought on Harry as she spoke. The image was all good, nothing like Greg Hoffmann or Ken.

Pam waited awhile, assessing her friend's composure as her own began to fail; 'So, what do you plan to do about it?' she asked, ordering another drink for herself.

'I've no idea... none at all,' responded Allison. 'We seemed to be getting on so well during the short time we spent together, but... well.'

Pam's mood changed quite suddenly. Allison wasn't at all surprised, simply sad. The mood swings were becoming more evident when Pam drank. 'Do you expect him to be running after you, Allison? A man in the position he's in at present? God, Allison, he was over there trying to find a cure to save his daughter's life!'

'You're right Pam,' said Allison meaning it despite Pam's erratic mood. 'It was hardly the best setting for anything.'

'Precisely,' agreed Pam. 'Why don't you give him a call. Take the initiative. The man's been under a great deal of pressure for a very long time. Make it easy for him - call him.'

Allison looked at her friend questioningly, surprised at the strength of feeling she was expressing. 'Think I should?' she asked almost rhetorically. Pam just smiled and nodded. She was pretty drunk now. 'O.K. I will...' Allison continued. 'When I get home this evening.'

'You have his number?' Pam slurred slightly.

'Yes, he gave it to me in Vienna.'

'Well then, that settles that.'

'I suppose it does,' Allison replied, relieved, despite the circumstances, that she had made a decision. 'Anyway, how are things going with you? I've noticed that you've been seeing quite a bit of young Gerry recently. Is it going well?'

'Well enough,' said Pam flatly, through her glass of Scotch. 'I'm pregnant.'

Alliosn was shocked at both the statement and its palce of entry into their conversation. 'With that young dodcotr's child?' she exclaimed.

'Who else's?' replied Pam casually drinking her drink and looking at her friend and blinking too frequently.

'I'm sorry, Pam, I didn't mean that. I meant... well. Why didn't you mention this before now? I didn't think you'd want to start a family just yet.'

'I didn't, but it's happened and so now I want to. It's baby time. Motherhood the whole bit. So, what do you think? Can the old soak pull herself together enough to see it all through?'

'I'm sure she can,' Allison said to her friend earnestly. 'Give it a try, Pam, get professional help. I'm sure you can.'

The remainder of the evening was dominated with talk of the child. Allison was surprised at her friend, who seemed to be resigned to things without having fully thought them through.

Allison didn't want to make any allusion to her concerns about Oviron and Unicorn. This was neither the time nor the place to do so. However, her curiosity though diminished, had not wholly gone and that *had* been the main purpose of asking Pam out.

'To change the subject for a moment, Pam. This porphyria thing with Unicorn. Do you know of anyone in the hospital who has looked at the disease in the *current* Royal Family?'

Pam gave her a searching look with her now very glazed eyes. 'I have.' she said glibly.

Allison was amazed. 'You have? she repeated, incredulously; 'But you've never mentioned this at any of the meetings... In what way?' she persisted her voice portraying her frank amazement. Pam continued looking at her, her eyes reflecting emotions of all types. Allison could barely breathe.

'Our eminence Sir William Mostyn, asked me to carry out a genetic profile of the current European royals, which of course included our *own* Royal Family.'

'And what did you find?' asked Allison.

'Sorry I can't say,' responded Pam, sobering slightly.

'Why ever not?' Allison remarked, surprised at her friend's reticense.

'I promised I wouldn't tell anyone,' Pam continued slurring again; 'and I'd better keep good to that promise.'

'Tell anyone what?' Allison ventured hopefully, the tension in her mounting.

'Whatever there is to tell.' Pam gave a short laugh and tears filled her eyes. 'Don't ask me any more, Al, please. I don't know what's going on. Bennett does though, as does our dear Sir

William and John Raynor. I've heard things, here and there... .
Nothing makes much sense. The Shadow Man's involved too.'

'The Shadow Man?' quizzed Allison.

'That's what Sir William calls him.'

'Calls who?' persisted the confused young woman.

'Greg Hoffmann,' said Pam. Allison felt sick.

Once she had calmed herself down with a few stiff drinks of
her own, Allison decided she'd asked her friend enough about
these matters and attempted to steer Pam towards consideration
of the pros and cons of having a child at this time.

Pam apparently saw no cons, which given the state she was
in was fair enough. Allison knew the future usually looked rosy
through a glass and this was Pam's fifth.

During all of this conversation, Allison found that her
considerations for her friend were complemented not only
by the lingering amazement of what she'd just said about her
colleagues, but also by a sense of loneliness and isolation within
herself.

While she couldn't have wished Pam anything but complete
happiness with her prospective child, she did feel desperately
lonely herself and wished that she, too, had something, someone
she could talk with intimately, share her confusion with.

Her thoughts automatically turned to Ken, Greg Hoffmann
and then irrevocably to Harry, and they ran back and forth
between them, going nowhere. To categorize her brief
relationship with Harry as an 'involvement' was, when she
reflected on it, nothing short of ridiculous.

Still, she was psychologist enough to know that the
association of ideas between children and Harry had a basis
in something unconscious within her. She knew, too, that
even if she became fully aware of what this something was,
then it would probably lead to nothing but more unhappiness.

Whatever she may be feeling deep down inside herself, it would appear that there was little chance of it being reciprocated by the man concerned.

With respect to the sheer common sense she needed now, however, there was no question that Harry Wright was the person to seek advice from. Not only did he have a first-class mind, which Allison was certain she badly needed to consult, he also knew the staff at the hospital. If there *was* some incredible nonsense going on in the place, Harry would be able to advise her objectively on what it all meant. Allison simply couldn't believe that there was something unprofessional, let alone illegal, happening around her, but the feeling that something was wrong persisted with her.

There was no point in brooding on it, however, and once she had taken Pam home, Allison turned the car in the direction of her flat and decided to take the bull by the horns. She'd call Harry as the unfortunate Pam had suggested. She wondered what sort of reception she'd get. Would he be pleased to hear from her? Displeased? Neither? Indifferent?

She drove home by a longer and more circuitous route than usual. Then, turning the car round full circle, she drove in the direction which was quickest and most direct for her. Where she wanted to go. She decided to address all her problems at once, including her personal problems and her personal needs.

When she finally arrived home, Allison took off her coat, hung it up and almost immediately went and sat down beside the telephone. She felt slightly nervous as she looked at the receiver, working up the courage to lift it. She did so. She dialed Harry's number quickly and heard the line click and then the phone at the other end ring. It seemed to ring a long time before it was picked up and a tired voice said 'Hello.'

'Hello, Harry, it's Allison,' she said. 'I thought I'd ring.'
There were a few moments silence; moments in which Allison
wondered if her call was welcome.

'I'm glad you did,' Harry said, with genuine warmth. 'I
really am. How are you?'

'Well,' Allison said, breathing a sigh of relief and feeling
ever so odd again at the sound of his lovely soft voice. 'Very
well indeed.'

Harry picked Allison up at seven thirty without having
made any formal arrangement about where they were going. It
had been decided that they would have dinner somewhere, but
where precisely had not as yet been decided. He drove carefully
in his quietly comfortable sedan, a sharp contrast in every way,
thought Allison, to the rather flash image Ken liked to present.

'I know a pleasant little place out by Lake Loddington,'
Harry said, referring to a small village by a lake some twenty
miles distant. 'It's nothing remarkable, but they have decent
food and it's quiet. I like it.'

'Let's go there, then,' said Allison. 'It sounds lovely.'

They drove out of the town and into the country roads
and Allison felt herself relax and begin to really enjoy herself.
Distracted somewhat by his driving, Allison noted that Harry
was really quite talkative. The hints she had caught from him
in Vienna, that he was a highly sensitive, amusing and informed
individual indeed, had been absolutely correct. He talked on
a range of subjects during the journey, always listening to her
response, considering it and making appropriate comment when
called for.

In time they arrived at the village of Lake Loddington and
just outside of the village Harry brought the car to a stop in the
car park of a small building of classic English Tudor design with
a thatched roof. A sign hung from the door *The Marlow Bridge*

Restaurant. It looked enchanting and candle light glowed from its leaded windows.

'It looks lovely,' said Allison. 'I've never been in this area before, despite it being so close. It does seem a rather elegant little restaurant. It must be very popular, is it?'

'It used to be very popular indeed,' replied Harry as he unbuckled his seat belt and made to open the car door. 'I don't imagine it's changed much. It's some time since I've been here, though I dare say the rather unique service it offers is still here. We'll see soon enough.' Allison wondered what he meant.

Almost as soon as they had walked through the door, a man dresed in formal evening wear rushed over to Harry and shook his hand:

'Doctor Wright,' he welcomed Harry. 'How marvellous to see you. How are you? My goodness, it's been a long time and you look so well. How are you?' he said again.

'Fine, Jerome,' replied Harry, turning to his companion. 'Allison, I'd like you to meet Jerome, the best maitre d'hote in Lake Loddington or anywhere else for that matter. Jerome, a friend of mine, Allison Young.'

'A pleasure,' Jerome said to Allison, taking her hand, shaking it and assisting her to remove her evening jacket all in one movement. Before she knew what was happening, her jacket and Harry's were hung up in the small cloakroom and they were seated at a small table by the window, the candle lit and the menu sitting open in front of them.

'That was fast,' said Allison with a smile.

Harry smiled back. 'He's efficiency with a capital E. 'You'll be surprised just *how* efficient. You'll see soon enough,' he said cryptically. 'But he has a lovely heart and serves even lovelier food. Would you like a drink to start? I'll have a small gin and tonic.'

'I think I'll have a dry sherry,' Allison replied.

Almost before she had finished her sentence, Jerome had appeared with a dry sherry in one hand and a small gin and tonic in the other. He placed the sherry on the table beside her and simultaneously placed the gin and tonic beside Harry. Allison gave a gasp of delighted surprise. 'You must be a mind-reader, Jerome,' she said laughingly.

'Lips,' said the waiter, quite seriously. Allison looked at him quizzically. 'I read lips,' the waiter continued. 'Helps a lot with my job.' With that, he whisked himself off to another table and Allison could barely stop herself from laughing out loud.

'I don't believe it!' she said, putting her hand over her mouth to control her laughter. 'He doesn't! Surely. He doesn't read lips. No!'

Harry laughed with her. 'He does!' he said, his laughter filling Allison with a deep pleasure. 'As I said he's efficient. But don't worry, he's very discreet I assure you. You can say whatever you want. Discretion's included in the service charge!'

During the remainder of their meal, Jerome took their orders by a combination of lip-reading and sign-language, only once actually coming to the table to clarify an order from them. Allison hadn't enjoyed a meal as much in years, not only because of the incongruous and unique waiter service, not only because, as Harry had said, the food was good too; but because the man opposite her gave her plently food for thought.

They were both relaxed and as they ate they chatted and laughed and looked serious and concerned and amused in turn. Harry was great company in this mood and Allison found that she sometimes deliberately detached herself from the conversation just to look at him objectively and observe what a lovely man he was. Strong, gentle, good-looking, sensitive, articulate and less troubled this evening than she had ever seen him, she wondered what it would take to keep him like this. For it was something worth keeping.

Despite the fact that she would rather have continued in this light vein, Allison decided that she'd attempt to broach the subject of her concerns about her colleagues, Unicorn Chemicals Ltd and Oviron with Harry. She decided to take a tactful approach and asked him only general questions, at least at first.

Allison soon ascertained that he knew all of the staff concerned - if that's what they were - very well indeed. She then became more specific.

'Can you think of any reason why John Bennett, John Raynor or Sir William Mostyn would have a particular interest in acute porphyria, Harry?'

The blueness of his eyes brushed over her; 'Why do you ask, Allison? I thought that porphyria was *your* forte.'

'So did I, responded Allison, 'but I was told something when I was in Japan recently, something that... .' she searched for the correct words to say, this could sound pretty stupid otherwise.

'...something that suggests there may be unprofessional conduct taking place at The London.'

'In what way?' asked Harry; serious now. Allison felt her mouth go dry. She wished she'd never mentioned the subject, not now at least.

'I don't really know,' she replied lamely; 'Oviron's being used experimentally to treat a porphyric patient and there's a lot of contact between our staff and Unicorn Chemicals.'

Harry looked at her closely, he smiled. 'What's so unprofessional about that? he asked amicably; 'Intimate contact between the Industry and hospital staff is quite common you know. Many of our consultant physicians are paid by the Industry. John Raynor's post at The London General for example is paid for by Unicorn. It saves the public sector a lot in wages.'

A memory of something tugged at Allison for a moment, something significant. It went as Harry continued: 'Intimate contact doesn't always equate with unprofessional behavior you know. In fact, most physicians funded by the various companies don't generally prescribe their own company's products. Though don't expect them to admit that!'

'So there's no link that you know of between the company and our colleagues,' Allison said; 'other than that which is normal between two such parties?' Harry reflected on her question for a time. His face became more serious.

'The only other connection which I know of pertains to the fact that Mostyn's an amateur historian and Unicorn occasionaly fund trips to Washington for him to attend the meetings of some society there.' Allison felt a rush of adrenaline.

'Do you know what it's called, Harry?' she asked with an urgency which surprised him.

'Mayflower something or other,' he replied; 'I remember the name because it struck me as pretty ornate. I heard it mentioned once by Mostyn to John Bennett. But there's nothing untoward about that. Mostyn fits his trips in when there are appropriate medical meetings on Stateside and he has professional contacts there too. It's not uncommon and certainly not unprofessional.'

Allison felt excited and was about to ask Harry more about this Society when he interrupted the pattern of her thoughts.

'I don't know if you've met a character called Hoffmann from Unicorn, he's a senior marketing man and a member of this thing too. He's pretty close to Mostyn. Another historian I believe. There's nothing unprofessional about that either.'

Allison flushed. Harry noticed. 'You okay?' he asked her.

'Fine,' she smiled which was far from true. Despite her fascination at what Harry was telling her, Allison was aware that she was changing the mood of the occasion and she determined to swing it back, leave The London and Unicorn for another time.

'Your right of course.' she said; 'I'm simply not *au fait* yet with the intricacies of hospital medicine. How did you find this place anyway. And what does it mean, "The Marlow Bridge"? It's like something from Dickens.'

Harry relaxed again. Whatever tension had entered his voice went immediately. 'You'd like to know the origin of the restaurant's name?' His gaze caught Allison unaware, his blue eyes glinting in the candlelight.

'"The Marlow Bridge"?' asked Allison puzzled. 'I've no idea. It sounds a bit familiar, but I can't place it at all. Tell me.'

'It's not very pleasant,' said Harry half-seriously.

'Go on,' she said. 'I think I might just be able to handle it!'

'O.K.' he continued, 'you've asked for it. Well, to this day at Eton, the boys sometimes shout a rather distasteful line at the occupants of barges which pass them on the river:

"Who ate puppy pie under Marlow Bridge?"

Harry had raised his voice a little and Allison, once again, couldn't help laughing at the ridiculous phrase. She realized that she felt very good indeed.

'Well, apparently,' he continued, 'many years ago, a housekeeper or cook at Eton had observed that some of her food disappeared from the larder every now and then when a barge passed by and she suspected some of the local barge owners of stealing it.'

Allison was amused and thoroughly enjoying herself. She conspired to make the most of it as Harry continued his story.

'Well, one day she found a sackfull of drowned puppies down by the river and she took them back to her kitchen and baked them into a pie.'

'No!' Allison exclaimed in mock-horror, 'Oh, how disgusting... .'

'Indeed,' continued Harry. 'Anyway, it too disappeared and was found sometime later under Marlow Bridge where it had apparently been discarded by the thieves. Partly eaten! The stealing stopped!'

Allison finally burst out laughing at Harry's exaggerated emphasis on the last few words.

'I don't believe a word of it,' she said.

'It's true I'm afraid, madam,' a stern voice said. It was Jerome, standing beside her, looking very serious indeed. 'Did you enjoy your meal?' he asked.

'Why, yes!' exclaimed Allison, smiling at the waiter. 'It was lovely.'

'We don't use puppies here,' he said, quietly walking off with a few used dishes. Allison's eyes met Harry's and another rush of laughter took them both. Within it she realized just how happy she was and what a charming man she was with.

It was almost ten by the time they left the restaurant. Jerome saw them right out to the car and ensured that they were seated safely within it before he returned to the soft-lit *Marlow Bridge Restaurant* to read more lips.

'What a delightful character,' Allison said as Harry drove off. 'What a pleasant change from the stiff formality of some places.'

'It is,' agreed Harry.; 'Isn't it just? I'm glad you enjoyed yourself.'

'Oh, I did,' said Allison, meaning it sincerely.

'Do you mind if we go for a short drive?' he asked her. 'It's early enough yet and I'd enjoy a drive if you would.'

'Why, no, I'd love to,' Allison replied quickly. 'Anywhere special?'

'Loddington Lake. It's lovely there.'

'I've never been. I've heard about it though. Is it really as nice as they say?'

'You'll see. Let's go and find out.'

They drove in contented silence and Allison sat back deeply in her seat looking out of the car window as the countryside flowed by and the sky darkened causing deeper shadows to form around them. It was a beautiful evening and she sat back relaxed in her seat, ruminating on many things, but in particular on the remarkable Jerome and his circus-like antics. Harry, too, and his delightful companionship. She doubted if she'd ever enjoyed a meal as much before.

At length, Harry turned into a small country lane which seemed invisible from the road and he drove carefully up its bumpy surface until at length they reached its end. He turned the car sharply to the left and stopped. Allison looked out of the window and in the dying light she could see the glistening expanse of the lake. He switched off the engine of the car and they were surrounded by almost total silence.

'It is lovely,' she whispered, as she discovered her new surroundings.

'Isn't it just,' replied Harry, almost thoughtfully, as Allison moved a shade nearer to him.

'Let's go for a walk,' he said, turning to look at her.

'Right,' she said. 'Let's.

They got out of the car and walked slowly over towards the water's edge. There was a small pebbly beach and it crunched beneath their feet as they slowly walked on it. Allison looked across the lake. It was beautifully surrounded by shadowy trees and shrubs and bushes of all sorts. She found it breathtaking and reached for Harry's hand. He took her's in his, his grasp firm but gentle, his skin soft and warm next to her's.

They walked along the edge of the water, pebbles crunching beneath them, the sounds of the water washing over them. They remained silent as they walked, content in each other's presence in this lovely setting. Allison wondered when she had last felt so much as peace, so happy and content. She saw the first fine edge of the moon rise into the sky and her hopes rose with it.

Still without speaking, they walked back towards the car. As they reached it, they stopped and hesitated, contact about to be broken, hand taken from hand. Effortlessly, they turned towards each other and Allison lifted herself slightly to reach Harry's lips with her's. She embraced him, held him close and they kissed.

He pulled her close, crushing her body next to his, holding her closer than she had ever been to anyone. As she pressed herself against him and felt the beginings of literal bliss creep through her, Harry froze and gently moved her away.

'I'm sorry Allison,' he said quietly as he made his way back to the car.

A coldness such as she had never known ran through Allison. The image of the beautiful woman in the photograph flooded through her mind and drowned her.

......

Over the next few days it was evident to her colleagues that something was wrong with Allison. Her usual cheery, efficient self had gone and had been replaced by someone who went about her tasks with professionalism but little enthusiasm. The change was obvious to every one of them and, while none of them could precisely place their finger on what it was that was different about her, they knew that they were dealing with a different Allison Young.

While no-one could fault her in what she did, neither could they say that she did it with the elan normally associated with her. This was most evident during their regular research meeting where Allison's contribution was dry and spiritless. She reported her latest thoughts and findings in a dull, routine manner, which was devoid of the scientific flair and fervour the group associated with her.

Most tellingly, during the meeting, once Allison has said her piece, she simply sat silently in her place. By now her colleagues were used to her being their most provocative foil, asking them penetrating questions, suggesting new leads, new lines of thought. Not now. Now she just sat there, listening but not participating. It concerned them all.

Pam knew that there had been some sort of scene or other with Harry. When she had asked Allison how their date had gone, Allison's look had said it all and her 'Not too well' was unnecessary. She had obviously not wanted to discuss it with Pam and her friend had respected her wishes and hadn't pursued the subject. It caused her great concern, however, to see Allison so distressed and she dearly wished she could do something about it. What she could do, however, she had no idea.

This situation continued for a few days more and then Doctor Bennet had a discreet word with Pam. He collared her in the corridor and asked her if she would mind having a brief chat with him about her friend, in his room. She was more than happy to do so.

'Do you know if there's anything in particular troubling Allison?' he asked her. 'She doesn't seem quite her usual self.'

'She isn't, Doctor Bennet,' Pam replied cautiously. 'It's nothing she's confided in me, however, though I imagine it's more personal than organic. She seems to be physically well enough, just a bit down.'

'Could you have a word with her, find out the problem if you can? We really don't want her being so preoccupied. She has important work to do here. See what you can do.'

'I will,' replied Pam, relieved that Doctor Bennet hadn't penetrated the issue too deeply. He wouldn't have approved of a member of his staff being so susceptible to the negative influences of inter-personal relationships.

'By the way,' he called after Pam as she walked along the corridor. 'Have we any of those recent results back yet on young Miss Wright?'

'They're due tomorrow,' Pam replied, a bit taken aback. 'The lab is rushing them through, giving them priority over other things, but it will still be tomorrow before they're ready.'

'Fine, let me know what they are as soon as you have them. She's a fighter, is our Miss Wright, an excellent person. So's her father, you know. I imagine you know Harry Wright, don't you? He's a good man. He's had his problems recently but he's a fighter, too. He'l get over them.'

'I...eh...' mumbled Pam. 'Yes, I do know Harry, I...'

'Have a word with Allison,' Doctor Bennet said once again somewhat abruptly, as he turned away. 'Find out what's wrong with her if you can. It shouldn't be too difficult.'

He went inside his office again and closed the door leaving Pam to think what a very observant man he was. And leaving John Bennet to wish that he'd remained the way he'd been before, before the promise of Oviron had seduced him - had seduced them all.

......

The following evening Pam at last convinced Allison to spend some time with her and to have a further chat. They sat together in Pam's small office drinking coffee - Pam's spiked as usual - and making idle chit chat for a while.

Even when doing this, Allison wasn't particularly communicative and Pam was continually frustrated in her attempts to direct the conversation round to Harry.

'All I can gather from you, Al, is that you had some sort of disagreement with Harry the other night. You seemed so happy about the date. What went wrong?'

'Nothing went wrong, Pam, we just don't get along as well as I'd hoped. Anyway, how are your own problems?'

Pam felt a twinge of hurt. 'Still drinking,' she said crisply. 'I know I shouldn't but there we are.'

After a time, she decided not to approach things so directly with Allison. Instead she very tactfully asked Allison what was wrong with her, pointing out that it was pretty evident that things weren't as good as normal since she'd returned from her trips abroad and that she had noticed this for some days now.

'It's nothing in particular,' Allison replied non-committally. 'There's just a few things I have to sort out. I'll be fine in a day or two, Pam, honestly.'

'Don't you want to talk about it?' her friend encouraged. 'Share it? Get it off your chest?'

'No, not really,' Allison replied a bit too quickly. 'I'd sooner let things sort themselves out, run their course. I've just been upset a bit. I'll get over it soon, honestly. And let me assure you that it's not all Harry... really!'

'You know, it would do you some good to talk a bit about it, whatever it is. You've been working very hard over the past few months and, if you're feeling a bit tired, things are probably way out of perspective. I'm hardly in a position to offer anyone advice, but I'm here ready to help... try me. Why don't you?'

Allison looked at her friend closely and affectionately. She took her hand, gave it a little squeeze and forced a smile:

'I'll be all right, Pam,' she said softly. 'Honestly. I'm still a bit tired, a bit upset, a bit.. well, it's been a hectic week or so, in one way or another. I'll be fine, I promise. You just take care of yourself and your baby.'

Pam wondered if she should mention that their colleagues had noticed the change in Allison's mood, that Doctor Bennet himself was showing concern, had spoken to her. That if Allison didn't get herself together soon it could perhaps affect her career. She decided not to.

There was no point in worrying Allison unduly and perhaps making her worse. Further, who was she to talk? The hospital had tolerated her drinking for God knows how long... still, Pam knew one of the major reasons for that and, as she thought on it, a mixture of anger, shame and grief gripped her.

'Well, look,' Pam said. 'The least I can do is to help take your mind off things for a while. I've got two tickets for the cinema this evening - Clients is showing, it's had excellent reviews - come with me. Gerry's on late and I'd like the company. It would do us both good. Will you come? Please, Allison. Keeps me away from bars.' She gave a slight derisory laugh, but Allison knew there was some truth in what she said.

Reluctantly, Allison agreed to go, and they arranged to go in Pam's car, after she promised Allison she'd have no more to drink and was 'safe' to drive. She picked Allison up at home half an hour before the feature started. Allison still didn't look or behave any better.

The film was good and Pam enjoyed it thoroughly. Allison, however, didn't seem to lose herself in it as much as Pam had hoped she would. Afterwards, while she made the obligatory noises and said she'd enjoyed herself, Pam knew she was still preoccupied with her problems. As she dropped her off home again, she watched her walk slowly to her door and wondered just what on Earth had happened to make her friend like this.

She wondered if she should have a word with Harry himself. She knew him reasonably well. Perhaps it wouldn't be out of place. She decided, however, that it would be. These were adults, after all, professional people who would have to sort things out for themselves. She had done what she could, what any friend would. As much and no more. As she drove off home she hoped that Allison would resolve her problems soon. Whatever they were.

Over the next two days Allison perked up a little but she was still far from her usual self. Her work wasn't sufferintg obviously, though, and she managed to maintain her highly successful bedside manner with her patients. The trained eye of John Bennet, however, knew how to spot a problem in the making and he decided to have a word with her directly.

Claire Sillars called Allison in her office and asked her to come along to Doctor Bennet's office at three in the afternoon. She duly did so and her chief called her in through his open connecting door and directed her to have a seat. He was sitting behind his desk and he smiled at her as she sat. He stood up, came from behind his desk and sat informally beside Allison. He handed her what was evidently an academic paper:

'A new reprint,' he said. 'It's an excellent paper, been published quickly, too. I think that it should interest you.'

Allison looked at the title: *Effective Drug Intervention in a Acute Intermittent Porphyria.* Beneath it, in the sub-heading entitled 'authors', she saw her name in bold type alongside Doctor Bennet's: Allison Young M.B. Ch.B. She felt a sudden surge of pleasure. It was her first publication and Doctor Bennet had timed her receipt of it very carefully indeed.

'So, that's your first publication, Doctor Young,' he said. 'An excellent one, too, if I may say so. Now, I believe, Allison,' he continued, 'that you have quite a bit of leave due to you and I'd like you to take some of it as soon as possible. That way we should ensure a steady flow of these,' he continued, directing his eyes at the paper.

'But I can't have a break at present,' responded Allison immediately. 'I've too much to do at present. I'm involved in...'

'We can't do without you?' Bennet asked ironically. 'The hospital can't run for a short time without Allison Young... the research group will fold, the infrastructure collapse?'

'Well, of course, I don't mean that, Sir, but I really...'

'Take a break, Allison,' said Bennet more firmly now. 'I want to see you back here in a week or two's time ready to make some more penetrating discoveries and perform your duties to your patients to the full. Meanwhile, I think we can manage well enough for a time without you.'

Allison felt confused, frustrated, angry and rejected. She looked at her chief and his eyes didn't flinch. He was every bit as determined as she was and she knew it.

'O.K.,' she said. 'I'll spend some time with my parents down South. I'll call them this evening. Take a break. You're right, I probably do need a few days away just now. Just a few.'

'Fine,' said Bennet. 'We'll see you in a week or so. Give Claire the details and have a pleasant break.'

'Thank you,' Allison said quietly, as she left his room.

After she had registered her leave with Claire, Alison went out into the corridor where almost immediately she bumped into Jennifer Wright.

'Hi, there,' Jennifer said. 'How are you? Haven't seen you for ages. How was the trip - New York, Tokyo - sounded fantastic! How about some coffee or something? Want to arrange a time just now?'

'Sorry, Jennifer,' Allison replied. 'I'm going off for a week or so, down to visit my parents, so I'll have to get things packed, arrange things. Let's meet up when I get back.'

'Why, of course,' Jennifer responded. 'Your parents will be pleased to see you and you them, I imagine. How lovely. Have you seen Harry recently, by the way? I haven't spoken to him for almost a week. I've been wondering what he's been up to.'

'No, sorry, Jennifer, I haven't,' Allison said quickly. 'Look, I must dash, things to do. I'll see you soon. Take care. Bye.'

'Bye,' Jennifer replied, looking after her. 'Have a lovely time.'

'My love to Tina,' Allison said finally, as she disappeared around a corner.

'Of course,' Jennifer responded, as she watched her friend dissappear from view and wondered if Harry knew that she was off on holiday, down to see her parents. He had seemed very keen on her, very keen indeed.

The following morning, after a brief phone call to her delighted parents and with a few necessities put together in a suitcase, Allison drove off in her car for the journey South.

Pam had agreed to pop into the flat once or twice in her absence to check on things and Allison had asked her to call her at her parents if anything important cropped up. What precisely she meant by that she wasn't sure, but Pam had a sneaking suspicion.

C HAPTER ELEVEN

The British Airways 747 left Heathrow Airport at 8 p.m. local time and arrived at Kennedy Airport in New York at 7 p.m. As promised Greg Hoffmann had accompanied Allison and he had made the journey both informative and enjoyable.

They were met at Kennedy by one of the employees of Unicorn who took their luggage cart and ushered them both to a waiting car. He drove them immediately to The Holiday Inn where Allison was staying and after checking her in there they saw her to her room. Greg told her to rest and that he'd come back and collect her at seven the following morning. He was staying at the service flat he kept in New York and which he always used on his frequent trips there.

'Try and get some sleep,' he had said to Allison. 'It's night -time for you now as you know, so sleep well. I've got some quick work to do over at the office here and back at the flat. I'll show you around tomorrow and then it's down to real work for both of us.' He shook her hand formally and then left her.

She walked about the room for a time, looked out of the window, wondered at the fact that she was in this city at all, but then she took Greg's advice and, feeling tired yet excited, she lay down for a nap that turned into a deep and restful sleep.

The following day, prior to her visit to Unicorn's Laboratories, Allison had seen the sights with Greg. Early in the morning they had visited Central Park and walked there for almost an hour. Then it was a fairly brief trip to the Empire State Building, the Statue of Liberty and Greenwich Village where they lunched in a Mexican restaurant where the food was excellent and Allison relaxed and casually absorbed the whole atmosphere of the place.

In the afternoon they visited the Museum of Modern Art and Saint Patrick's Cathedral and finally, at Allison's request, they paid a quick visit to the Whitney Museum of American Art where Greg once again showed his encyclopaedic knowledge of things cultural.

Allison enjoyed her sight-seeing immensely as she did Greg's role as a guide which he did adeptly. But even more than this, she enjoyed his company. He was a very enjoyable companion and his combination of wit, knowledge, caring attention, and sheer good looks were a stunning combination.

By the end of her second day in New York City Allison was very tired indeed. That day she had spent touring Unicorn's laboratories which were linked with facilities from the State University of New York.

The laboratories were extensively equipped with the most modern of bio-engineering and other euiptment and were staffed by some of the best minds in the country in turn taken from the international elite. She had enjoyed her tour of the laboratories but had not learned a great deal that was new to her, other than how the management structure of a commercial laboratory was different to the purely academic ones she was familiar with.

In academic laboratories in the U.K. - those she had seen in the University, the National Health Service and funded by the Medical Research Council - Allison was used to a relatively casual approach to things. Plenty of good work was done, but it tended to be done in no great hurry and to be sometimes *ad hoc,* jumping from one interesting finding to another as any given project went on. No so here.

Here, the research team worked as if they were on an assembly line and every aspect of every hour and what was being done with it was accounted for. The atmosphere was brimming with industry, as thought and method were combined in a collective scientific efficiency towards the given end, the discovery of and screening for activity of new drugs.

She was shown the screens that were being used to test Oviron for anti-porphyric activity. The so called 'animal models' of the disease in humans. These consisted of rats who had been injected with the drug, after they had received one or two other drugs which induced porphyric-like signs in them. Their tissues were then removd and analysed for various enzymatic changes.

Allison fully appreciated the significance of the work as it may apply to humans with the disease. She appreciated too, however, that it was a far cry from these studies to justifying administering the drug to humans. That Oviron had potential anti-porphyric activity seemed in no doubt but then Allison had already known that before her visit.

One particular set of experiments interested Allison more than the rest. A group of bio-engineers were attempting to incorporate the human gene which allegedly caused porphyria into the embryos of guinea pigs. The hope was that these mammals - which along with human beings, were the only ones who could not produce their own vitamin C - would produce offspring who were 'porphyric'.

Such transgenic offspring had not yet been produced, but the technicians intimated to Allison that they were certain that they'd soon be successful. The whole process did give Allison some cause for reflection. Why should an industrial laboratory be so geared towards assessing a product for its anti-porphyric activity when the market was infinitesimal? Indeed they'd make more money if they marketed vitamin C!

She didn't ask any of the laboratory staff, however, and if she had they wouldn't have known. Indeed they themselves wondered what a relatively junior hematologist was doing there at all.

On her final evening before her onward trip to Tokyo, Greg took Allison to the *Four Seasons* restaurant on Park Avenue at Fifty Second Street. The surroundings were beautiful, being suggestive of money with taste rather than mere opulence for its own sake.

Allison noted the Picasso on the lobby wall. It was an operatic stage impression, an original work as discretely set in its surroundings as Greg Hoffmann's thoughts were in his head. She looked around. The decor was to her English taste. It was conservative, understated, almost plain. It was in keen contrast indeed to some of the other restaurants she'd visited or seen over the past two days.

Of the two possible restaurants in the hotel they chose the Grill Room; Greg preferred it. It was less pretentious than the Pool Room with its pond and palm trees and its artificial ambience of the South Seas.

The maitre d'hote approached them smiling as ever: 'Your table's ready, Mr Hoffmann, Madam.'

'Thank you,' said Hoffmann courteously escorting Allison by the arm to the table.

They began with an aperitive. A very dry Martini which drew in Allison's breath like liquid blotting paper. They continued with Beluga caviar which was salted perfectly and placed delicately on cold, crisp, crackers.

Gazpacho soup followed, which Allison had never tasted before but which appealed to her palate enormously and this was followed by smoked salmon served with brown bread and butter, which was in turn followed by a green salad. As Greg said, 'It cleans the palate before the main course.'

The main course was Wild Duck shot in Maine and it was garnished with blueberry sauce. It, and the crisp, fresh vegetables served with it, was simply delicious.

To finish, Allison had some Crown Stilton and Greg some genuine Scottish Cheddar with Orkney oatcakes. The coffee and the tequillas which followed - and which Greg insisted they have - were simply the perfect end to a perfect meal.

'Why tequilla, Greg?' Allison had asked. 'I had thought about having something different - cognac, perhaps. I don't mind though, I enjoyed it. I just wondered why?'

'Well,' he replied. 'New York City has a population of around eight million people. It's the largest city in the States. When I was at college I once made a trip here by Greyhound Coach and I was caught in a snowstorm while on my way to the coach station. I reached the coach virtually frozen and people sat either looking at me vacantly or else studiously ignoring me.'

Allison listend with interest. This was the first time Greg had spoken about himself in a personal context. She was intrigued. What did he have to say about himself?

'Suddenly an elderly woman with a handful of kids approached me and helped me off with my over-clothes. She gave my arms and face a good rub and produced a small bottle of tequilla from somewhere in her bag. She made me drink some. I've never forgotten that.' He looked reflective, almost sad and Allison's interest deepened.

'In a city of almost eight million people, one, and one of the least fortunate at that, took the time and had the heart to attend to another unfortunate kid. So every time I have a decent meal over here, I finish it with a tequilla. In memory of my absent good samaritan.'

Allison observed him closely. She could have sworn there was some clouding in his eyes, the hint of a deeper emotion. She smiled at him and said nothing. He had said enough. There was more to Greg Hoffmann than met the casual eye.

Greg had arranged for them to be picked up by a car at the door of the restaurant. They fell laughing into the luxuriously upholstered back seat of the black limousine. They were having a good time. Allison looked at the sights of Park Avenue as the car sped towards her hotel. The place was alight with night-life and neon signs and Allison had an errant thought of Audrey Hepburn standing alone here in that classic early morning scene of *Breakfast at Tiffany's*.

They drove back to Allison's hotel and Greg, quite naturally, escorted her to her room. Again, quite naturally, he went in with her, went to the courtesy bar and poured Allison a glass of white wine and himself a tonic water.

'Don't you want something stronger?' asked Allison.

'I just drink tequilla,' said Greg politely, 'And then only in New York, though I'll occasionally do so elsewhere if there's good reason. There's none in the bar anyway.'

'Would you like me to order some from room-service?'

'No, thanks,' Greg replied as he sat down by the small table in the center of the room and cradled his drink in his hand:

'And what did you think of the anti-porphyric screens, Allison?' he asked, almost formally, surprising her with the sudden switch in mood.

'In what way, Greg?' Allison replied, as she sat on the bed and sipped at her wine.

'You think that they're showing anything? Anything that we can use?'

'Well, of course. They're showing what we were already pretty sure of, that ALA synthetase is blocked...'

Greg held up his hand: 'Spare me the technical stuff, please,' he said. 'I just want to know if we can use that stuff to sell our drug.'

'Well, if it works in human porphyrics, you can. If not, I don't see how it can help you.'

'You don't?'

'No, I don't. I mean porphyria is hardly a widespread disease. If you want to sell your drug you'd be better doing some more work on its antibiotic profile and this anti-obesity thing.'

'You know about that?'

'I heard it mentioned by Sir Abe Wilder at John Raynor's dinner party. He mentioned it to me almost in passing.'

'And you don't see how an anti-porphyric indication could help us that way? I mean, in the anti-obesity market?'

Allison looked at Greg closely, at his handsome face and burning brown eyes. 'No, I don't,' she replied. 'There's just no relationship between the two things. Medically they're quite, quite different. There's no medical relationship at all.'

'Has anyone suggested that there was?' added Greg Hoffmann, standing up to full height and walking to the bar to replenish their drinks. 'Any medical relationship?'

'No, but... .' Alliosn paused; 'You seem to be linking them in some way. Some way that eludes me.'

'There's not a lot eludes you Allison,' Greg said, as he walked towards her with the small bottle of white wine. 'Not a lot at all. You're a pretty good lateral thinker, Allison. Are you certain that you couldn't find something advantageous in an indication for Oviron in porphyria, given your nationality for example?'

'I really don't understandd,' Allison continued, searching his face, looking confused, vulnerable. Exciting the Shadow Man.

She continued looking up at him and their eyes met. She felt the mood change again and there was a tingling sensation inside her, like a faint electrical pulse. He poured her some more wine then took the glass from her hand and placed it on the table.

He bent over and kissed her gently. Despite herself, the combination of wine, physical need, this attractive man and the intimacy of the hotel room, she responded immediately.

She put her arms around his neck and pulled him down onto the bed. She could feel him against her as he began to kiss her neck and his hands slipped inside her dress and he squeezed her breasts.

'Oh, Greg,' she whispered aroused by this man of fascinating contradictions. An enigma which was resolving itself: 'Oh Greg, love me!'

Suddenly he stopped, froze. He pulled himself from her and sat up rigidly on the bed shaking his head. Confused.

'What's wrong?' she asked, surprised both at him and herself.

'Nothing.' he said in a voice that Allison could tell was close to breaking. She was amazed.

'What's wrong, Greg.' she repeated trying still to get close to him, repossessing him in her arms, pulling him down again: 'Love me.' she whispered.

Hoffmann rose: 'Shut up! 'he snapped, walking away then sitting on the solitary chair.

Allison fell back onto the bed more in shock and defense than from the force of the blow. She looked at him as he half-turned towards her. There were tears in his eyes. He was weeping.

Allison said nothing as he rose and muttered some brief apology then left the room. She lay there, astonished. The great Greg Hoffmann, Marketing and Sales Director of Unicorn Chemicals, international man, man of many parts and many cultures, reduced to tears by... what?

Despite her shock, Allison wondered and wondered but she couldn't for the life of her account for what had happened.

......

The following morning Allison phoned Greg at his office. A secretary told her that he wasn't there, but that she could contact him at his club. Allison waited to be put through, heard the number ring and after the obligatory, 'Have a nice day.' the secretary hung up.

Allison felt quite nervous as she waited, but she had to speak to the man. She got through to the club without any trouble and asked the manager who she was referred to if she could speak with Mr Hoffmann. Within seconds he was on the phone.

He spoke to her as if the incident had never occurred. He wished her a safe and rewarding journey to Tokyo and said that a car would pick her up at the hotel an hour before her check-in time.

Allison thanked him for all he'd done and intentionally made no mention of the incident in her hotel room. She still burned with a desire to discover what had triggered it, however, for she knew as certainly as a large red sun shone in Japan awaiting her, that something had triggered this behavior in Greg Hoffmann and that if it had done so once, it could do so again. The Shadow Man, she was amazed to discover, was mentally unstable.

The car arrived for her as promised as yet another representative of Unicorn eased her through the hotel check-out procedures. The bill had already been paid, and her luggage was carried to the waiting car which was to take her to Kennedy airport.

The cheery young chauffeur left her sitting with a good ten minutes to wait until her check-in time for her flight to the capital of Japan. He asked her if there would be anything else? Allison considered calling Greg again, felt, for some reason, that she should tell him that the incident was forgotten. She looked at the young man, responded to his question:

'Just one thing,' she said. 'I may wish to call Mr Hoffmann. He's at his club at present, I believe, do you have the number by any chance?'

'Sorry Ma'am,' said the young man still smiling; 'I don't. But you can get it from enquiries.'

'Thank you.' said Allison, asking if there was a particular number to dial for enquiries on New York numbers.

'Oh it's not in New York, Ma'am,' he replied to her intrigue; 'It's in Washington. Mr Hoffmann flew there last-night. It's called the Mayflower Charter.' Allison was quite taken aback at Hoffmann being in Washington, but decided against making the call. It might disturb the man. And what an odd name for a club.

She thought briefly on all that had happened to her in the space of just a couple of days in New York and she wondered what the Orient held for her. Whatever it was, the prospect excited her enormously. Somewhere, however, she still wondered why. Why should someone as junior as she was be jet-setting in such a manner? The though flew from her mind the moment the large jet lifted off from the runway.

Allison's Boeing 747 touched down at Tokyo International Airport, Narita, at three thirty in the afternoon precisely. Though very tired, she was also very excited. To have made the trip to New York had been one thing - to come to the Far East quite another. Here she was in the Orient and no matter how post-war Japan had become she knew it still bristled with traditional places, customs and values.

As promised, Yukio Yoshimura was standing waiting for her among the milling crowds in the airport's arrival hall. He looked calm, relaxed, at peace with himself amidst the turmoil of people and noise. He, just as she remembered him.

He had already taken her luggage trolley and was pushing it with ease before they even had a chance to say anything to each other except 'Hello' and 'Welcome'.

Smiling, Yoshimura led her to a special V.I.P. area where his car was parked with a chauffeur waiting behind the wheel. Allison wondered why the chauffeur hadn't come to help with her luggage as he was doing now. She then realized that this was some acknowledgement by Yoshimura of his respect for Allison. That he had taken her baggage himself meant a great deal she was sure, with respect to the esteem he held her in.

They sat in the back of the limousine and Allison looked out at the streets of Tokyo with their collage of Western and traditional Japanese sights. Japanese lettering fought for space with Coca-Cola Signs and neon lights flickered on and off the way she imagined fireworks once did in this magnificent city which was once called Ebo and which contained some thirty million souls within a thirty-mile radius of the Imperial Palace.

They drove straight to Allison's hotel, the Imperial, which was situated right within the business community of the city. Allison gasped as she saw the beautiful fountain spraying its water up in front of the hotel and it seemed only a matter of minutes after their arrival that she was being led into her room by the attendant who carried her luggage, accompanied by Yoshimura who tipped the young man generously.

Her room was lovely. It was surprisingly large and air-conditioned with a television, a courtesy bar and a magnificent bed. She walked over to the window and looked out:

'That's the Imperial Palace,' said Yoshimura,' and Hibiya Park. We will go and visit them and a few more sights tomorrow if you would like to. Would you?'

'Why, that would be marvelous,' replied Allison. 'Are you certain you have the time, that I have it, that we have it?' She laughed. Her excitement had spilled over her.
Yukio Yoshimura smiled; 'I have plenty time,' he said, 'And so have you.'

......

The following day Yoshimura showed Allison the major sights of Tokyo. They travelled on the Yamanote Loop Line of the Tokyo Underground, by far the fastest and best way to get around the city quickly and see the sights.

They started by getting a view of the whole city from Tokyo Tower itself with Yoshimura picking out the landmarks for her. They then descended to the streets and made their way to view them properly.

Allison was taken first to the Assakussa Kannon Temple - where she did some interesting shopping in the arcades there; then on to the Imperial Palace East Garden and then to the Happo Enn Garden where she witnessed an exhibition of the traditional Japanese tea-ceremony. She found it delightful and Yoshimura supplemented her delight by his detailed explanation of it and its significance.

After lunch - which they had in a small riverside restaurant -Yoshimura took her for a short cruise on the river Sumida where Allison with the fine breeze tousling her hair, found herself amazed at the diverse number of sailing craft they passed, some of which she thought shouldn't be able to stay afloat.

Later that afternoon they went to the Tasaki Pearl Gallery where Allison was enchanted by an exhibition of flower arranging such as she'd never seen in her life before. The delicacy of touch and color, the matching of shade and contrast here, were nothing short of perfect and she left with a burning image in her mind of how really beautiful flowers could be when properly arranged.

As an end to her sightseeing for the day, Yoshimura drove Allison along the Chuo Expressway where they stopped off at a station well up the side of Mount Fuji. He spoke a great deal about the mountain and its symbolic significance for the Japanese. Allison was enchanted. On the way back he skirted Lake Ashi where they saw cruise boats taking people here and there and no where in particular.

By the time dinner time came Allison was exhausted but she had been promised one more day's sightseeing 'before work'. That was to be on the following morning.

Arriving early in the morning, Yoshimura drove Allison out of Tokyo and into the mountainous country by Lake Chuzenji. Surrounded by volcanoes Allison watched in sheer ecstasy as tons of water tumbled down in a magnificent spray from the spectacular Kegon waterfall. She looked at Yoshimura and smiled. It really was a fascinating sight, an inspiring one. He caught her look and smiled back.

'Like it?' he asked, looking small and vulnerable against this contrasting giant of water.

'Very much,' said Allison; 'It's beautiful.'

'So, you like Japan, eh?'

'I like Japan, yes!' Allison said, 'very much indeed.'

When they returned to Tokyo, Yoshimura took Allison to a building near the city center. It was the Association of Haiku Poets, he explained to her and he wanted to collect a book from them. The book was waiting for him and he showed it to Allison. She didn't understand a word, of course, but the poems all looked similar in format to her. Yoshimura explained:

'Haiku is one of the major forms of Japanese poetry. It has a very formalised structure and there are few adults in Japan today who have not at one time or another written such a poem.

'There must be around six to seven hundred Haiku groups in Japan today with a total membership of some 1,000,000 people. Surprised, eh?'

'Why, yes,' Allison responded honestly, thinking of Byron and Keats and the number who still followed them. 'And do you write Haiku, Yukio?' she asked.

'Sometimes,' the Japanese said, 'when the mood takes me. But this one,' he said, pointing to a particular poem in the book. 'I wish to translate into English... perhaps you could help me do so?'

'Of course,' Allison said with alacrity, 'but I'll warn you now, I'm no literary buff. I'll do my best though. How shall we start?'

'By going somewhere quiet for a period, to relax and reflect for a time,' said Yoshimura, 'and then we shall tease out the words from the seventeen Japanese Syllables into English.'

'What's the poem called?' asked Allison, delighted at the prospect of the translation.

'Oh, something like. Mmm... *The Way Life Runs In A Steady Pattern*' or something. No, that's too long. That's the problem. '*The Run Of Life* As...'

'*Life Flow?*' suggested Allison quietly.

Yoshimura looked at her, met her eyes, laughed. She tingled.

'That will do nicely, Allison,' he said softly and gently. With respect.

That evening they went to a small reception room in the hotel which was very quiet indeed and which was empty. It had been reserved for Allison's talk the following morning and hence was available to them now.

They sat there for a couple of hours as they attempted to get the best fit of English words to match those of the Japanese. At the end of their session Allison felt very pleased with herself indeed and she knew the English form of the Japanese poem by heart.

The following morning Allison gave her talk. It lasted longer than usual - one hour - and was followed by a similar time taken up by answering questions. She spoke about all the work, findings, ideas and theories her research group had elucidated and suggested another few speculative lines of thought which had her audience very interested indeed.

Question-time had been a pleasure. It had been very formal and while there had been a few testing questions, there had been nothing Allison couldn't answer satisfactorily or at least refer back to another member of the research group, promising to follow it up with them.

The only really difficult moment was when one member of the invited audience asked Allison about Oviron:

'And why, Doctor Young, do you want to prove that Oviron works so well in porphyria, given that all you have with it is Streptococcal throats?'

Allison didn't understand the question and said so. Yoshimura, who was chairing the meeting, intervened:

'Doctor Young is not here as a representative of Unicorn Chemicals but as a member of the porphyria research team at The London General Hospital. Such issues would not concern her.'

The man who had questioned her did not look satisfied with the answer but did, nevertheless, desist from further questioning.

At length the meeting finished, the delegates headed for a buffet lunch and Allison felt very pleased with herself indeed.

......

The following day Yoshimura and Allison made the short flight from Narita airport in Tokyo to Osaka. This was Allison's choice, having been offered the option of making the journey on the 150 miles per hour 'Bullet' train. Outside the airport Yoshimura's wife was waiting for them.

She looked a delightful woman and, much to Allison's surprise, she wore modern Western clothes. Allison had expected some kimmonoed chalk-faced lady; what she got instead was a warm, welcoming thoroughly Westernised elderly woman who Allison could see must have been very beautiful indeed when she was younger. Fine looking people now, Allison sensed that these two must have made a marvellous couple in every way when they were young.

As promised back in London, Allison was staying with the Yoshimuras during her brief visit to Kyoto and, on her first morning there, Yoshimura's wife told her that she was once again going sightseeing, this time with both of them and only 'for one day'.

She explained that Kyoto was the old Imperial capital of Japan and had been its center of culture for a thousand years. Here, more than anywhere else she told her, the people followed a traditional way of life and this was to be glimpsed everywhere, if you knew what to look for and where.

In a hectic morning they managed to visit The Old Imperial Palace, the marvellous wooden Nijo Castle which was positively brimming with marvellous paintings and the Golden Pavilion at the Kinkakuji Temple.

After an early lunch they drove far out of the city heading south to the city of Nara to see the Todaiji Temple which contains the largest wooden construction in the world - the great hall of the temple. Inside the temple Allison felt simply humble as she looked on at the great bronze Buddha who sat 53 feet high and weighed 450 tons.

She had a similar feeling, too, at the Kasuga shrine at Nara where some 3000 bronze lanterns burned in the grounds. There was an atmospheric difference between Tokyo and its vicinity and Kyoto and its vicinity and Allison was beginning to feel it.

That evening, Allison sat with the Yoshimuras in their home - a rare honour which was enhanced by the lovely meal they had. both of her hosts were dressed in real kimonos. These were the expensive formal dress worn at special occasions and confused with the cheaper cotton robe or yukata which has no vents and is often worn for everyday use.

The meal started with the Yoshimura's housekeeper bringing them a pot of Ocha, the lovely green Japanese tea, together with a flask of sake which she poured into fine porcelain cups.

Yukio lifted his cup in a toast to Allison:

'Kampai,' he said, 'Cheers.'

'Kampai,' Allison responded, as she brought the blood warm liquid to her mouth and sipped its aromatic flavour gently.

There soon followed a number of dishes and each was sculpted like a mosaic so that it appealed to the eyes as much as to the stomach.

There were three types of noodles, soba, ramen and udon - a delightful fish soup - rice cooked in saffron and a sarada or salad which had been presented so delicately and delightfully that Allison felt it almost sacrilege to eat it.

To the Yoshimuras delight, she used 'hashi' - chopsticks, to eat her food, taking each bite-sized bit and eating it carefully, savouring it and washing it softly down with sake or tea.

The sashima, the cold raw fish, was something Allison enjoyed greatly, though it was her first attempt at it. She also enjoyed the beef they had, however, - an expensive commodity in Japan, but a familiar thing to her in such a different world.

There were so many different and varied vegetables that Allison didn't know what was what and before each course she was soon reflexly saying 'Dozo' – *bon appetite* - to her hosts.

The meal was quite delicious and during it they spoke of a great many things. At length, Yoshimura's wife left them alone together and after they had made some more casual chat and drunk some more sake and ocha Yoshimura approached another subject:

'I wonder, Allison,' he said, 'if you really understand all that is involved in working with Unicorn on their drug Oviron.'

'How do you mean?' she responded.

'Do you know much about what the drug does and why Unicorn are so keen to market it?'

'I think so,' Allison said unevenly. 'It has a strong anti-streptoccocal action, it may work in acute porphyria and other forms of the disease and, what is particularly promising from their point of view, is that it appears to reduce body weight in some obese people without dietary control.'

'And which of those things is most imortant?' asked the Japanese.

'Why, I don't know,' Allison remarked truthfully. 'All of them, I suppose, if the drug is good enough.' Yukio Yoshimura smiled at her, at her naivity:

'Forget the humanitarian aspects, Allison.' he continued 'There's only one indication that's lucrative financially. It's potential use in obesity. The other two would actually cost the company money if they marketed the drug for them alone.'

'I did wonder at the interest in porphyria from a commercial point of view,' admitted Allison; 'Though I thought another anti-biotic was always welcome. So why do they want to proceede with all three if they're not all commercialy viable?' she asked, slightly bewildered.

'Why do you think?'

'I've no idea.'

'Promotion, advertising, good-will, confidence, repectability. Smokescreens!' came the reply, with distinct hint of distaste.

'I don't think I follow, Yukio, could you elaborate?'

'Of the three, which of those potential indications is the most dramatic, promotionally?'

'Why, obesity, of course. If they have got a lipolytic agent they could announce it to the world and the world would listen.'

'Only if they had a license for the product and it was safe,' he continued quietly now, almost sombre. 'Anyway, with all respect, you're incorrect, Allison. That's not the most exciting promotional aspect. They have something guaranteed to make the drug internationally known overnight.'

Allison thought carefully. "Strep. throats, urinary tract infections, porphyria, impossible! Why, they'd bore the general public. They'd even bore the medical profession." She caught Yoshimura's eyes, they seemed to convey something to her. She considered the question again. An unthinkable thought inserted itself. Her eyes widened in incipient amazement: 'Unless...,' she said quietly, unless... .'

'Who do you know who has, or may have, acute intermittent porphyria, Allison; 'In addition to the young woman you gave the excellent presentation on in Tokyo?'

Allison froze. 'No, I can't accept that. You cannot be serious.' said Allison fully realizing now where Yukio Yoshimura's thrust was leading. She remembered her discussions with Greg Hoffmann in New York, his innuendoes. She remembered other things all at once.

'Are you trying to tell me that Unicorn would leak the fact that the European royalty may have this disease, in order to promote their drug in obesity?'

'I'm trying to allow you to see what is staring you in the face, Doctor Young.'

'I still can't believe that.' murmured Allison, bemused. Her world didn't include such a mind-set.

'As you wish,' said the Japanese. 'But tell me, Allison, what were the precise circumstances of the re-admission of your young porphyric patient. Why did you try Oviron on her and tell me about Mrs Bailley's baby?'

Allison was shocked and amazed. 'How do you know about that! You couldn't possibly...'

'I have my sources in London,' interrupted Yoshimura. 'Inside and outside your hospital. I am a very important man, Allison, I was for many years the personal physician to the late Emperor and I know very important people in London and elsewhere, who have access to all sorts of information.'

'I wasn't aware of that,' Allison said with respect; 'I was under the impression that you were associated with Unicorn in a formal capacity.'

'I am,' Yoshimura interrupted once more; 'But that was as a consequence of the wishes of the health authorities in Japan. It was not a choice I made personally.'

Allison reconsidered the diminutive man who stood before her. Questions fell through her like the waterfall she'd seen only the day before. She could tell from Yoshimura's demeanour that there was more to this than he'd already told her. She determined to know the worst:

'What is really happening?' she asked quietly; 'I'd be grateful if you would tell me.'

Yoshimura took a few paces away from her, looked at the sun, the large red sun which so dominated his beautiful country:

'The heirs to the British throne have been diagnosed positive for acute intermittent porphyria,' he responded gently; 'Unicorn have this information and, I believe, intend to use it inappropriately.'

'In what way?' the young doctor asked, subdued now, calm.

'I believe your eminent colleague Sir William Mostyn would like to make some sort of deal with the royal family. Part of it seems simple enough, but there are other aspects... .' Yoshimura shook his head in puzzlement, it was all far from clear to him either: 'No one is quite certain,' he continued; 'However, they certainly intend making public the fact that your monarchy have this disease.

'This information could only have come from your colleague and, given the other facts which I have, from other colleagues too.'

'But that would suggest that Doctor Bennet, perhaps John Raynor. Pam! I can't believe it, Yoshimura-San. It's out of the question. impossible.'

'There is evidence to suggest that it's not.'

Confused as she was Allison went along with the Japanese for the moment: 'But, if it is true, then someone has to stop them?'

'A difficult thing to do,' said Yukio Yoshimura; 'They are breaking no fiscal law.'

'No, but it's immoral,' said Allison firmly; 'And that's just as bad.'

'I thought you might say that,' said Yoshimura gently. 'Come, I'd like to take you somewhere, see something. It's not far away.' He took Allison by the hand and she followed him to the car.

Yoshimura drove off heading West and Allison saw the magnificense of the giant deep red sun.

After about a half-hour drive, they suddenly came across a small temple almost completely hidden by small trees and bushes. When the car's engine had been shut off Allison noticed just how quiet it was. How tranquil the whole place felt. She walked slowly towards the small shrine leaving Yoshimura in the car. She recognized it immediately as a Shinto shrine - a shrine to the spirits of nature and of life.

There was a small stream nearby and the sunlight fell around her causing a remarkable sensation to unfold within her. This was beauty, real beauty. It was ineffable. In the distance there were mountains flirting with mist.

Allison heard the trickle of the stream as it flowed from the shrine. She thought on Yoshimura's poem; the traditional haiku form he had helped her translate into English. She had translated it:

Life Flow
"Water is sacred,
Where is life?
It flows;
A fresh stream,
In springtime."

She looked far away into the distance. The air seemed alive, mists hung white around the mountains. She felt something. Something touched her at the base of her neck. She shivered and turned round. Yoshimura was looking at her. He smiled. Allison returned his smile. She had begun to make her decision.

That night, Allison was taken to her small discreet room where a futon lay spread over a tatami straw matted floor. She had never slept on a futon before, but found it very comfortable indeed despite its lowness. When she had made her goodnights to the Yoshimuras, she lay thinking about her trip home tomorrow and the decisions that faced her. Outside the moon was pale and a cold wind, swept moonlit clouds across a dark blue sky.

CHAPTER TWELVE

Allison paid another visit to her parents. As soon as they discovered her intentions, Allison's parents helped her pack what she required and after reminding her to drive carefully, they watched their daughter drive off into the falling night. Her father's face in particular was fixed rigid with a very serious look indeed. His daughter had very serious business to attend to.

Allison drove fast. Against her better judgement she decided to stop only to refuel and hoped in this way to reach the hospital within a few hours. As her car sped along swiftly and easily, images flitted through her mind, of Harry and Tina, of Dr Bennett and John Raynor of a secret society, of conspiracy in royal circles. Of everything she was going to.

To distract her thoughts she switched on her radio and turned the dial. She moved it along absentmindedly until she was tuned into one of her favorite stations and programs. It was light, popular though at present the newscaster was talking about some terrorist outrage in the State. Its familiarity seemed welcoming at first, reassuring, solid.

She tried to remember the times she had listened to this program before; tried to recall the various episodes of her life that had been going on then, but it was no good. The images of what awaited her continued to trickle through and disturb her and at last she turned the radio off, set her face in a fixed determined look and drove on in silence into the night-time.

She made good time and it was in the early hours of the morning when she arrived at the entrance to the hospital. The sign saying The London General Hospital was lit up outside the entrance and as she turned the car by it, Allison briefly remembered her first day there. Her nervousness, her meeting with Jennifer, with Harry. It now seemed like a very long time ago indeed.

Allison parked the car as close as she could to the ward and moved quickly through the doorway and into the long corridor. She walked briskly along it, thoughts tumbling through her head, concern gripping her tightly. She finally turned into the ward, walked along the small corridor within it, entered Tina's room and saw the child's bed.

Harry was sitting on it speaking to Pam who was standing beside him. Jennifer was also there, standing vacantly, out of uniform, obviously called from home and sleep and looking very concerned indeed.

Allison's heart sank as she took it all in. Tina was lying prepared for surgery and she looked very, very weak.

Weak as she was, it was the child who was first to speak:

'Hello, Dr Young,' she said.

'Hello,' replied Allison feeling flustered. 'How are things? How are you?' she continued, turning her attention to Tina.

The child smiled at her. 'O.K.' she replied in a very weak voice. 'This is my dad.'

'I know,' said Allison. 'We've met.'

'He's lovely, isn't he?' said Tina.

Allison felt herself flush. 'Yes' she said with a smile.' Any complaints, young lady?' Tina shook her head. 'Well,

I thought I'd just pop in and see how you were doing,' she continued. 'I see you're going off to get things sorted out once and for all.'

'This is good of you,' Harry interupted; 'Tina tells me you dropped in on her quite often. She enjoyed the company, didn't you, love?' The girl nodded briefly. 'So you got back from the meeting O.K., then?' Harry said, intentionally making even conversation to keep Tina's mind - and his own - off the immanent surgery.

'Yes,' Allison responded. 'I did. And you?'

'Yes, no trouble. I left a bit early to get back to this young lady here. I called 214 a few times but there was no reply.'

Allison wondered what he was referring to. '214?' she repeated, confused.

'Yes, your room number, at the hotel. I called to say I was going, but there was never any reply. The desk clerk was no help either. Simply said you weren't there.'

'I wasn't,' Allison said bemused. 'I was in room two ones four -114 - that's why you didn't get through! The desk should have checked the register, however, I-'

'- Well, they didn't,' Harry said quietly.

'No,' said Allison, wondering what to say next, when the porters came for Tina.

'Come on, young lady,' said the nurse who accompanied the porter with the trolley. Tina was helped on and they wheeled her off to theatre with Harry being allowed to go as far as the pre-med room with her. Allison gave Tina and Harry a brief wave. Tina waved weakly back, but Harry, walking there handsome and tormented didn't respond at all.

He returned and without saying anything about his daughter turned to Allison, extending his arm as he did so and taking her hand in his own.

'It was good of you to drive up. There was no need to, but I'm glad you did.' Allison noticed that his voice was very controlled, it showed no trace of emotion whatever. It was his professional voice, measured and careful.

'Tina?' asked; 'What's happened to her?'

'She's in surgery now, Allison,' Harry continued, as Pam and Jennifer looked on quietly. Allison noticed now that Jennifer had been crying. She wasn't at all surprised. But Harry was in control now. The situation was bringing things together within him. He was already accepting the worst. In a sense he was returning rapidly to normal.

'I called a young surgeon I know...' he continued.

'Yes, I've met him briefly,' said Allison absently as Harry elaborated.

'He's been doing some highly experimental work and has developed a new surgical procedure which could just work with Tina. It's a very long shot indeed but it's all we have. He received permission from the ethical committee to go ahead just over an hour ago, and he's operating on Tina right now. It's her only chance - we had to take it.'

'Of course you did,' agreed Allison, looking up at Harry as she sat down in a chair and Pam went off to find her a cup of coffee. She noted that he looked very different from the man she had held so tightly by the lake, the man who had so distressed her. He was disciplined and controlled and handling the situation with uncommon clarity of thought and objectivity given the circumstances.

This, she knew, was the real Harry, the successful man and physician. The man everyone loved and respected so much. The crisis in his daughter's illness had indeed brought him together again, reformed him. His eyes glowed with a deep penetrating blueness. Allison knew without doubt that she loved this man. In a way which the poet alone understood.

They sat around talking, keeping their minds as far as possible from the events in the operating theatre. Every new movement, however, from any of the staff around drew their attentions to it and to the fact that Tina was facing a life-or-death battle at that very moment under the skilled hands of the young surgeon.

Allison distracted them as much as she could with a few observations on the time she'd spent with her parents. Pam brought her up to date with what had been happening in the hospital in her absence and Jennifer, still very tired looking, supplemented this where and when she could.

These efforts, however, could barely remove their attention for long from the patient and interspersed with such talk, the conversation always turned back to the child and how she might be faring. Harry said little about his daughter, however, preferring to 'Just wait and see.' rather than speculate any further on the possible outcome of the highly speculative surgery.

At length, they persuaded Pam to excuse herself and go off to try and catch an hour or so's sleep. She was on duty very early and they were insistent, promising they would let her have any news as soon as it was available. Reluctantly she went off, also looking very tired and very concerned indeed.

As the hands of the clock moved towards 5 a.m., Allison realized that Tina had now been in surgery for over four hours. She wondered just how much trauma the frail little girl could take, how she could possibly cope for so long with the anaesthesia and the surgery. It didn't seem possible that she could survive.

At length, one of the theatre nurses approached them and beckokned to Harry: 'Doctor Wright,' she said. 'Could I have a word with you?' Harry stood up and walked over to her and they spoke quietly together. Harry turned to look at Allison and Jennifer: 'Excuse me,' he said to them firmly; 'I have to go.' With that he accompanied the nurse out of the ward and into the corridor. Allison and Jennifer looked at each other. For a few supportive moments, they took each other's hand.

About half an hour later, Harry returned. As he made his way towards them, both Allison and Jennifer were rigid with anticipation. His appearance betrayed nothing, gave no hint as to how Tina had progressed. He walked over to them and sat down.

'The surgeon says that there's a chance,' he said. 'She's still in the recovery room and by some miracle has survived the procedure relatively intact. He managed to remove the whole tumor mass which, if nothing else, is an enormous success for him and his technique.

'The problem now, however, lies with Tina's vital functions. They're understandably pretty labored and the staff are worried about respiratory or cardiovascular collapse. We won't know how things are going to turn out for some time yet. All we can do now is go home and get some sleep. The staff will call me immediately they have any news.'

'Let me know immediately you hear something, Harry,' said Jennifer.

'Me too, Harry,' Allison added. 'Please call me straight away. I'll be at home.'

'I'll do that,' said Harry, addressing both of them simultaneously. 'Now, let's all get some rest. There's nothing more we can do here for now.'

Allison drove home through the early morning streets with her tired mind ruminating on the events of the night. She hoped with all her might that Tina would recover. That the dramatic success of the surgery would not be made useless by post-operative complications and that the lovely little girl would have the chance at life she so richly deserved.

She knew, however, the risks involved and the unlikelihood of success that existed. She had rarely known of a patient so compromised who had survived any procedure and all she could do was hope that Tina was one of the few exceptions.

More than anything, however, what held her mind most was her image of Harry. Authoritative, decisive, confidant and controlled in the face of his daughter's possible death. And gentle and considerate too. Despite the seemingly sudden change which had enabled him to integrate himself once more, he had maintained the gentility she had do loved about him. A gentility based on strength and caring and which complemented perfectly those other aspects of him which she also loved so much.

Allison wondered what other aspects of his prior state Harry had maintained. In particular, she wondered if he had now managed to expel enough grief to give her the opportunity of entering his life and filling the vacuum the death of his former wife had left.

As she lay down on top of her bed and pulled the duvet over her very tired body, she continued to think on these things and on the others too; and they fluttered through her thoughts keeping her awake with uncertainty and anticipation. At length, she fell asleep and very soon she was dreaming. And as she so dreamt, a warmth such as she had never known, enfolded her.

She woke abruptly to the ring of the telephone. Reflexly she reached out, grabbed it and brought it to her face:

'Hello, Allison?' the voice said. Through her sleepiness Allison realized that it was Harry. Instantly she was fully awake and a sinking sensation grabbed at her stomach.

'Yes, Harry,' she said. 'How are things? Are things O.K.?' she rephrased, sensing that they weren't.

'We don't know yet. I was in again this morning and there was no change. The mite is holding her own, but she's weak. She's putting up a tremendous fight, but it's still touch and go.'

As he spoke, Allison looked at her bedside clock. It was almost eleven o'clock. She had slept a great deal later than she had intended. Even as she wondered at this, Harry continued:

'Look, Allison,' he said. 'The main reason I telephoned, was to ask you if you'd mind coming over to spend the day with me here, if you're free to do so. I was going to pop in and out of the hospital fairly frequently, but have decided it's fairer on them if I wait here for some definite word. It's going to be a long day and I'd appreciate the company.'

'Why, of course I will,' responded Allison immediately. 'I'll be over within the hour. How, precisely, do I get to you?'

Harry gave her detailed instructions on how to reach his home and within the hour Allison had showered, dressed, rummaged through her back mail, had a quick cup of instant coffee and was in her car driving towards Harry's house.

As she attempted to follow the rough map she had drawn to simplify his directions, she felt all sorts of feelings run within her. All of them concerned her, but some were of a very different nature to the others.

Allison turned into the street where Harry lived and immediately saw his house. It *was* imposing and very impressive indeed. She wondered how Harry managed to run it on his own.

As she drove into the driveway, the door opened and Harry came out to meet her. He waved and smiled at her, but through his solid composure Allison knew he must be very worried. She waved back, stopped the car and switched off the engine. A silence fell around her as if she were miles from the town. It was a lovely house and a lovely place to live. She got out of the car and closed the door behind her.

Inside, the house was as impressive as it was outside and after they had briefly discussed Tina, there being no further news, Allison decided to distract Harry's attention by asking him about his home.

Before she could do so, the phone rang. Harry picked it up.

'Hello,' he said. 'Doctor Wright speaking.' He listened for a time and said nothing. A grim, determined look tightened his face. 'I'll be right over,' Putting the phone down. He turned to Allison. 'I'll have to go over to the hospital. Things are critical. She's still fighting away but they'd rather I be there over the next hour or so. Yo're welcome to stay here if you'd like to.'

Harry gave Allison a deep, intimate look, one that told her he wanted her to stay.

'I'd like to,' she replied, walking over to him and squeezing his shoulder in mute support.

'Fine,' he said. 'See you when I get back. Help yourself to whatever you need.' With that, he went to a small cloakroom, pulled on a driving jacket and went out of the door into his car and drove off. When the sound of the car had gone it was very quiet indeed.

Allison sat for a while looking around the lounge which was traditionally furnished and which had, along one wall, a beautiful chaise-longue. In one of the corners there was a period mahogany cabinet on top of which there was a framed photograph of Harry's former wife. Allison went over and looked at it, at the beautiful woman, at the wife and mother he and Tina had lost. And that's precisely how things were. The woman was dead.

No jealousy clouded her thinking now, no sense of inferiority, or irrational anger that he had loved this woman, and still did so in his way. All that she felt was a deep and profound sadness that such tragedy had struck this lovely man and his daughter and she also felt an equally deep and profound hope that things would go better for him now.

She sat there for a time flicking through the morning paper which had obviously remained untouched since its delivery. She couldn't really concentrate on it, however, her thoughts constantly flitting to Harry, the hospital, Tina and the drama which was unfolding and surrounding the three of them.

At length she heard a noise at the front door - a key fumbling in the lock. She put the paper down and rushed through to the entrance hall. As the door swung open her heart was thumping hard in her chest:

'Hello,' the woman said. 'I'm Mrs Mawson, Doctor Wright's receptionist. You must be a friend of his. How's Tina?' Her voice was genuinely concerned.

'Well, yes, I'm Allison Young. Not so good, I'm afraid,' Allison immediately took to the woman, there was a genuine caring in her enquiry that she liked. 'At least, we're not quite sure yet. Doctor Wright's with her now.'

'I hope she gets well,' said the woman, looking with sincerity at Allison. 'She's a brave little thing, so lovely too.'

'I hope so too,' Allison said softly. 'I really do.'

For the next hour or so, Allison sat around chatting occasionally with Mrs Mawson while she went about her work. At length it was completed and with some more expressions of concern for Tina, the woman left and Allison was immersed within the silence again with her thoughts. It was late afternoon now and she wondered just what was happening at the hospital.

Once or twice she had considered phoning to see what she could discover, but on each occasion she had finally decided against it. It would add more to the very busy workload they had there and anyway, she would know in time.

The sky seemed to dull a little and Allison looked out of the lounge window. Harry's car was approaching the house and within a short second, she found it had entered the driveway and was parked outside. She rushed to the door, opened it and waited. She held her breath as Harry walked towards her looking very determined and serious.

He said nothing until he entered the house and closed the door behind him. His eyes met Allison's:

'She's going to pull through,' he said. 'She'll make it now. She'll be fine.'

'Oh, Harry, I'm so glad.' Allison rushed to him and buried her head in his chest. She pulled herself close and his arms surrounded her. He held her tight and firm as if he would never let her go. She felt herself sink into him and felt a wave of relaxation and relief wash over her, freshening her thoughts, clearing them.

They stood that way for some minutes, expressing their mutual relief in mutual silence and proximity. At length, Allison felt a change occur in herself and in him. She could sense his masculinity now, his strength, his controlled passion. She tilted her head and looked at him. Their eyes met again and this time a look passed between them which made her feel something she had never felt before in her life.

She raised her hand and ran it along the back of Harry's neck. Simultaneously he let his own fall down her back, his nails gently stroking her back through her light dress, dropping lower and coming round across her breasts, brushing her nipples, making them harden with a powerful excitement.

She kissed him full in the mouth and his tongue entered her, soft as velvet, warm, exploring her as she in turn responded, mixing her warmth and moistness with his.

His hands went to the straps of her dress and loosened them. The top of her dress fell from her and he traced his tongue along her cheek, down her neck to her breasts. He nibbled gently on her nipples as he released her bra and it fell from her leaving her trembling with excitement.

Still kissing her, Harry lifted Allison in his arms and carried her through the lounge to his bedroom. He placed her on the bed and lay beside of her, kissing her, licking her skin, finishing undressing her and dropping her remaining clothes upon the floor.

'I love you,' she whispered as she began to undress him, unbuttoning his shirt, easing his trousers from his firm, muscular body the odour of which aroused her like a potent aphrodisiac.

'Me, too,' he responded genttly, licking her ear, blowing warm breaths into it; sending shivers of pleasure through her with the deft use of his hands.

Allison turned over fully and pulled him on top of her. She was swimming in blissful sensations and emotions as she felt his strength above her, smelled deeper of his deep masculine smell, held him tight:

'Love me, my Harry,' she gasped. 'Oh, love me, love me!'

'Allison,' he whispered, even as he continued to excite her. 'I want to so much, so very, very much.' He pulled her even tighter to him, entered her, hard warm wide; riding her hard as she gasped deeply, deeper than she ever had before.

As the sky fell darker and the afternoon progressed, they meged with one-another completely and totally. They consummated, with thrilling passion, the potent love they felt for one another. It was a long time later that, in emotional and physical exhaustion, they came together again and, arms entwined, fell asleep.

It was a full four hours later when they awoke. They made love again, gently and tenderly. Afterwards Harry telephoned the hospital to check on Tina's condition. It was stable and improving. He came back into bed beside Allison and they lay together, holding one another, talking and loving as the evening deepened and the shadows fell.

Later they both paid a brief visit to see Tina. She couldn't speak partricularly coherently as yet, but she looked a great deal better and was obviously very happy to see them. The medical view now was that she could potentially make a full recovery though it would take some months to be certain.

As they made to leave, Allison realized that Tina was trying to say something to her and was determined to do so. She bent down to hear the tired girl's whispers and strained to hear:

'I'll get to the concert now,' she said. 'Cat Machine. Do you remember, Doctor Young? My favorite group?'

'I remember,' Allison smiled. She was getting better. 'You'll get to a concert, Tina, I promise you. Cat Machine,' she repeated. 'You'll get to see them, I promise.

Tina lay back seemingly content as Harry and Allison left her to rest and recuperate.

As they made their way back to Harry's house he turned to Allison and made her day perfect:

'I wonder,' he asked her, 'If you'd like to spend the next few days with me when we're free. I've got a few patients to see and have to attend to Tina, of course, but otherwise... well. You may as well spend what's left of your holiday with someone? Why not with me?'

'I can't think,' Allison replied non-committally.

'Think what?' Harry asked, slightly bewildered.

'Of anyone I'd rather spend it with.' she said, as she briefly squeezed his hand and kissed him gently on the cheek.

'Settled then?' asked Harry.

'Very settled!' Allison replied.

As the night-time brushed the sky, the moon rose slowly full.

The remainder of the week was on the happiest periods of Allison's life. She and Harry spent every free moment they had together and they talked about themselves and their lives and they shared moments of sadness and tenderness together and discovered each other every day as new.

Although Allison spent her nights at her flat, she also spent a great deal of time at Harry's place and she grew to love the house and its magnificent rooms and rambling garden. The surgery and consulting room were superb and as well-equipped as any you would find anywhere. It was evident that Harry had spared no cost in his preparations for treating his patients properly and she knew that, in time, his practice would return to being the enormous success it had been.

Allison watched how, now that Tina was beginning to become well again, Harry threw himself back into his work and into getting his affairs and practice ship-shape again. She helped him as much as she could with advice on his paperwork and even ventured an opinion or two on a few of his most difficult medical cases.

They visited Tina twice daily at the hospital and it was evident - even after so little time - that she was improving slowly but surely. Color was coming back to her face and for the first time since she'd met her, Allison began to realize what a lovely looking little girl she was.

She was speaking more and more each day and by the end of the week, she was able to speak for quite a few minutes without becoming breathless. Even to Allison, experienced as she was in dealing with such cases, Tina's progress was remarkable and she discerned in it all the fighting spirit she knew her father had.

After the hospital visit, when he'd seen the last of his patients in the evening, Harry would drive Allison out deep into the country where they would go for a walk, have dinner, then drive somewhere to sit and talk about all the things they wanted each other to know. These evenings were idyllic for Allison and, each night before she went to sleep, she went over them in her mind, recapturing special moments, lovely ones - ones she'd never lose.

It was during one of these talks in the car after a long walk and dinner had made them especially relaxed and peaceful that Harry had told Allison about Ann. This was a subject she had only now come to realize she could listen to him discuss, without undue and inappropriate emotional involvement. He had told her that he wanted to tell her about their relationship and Allison had indicated for him to do so, assuring him that she was a sensitive and willing audience.

'We met when we were undergraduates,' Harry began, smiling at the reminiscence. 'Me a wet behind the ears medical student and Ann a linguist, majoring in French and German.'

'We were both just seventeen when we met - in fact she was a few months older than I was - and it seemed the most natural thing on Earth for us to get together and stay there. We were quite inseparable and we were married almost exactly two years after first meeting.

'We had Tina two years later, much to the dismay of our parents and teachers. It made no difference to our studies though, except that Ann couldn't go abroad for the year she was required to, in order to obtain her degree with honors. She did without the honours and Tina became part of us instead. We always felt that she should have been there to pick up a scroll herself, when first Ann and then I, graduated.

'From the beginning of our relationship, everyone was predicting dire things. Financial and academic ruin, a quick marriage followed by an even quicker divorce, everything imaginable.' He paused, reflecting on times past

'Somehow, we managed to sail through life without these things occurring, without any of the troubles many young people face in such a situation. I was fortunate enough to get a few lucky breaks with placings with good people like John Bennet and to succeed in private practice without any apparent major effort.'

At the mention of John Bennet's name Allison chilled. She'd managed to keep that issue out of Harry's way for the past week. She appreciated that she'd have to tell him about that particular madness sometime soon, but not yet. She didn't want to quite yet.

'Ann taught for a while which helped financially,' he continued. Then, as the practice grew and I brought in some good income from some financial dealings of my own, she gave that up and managed the practice full-time.

'She was a good administrator and as deft with the paperwork and my patients as she was with her languages. Everything was going so well, very well indeed. I suppose there was a surplus of riches in every sense.'

Allison caught the brief change in his tenor, his down-swing of mood and she encouraged him to continue: 'It sounds as if you were a great match,' she said with encouragement; 'You were both very lucky indeed, to have what you did have, even if it ended as it did.'

Harry looked at her, slightly distant, preoccupied with the memory of such tragedy. 'We were,' he went on. 'I see it that way now, though I didn't until very recently. There's a special reason for that, you see, something almost no-one knows about.

Things were great for a number of reasons, marvelous, that's why the whole thing was so awful.

'You see, Allison, not only was the practice doing well and Tina blossoming, but Ann was pregnant again. We even had amniocentesis carried out to determine the baby's gender. It would have been a boy. The perfect complement to Tina.'

'Oh!' Allison was quite shocked and suddenly hurting terribly for him. 'Oh, Harry, I'd no idea...'

'Anyway, the irony is that it was on a routine trip to see Ann's gynecologist when a car on the opposite lane of the motorway had a blow out and hit Ann's car head on.

'All those years of plenty were called in within a second. I was talking to our housekeeper when I received the call. We were discussing how best to clean one of the carpets. The message was simple. My wife and unborn child were dead.'

'It was only the thought of Tina that kept me going then. It was pretty awful. I did love Ann a great deal, you know, a great deal. That's something that won't ever change.'

'I know,' Allison said softly to him. 'I know that, Harry, it can't change and it shouldn't. It must have been terrible for you, terrible.'

'I'm over it now, Allison, over the worst of it. Yes, I'm glad of the time Ann and I had and I've got Tina to show for it and lots of happy memories. I was very lucky indeed, exceptionally so and I still am.'

They sat in silence for a time, each ruminating, sifting through thoughts and emotions, wondering about the past, the present, the future; what it held, what it might bring to them. After a time, Harry spoke again. He sounded interested, concerned.

'Ever been in love yourself?' he asked. 'Really in love?'

Allison sat quietly for a while wondering how she could answer such a question. After hearing what Harry had just told

her it seemed a difficult question to answer. Love was about
many things and, it seemed, he had known most of them. For
her part what could she say by comparison?

'I had a relationship for a while with someone,' Allison
began. 'But I don't imagine you could call it real 'love' - whatever
that means. As I see it now, it was more like a maternal rush'
she said. 'One that lasted far too long.'

'I don't know if you'd understand that sort of thing. It
seems, well... a bit feminine, really, I suppose. I think I was
attracted to a child in a way, a grown-up child, mark you, but
a child just the same.'

'I understand, Allison,' he said softly. 'I know the sort of
thing you mean. It isn't uncommon or easy to handle either.'

Allison told Harry about Ken and his crippling possessiveness.
He seemed interested, but not unduly so. She wondered how she
could possibly have had such a relationship, now that she had
discovered this man.

'It's all over now, though,' she reflected, ending her brief
account of the relationship with a depth of feeling that was
clear in her voice. 'All over, very much. Very much indeed.'
Harry turned to her and she was expecting him to make some
comment on what she had just told him. He didn't.

'Tomorrow,' he said, instead; 'I'm going to take you to *The
Marlow Bridge* again. Are your lips up to it?' Allison laughed
softly:

'I don't know,' she replied as she turned to him and put her
hand behind his head pulling him to her. 'But they're up to
this,' she kissed him soft and warm, expressing her love for him
as deeply as she could.

That night, Allison returned to her flat feeling almost
overcome with her love for Harry. The details he had given her
of the circumstances of his wife's terrible accident enabled her to

appreciate more fully just what he had been through and what he had emerged from.

Gone now, completely, were her thoughts of comparison, her juvenile jealousies. In their place, there was a desire to make herself a fitting companion for this marvellous man and the hope that he would see her as such and perhaps, in time, become her husband.

There was a knock on her door and as she moved towards it to open it, she looked at her watch wondering who in the name of God would call at this time. She wondered if it was Harry, if he had returned for some reason. As she reached for the door-knob, she cautiously asked who was there. A voice replied at once:

'It's me, Allison. Sorry to disturb you. I saw the light on and...'

Allison felt quite unreal. She recognized the voice immediately. It was Ken.

She let him in and directed him towards a seat. It was evident that he was very distressed about something and Allison wondered what.

'I had to see you, Allison,' he started. 'I've decided to leave general practice and go into hospital medicine. I thought you should know.'

Allison looked at him carefully. She sensed something was wrong. There was something different about him. Then, all at once she realized that perhaps there was nothing different about him at all, that the difference was in her:

'Why, Ken? Why should I know?' she asked him abruptly.

'Because it might just alter your attitude to us. I've thought of little else, Allison, since the evening we left that laboratory. We have too much to give each other to throw it away, too much we can share and make a decent life with together. So

I've decided to give up my job for you. We can be together, as we always wanted to be.'

Allison was incredulous. She observed him closely, his posture, his eyes:

'Have you been drinking?' she asked.

'Just a little,' he admitted, noticeably flushed now. 'Why not? A celebration. A get-together.' He laughed: 'So what's wrong with that?'

'There's plenty wrong, Ken, plenty wrong with that and with just about everything else you've said.'

'We're finished Ken. I made that perfectly clear to you... finished for good. There is no question of that situation changing, none whatsoever. Now, if you'd like to go, I would be very grateful indeed.'

'Is there someone else?' he asked aggressively. 'Has someone else moved in already? Well, is there?'

Allison was beginning to lose her temper, fast. She was tired and had been so happy this evening. This was the last thing she needed. As she stared intently at Ken, ready to give him a real piece of her mind, the phone rang. Still looking at him angrily, she lifted the receiver:

'Hope I'm not disturbing you,' the familiar voice said. 'Just thought I'd call to say what a lovely evening I had.' It was Harry and his voice was soft and gentle. 'You're very special to me, Allison, very special indeed. I wanted you to know that, yet again.'

'I... oh thanks,' Allison garbled uncomfortably. 'Thanks, Harry, I...'

'Is there someone there?' Harry asked, obviously detecting the strain in her voice.

'No, not really, just...'

'So, there is someone else. Already!' Ken shouted, loud enough to be heard over the telephone. 'Marvelous - you didn't waste any time hanging about, did you, Allison? Who's the lucky man then? Your boss perhaps, or someone else who can advance your almighty career such as your laboratory friend... is that him eh?'

Allison could hear Harry's voice still speaking: 'Sorry, Allison, didn't think you'd have company at this time. I'm sorry to have called. I...'

'No, Harry!' Allison said, filling with rage and confusion. 'It's Ken. He's turned up out of the blue and...' but before she could finish, she realized that the receiver had been put down and there was just the solitary noise of the dialing tone. She looked at Ken with a look he had never seen in her before:

'You...' she began, pointing at him, speechless for a second. 'Get out of here, you drunken shit. I never realized until this moment what a spoiled, self-centered, egocentric little bastard you were. I should have realized it long ago. I wish to God I had. Get out of here, Ken - now - or I'll call the police and have them arrest you.'

'You bitch,' he said, walking towards her. 'You would, too, wouldn't you? Just because someone else shows an interest... Excites you, does he? Good between the sheets? You whore! You couldn't even wait a decent interval. Yo've always been the same. I give up my job for you, I put my career in jeopardy, I get involved with those bastards at Unicorn Chemicals to make some money for us and...'

As Allison moved to open the door, he grabbed hold of her and attempted to kiss her. His hands grabbed at her breasts fumbling and pressing as he squeezed hard through the light fabric of her dress, hurting her.

'Out!' Allison shouted, pushing him away from her and pointing to the door, attempting to get to it, to pull it open.

'You dirty little...' Before he could say anything more, Allison had managed to grab him by the back of his jacket, bring her knee up hard against his groin and as he doubled over with the pain, managed to drag him towards the door and push him out. She slammed the door behind him and locked it in one quick movement. She could hear him continue to rant outside but she didn't give a toss.

She sat down for a moment or two to compose herself and heard him leave, still cursing her and using all sorts of exotic epithets.

Her hands trembling, she reached for the telephone to call Harry. She dialed his number and listened to the first few rings. There was a click at the other end and his telephone machine answered her. It asked whoever had called him to leave a message.

For a multitude of reasons, Allison walked to her bed, lay down on top of it, and wept. It was only later, just before she fell asleep, that the fact that Ken had mentioned Unicorn Chemicals impressed itself upon her. She was too drained to care.

The following morning Allison woke early after a fitful night's sleep. Scenes of Ken's abusive behavior towards her and of Harry's interrupted telephone call flashed through her mind. The contrast between the two men couldn't have been more emphatic and as she lay there in the forming light, she hoped with all her heart that Ken's sudden and unexpected intrusion back into her life hadn't been misunderstood by Harry.

She decided to wait until around eight to call him and apologize for the debacle of the previous night. He would have had breakfast by then and would be free before seeing his first patient at eight thirty. She would arrange to see him that lunch-time and make up for her lack of response to the sentiments of his call.

She duly called at eight and Harry answered on the first ring:

'Oh, Allison,' he said, sounding almost cool to her. 'How are you?'

'Fine, Harry. Look, about last night. I'm very sorry. Ken turned up here drunk and...'

'There's no need to explain, Allison,' he said. 'No need at all. Look, forgive, me but I must get back to some notes I've been reading. I have to finish them before my first patient arrives and they're fairly hefty reading.'

'Why, of course. I'm sorry. I wondered if? What are you doing for lunch?'

'I'm tied up today, Allison. In fact I've had a load of mail this morning - the practice is recovering and I'm afraid I don't think I'll be able to make it this evening either. I hope you don't mind but I'm sure you understand that...'

'Of course,' Allison interrupted. 'Of course, I understand, Harry. I'll call you later.'

'Do that. Bye.'

'Bye,' Allison repeated as she placed the receiver back in its place and felt a wave of what was almost naked fear pass through her. Ken's appearance had disturbed Harry. It was not surprising. His first relationship since the tragedy, the first open expressions of that relationship and he discovers Allison at home at night with her former lover. What else could he think? How else could he react? What else did she expect?

She called Pam and arranged to have lunch with her. It helped distract her from thoughts of Harry and gave her the opportunity to catch up on what was happening at the hospital medically and personally. As ever, it was the latter which gradually dominated the conversation:

'And Jennifer's been seeing Gerry's friend, Michael, quite a bit. They seem quite attached. Wouldn't surprise me if they didn't end up married.'

'But he's such an odd young chap,' Allison said surprised. 'You know I've met him once or twice and I don't think I've heard him speak once.'

'He doesn't say much,' Pam agreed, laughing. 'But what he does say obviously has effect. Jennifer thinks so anyway. They've apparently been inseparable for months and few of us knew anything about it. Gerry only told me yesterday. Anyway, how are things with you and Harry?'

'Troubled,' Allison said to her friend and explained what had happened the night before.

'I think you may have got things a bit confused,' said Pam in response. 'You'll probably find that Harry is busy, that he has got a great deal to do today that's come up unexpectedly. I think you'll find too that the incident with Ken has barely crossed his mind and that, if it has, he appreciates it for precisely what it was. His apparent coolness towards you probably exists only in your imagination.

'You spent a long time with Ken, Allison, and a lot of your experiences and expectations of and from a relationship are based on what you learned from his responses, not from someone like Harry.

'I may be wrong, but I'll bet Harry's missing you today as much as you're missing him. He's just very busy getting his life together again. He's not Ken - don't expect him to behave like him.'

Allison listened to her friend, was surprised at her insight into her and felt very confused. "Was this true? Was Harry merely very busy?" She would have liked to have thought so, but...

'Believe me,' continued Pam, seeing her friend's confused expression. 'I know Harry well enough now to assess the man and I'm not blinded by love for him. I'm right. You'll see.' As Allison asked Pam how the pregnancy was coming on, she certainly hoped that she would see and soon.

When asked about her pregnancy Pam had looked distressed. She lit a cigarette and, inhaling the smoke deeply, addressed her friend with a directness that Allison had never seen in her before.

'Would you mind, Allison, if we dropped that topic for good. For now anyway?' She inhaled again and sipped from her drink, a glass of light wine, which surprised and pleased Allison. At least some attempt was being made to deal with her drinking.

'The situation is a great deal more complicated than I've intimated to you,' she confided; 'and it would be best all round if we didn't discuss it.' Allison was taken aback, but understood her friend's sentiments. She wondered however precisely *what* was "more complicated" and she realized that the time was fast approaching when she'd have to confront *someone* with the knowledge she had.

'I'm sorry, Pam. Of course I'll respect your wishes,' she said in an understanding tone. There was little, however, that she did understand. It was about time to start doing so.

It was evening before she called him and he still seemed distracted and distant to her. He said that he was very busy indeed and that if she didn't mind he'd cancel The Marlow Bridge for that evening. Allison said that was fine, that she understood.

'I could pop over later, though,' Harry said, unexpectedly. 'Around ten or so, if it's not too late. We could go for a short run or something. If you'd like to.'

'Of course!' Allison said immediately. 'Of course I'd like to.'

'I'll pick you up around ten, then,' he said. 'See you then.'
He hung up and Allison began to realize that Pam had been correct after all.

After dinner alone, Allison dressed very carefully and applied the slight touches of make-up which were barely necessary to define her lovely features. She was ready far too soon and ended up pacing back and forth across her lounge floor, waiting impatiently for the sound of Harry's car.

After what seemed a very long time indeed, she heard the car pull up outside and without waiting, she made her way out of the door and walked briskly towards it. Harry was sitting at the wheel, a bit tired looking, but obviously pleased to see her:

'Hello,' he said, smiling. 'That was quick. You're better than Jerome. Reading minds now, are we?'

With those few words Allison realized just how wrong she'd been. Harry was a man such as she had never met before, Ken had never allowed her the opportunity to do so.

She briefly explained to him about Ken's unexpected appearance at her flat and Harry's reponse was initially one of concern for her safety. As her description of events continued, however, it gradually changed to one of amusement.

'I don't imagine he'll be troubling you again,' he said. 'Seems you can handle troublemakers O.K. Maybe you're in the wrong profession!'

'I don't think so somehow,' Allison replied, now amused at the fracas herself. 'I think I'll stay put, just where I am.'

They drove out deep into the countryside and along the dark country roads. The headlights of Harry's car shone out brightly in front of them, but otherwise they were surrounded by darkness with not even the reflected light of the town to lighten the sky.

Allison watched a few moonlit clouds rush by the moon as the car drove steadily on until they reached the entrance to a country park where Allison had never been before. Harry drove the car in, brought it to the edge of a small ridge which overlooked a wide expanse of shadowed flat countryside and pulled it to a stop. He switched the engine off and there was utter, total, silence.

'It's lovely here,' said Allison quietly. 'So quiet, isolated. Perfect.'

'It is, isn't it?' Harry responded. 'It's one fo my favorite places. I used to come here often when I'd a major decision to make. I remember sitting here just like this before deciding to leave Saint Luke's I agonised for weeks over that and resolved it here in just a few, quiet, hours of peaceful reflection.'

'I'm not surprised,' continued Allison, as a strange sense of excitement began to creep over her. 'It's a beautiful place, a place where things could be resolved, decided.

'Yes,' said Harry. 'That's why I'm here now!'

'Why?'

'To resolve something.'

'What?'

'Whether or not you'd like to become my wife.'

Allison was pleasantly stunned. In her wildest dreams she never thought she'd hear these words from him so soon. She turned and looked at the man, her eyes filled with him, shining with him in some stray beams of moonlight:

'I've never wanted anything more in my life,' she said quietly.

Harry said nothing. He merely put his arms around her and kissed her with a strength and tenderness that she would never forget for the rest of her life.

CHAPTER THIRTEEN

Allison had decided to pay her parents another visit. She had visited more frequently since she had started her new job. She was barely out of the car when her father had his arms around her and was hugging her with all his might. He was not normally a demonstrative man but, as in everything else, he made an exception to this with his daughter.

She had an elder brother who had emigrated to Australia when she had been quite young and, even on his occasional visits home with his family, her father didn't openly show as much feeling as he demonstrated each time his daughter visited.

'Father!' exclaimed Allison, hugging him back, feeling his support. 'It's good to see you.' She felt a few tears form in her eyes, tears which streamed from a sense of relief, a sense of being where she was secure and unconditionally cared for.

She could feel a strange sensation around her feet and looking down she saw the ancient family spaniel, Old Sam, scratching at them and looking up at her with expectant, affectionate eyes.

'Well, Sammy boy,' she said, bending down to stroke him. 'You look well enough.' The dog wagged his tail, stood up and wandered slowly but surely back into the house.

'Hasn't been that great,' her father said almost guiltily, looking at his beloved dog.

'Nonsense,' said Allison firmly, smiling at him: 'You're always going on about that dog's health. He's as well as you are and you know it.'

Her mother came out and joined them.

'Come in, darling,' she said to Allison. 'You must be exhausted after the drive. We'll have some tea and a bite to eat, then let us have all your news. Your trip, the hospital. First things first.'

Allison followed her parents into their rambling country house, leaving her luggage in her unlocked car. She felt herself relax almost immediately as she entered the sprawling lounge filled with familiar things. It was good to be home.

Later in the afternoon, Allison went out for a walk on her own, wandering about the country lanes and pathways she had known since childhood. It was a bit overcast with just a slight drizzle of rain. So, she wore her green wax jacket and matching Wellington boots and carried her old riding crop which matched the well-used crash cap and jodhpurs she also wore as a bit of nostalgia.

The clothes reminded Allison of the many happy days she had spent when she was younger riding her lovely 'Two P', the horse her parents had bought her for her fourteenth birthday. As she walked by the fields she used to ride in, she remembered him and the long, lazy days when the sounds of his galloping across the short green grass and the feeling of him beneath her as the wind he created blew in her face had thrilled her so much.

When she had gone up to medical school they had sold 'Two P' to some friends of Allison who ran a riding school. She had managed over once or twice to see the old boy and he was still in good condition. She still missed him, however, and as she wandered about the old-haunts she had shared with him she realized that she missed the protected security of that childhood too.

'Penny for your thoughts or should it be "Two P"?'. Allison turned round startled out of her reverie. It was an old friend of hers, Katie, Katie Langford.

'Why, Katie!' she said delighted to see her friend. 'How are you? My goodness, you do look well.' Allison remembered the times she and Katie had gone riding together and how on occasions when one or other horse had been laid up for one reason or another, one had ridden on horseback, the other on a bicycle, taking turn after turn on each.

'I'm well,' Katie said, excited at seeing her friend so unexpectedly. 'And you look marvelous yourself, Allison. I hear you're making quite a name for yourself up at The London. The best physician they've ever had, I'm told. Already!' Katie laughed and Allison joined her:

'Father!' she exclaimed with mock disapproval. 'Whatever has the old tike been saying about me?'

'Oh, just that you're already the best physician they've ever had and the best research worker too. I hear there's talk of a Nobel Prize. if not this year...'

Allison and her friend laughed together. 'He's really proud of you,' said Katie; 'You can't blame him if he, well, exaggerates ever so slightly. Can you?'

'I suppose not,' Allison replied, still smiling at her father's outrageous comments on her progress. 'Anyway, what are you doing with yourself now? It seems ages since I heard from you, let alone saw you. Last I heard you were finishing Vet School and thinking of going into practice down here.'

'I've done both,' replied Katie. 'I have a surgery at Thorpe Manor. It's marvelous and I'm really enjoying it. In fact, I'm over here to have a look at Old Sam. He's not been too well apparently and your father still considers me a slip of a girl enough to expect me to come to him, rather than him to me. I don't mind, of course. It's nice to be complimented on one's age, even in that way. What's wrong with Old Sam anyway... something serious?'

'Doubt it,' Allison said to her old friend. 'He looked well enough to me. Father has canine hypochondria where it concerns that dog. Make sure you reflect it in your fee! Discourage him a bit.'

'I will,' responded Katie. 'Can I give you a lift up to the house?' she asked.

'No, thanks,' Allison replied. 'A bit of air's what I'm out for and I'd best get it. Thanks, anyway. Give me a call over the next day or so and we'll get together.'

'I'll do that,' said Katie eagerly. 'Anything in particular to brag about, by the way?' she asked cheerfully. 'Other than being the medical protege of the century?'

'Not particularly,' said Allison. 'Yourself?'

'Well, I'm engaged to Tom at last,' she said proudly. 'We're getting married next year. I hope you'll make the wedding. You'll be receiving an invitation shortly, anyway.'

'Why, yes,' Allison replied, as spontaneously as she could sound. 'Congratulations,' she shouted as her friend made her way to her Land-Rover which was parked some distance away.

'Thanks,' Katie called back over the sound of the engine as she left, leaving Allison alone with her countryside, her memories and her thoughts.

That evening over dinner, Allison brought her parents up to date with what she stressed were the true facts of her progress at The London and she briefly gave them the major points which would interest them with respect to her trips abroad.

Her father uncharacteristically looked sheepish enough as she did this for her to feel no need to labor the point of his hyperbole. Both her parents were obviously very proud of her and in deference to this she gave them the copy of the paper Doctor Bennet had given her.

'I'll get loads of reprints later,' she told them. 'More than I'll be able to get rid of.' Her father sat reading it word by word, line by line.

'Good stuff,' he muttered, looking proudly at Allison over the dinner dishes. 'You're making your mark young woman. I knew you would.'

After dinner, Allison helped her mother wash up, while her father went his evening walk with Old Sam. As they washed and dried the dishes and cutlery and put them away in their places, they spoke about all sorts of things.

Her mother brought her up to date with her brother's progress and that of his family. She told her all the local gossip and, it seemed, everything of any import which was going on throughout the county. She spent some time discussing the state of the Practice and stressed that it looked as if when her husband retired, it would cease to exist.

'Your father can't find an acceptable partner,' she said. 'He's had one or two people over for a time, but none of them seemed to suit. When he retires, I think the group practice in Market Harbour will have to absorb his patients.'

While Allison felt that this was sad, she couldn't help but smile. 'I wonder just *why* he can't find anyone suitable,' she said. 'Is it because he's maybe not the easiest of general physicians to work with? Surely that was why he was so succesful as a psychiatrist! The only creature I can ever remember getting along with father in any sort of shared practice is Old Sam,' she continued. 'Does he still take him on his rounds?'

Her mother laughed. 'Yes,' she said; 'He sits in the back of the car watching expectantly like a professional auxiliary. You're probably right, he's not the easiest of men to work with, but he's still a good doctor, he's adapted well to his changed status. He's dedicated, hard-working and is remarkably familiar with current General Practice. He's Old School, Allison, Never be anything else.'

'The best,' Allison agreed with conviction as she wiped silver cutlery with a towel.

'The very best,' replied her mother, smiling at her making her feel very much at home.

......

For the next few days Allison took things easy. She went for long walks, enjoyed her mother's marvellous cooking and listened attentively as her father discussed his practice and the various problems he had with it.

Neither parent asked her about her personal life at all, both recognising the fact that if and when she wanted to discuss it with them she would do so.

For her part, Allison began to get herself together again emotionally. The fresh air, the happy memories and the general warmth which surrounded her, helped dispel the fall in mood she had felt since the events of New York and Tokyo and her ruined night with Harry. Thoughts of conspriacies seemed reckless indeed in this setting, though the same could not be said of what she thought of Harry.

She was still unsure of her emotions, of course, and thought on him with care; but gradually she was able to do so with a little distance and a dgree of healthy perspective. She still wondered, still hurt, but it was less naked, more tolerable.

Allison had been brought up in a liberal enough environment. Her father had never desired her to suffer neuroses from inappropriate sexual and other inappropriate repressions. However she had never been prepared for the intense feelings she was having now. She remembered having once asked her father how he'd define love, psycho-analytically. He had laughed; 'Even we Freudians leave that to the poets,' he'd replied and that had been that. Allison understood what he'd meant.

She called Katie, as arranged, who made arrangements for them to spend a day riding together. It was just like old times and, though Allison was a bit rusty, she soon recovered the considerable skill she'd had as a horsewoman and found herself enjoying the ride almost as much as she'd done when she had been younger, fitter and at the peak of her ability.

The horse Katie brought for her to ride was a gelding called 'Buttermilk' and Allison found him enchanting. He was very placid and calm and he nuzzled her almost immediately they were introduced to one another. Allison mounted him with ease and he murmured his pleasure. They set off at a trot and within a very short time they were cantering towards the fields Allison had known so well in her childhood. She looked at Katie and they exchanged a smile:

'Got your bike?' Allison asked her friend jokingly, light, relaxed.

'I'm on it,' she replied, laughing at Allison's reference to their early adventures together. 'Let's go, girl!' Katie commanded as, given the prompt, the two horses broke into a gallop and carried them back through the years to those very happy times.

They rode deep into the countryside and then stopped for a picnic lunch. The horses grazed nearby as they unpacked the food and drink and settled down to eat and drink and chat. It was idyllic. Allison had forgotten just how good it could be to be outdoors in the fresh air, steeped in the countryside, far from the constricting confines of the town.

She began to wonder if perhaps she would not be better suited to a life in the country. Even as she conversed with Katie on other matters, the thought took hold of her. A country practice, a country life - fresh air, horses, garden fetes, quietness. It really did appeal to her.

In particular, she had once wanted not only to ride horses, but to breed them too. That was not impossible if she could find the right people to help finance and run such a business. Katie would be interested, she knew.

Should she consider a change? Allison thought. Was she considering one? Time would tell.

After lunch was finished, they rested for a while and talked a bit about old times. Katie was eating idly at a spare crisp which had been left in the packet they'd shared. The sound she made as she ate it suddenly reminded Allison of the crisp salad she'd had in New York which in turn made her think on Greg Hoffmann and the friend he'd told her about who'd been treated by her father. She hadn't got a name, of course. Still, there might be some way of finding out. But finding out what? she wondered.

They packed up and rode back over the fields in the direction of Allison's parent's home. As the horses' hooves thumped at the earth, she felt more and more certain that this was the life that she was more suited to. No more the long antiseptic corridors of The London, the cramped lonely walls of her town flat, the noise of the traffic, the routine of ward rounds, case notes, meetings and more meetings. A life added to now by conspiracy theories!

She seriously considered assisting her father, then in time, taking over from him, continuing the practice, keeping it in the family. She could continue the family tradition and, in doing so, find herself. It made perfect sense to her and it would to him, too. She would discuss it with him as soon as possible.

As she said goodbye to Katie and watched her as she rode off with Buttermilk following her, shaking his head and flicking his tail; Allison felt that she had made a memorable decision. She would speak to her father about it that evening. He would be pleased about it, very pleased. Amidst her continuing confusion, that much she knew.

That evening, after dinner, Allison joined her father in his walk with Old Sam. They walked at the dog's pace which wasn't very fast and Allison wondered how she could best broach the subject of her joining the practice. The words kept running around in her head, but she didn't quite know the best way to start. At length, she gave up attempting to assemble them in any specific order and just expressed them as they came to her.

'I've been thinking, father,' she started, 'I think I might like to give up hospital medicine and come down here and work with you. I've thought carefully about it, weighed up the pros and cons and that's the decision I've reached.'

'Really?' her father replied, nonplussed; 'That sounds a good idea, Allison. What's brought this on so suddenly?'

'I've been thinking about it for some time,' she continued, 'and I've decided that's what I want to do, with your approval, of course.'

'If that's what you want, you have my approval. You should know that,' he said.

'Well then, that's settled,' Allison responded; feeling less releived than she thought she would. 'I would have to work notice at The London, but that's no problem is it?'

'None at all. By the way, I think the old boy's got something wrong with his legs. Rheumatism I imagine.'

'What?' asked Allison, wondering what her father was referring to.

'Old Sam,' he went on. 'Bet he's got rheumatism. Look at how he's walking.'

'Maybe,' Allison muttered quickly, almost in irritation. 'I don't know how soon I could get down here, but I'll let you know as soon as I get back.'

'Do that,' her father said softly, 'And while you're doing so, why don't you tell me what's really wrong? If you want to join your old man and his dog you're welcome to, but not as an escape from whatever it is that's really troubling you. Do you want to tell me about it now or later?'

Allison looked at him. He was watching her carefully, his eyes filled with his affection for her and her own filled with tears. She'd been raised to express her emotions and did so without any embarrassment.

'Later,' she said, putting her arms tight round him and holding him close as the tears stung at her eyes.

'Fine, then,' her father said gently. 'Let's see if Old Sam's rheumatoid legs will carry him to that tree. He seems determined to reach it for some reason or another. I can't imagine why.'

For the first time in days, Allison felt her mood really lighten back to normal and through her tears she heard herself laugh out loud.

'So, this Harry of yours had the audacity to let his grief intrude. In a moment of deep affection and sensitivity, probably his first for a very long time, the poor man has become a little confused, probably recollects his late wife, hurts, and suddenly my daughter feels rejected, disowned and utterly humiliated!

'For someone who has told me in detail of the man's interest in Freud, it seems to me that there's a great lack of understanding as to the nature of a Freudian slip. A slip of the tongue, of the pen, or of emotions; in a state of grief is not an uncommon thing. It's merely an expression of that grief - a good thing - or didn't my gifted daughter know that?'

Allison felt her face burn, felt that her father wasn't being fair to her.

'It wasn't just that!' she exclaimed; 'I don't believe that he'll ever get over her. They were very much in love and I know he'll never be able to find another woman like her. He's as good as said so.'

'And he's probably correct,' her father continued, more sympathetically now, softer. 'The man's been through a great deal, Allison - is going through a great deal. Grief is a potent emotion. Within it we have to accommodate bonds that are broken suddenly, reintegrate them in a way that's acceptable to us. It can be a long process and a very difficult one.' His daughter listened carefully, feeling young again, the bright schoolgirl who'd adored and respected this man and still did so.

'No, your Harry may never find another woman like his late wife. Why should he? But in time, he'll find another one, one he can care for every bit as much. You can be sure of that. He sounds like an exceptional young man - there'll be no shortage of sensitive women around when he's ready to start a new relationship, you can be sure of that too.'

Allison looked at her father closely. He was right of course, as ever. She supposed she had behaved in a rather juvenile manner. In fact, she was sure she had. She wondered why? She wasn't given to such behavior normally. Why on this occasion? Her father seemed to read her thoughts:

'Your reaction is quite understandable, Allison,' he said. 'You obviously care for the man a great deal and given that, the workload you've been carrying, your travels abroad, your break with Ken...' he raised his hands. 'What do you expect?

You're as human as the rest of us. An over-reaction, a perfectly understandable over reaction. No harm done, I imagine, not really. The thing now is, what are you going to do about it?'

She sat still, pondering the situation, wondering what indeed she should do, thinking about The London, her work, Tina, Harry, Yukio Yoshimura, The Mayflower Compact. Odd how that name had come back to her.

'Of course, you'll have plenty of time to sort things out when you pack up your job,' her father continued with perfectly disguised irony; 'when you come down here to lance a few boils with me, apply procaine to hemorrhoids. Plenty of time. You'll be able to take things easy, work everything out. Good country air, taking Old Sam for walks to help his rheumatics.'

Allison smiled, knowing what her father was doing, loving him for it.

'I may not be down,' she said.

'I rather gathered that,' he went on. 'Still, I'm always here if I'm needed and so's the practice. If you ever decide for some very good reason that hospital medicine's not for you, then it's all yours. I doubt, however, if that will ever happen and I must say I'm rather glad that it won't.'

Allison smiled at him and then her face went serious again. 'There was something else, father. Something... well, I don't know, strange. About a company, Unicorn Chemicals and a drug called Oviron.'

She told her father everything she could remember about the drug and about the company and its personnel including Greg Hoffmann, judiciously omitting the account of the slap he'd given her. Her father looked very pensive indeed.

'You'd best be careful, Al. I'm sure it's all a misunderstanding but you never know. These industrial boys sometimes get a bit carried away with themselves. Just watch the legal side, protect your back. All I can do right now is assure you that if you ever need anything, cash, a place to think things over, a job!... you've got them. I can also make a few telephone calls.'

'Who to?' Allison asked, expectantly.

'I still have friends in Harley Street who are well connected,' he replied; 'Give me ten minutes and I'll see what I can come up with about what this Japanese said. What was the name of this society you mentioned?

'"The Mayflower *Compact*" her father said not ten, but fifty minutes later, when he'd returned from his study looking very serious indeed. 'That's what it's called. As you said it's based in Washingtom, though it has a few European members including Mostyn as you know.' Allison didn't respond. She knew that when her father was serious there was something to be serious about and that he'd tell her what it was in his own good time.

'By all accounts Mostyn is a strange one. Has some pretty bad habits I'm told and, yes, he's quite an historian. In fact I believe he once considered leaving medicine for politics, but his political notions were as extreme as his other habits. He was too far to the right to be a serious nominee for a seat, so he gave that idea up, at least oficcially.' Allison was intrigued, but still she said nothing. She knew she'd get more information, quicker, that way. Her father was systematic and comprehensive in all that he did. There would be no exception here.

'Apparently he still dabbles in politics. This Mayflower Compact is quite respectable, it's an historical society which attracts rich republicans. It also attracts the likes of Mostyn and it seems that there's more to his type than meets the eye.'

Allison could no longer contain herself: 'In what way?' she asked her father quietly.

'Well the person I spoke with intimated that there has been some talk years back of the Society being a front for a pretty radical right-wing group of political activists, collectively known as the Society of the Sans Graal.'

'The Sans Graal,' Allison thought for a moment, made the translation, 'The sacred cup? The Holy Grail?' she asked incredulously.

'Apparently,' her father replied before continuing; 'Anyway it seems that U.S.A. special services had a look at them once, but found no evidence of anything criminal. Their members, individually, help fund Republican congressional or senatorial candidates who are to the right of their party. There's nothing wrong about that.

Allison began to feel disoriented. Here, in the wilds of the English countryside, her own father was telling her about a putative group of American political extremists.

'Who told you this?' she asked, her credibility strained to breaking point.

'An old friend and former patient from Whitehall,' he replied non-commitally. 'And he told me something else too.' Allison was perfectly still, her father had her total concentration. 'It seems that the parent Society, this Mayflower Compact, have a significant shareholding in Unicorn Chemicals. Not qute a controlling interest but one large enought to interest the Ministry of Trade.'

Allison was beginning to sense that there was something very wrong here. For the first time since she'd spoken with Professor Yoshimura in Osaka she began to believe that there was indeed something very much amiss and that, in some way, she was a part of it.

'Go on,' she said to her father redundantly as he was already looking at her with a concern which intimated that there was something he wanted very much to tell her.

'I spoke with someone else, Allison, someone I came to know very well indeed some years ago when I helped advise on the bulimia and anorexia issue.' Allison passed no comment. She knew her father had been consulted on this issue as eating disorders were one of his major area of expertise. But they didn't talk about it. Not only would it have been unprofessional, it would also have transgressed his sense of propriety in general terms.

'His name is Charles U'Prichard and he's currently the Prince's Private Secretary. He tells me that the Prince's personal physician has diagnosed existing cases of acute intermittent porphyria in the immediate family.'

It was as if Allison had been physically struck. The impact was incredible. As the rush of adrenaline flowed in response *to* it, she thought with a clarity that had been absent for weeks.

'Has this diagnosis been confirmed?' she asked, her voice composed and betraying no sign of the conflicts within her.

'Yes,' replied her father; 'By Sir William Mostyn of all people. Apparently his team at The London General have confirmed these findings. In particular the diagnosis was made through biochemical assay by an eminent clinical biochemist, Dr John Raynor. His chief, Dr John Bennett, countersigned the medical report. Of course you would know all about that.' Allison was quite simply amazed as her world reformed itself.

It was late now or, to be more precise, early. The fire burned warmly in the hearth, Old Sam lay stretched in front of it as Allison told her father virtually everything. She soon found that the surprises of the evening were far from over.

'Now, as for the marketing man you mention who said he had a friend who was a patient of mine, Hoffmann, Gregory Hoffmann.'

'Yes,' Allison responded? as her father gave her one of his far away looks which meant he was focusing on something important.

'There was no friend of his any patient of mine to my knowledge.'

Allison was not particularly surprised at this. No doubt Greg Hoffmann had carried out his research on her, just as he had done on everyone else. It was the nature of the beast. 'I probably shouldn't be so candid but I've no option here. He was a patient of mine for about two years.

Greg Hoffmann!' exclaimed Allison.

'Yes, Greg Hoffmann,' replied her father; 'He underwent psycho-analysis with me. It was unsuccessful.'

For almost an hour Allison's father gave her the details of Greg Hoffmann's history. The ethics of the issue were secondary to his daughter's welfare. Allison was horrified. Greg Hoffmann was indeed an unstable man, but the reason for his instability went back to a childhood which had inflicted greater pain on the young Greg than he had probably ever inflicted on anyone himself.

She soon understood now why he'd slapped her. His mother had not only exposed him to the sorts of scenes no child should ever be exposed to, she had also made him take part. He'd had an incestuous relationship with her. It had lasted six years. He was, no doubt a misogynist but not, in Alliosn's father's opinion, a genuine sadist.

'He might well give a woman a spontaneous whack,' he said, 'but he wouldn't really harm her. It would be most likely to occur if she said something intimate to him. Allison felt her cheek blush, right where Greg had hit her.

'"Love me," for example,' she asked.

'Yes, that would do it, under the correct circumstances.'

Unstable indeed, Greg Hoffmann had terrible reasons for being so and Allison felt very sorry for him. He was a product of a childhood hell. She remembered the tequilla, the story he'd told her about the woman and the boy. He had been talking about himself.

Two hours later, when they had finished talking, Allison stood up, walked over to her father and gave him a quick kiss on the cheek:

'Thanks for all your help and support,' she said, 'I really appreciate it. She became lost for further words as she made her way out of the room to go, at last, to bed.

'And one other thing before you go,' her father continued, his voice losing the urgency it had held as they'd discussed the matters which had kept them there. Allison turned, 'I'd give that chap Harry a call sometime soon,' he said with a smile; 'Before he forgets about you altogether.'

'I'll do that,' Allison said. 'I'll do it tomorrow. Thanks father. Thanks a lot.'

'Pleasure,' he replied. 'Would you check Old Sam's legs on your way out, see if they're swollen at all?' He allowed himself a brief smile as he heard his daughter groan her disapproval. At least her sense of humor was intact. She'd need it.

The following morning, Allison woke completely refreshed. It seemed as if some dark cloud had lifted from her and as she looked out of the window of her room at the morning sky she was filled with a freshness she hadn't felt for a very long time indeed.

Her first formed thought was of Harry. She would call him this evening, apologise, arrange to see him when she got back. As her father had said, it took time and she hoped that in that time she would find herself a part of his plans.

Meanwhile, her first priority was to get herself as refreshed as possible for reocmmencing work at The London General, the place where she wanted to be with all her heart. There were things to be done there and by God she'd do them or die trying. She did not, of course, mean this literally.

She rose and after breakfast she went out for yet another long walk in the familiar haunts of her childhood. It was raining and she was well wrapped up. She enjoyed walking in the rain and smelling the rich green smell which surrounded her from the trees and the bushes and the grass.

A few minutes after beginning her walk she noticed Katie's Land Rover driving along the road towards the house. Katie stopped when she saw her and waved. Allison waved back and walked over to speak to her. She began to feel embarrassed. Surely not...!

'Rheumatism?' she asked her friend.

'That's what he said,' she replied; 'You don't think so?'

'I certainly don't!' Allison said briskly. 'My goodness, he must think you have nothing else to do but attend to that dog. It's geriatric. It's about twenty three years old, that's about a century and a half in human terms. What does he expect?'

Katie laughed: 'Miracles. It keeps me in a job anyway.'

'I'll have a word with him,' said Allison. 'Rheumatism, my foot! An ancient spaniel, that's what Old Sam is. Nothing else!'

Katie drove off towards the house, still smiling and Allison found herself smiling too at the obstinacy of her father. He was a delightful man whose only concern after the revealations of the previous night, was undue concern about a geriatric spaniel. He could be a lot worse, Allison decided, a lot worse indeed.

When evening finally came, Allison helped her mother wash up again after dinner. She then decided that it was time to telephone Harry. She felt apprehensive as she approached the telephone but her apprehension was tempered by her wish to hear him again, to speak to him. About everything. She dialled his number and waited. The line clicked once or twice and she held the phone tightly in anticipation.

It was engaged, so she put the phone down and waited for a few minutes. She dialed again. It was still engaged. She went out into the garden, walked around, came in, tried again. The same result. She wondered what was keeping Harry occupied on the phone for so long. She would keep trying until she got through to him.

She waited a good half-hour before trying again and this time there was no answer at all. He'd obviously gone out since she'd last called. The phone rang, ring after ring, and Allison felt very frustrated indeed.

'Shit!' she said to herself. 'Where are you, Harry? When will you be back?' She turned to walk out of the room again when suddenly the phone rang. It made her start. She walked over and picked it up:

'Hello,' she said: 'Maybridge 522632.'

'Hello, Allison?' She recognized Pam's voice immediately. It was ever so slightly slurred.

'Yes, Pam,' she said, suddenly feeling rather nervous. 'Is there anything wrong?'

'I'm calling from the hospital,' her friend said. 'It's little Tina. She's critical, Allison. I thought you'd want to know. I don't think there's much hope - an intracranial hemorrhage. It looks very bad indeed.'

'And Harry?' Allison asked, her heart sinking. 'How's he? Does he know?'

'He's here, too, at her bedside. He's just arrived,' said Pam. 'He was asking about you. I told him you were at your parents.'

'Not for long,' said Allison. 'I'm leaving immediately, Pam. I'll be up soon, tell him that. I'll be up there within a few hours.'

'I'll do that,' said Pam. 'But there's no need...'

'But there is,' said Allison with a fierce certainty. 'Oh yes, there is.'

CHAPTER FOURTEEN

As soon as they discovered her intentions, Allison's parents helped her pack what she required and after reminding her to drive carefully, they watched their daughter drive off into the falling night. Her father's face in particular was fixed rigid with a very serious look indeed. His daughter had very serious business to attend to.

Allison drove fast. Against her better judgement she decided to stop only to refuel and hoped in this way to reach the hospital within a few hours. As her car sped along swiftly and easily, images flitted through her mind, of Harry and Tina, of Dr Bennett and John Raynor of a secret society, of conspiracy in royal circles. Of everything she was going to.

To distract her thoughts she switched on her radio and turned the dial. She moved it along absentmindedly until she was tuned into one of her favorite stations and programmes. It was light, popular though at present the newscaster was talking about some terrorist outrage in the State. Its familiarity seemed welcoming at first, reassuring, solid.

She tried to remember the times she had listened to this programme before; tried to recall the various episodes of her life that had been going on then, but it was no good. The images of what awaited her continued to trickle through and disturb her and at last she turned the radio off, set her face in a fixed determined look and drove on in silence into the night-time.

She made good time and it was in the early hours of the morning when she arrived at the entrance to the hospital. The sign saying The London General Hospital was lit up outside the entrance and as she turned the car by it, Allison briefly remembered her first day there. Her nervousness, her meeting with Jennifer, with Harry. It now seemed like a very long time ago indeed.

Allison parked the car as close as she could to the ward and moved quickly through the doorway and into the long corridor. She walked briskly along it, thoughts tumbling through her head, concern gripping her tightly. She finally turned into the ward, walked along the small corridor within it, entered Tina's room and saw the child's bed.

Harry was sitting on it speaking to Pam who was standing beside him. Jennifer was also there, standing vacantly, out of uniform, obviously called from home and sleep and looking very concerned indeed.

Allison's heart sank as she took it all in. Tina was lying prepared for surgery and she looked very, very weak.

Weak as she was, it was the child who was first to speak:

'Hello, Dr Young,' she said.

'Hello,' replied Allison feeling flustered. 'How are things? How are you?' she continued, turning her attention to Tina.

The child smiled at her. 'O.K.' she replied in a very weak voice. 'This is my dad.'

'I know,' said Allison. 'We've met.'

'He's lovely, isn't he?' said Tina.

Allison felt herself flush. 'Yes' she said with a smile.' Any complaints, young lady?' Tina shook her head. 'Well,

I thought I'd just pop in and see how you were doing,' she continued. 'I see you're going off to get things sorted out once and for all.'

'This is good of you,' Harry interrupted; 'Tina tells me you dropped in on her quite often. She enjoyed the company, didn't you, love?' The girl nodded briefly. 'So you got back from the meeting O.K., then?' Harry said, intentionally making even conversation to keep Tina's mind - and his own - off the immanent surgery.

'Yes,' Allison responded. 'I did. And you?'

'Yes, no trouble. I left a bit early to get back to this young lady here. I called 214 a few times but there was no reply.'

Allison wondered wehat he was referring to. '214?' she repeated, confused.

'Yes, your room number, at the hotel. I called to say I was going, but there was never any reply. The desk clerk was no help either. Simply said you weren't there.'

'I wasn't,' Allison said bemused. 'I was in room two ones four -114 - that's why you didn't get through! The desk should have checked the register, however, I...'

'Well, they didn't,' Harry said quietly.

'No,' said Allison, wondering what to say next, when the porters came for Tina.

'Come on, young lady,' said the nurse who accompanied the porter with the trolley. Tina was helped on and they wheeled her off to theatre with Harry being allowed to go as far as the pre-med room with her. Allison gave Tina and Harry a brief wave. Tina waved weakly back, but Harry, walking there handsome and tormented didn't respond at all.

He returned and without saying antthing about his daughter turned to Allison, extending his arm as he did so and taking her hand in his own.

'It was good of you to drive up. There was no need to, but I'm glad you did.' Allison noticed that his voice was very controlled, it showed no trace of emotion whatever. It was his professional voice, measured and careful.

'Tina?' asked; 'What's happened to her?'

'She's in surgery now, Allison,' Harry continued, as Pam and Jennifer looked on quietly. Allison noticed now that Jennifer had been crying. She wasn't at all surprised. But Harry was in control now. The situation was bringing things together within him. He was already accepting the worst. In a sense he was returning rapidly to normal.

'I called Shaun Bates, a young surgeon I know...' he continued.

'Yes, I've met him briefly,' said Allison absently, as Harry elaborated.

'He's been doing some highly experimental work and has developed a new surgical procedure which could just work with Tina. It's a very long shot indeed but it's all we have. He received permission from the ethical committee to go ahead just over an hour ago, and he's operating on Tina right now. It's her only chance - we had to take it.'

'Of course you did,' agreed Allison, looking up at Harry as she sat down in a chair and Pam went off to find her a cup of coffee. She noted that he looked very different from the man she had held so tightly by the lake, the man who had so distressed her. He was disciplined and controlled and handling the situation with uncommon clarity of thought and objectivity given the circumstances.

This, she knew, was the real Harry, the successful man and physician. The man everyone loved and respected so much. The crisis in his daughter's illness had indeed brought him together again, reformed him. His eyes glowed with a deep penetrating blueness. Allison knew without doubt that she loved this man. In a way which the poet alone understood.

They sat around talking, keeping their minds as far as possible from the events in the operating theatre. Every new movement, however, from any of the staff around drew their attentions to it and to the fact that Tina was facing a life-or-death battle at that very moment under the skilled hands of the young surgeon.

Allison distracted them as much as she could with a few observations on the time she'd spent with her parents. Pam brought her up to date with what had been happening in the hospital in her absence and Jennifer, still very tired looking, supplemented this where and when she could.

These efforts, however, could barely remove their attention for long from the patient and interspersed with such talk, the conversation always turned back to the child and how she might be faring. Harry said little about his daughter, however, preferring to 'Just wait and see.' rather than speculate any further on the possible outcome of the highly speculative surgery.

At length, they persuaded Pam to excuse herself and go off to try and catch an hour or so's sleep. She was on duty very early and they were insistent, promising they would let her have any news as soon as it was available. Reluctantly she went off, also looking very tired and very concerned indeed.

As the hands of the clock moved towards 5 a.m., Allison realized that Tina had now been in surgery for over four hours. She wondered just how much trauma the frail little girl could take, how she could possibly cope for so long with the anaesthesia and the surgery. It didn't seem possible that she could survive.

At length, one of the theatre nurses approached them and beckoned to Harry: 'Doctor Wright,' she said. 'Could I have a word with you?' Harry stood up and walked over to her and they spoke quietly together. Harry turned to look at Allison and Jennifer: 'Excuse me,' he said to them firmly; 'I have to go.' With that he accompanied the nurse out of the ward and into the corridor. Allison and Jennifer looked at each other. For a few supportive moments, they took each other's hand.

About half an hour later, Harry returned. As he made his way towards them, both Allison and Jennifer were rigid with anticipation. His appearance betrayed nothing, gave no hint as to how Tina had progressed. He walked over to them and sat down.

'Shaun says that there's a chance,' he said. 'She's still in the recovery room and by some miracle has survived the procedure relatively intact. He managed to remove the whole tumor mass which, if nothing else, is an enormous success for him and his technique.

'The problem now, however, lies with Tina's vital functions. They're understandably pretty labored and the staff are worried about respiratory or cardiovascular collapse. We won't know how things are going to turn out for some time yet. All we can do now is go home and get some sleep. The staff will call me immediately they have any news.'

'Let me know immediately you hear something, Harry,' said Jennifer.

'Me too, Harry,' Allison added. 'Please call me straight away. I'll be at home.'

'I'll do that,' said Harry, addressing both of them simultaneously. 'Now, let's all get some rest. There's nothing more we can do here for now.'

Allison drove home through the early morning streets with her tired mind ruminating on the events of the night. She hoped with all her might that Tina would recover. That the dramatic success of the surgery would not be made useless by post-operative complications and that the lovely little girl would have the chance at life she so richly deserved.

She knew, however, the risks involved and the unlikelihood of success that existed. She had rarely known of a patient so compromised who had survived any procedure and all she could do was hope that Tina was one of the few exceptions.

More than anything, however, what held her mind most was her image of Harry. Authoritative, decisive, confidant and controlled in the face of his daughter's possible death. And gentle and considerate too. Despite the seemingly sudden change which had enabled him to integrate himself once more, he had maintained the gentility she had do loved about him. A gentility based on strength and caring and which complemented perfectly those other aspects of him which she also loved so much.

Allison wondered what other aspects of his prior state Harry had maintained. In particular, she wondered if he had now managed to expel enough grief to give her the opportunity of entering his life and filling the vacuum the death of his former wife had left.

As she lay down on top of her bed and pulled the duvet over her very tired body, she continued to think on these things and on the others too; and they fluttered through her thoughts keeping her awake with uncertainty and anticipation. At length, she fell asleep and very soon she was dreaming. And, as she so dreamt, a warmth such as she had never known, enfolded her.

She woke abruptly to the ring of the telephone. Reflexly she reached out, grabbed it and brought it to her face:

'Hello, Allison?' the voice said. Through her sleepiness Allison realized that it was Harry. Instantly she was fully awake and a sinking sensation grabbed at her stomach.

'Yes, Harry,' she said. 'How are things? Are things O.K.?' she rephrased, sensing that they weren't.

'We don't know yet. I was in again this morning and there was no change. The mite is holding her own, but she's weak. She's putting up a tremendous fight, but it's still touch and go.'

As he spoke, Allison looked at her bedside clock. It was almost eleven o'clock. She had slept a great deal later than she had intended. Even as she wondered at this, Harry continued:

'Look, Allison,' he said. 'The main reason I telephoned, was to ask you if you'd mind coming over to spend the day with me here, if you're free to do so. I was going to pop in and out of the hospital fairly frequently, but have decided it's fairer on them if I wait here for some definite word. It's going to be a long day and I'd appreciate the company.'

'Why, of course I will,' responded Allison immediately. 'I'll be over within the hour. How, precisely, do I get to you?'

Harry gave her detailed instructions on how to reach his home and within the hour Allison had showered, dressed, rummaged through her back mail, had a quick cup of instant coffee and was in her car driving towards Harry's house.

As she attempted to follow the rough map she had drawn to simplify his directions, she felt all sorts of feelings run within her. All of them concerned her, but some were of a very different nature to the others.

Allison turned into the street where Harry lived and immediately saw his house. It *was* imposing and very impressive indeed. She wondered how Harry managed to run it on his own.

As she drove into the driveway, the door opened and Harry came out to meet her. He waved and smiled at her, but through his solid composure Allison knew he must be very worried. She waved back, stopped the car and switched off the engine. A silence fell around her as if she were miles from the town. It was a lovely house and a lovely place to live. She got out of the car and closed the door behind her.

Inside, the house was as impressive as it was outside and after they had briefly discussed Tina, there being no further news, Allison decided to distract Harry's attention by asking him about his home.

Before she could do so, the phone rang. Harry picked it up.

'Hello,' he said. 'Doctor Wright speaking.' He listened for a time and said nothing. A grim, determined look tightened his face. 'I'll be right over,' Putting the phone down. He turned to Allison. 'I'll have to go over to the hospital. Things are critical. She's still fighting away but they'd rather I be there over the next hour or so. Yo're welcome to stay here if you'd like to.'

Harry gave Allison a deep, intimate look, one that told her he wanted her to stay.

'I'd like to,' she replied, walking over to him and squeezing his shoulder in mute support.

'Fine,' he said. 'See you when I get back. Help yourself to whatever you need.' With that, he went to a small cloakroom, pulled on a driving jacket and went out of the door into his car and drove off. When the sound of the car had gone it was very quiet indeed.

Allison sat for a while looking around the lounge which was traditionally furnished and which had, along one wall, a beautiful chaise-longue. In one of the corners there was a period mahogany cabinet on top of which there was a framed photograph of Harry's former wife. Allison went over and looked at it, at the beautiful woman, at the wife and mother he and Tina had lost. And that's precisely how things were. The woman was dead.

No jealousy clouded her thinking now, no sense of inferiority, or irrational anger that he had loved this woman, and still did so in his way. All that she felt was a deep and profound sadness that such tragedy had struck this lovely man and his daughter and she also felt an equally deep and profound hope that things would go better for him now.

She sat there for a time flicking through the morning paper which had obviously remained untouched since its delivery. She couldn't really concentrate on it, however, her thoughts constantly flitting to Harry, the hospital, Tina and the drama which was unfolding and surrounding the three of them.

At length she heard a noise at the front door - a key fumbling in the lock. She put the paper down and rushed through to the entrance hall. As the door swung open her heart was thumping hard in her chest:

'Hello,' the woman said. 'I'm Mrs Mawson, Doctor Wright's receptionist. You must be a friend of his. How's Tina?' Her voice was genuinely concerned.

'Well, yes, I'm Allison Young. Not so good, I'm afraid,' Allison immediately took to the woman, there was a genuine caring in her enquiry that she liked. 'At least, we're not quite sure yet. Doctor Wright's with her now.'

'I hope she gets well,' said the woman, looking with sincerity at Allison. 'She's a brave little thing, so lovely too.'

'I hope so too,' Allison said softly. 'I really do.'

For the next hour or so, Allison sat around chatting occasionally with Mrs Mawson while she went about her work. At length it was completed and with some more expressions of concern for Tina, the woman left and Allison was immersed within the silence again with her thoughts. It was late afternoon now and she wondered just what was happening at the hospital.

Once or twice she had considered phoning to see what she could discover, but on each occasion she had finally decided against it. It would add more to the very busy workload they had there and anyway, she would know in time.

The sky seemed to dull a little and Allison looked out of the lounge window. Harry's car was approaching the house and within a short second, she found it had entered the driveway and was parked outside. She rushed to the door, opened it and waited. She held her breath as Harry walked towards her looking very determined and serious.

He said nothing until he entered the house and closed the door behind him. His eyes met Allison's:

'She's going to pull through,' he said. 'She'll make it now. She'll be fine.'

'Oh, Harry, I'm so glad.' Allison rushed to him and buried her head in his chest. She pulled herself close and his arms surrounded her. He held her tight and firm as if he would never let her go. She felt herself sink into him and felt a wave of relaxation and relief wash over her, freshening her thoughts, clearing them.

They stood that way for some minutes, expressing their mutual relief in mutual silence and proximity. At length, Allison felt a change occur in herself and in him. She could sense his masculinity now, his strength, his controlled passion. She tilted her head and looked at him. Their eyes met again and this time a look passed between them which made her feel something she had never felt before in her life.

She raised her hand and ran it along the back of Harry's neck. Simultaneously he let his own fall down her back, his nails gently stroking her back through her light dress, dropping lower and across her breasts. She kissed him full in the mouth. Still kissing her, Harry lifted Allison in his arms and carried her through the lounge to his bedroom. He placed her on the bed and lay beside of her.

'I love you,' she whispered.

'Me, too,' he responded gently.

'Love me, my Harry,' she whispered. 'Love me!'

'I want to so much, so very, very much.' He pulled her even tighter to him. She felt happier than she ever had before.

As the sky fell darker and the afternoon progressed, they merged with one-another completely and totally. They consummated, with thrilling passion, the potent love they felt for one another. It was a long time later that, in emotional and physical exhaustion, they came together again and, arms entwined, fell asleep.

It was a full four hours later when they awoke. They made love again, gently and tenderly. Afterwards Harry telephoned the hospital to check on Tina's condition. It was stable and improving. He came back into bed beside Allison and they lay together, holding one another, talking and loving as the evening deepened and the shadows fell.

Later they both paid a brief visit to see Tina. She couldn't speak particularly coherently as yet, but she looked a great deal better and was obviously very happy to see them. The medical view now was that she could potentially make a full recovery though it would take some months to be certain.

As they made to leave, Allison realized that Tina was trying to say something to her and was determined to do so. She bent down to hear the tired girl's whispers and strained to hear:

'I'll get to the concert now,' she said. 'Cat Machine.' Do you remember, Doctor Young? My favorite pop group?'

'I remember,' Allison smiled. She was getting better. 'You'll get to a concert, Tina, I promise you. 'Cat Machine,' she repeated. 'You'll get to see them, I promise.

Tina lay back seemingly content as Harry and Allison left her to rest and recuperate.

As they made their way back to Harry's house he turned to Allison and made her day perfect:

'I wonder,' he asked her, 'If you'd like to spend the next few days with me when we're free. I've got a few patients to see and have to attend to Tina, of course, but otherwise... well. You may as well spend what's left of your holiday with someone? Why not with me?'

'I can't think,' Allison replied non-committally.

'Think what?' Harry asked, slightly bewildered.

'Of anyone I'd rather spend it with.' she said, as she briefly squeezed his hand and kissed him gently on the cheek.

'Settled then?' asked Harry.

'Very settled!' Allison replied.

As the night-time brushed the sky, the moon rose slowly full.

The remainder of the week was on the happiest periods of Allison's life. She and Harry spent every free moment they had together and they talked about themselves and their lives and they shared moments of sadness and tenderness together and discovered each other every day as new.

Although Allison spent her nights at her flat, she also spent a great deal of time at Harry's place and she grew to love the house and its magnificent rooms and rambling garden. The surgery and consulting room were superb and as well-equipped as any you would find anywhere. It was evident that Harry had spared no cost in his preparations for treating his patients properly and she knew that, in time, his practice would return to being the enormous success it had been.

Allison watched how, now that Tina was beginning to become well again, Harry threw himself back into his work and into getting his affairs and practice ship-shape again. She helped him as much as she could with advice on his paperwork and even ventured an opinion or two on a few of his most difficult medical cases.

They visited Tina twice daily at the hospital and it was evident - even after so little time - that she was improving slowly but surely. Color was coming back to her face and for the first time since she'd met her, Allison began to realise what a lovely looking little girl she was.

She was speaking more and more each day and by the end of the week, she was able to speak for quite a few minutes without becoming breathless. Even to Allison, experienced as she was in dealing with such cases, Tina's progress was remarkable and she discerned in it all the fighting spirit she knew her father had.

After the hospital visit, when he'd seen the last of his patients in the evening, Harry would drive Allison out deep into the country where they would go for a walk, have dinner, then drive somewhere to sit and talk about all the things they wanted each other to know. These evenings were idyllic for Allison and, each night before she went to sleep, she went over them in her mind, recapturing special moments, lovely ones - ones she'd never lose.

It was during one of these talks in the car after a long walk and dinner had made them especially relaxed and peaceful that Harry had told Allison about Ann. This was a subject she had only now come to realize she could listen to him discuss, without undue and inappropriate emotional involvement. He had told her that he wanted to tell her about their relationship and Allison had indicated for him to do so, assuring him that she was a sensitive and willing audience.

'We met when we were undergraduates,' Harry began, smiling at the reminiscence. 'Me a wet behind the ears medical student and Ann a linguist, majoring in French and German.'

'We were both just seventeen when we met - in fact she was a few months older than I was - and it seemed the most natural thing on Earth for us to get together and stay there. We were quite inseparable and we were married almost exactly two years after first meeting.

'We had Tina two years later, much to the dismay of our parents and teachers. It made no difference to our studies though, except that Ann couldn't go abroad for the year she was required to, in order to obtain her degree with honors. She did without the honors and Tina became part of us instead. We always felt that she should have been there to pick up a scroll herself, when first Ann and then I, graduated.

'From the beginning of our relationship, everyone was predicting dire things. Financial and academic ruin, a quick marriage followed by an even quicker divorce, everything imaginable.' He paused, reflecting on times past

'Somehow, we managed to sail through life without these things occurring, without any of the troubles many young people face in such a situation. I was fortunate enough to get a few lucky breaks with placings with good people like John Bennet and to succeed in private practice without any apparent major effort.'

At the mention of John Bennet's name Allison chilled. She'd managed to keep that issue out of Harry's way for the past week. She appreciated that she'd have to tell him about that particular madness sometime soon, but not yet. She didn't want to quite yet.

'Ann taught for a while which helped financially,' he continued. Then, as the practice grew and I brought in some good income from some financial dealings of my own, she gave that up and managed the practice full-time.

'She was a good administrator and as deft with the paperwork and my patients as she was with her languages. Everything was going so well, very well indeed. I suppose there was a surplus of riches in every sense.'

Allison caught the brief change in his tenor, his down-swing of mood and she encouraged him to continue: 'It sounds as if you were a great match,' she said with encouragement; 'You were both very lucky indeed, to have what you did have, even if it ended as it did.'

Harry looked at her, slightly distant, preoccupied with the memory of such tragedy. 'We were,' he went on. 'I see it that way now, though I didn't until very recently. There's a special reason for that, you see, something almost no-one knows about. Things were great for a number of reasons, marvelous, that's why the whole thing was so awful.

'You see, Allison, not only was the practice doing well and Tina blossoming, but Ann was pregnant again. We even had amniocentesis carried out to determine the baby's gender. It would have been a boy. The perfect complement to Tina.'

'Oh!' Allison was quite shocked and suddenly hurting terribly for him. 'Oh, Harry, I'd no idea...'

'Anyway, the irony is that it was on a routine trip to see Ann's gynecologist when a car on the opposite lane of the motorway had a blow out and hit Ann's car head on.

'All those years of plenty were called in within a second. I was talking to our housekeeper when I received the call. We were discussing how best to clean one of the carpets. The message was simple. My wife and unborn child were dead.'

'It was only the thought of Tina that kept me going then. It was pretty awful. I did love Ann a great deal, you know, a great deal. That's something that won't ever change.'

'I know,' Allison said softly to him. 'I know that, Harry, it can't change and it shouldn't. It must have been terrible for you, terrible.'

'I'm over it now, Allison, over the worst of it. Yes, I'm glad of the time Ann and I had and I've got Tina to show for it and lots of happy memories. I was very lucky indeed, exceptionally so and I still am.'

They sat in silence for a time, each ruminating, sifting through thoughts and emotions, wondering about the past, the present, the future; what it held, what it might bring to them. After a time, Harry spoke again. He sounded interested, concerned.

'Ever been in love yourself?' he asked. 'Really in love?'

Allison sat quietly for a while wondering how she could answer such a question. After hearing what Harry had just told her it seemed a difficult question to answer. Love was about many things and, it seemed, he had known most of them. For her part what could she say by comparison?

'I had a relationship for a while with someone,' Allison began. 'But I don't imagine you could call it real 'love' - whatever that means. As I see it now, it was more like a maternal rush' she said. 'One that lasted far too long.'

'I don't know if you'd understand that sort of thing. It seems, well... a bit feminine, really, I suppose. I think I was attracted to a child in a way, a grown-up child, mark you, but a child just the same.'

'I understand, Allison,' he said softly. 'I know the sort of thing you mean. It isn't uncommon or easy to handle either.'

Allison told Harry about Ken and his crippling possessiveness. He seemed interested, but not unduly so. She wondered how she could possibly have had such a relationship, now that she had discovered this man.

'It's all over now, though,' she reflected, ending her brief account of the relationship with a depth of feeling that was clear in her voice. 'All over, very much. Very much indeed.' Harry turned to her and she was expecting him to make some comment on what she had just told him. He didn't.

'Tomorrow,' he said, instead; 'I'm going to take you to *The Marlow Bridge* again. Are your lips up to it?' Allison laughed softly:

'I don't know,' she replied as she turned to him and put her hand behind his head pulling him to her. 'But they're up to this,' she kissed him soft and warm, expressing her love for him as deeply as she could.

That night, Allison returned to her flat feeling almost overcome with her love for Harry. The details he had given her of the circumstances of his wife's terrible accident enabled her to appreciate more fully just what he had been through and what he had emerged from.

Gone now, completely, were her thoughts of comparison, her juvenile jealousies. In their place, there was a desire to make herself a fitting companion for this marvelous man and the hope that he would see her as such and perhaps, in time, become her husband.

There was a knock on her door and as she moved towards it to open it, she looked at her watch wondering who in the name of God would call at this time. She wondered if it was Harry, if he had returned for some reason. As she reached for the doorknob, she cautiously asked who was there. A voice replied at once:

'It's me, Allison. Sorry to disturb you. I saw the light on and...'

Allison felt quite unreal. She recognized the voice immediately. It was Ken.

She let him in and directed him towards a seat. It was evident that he was very distressed about something and Allison wondered what.

'I had to see you, Allison,' he started. 'I've decided to leave general practice and go into hospital medicine. I thought you should know.'

Allison looked at him carefully. She sensed something was wrong. There was something different about him. Then, all at once she realized that perhaps there was nothing different about him at all, that the difference was in her:

'Why, Ken? Why should I know?' she asked him abruptly.

'Because it might just alter your attitude to us. I've thought of little else, Allison, since the evening we left that laboratory. We have too much to give each other to throw it away, too much we can share and make a decent life with together. So, I've decided to give up my job for you. We can be together, as we always wanted to be.'

Allison was incredulous. She observed him closely, his posture, his eyes:

'Have you been drinking?' she asked.

'Just a little,' he admitted, noticeably flushed now. 'Why not? A celebration. A get-together.' He laughed: 'So what's wrong with that?'

'There's plenty wrong, Ken, plenty wrong with that and with just about everything else you've said.'

'We're finished Ken. I made that perfectly clear to you... finished for good. There is no question of that situation changing, none whatsoever. Now, if you'd like to go, I would be very grateful indeed.'

'Is there someone else?' he asked aggressively. 'Has someone else moved in already? Well, is there?'

Allison was beginning to lose her temper, fast. She was tired and had been so happy this evening. This was the last thing she needed. As she stared intently at Ken, ready to give him a real piece of her mind, the phone rang. Still looking at him angrily, she lifted the receiver:

'Hope I'm not disturbing you,' the familiar voice said. 'Just thought I'd call to say what a lovely evening I had.' It was

Harry and his voice was soft and gentle. 'You're very special to me, Allison, very special indeed. I wanted you to know that, yet again.'

'I... oh thanks,' Allison garbled uncomfortably. 'Thanks, Harry, I...'

'Is there someone there?' Harry asked, obviously detecting the strain in her voice.

'No, not really, just...'

'So, there is someone else! Already!' Ken shouted, loud enough to be heard over the telephone. 'Marvelous - you didn't waste any time hanging about, did you, Allison? Who's the lucky man then? Your boss perhaps, or someone else who can advance your almighty career such as your laboratory friend... is that him eh?'

Allison could hear Harry's voice still speaking: 'Sorry, Allison, didn't think you'd have company at this time. I'm sorry to have called.'

'No, Harry!' Allison said, filling with rage and confusion. 'It's Ken. He's turned up out of the blue and...' but before she could finish, she realized that the receiver had been put down and there was just the solitary noise of the dialing tone. She looked at Ken with a look he had never seen in her before:

'You...' she began, pointing at him, speechless for a second. 'Get out of here, you drunken shit. I never realized until this moment what a spoiled, self-centered, egocentric little bastard you were. I should have realized it long ago. I wish to God I had. Get out of here, Ken - now - or I'll call the police and have them arrest you.'

'You bitch!' he said, walking towards her. 'You would, too, wouldn't you? Just because someone else shows an interest... Excites you, does he? Good between the sheets? You whore! You couldn't even wait a decent interval. You've always been the same. I give up my job for you, I put my career in jeopardy, I get involved with those bastards at Unicorn Chemicals to make some money for us and...'

As Allison moved to open the door, he grabbed hold of her and attempted to kiss her. His hands grabbed at her breasts fumbling and pressing as he squeezed hard through the light fabric of her dress, hurting her.

'Out!' Allison shouted, pushing him away from her and pointing to the door, attempting to get to it, to pull it open.

'You dirty little...' Before he could say anything more, Allison had managed to grab him by the back of his jacket, bring her knee up hard against his groin and as he doubled over with the pain, managed to drag him towards the door and push him out. She slammed the door behind him and locked it in one quick movement. She could hear him continue to rant outside but she didn't give a toss.

She sat down for a moment or two to compose herself and heard him leave, still cursing her and using all sorts of exotic epithets.

Her hands trembling, she reached for the telephone to call Harry. She dialled his number and listened to the first few rings. There was a click at the other end and his telephone machine answered her. It asked whoever had called him to leave a message.

For a multitude of reasons, Allison walked to her bed, lay down on top of it, and wept. It was only later, just before she fell asleep, that the fact that Ken had mentioned Unicorn Chemicals impressed itself upon her. She was too drained to care.

The following morning Allison woke early after a fitful night's sleep. Scenes of Ken's abusive behavior towards her and of Harry's interrupted telephone call flashed through her mind.

The contrast between the two men couldn't have been more emphatic and as she lay there in the forming light, she hoped with all her heart that Ken's sudden and unexpected intrusion back into her life hadn't been misunderstood by Harry.

She decided to wait until around eight to call him and apologize for the debacle of the previous night. He would have had breakfast by then and would be free before seeing his first patient at eight thirty. She would arrange to see him that lunchtime and make up for her lack of response to the sentiments of his call.

She duly called at eight and Harry answered on the first ring:

'Oh, Allison,' he said, sounding almost cool to her. 'How are you?'

'Fine, Harry. Look, about last night. I'm very sorry. Ken turned up here drunk and...'

'There's no need to explain, Allison,' he said. 'No need at all. Look, forgive, me but I must get back to some notes I've been reading. I have to finish them before my first patient arrives and they're fairly hefty reading.'

'Why, of course. I'm sorry.... . I wondered if? What are you doing for lunch?'

'I'm tied up today, Allison. In fact I've had a load of mail this morning - the practice is recovering and I'm afraid I don't think I'll be able to make it this evening either. I hope you don't mind but I'm sure you understand that...'

'Of course,' Allison interrupted. 'Of course, I understand, Harry. I'll call you later.'

'Do that. Bye.'

'Bye,' Allison repeated as she placed the receiver back in its place and felt a wave of what was almost naked fear pass through her. Ken's appearance had disturbed Harry. It was not surprising. His first relationship since the tragedy, the first open expressions of that relationship and he discovers Allison at home at night with her former lover. What else could he think? How else could he react? What else did she expect?

She called Pam and arranged to have lunch with her. It helped distract her from thoughts of Harry and gave her the opportunity to catch up on what was happening at the hospital medically and personally. As ever, it was the latter which gradually dominated the conversation:

'And Jennifer's been seeing Gerry's friend, Michael, quite a bit. They seem quite attached. Wouldn't surprise me if they didn't end up married.'

'But he's such an odd young chap,' Allison said surprised. 'You know I've met him once or twice and I don't think I've heard him speak once.'

'He doesn't say much,' Pam agreed, laughing. 'But what he does say obviously has effect. Jennifer thinks so anyway. They've apparently been inseparable for months and few of us knew anything about it. Gerry only told me yesterday. Anyway, how are things with you and Harry?'

'Troubled,' Allison said to her friend and explained what had happened the night before.

'I think you may have got things a bit confused,' said Pam in response. 'You'll probably find that Harry is busy, that he has got a great deal to do today that's come up unexpectedly. I think you'll find too that the incident with Ken has barely crossed his mind and that, if it has, he appreciates it for precisely what it was. His apparent coolness towards you probably exists only in your imagination.

'You spent a long time with Ken, Allison, and a lot of your experiences and expectations of and from a relationship are based on what you learned from his responses, not from someone like Harry.

'I may be wrong, but I'll bet Harry's missing you today as much as you're missing him. He's just very busy getting his life together again. He's not Ken - don't expect him to behave like him.'

Allison listened to her friend, was surprised at her insight into her and felt very confused. "Was this true? Was Harry merely very busy?" She would have liked to have thought so, but...

'Believe me,' continued Pam, seeing her friend's confused expression. 'I know Harry well enough now to assess the man and I'm not blinded by love for him. I'm right. You'll see.' As Allison asked Pam how the pregnancy was coming on, she certainly hoped that she would see and soon.

When asked about her pregnancy Pam had looked distressed. She lit a cigarette and, inhaling the smoke deeply, addressed her friend with a directness that Allison had never seen in her before.

'Would you mind, Allison, if we dropped that topic for good. For now anyway?' She inhaled again and sipped from her drink, a glass of light wine, which surprised and pleased Allison. At least some attempt was being made to deal with her drinking.

'The situation is a great deal more complicated than I've intimated to you,' she confided; 'and it would be best all round if we didn't discuss it.' Allison was taken aback, but understood her friend's sentiments. She wondered however precisely *what* was "more complicated" and she realized that the time was fast approaching when she'd have to confront *someone* with the knowledge she had.

'I'm sorry, Pam. Of course I'l respect your wishes,' she said in an understanding tone. There was little, however, that she did understand. It was about time to start doing so.

It was evening before she called him and he still seemed distracted and distant to her. He said that he was very busy indeed and that if she didn't mind he'd cancel The Marlow Bridge for that evening. Allison said that was fine, that she understood.

'I could pop over later, though,' Harry said, unexpectedly. 'Around ten or so, if it's not too late. We could go for a short run or something. If you'd like to.'

'Of course,' Allison said immediately. 'Of course I'd like to.'

'I'll pick you up around ten, then,' he said. 'See you then.' He hung up and Allison began to realize that Pam had been correct after all.

After dinner alone, Allison dressed very carefully and applied the slight touches of make-up which were barely necessary to define her lovely features. She was ready far too soon and ended up pacing back and forth across her lounge floor, waiting impatiently for the sound of Harry's car.

After what seemed a very long time indeed, she heard the car pull up outside and without waiting, she made her way out of the door and walked briskly towards it. Harry was sitting at the wheel, a bit tired looking, but obviously pleased to see her:

'Hello,' he said, smiling. 'That was quick. You're better than Jerome. Reading minds now, are we?'

With those few words Allison realized just how wrong she'd been. Harry was a man such as she had never met before, Ken had never allowed her the opportunity to do so.

She briefly explained to him about Ken's unexpected appearance at her flat and Harry's reponse was initially one of concern for her safety. As her description of events continued, however, it gradually changed to one of amusement.

'I don't imagine he'll be troubling you again,' he said. 'Seems you can handle troublemakers O.K. Maybe you're in the wrong profession!'

'I don't think so somehow,' Allison replied, now amused at the fracas herself. 'I think I'll stay put, just where I am.'

They drove out deep into the countryside and along the dark country roads. The headlights of Harry's car shone out brightly in front of them, but otherwise they were surrounded by darkness with not even the reflected light of the town to lighten the sky.

Allison watched a few moonlit clouds rush by the moon as the car drove steadily on until they reached the entrance to a country park where Allison had never been before. Harry drove the car in, brought it to the edge of a small ridge which overlooked a wide expanse of shadowed flat countryside and pulled it to a stop. He switched the engine off and there was utter, total, silence.

'It's lovely here,' said Allison quietly. 'So quiet, isolated. Perfect.'

'It is, isn't it?' Harry responded. 'It's one of my favorite places. I used to come here often when I'd a major decision to make. I remember sitting here just like this before deciding to leave Saint Luke's I agonized for weeks over that and resolved it here in just a few, quiet, hours of peaceful reflection.'

'I'm not surprised,' continued Allison, as a strange sense of excitement began to creep over her. 'It's a beautiful place, a place where things could be resolved, decided.

'Yes,' said Harry. 'That's why I'm here now!'

'Why?'

'To resolve something.'

'What?'

'Whether or not you'd like to become my wife.'

Allison was pleasantly stunned. In her wildest dreams she never thought she'd hear these words from him so soon. She turned and looked at the man, her eyes filled with him, shining with him in some stray beams of moonlight.

Afterword

It didn't take long to quell the conspiracy. Irrespective of the power and influence of the conspirators, those who wielded real power were soon contacted by people of equal or greater power and influence whom Allison and Harry knew. It was soon neutralized.

Accordingly, Allison, Harry and those of her colleagues who were deserving of it, went on to have successful and happy lives. And Allison was more fulfilled than she had ever dreamed possible.

Printed in the United States
By Bookmasters